Second World
The Warnings 212

B. N. Holmes

Book Cover Design: BNHolmes

Interior Layout: Sam Wright

Editors: Sam Wright, Tyler Jubirt

For bulk ordering information: www.bnholmes.com

ISBN print: 979-8-218-15524-7.
ISBN eBook: 979-8-218-15528-5

Contents

Todd Markley 6

Chapter 1: Hiding..9

BEFORE THE FIRE..14

Chapter 2: Blue Lights and Code Red 15

Chapter 3: Cocooners 29

Todd Markley 40

Chapter 4: The Market.................................... 41

Chapter 5: Your Neighbor's keeper...........................50

Chapter 6: Night Vision 58

Chapter 7: Family Vacation................................ 60

Todd Markley 69

Chapter 8: D-Day....................................... 70

Chapter 9: An Eye for a Blue Eye........................... 76

Todd Markley 85

Chapter 10: What Happens Now? 86

Chapter 11: Behind Closed Doors.......................... 90

Todd Markley 101

Chapter 12: The Fruit Falls Far From the Tree 102

Chapter 13: Vision of One Leader.......................... 106

Chapter 14: Stealing Time 110

Chapter 15: Aurora Comes for Dinner 118

Chapter 16: Suspicions.................................... 127

Chapter 17: Time Waits For No One 137

Chapter 18: Seeing Double 144

Chapter 19: When it Rains, it Pours 151

Chapter 20: A Warning-Dead Quiet 160

Chapter 21: All Gone 165

Chapter 22: Digital Detox 181

Chapter 23: Consumed with Loneliness 191

Chapter 24: Elders Against Devices 198

Chapter 25: Silence Order 208

Karina Wiseman 216

Chapter 26: Digital Dare 217

Chapter 27: Come Home 234

Chapter 28: Kyle and Knox Wiseman 238

Chapter 29: 212 Degrees - Solomon's Boiling Point 246

AFTER THE FIRE 255

Chapter 30: Forever Changed 256

Deiderick Dollard and the Dollard Family 261

Chapter 31: Unwanted Responsibility 262

Chapter 32: Secrets 275

Chapter 33: The Mystery Man 277

Chapter 34: Missing Dinner Guest 284

Chapter 35: A Fallen Empire 287

Crossing Paths Wiseman, Dollard, Greybottom, Cook and the Others...298

Chapter 36: The Cats Out of the Bag.......................... 299

Chapter 37: Deidcrick and Solomon's Encounter 309

Chapter 38: Solomon's Decision.................................320

Todd Markley 323

Chapter 39: The Set Up.. 325

Chapter 40: Where is Solomon?................................. 339

Chapter 41: World is Excited About the app 343

Chapter 42: Trapped 352

Todd Markley...359

Chapter 43: Three Days Before the App Release.................. 360

Chapter 44: Two Days Before the App Release 370

Chapter 45: The Day of the App Release 376

Chapter 46: Thirty Minutes Before the App Release............383

Chapter 47: Five Minutes Before the App Release 388

Todd Markley 391

Todd Markley

Hello, My name is Todd Markley. You will learn about me a little bit later, but right now, I will act as your guide through the end of the 22nd century. You may not believe it, but the story I am about to tell you is true. I know because I was there. Well, I was there until I met my unfortunate end.

I feel it is important to provide you with some context. By the end of the 22nd Century, the world was on the verge of its first global leader. A man by the name of Yusef Aesis was making his way to be the One World Ruler. But he was not really the one running things. The real leader was a man by the name of Deiderick Dollard. The YSW praised Mr. Dollard for his technological inventions. Even Yusef Aesis, the future ruler of the world, paid homage to Deiderick Dollard and used his technology to advance his political platform.

From outside appearances, Mr. Dollard had it all. He was worshiped by the YSW like a god. But Deiderick didn't ask for this popularity. He would have shied away from it completely, but then he would have denied his gift. Simply put, he was a creative genius who invented a computer coding language that was compatible with every device. He ran nearly every facet of the Second world, the world Jah created after the great floods destroyed the first world.

With his power came a massive following. Society has always been obsessed with the rich and famous, but Deiderick Dollard was the richest man in the world. His following began with young people amazed by his devices, games, artificial intelligence, and security systems. You name it, and somehow, Deiderick Dollard created it.

He started his company when he was only 23 years old. He named it the DEAD company because of a record collection passed down to him 5 generations ago. The Grateful Dead albums began his interest in simple technologies. He was the proud owner of a 300-year-old record player and remembered watching those albums spin on the old relic left in an attic of his great, great, great grandfather. He created an acronym for DEAD which stood for (Device Engineering & Advancement Design), and from there, things took off. The YSW thought the name was cool and felt it added to the creative genius behind the products.

His following of young people gave themselves a name and the YSW, which stands for Youth of the Second World. As the fan club grew, so did the members who joined. Soon the YSW expanded beyond the young and hip. It included doctors, lawyers, politicians, school systems, and entire governments. They all wanted to be part of Deiderick Dollard and the DEAD company.

Social Media platforms and businesses switched to Deiderick Dollard's computer programs because his systems were the best. Deiderick Dollard was running the world. So, naturally, when he discovered that a simple fire took down one of his networks, he was curious as to the identity of this mystery man who started the fire.

So, who was that mystery man? His name was Solomon Wiseman. Solomon lived in the 212-area code, in a place called the Inbetween. The Inbetween was like your altitude and determined your status.

7

The rich lived in a higher altitude than everyone else. Solomon lived at a much lower altitude than the rich and was just above the homeless. He and I lived in the Inbetween district of the 212-area code.

When I was alive, Solomon was my only friend. He was a good man, a loving husband to his wife Kristen, and a devoted father to his children. Solomon had a daughter and two sons. Solomon and his wife made a promise that they would not conform to the YSW. He wanted his children to see life differently than the mirage of a life the YSW offered. But his children didn't understand why they had to go without just to prove a point to the YSW. They had a difficult time seeing the bigger picture, not giving into the YSW was better than living a life controlled by them.

Solomon's daughter desperately wanted to go off to school, but they couldn't afford the good schools because they were all owned by the YSW. This caused a rift between Solomon and his daughter.

Solomon was met with other challenges as well. He and his wife fought to provide boundaries for their children in a world where anything goes. But technology was everywhere, and it was a struggle to keep their kids focused on what he and his wife deemed valuable.

In the second world, everything was expensive except for alcohol, cigarettes, and powdered food. Clean water and organic food were scarce due to the diseases that plagued farms about twenty years ago. A war that ended five years ago left the world with a dusty reddish hue, blocking sunlight and causing plants not to grow. To eat healthy, you paid a high price. But you paid an even higher price if you didn't join the YSW.

The Wiseman family was one of the last families who refused to join the YSW. It was their ability to not conform to the pressures of the YSW that drew unwanted attention.

Solomon became the focus of even more attention when he started the Digital Detox fires. This is where we will begin our story.

Chapter 1: Hiding

If you protect the words of the Writ, then Jah, seeing your love for
his word, will protect you.
(Warning from the Writ)

"Jah, Jah, Jah, please help me," a panting Solomon thought. He
did everything he could to calm his breathing.

"I don't think they saw me." He could hear the buzzing of the
drones and the footsteps of the Youth of the Second World close
behind. He prayed the blue eyes somehow missed his leap into the
dumpster. He was surprised he was able to hide, well, at least for
the moment.

His heavy breathing fogged up his Code Red mask, and the
stench from the dumpster seeped through. An unbearable smell,
but he knew better than to move. The parades of protestors
walking past, for once, proved themselves beneficial and acted as
a distraction allowing Solomon's escape.

Solomon patted his long leather coat to feel the book deep
within the inner pocket. "Thank Jah, it is still here." Hunched in

the corner of the dumpster, he took the *Writ* from its hiding place, opened the cover, and unfolded a picture of his family at the beach. A few months prior, Solomon would have never imagined wanting to protect something with his entire life. But the *Writ* must remain unharmed. Solomon kissed the picture of his family, folded it, and placed it back into the sacred book.

THUD! The banging noise jolted Solomon from his moment of thought. THUD! There it was again. A nervous breath in and a controlled exhale out. He dared not peek. He would wait in the dumpster's dark, moist stench before revealing his location. *Voices*, Solomon stiffened.

"You heard about the man they are looking for?" the voice of a young man said. It sounded as if he were pressed up against the dumpster.

"What man is it now? They are always looking for someone." Another male voice, this one slightly deeper, was also nearby. The smell of cigarette smoke accompanied the dumpster stench.

"The one who started the fires. He is trying to save some book. He's an idiot if you ask me. Can't believe he would be stupid enough to start a fire with all the eyes watching."

"Ah yeah, I heard about him. I heard he was running in this direction. He could be right there in the dumpster."

Solomon's breathing all but stopped. He could feel his leg tremble. He put his hand on top of his leg to prevent vibration.

"You know they are offering a reward for finding the fire starter, and I will make it even more interesting, I will zip you five-hundred one world dollars if you crawl into that dumpster to find him."

Solomon could hear a long pause in their conversation. He braced himself for his big reveal. In the dark, he looked around for something to throw at them or stab them with. He couldn't be caught now; he was too close to home. His fingers began to rummage quietly into the trash but immediately paused when light filled what was once a dark void of filth.

Solomon grabbed hold of the item nearest him. He was about to lunge but heard the male with a slightly deeper voice. "Dear Jah, this smells like crap in here. I ain't doing it."

"Then I guess you don't want five-hundred one world dollars."

"You can keep your money."

"You're a punk."

"You're a punk, and your mama's a droid."

Laughter erupted, and the top slammed back down. The voices mixed with the noise of the streets and soon faded into the distance.

Solomon lifted the top of the dumpster with his left hand, and a small slither of light filled the space. "Ahh!" He screamed as a rat crawled on top of his right hand. He crashed back down into the rubbish but quickly sprung back up to avoid any other vermin that may be running about. A group of YSW were rioting. Solomon observed the words "HUMAN OWNED BUSINESS" being sprayed across windows. He would have usually been irritated by the rioting, but the chaos masked his appearance. *Now,* he thought, *just to stay away from the blue lights.*

The air was filled with noise. "Legalize Humans and Droid marriage!" was being chanted on Solomon's left. In front of him was a large group of One Racers. "One Race, One Gender, No Hate!" echoed down the street. The One Racers accompanied their chants with digital messages about the next mixer event. The passionate One Racers held their wrists in the sky where images filled the air.

Solomon didn't have time to be disgusted by the thought of people fornicating in the streets to eliminate racism, sexism, or whatever other "ism" the YSW was fighting for.

His fleeting thoughts were soon interrupted by the spy bots zinging in and out of the pandemonium, searching for him, the mystery fire starter. Solomon kept his Code Red mask on and scrunched his 6-foot frame, doing his best to weave in and out of the reckless crowd of YSW revolutionaries without being spotted.

The adrenaline from the chase was wearing off, and the throbbing pain from his fall became more noticeable. Solomon clenched his arm closer to his chest to not lose the *Writ*. It was in his coat pocket, being held close to his body with his arm, and he found a quick moment to feel around and see how much damage was done to his arm.

The sensor that all citizens wore, letting the government know who is a member of the YSW and who is not, had been significantly damaged from the crash of the droid. Another miracle of Jah. The damage made it difficult to be detected by surveillance droids and spybots, or, at least that's what he assumed when one of the spybots flying directly overhead passed him by without as much as a body scan.

Before he knew it, Solomon was in front of the EAD hide-a-way. The Elders Against Devices hangout became Solomon's safe place. He ran in. Quantas was in her usual spot.

"Look...I don't think I can go back home for a little while."

"What in the second world is going on?"

Before Solomon could explain trying to save his sons, the fire, and his fall from the airlifter, the silence order hours went into effect, and immediately an eerie hush consumed the 212 area code. All but the most elite of the YSW grew quiet.

Solomon hid in the corner of the EAD basement. It was dimly lit and musty but felt comfortable to Solomon. He removed the Writ from under his arm and gently placed it on the sticky wooden bar table, which seemed as if it hadn't been cleaned since before the One World Order took over. He rubbed his arm in hopes of removing the pain. "Ah." Solomon winced.

"Shhhh!" Quantas reminded him.

Quantas pointed to the blinds. She could see a glimmer of blue light easing through the crack. Quantas motioned for him to move away from the window. She feared that her cover was blown. She had no clue what Solomon had done but couldn't imagine losing her hide-a-way because he had done something stupid. While Quantas worried about the store, Solomon wondered how he ended up in this situation. He thought back on everything. It all went so wrong so fast.

BEFORE THE FIRE

Chapter 2: Blue Lights and Code Red

There will come a time when the Earth will no longer protect its people because the people did not protect the Earth.
(Warning from the Writ)

The ash came down like snow and blanketed the towering concrete structures and digital sidewalks of the 212 area code. The war left its mark, the New World Order, the One World Digital Currency, and the constant ash falling from the sky causing Code Reds. The war had been over for nearly 5 years, so Solomon had gotten used to most of the change, but the ash seemed to get on his nerves most.

The dark tint of his Code Red mask made it nearly impossible to see. Making it worse was the constant grayish hue of the once-blue sky.

"Used to be a lot more birds flying around. Seems like there are fewer each day," Solomon thought to himself. His eyes darted over to the miniature bird perched on a light post.

"Realistic, but *they are not fooling anyone."* He thought to himself. The bright blue eyes of the bird let Solomon know he was being watched.

"I would be at work already if I wasn't so self-righteous." He chuckled to himself. He thought about what an idiot he was for not conforming. He watched as hovercrafts flew above. *"It's better to walk anyway."*

Solomon continued to wipe the rust-colored buildup off the dark lens of his mask.

The war trapped them in the house for so long that he preferred to take in whatever good was left in 212.

Solomon came to a dusty metal door on the left side of a long alley. The alley ended with a brick wall sprayed with the letters YSW and a mural of Yusef Aesis, the One World Leader. In the corner, another robotic bird was perched on a fence. Its eyes glimmered as Solomon stood in front of the retinal scanner waiting to enter the door whose sign read "Reader's Publishing est. 1984." BUZZ, CLICK, the door opened. Kevin was already there when Solomon walked into the small Readers Publishing office.

"Hey Kevin, how's it going?" Solomon asked.

"Could be better. I don't know how much longer I can hold out." Kevin turned on the computer, an old relic from the 21st century. Kevin's dark brown hair and bushy eyebrows were streaked with silver.

Kevin grumbled, "No one is buying this stuff anymore. This job is not paying the bills. I might as well join the YSW. I mean, who are we kidding? We're still using technology but with *none* of the YSW perks. What kind of sense does that make?"

"Something about not giving in makes me feel like I still have some control."

"I don't care about control anymore. I want to put food on my table." Kevin huffed.

Kevin was frustrated with his work at Reader's Publishing, which, at one time, was the largest publishing company in the nation. Now, Reader's Publishing has been taken over by YSW techies, who converted most books into digital text, films, virtual reality games, and other digital media. They did away with the entire print department long ago, but with one exception; Collectors of vintage prints who pay astronomical sums of money to have copies of classic books or other materials in print.

Solomon liked the print department. He had been there for over 25 years. His job made something feel normal in this new, crazy digital world. Plus, he realized long ago that once things were removed from print, they could be altered.

"So the smell of books doesn't do it for you anymore?" Solomon chuckled. Solomon stripped off the layers of protective gear, stretched his arms, and popped his back. He could feel a slight twinge of pain in his bones. A sign he was no longer in his fifties. He plopped himself in an old metal chair that had leather cushions with most of the foam stuffing exposed, swiveled the chair around, and reached for his favorite coffee mug that said, "Number 1 Dad."

"Suit yourself," Kevin replied. He was rubbing his forehead and walking around the small 10x10 foot room with a little digital screen, printer, piles of paper, and a wall of shelves that appeared to be filled with thousands of classic books. Despite the width of the room, the ceilings spanned nearly 40 feet.

Solomon picked up a book and gave it a whiff. "For them to allow us to work around these gems, they must trust us. Paper alone is worth hundreds of one world dollars."

"Nah...it's not that. We are just so old, we remember when there was actually printed text. They probably realize that we don't have a need to steal them." Kevin's voice rumbled.

Solomon placed the book back on the shelf. "Maybe you're right. If I had been smart, I would have saved all of my old books, but I didn't see any of this coming. I know they are worth a fortune. Do you see how much people are buying them for?"

Kevin lifted his rough, dry hands to his chin and rubbed through the salt and pepper hair on his face. "I know. It's crazy. I still think I have a box of magazines in my house somewhere."

"Nudy magazines?" Solomon chuckled. "I thought you had grown too old for those, not gettin' any at home?" His chuckle grew into a laugh.

"I'm not!" Kevin belted out a laugh as well. "I am going to miss you, Solomon. You made working here enjoyable. But I have got to do something else."

"What do you want to do?"

Kevin was nervous. "I...um...I have entertained an offer from the DEAD company?"

A silence filled the room and several awkward seconds passed before Solomon broke the silence. "The DEAD company?"

"I know. I know exactly what you are going to say." Kevin looked down, hoping to avoid making eye contact with Solomon.

"You have to do what you have to do. It has been really tough, so I understand."

Kevin looked relieved. "You never cease to amaze me. I didn't think you were going to say that."

"Seriously, what am I trying to prove anymore? So, tell me about this offer?" Solomon hated to admit that deep down, he was also contemplating leaving to make more money by working for the YSW.

"Well, it is an entry-level position where I would be a data reader. It offers twice what I'm making now. I need it," Kevin said.

"Look." Kevin pointed to his arm. Solomon leaned in and looked closely at Kevin's arm."

"I got my currency chip put in during my interview so I can get the money zipped to me."

Solomon rubbed his arm and felt the tracking device placed in his arm after the war. He looked back at Kevin, who now had two chips in his arm.

"Wow, so this is really happening huh?" Solomon was in shock. "I understand. I really do. My daughter is about to go off to school. Things are just so tight, but I don't know...I just can't....or at least I can't right now. I have spent so much time proving that I can make it without them. It just seems like everyone who works for the 'tech lords' ends up, I don't know, just different. Plus, I am pretty sure my wife would kill me." Solomon chuckled.

Kevin laughed. "Your wife, she's something else....You know, you can save money by letting your daughter attend the virtual universities."

"I don't want her to miss out on the experiences. College was one of the best times in my life. She deserves to have the same experience. Besides, the virtual universities that I can afford are pieces of crap," Solomon said.

"True. The YSW controls all of the best virtual universities and brick-and-mortar schools in the nation. There's almost no way around it."

"It feels like there is no way around it. So I'm done here, my friend. Next week is my last week here. I have already turned in my notice," Kevin responded.

Solomon was dismayed. Both men fumbled around in the room, looking for something to break the tension. A few awkward moments later, Solomon spoke. "Well, since your decision has been made, no need to dig any deeper. Maybe we should just celebrate. Hell, I could use a reason to celebrate right now. I would say let's get out of here and grab a drink now but..." Solomon looked up to the corner at the small blue dot he knew was recording their every move.

"Look busy," Solomon whispered. Both men laughed.

Solomon pulled up his leather chair next to a small speaker and a digital screen about 7x11 inches in size. Kevin grabbed plastic totes and prepared them for shipping.

"On," Solomon said to the small speaker.

"Do you ever wonder why they didn't replace us with machines?" Kevin inquired.

Solomon placed his hands over the speaker and then turned to Kevin. "You know why they didn't. They want to look down on us and laugh at the last two idiots who would actually stay with this department."

Kevin laughed. "You may be right."

Solomon removed his hand off the speaker and worked on getting the orders for the day. "Order report," Solomon said.

"Order report granted. Prepare fourteen orders. Two classics, *To Kill a Mockingbird* and George Orwell's *1984,* will need to be shipped to Unit 5 on 42nd Ave. Ten copies of the *Writ* need to be delivered to 403 twenty-first street, two copies of the classic, *Catcher and the Rye* need to be delivered to 22nd street," the speaker reported.

"I will get the dropcraft ready," Kevin said to Solomon. As the speaker called out the addresses, Kevin double-checked to make sure the addresses were properly recorded in the dropcraft. Solomon grabbed the books he could reach and loaded the dropcraft. "Bubbles, find *1984*."

Immediately a large chrome-plated spider made its way over to Solomon. Its twelve 'eyes' looked like large clear bubbles with all sorts of lights and computer pieces gleaming inside of the clear domes. It hopped on the shelf in front of Solomon, climbed nearly 40 feet high, grabbed 1984 and brought it down to Solomon. Solomon patted Bubbles on its head, and Bubbles scurried off into the corner where its recharging station was located.

The dropcraft's claw-shaped device was perfect for deliveries. Solomon attached totes to the claws, and once he was finished, propellers spun around fast enough for it to lift into the air carrying the orders with it.

"Smaller shipment than usual," Solomon said as he reviewed the orders.

"Yep, but I have noticed more copies of the *Writ* being requested," Kevin replied.

"Same here. I guess some people are trying to get right with Jah." Solomon replied while working on the next order.

"I guess. Hey...have you ever read it?" Kevin asked curiously.

"Naw...I read a little of the *Writ* when I was younger. I remember my parents used to make me memorize a scripture a week, but, I don't know, it all seemed like fantasy to me. I tried to pick it back up when I was in my 30s. Kristen wanted us to start going to the temple more, so I thought it would be best if I attempted to read it again, but I couldn't get through it. I would fall asleep every time I tried."

Kevin chuckled. "Me too."

A few more filled orders, organizing papers, and recreating copies of books and the day was almost over. "I guess you won't miss these long boring days."

Solomon grabbed his long dark brown coat and put it on. Kevin wrapped his scarf around his neck and put his cap on his head.

"Closing," Kevin said and all of the lights shut off, making the blue piercing light from the corner of the office appear to glow brighter.

"Thirty seconds until the alarm sets." The voice sensor counted down.

"Let's get out of here and get a drink."

"Sounds good," Solomon said.

The street sounds, nonstop advertisements, and flying hovercrafts made the walk unpleasant. The air was filled with the dull red hue. Within seconds, the men's coats had a light covering of dust. Solomon pulled a mask out of his pocket, covering his nose and mouth.

"Crap, I forgot mine," Kevin said.

"Too dangerous to forget. It's been a Code Red for nearly three months. I can't risk it."

"You're right" Kevin wrapped his scarf over his nose and mouth and tried not to breathe in too hard.

"Hey, watch out!" Kevin said to a stranger who bumped into him. The stranger was blinking incessantly and staggering.

"He's got the latest model from the DEAD company," Kevin bragged.

Solomon chuckled. "Oh yeah, you'll be working there soon, helping to create more zombies. It's like they really don't see anyone anymore," Solomon said, shaking his head. "Promise you won't become like that when you become part of the DEAD company."

Kevin didn't respond.

They continued walking a few blocks before ending up at Shooters, a local bar at 57th and 4th Ave. The men frequented there for happy hours many times after work.

"Hey Solomon, Kevin, I can get you guys right here." Barkley was an older, white-haired man with dark skin and a deep, scruffy voice. He wore sunglasses all day. If you didn't know Barkley, you would think he just did that to keep a cool, mysterious presence in the bar, but those close to him knew he wore them because he was born blind. His glasses allowed him to see everything. Barkley stood 6ft 5in, with dark black glasses and a beer-stained shirt that barely covered his large protruding belly.

"How are y'all doing today?" Barkley's deep voice boomed in that small bar.

"Kevin here is thinking about leaving the wonderful world of print and going to the DEAD company." Solomon jabbed Kevin in the chest.

"Aw no, don't do it, man," Barkley said, pouring a dark brown drink into a small glass.

"What's so wrong with wanting to provide for my family?" Kevin asked, slightly smiling, slightly annoyed.

"Nothing. I just thought it was cool that I knew at least two people who didn't work for them somehow."

Solomon looked around. "Not many people are here today."

"Tell me about it. It will pick up later. The YSW haven't started their party hours yet. That's when the real money comes in."

"So, are you suggesting that me and Kevin here are not real money?" Solomon laughed before quickly turning up that small glass with the brown liquid.

"Hey, you said it, not me. So, if Kevin leaves, are you leaving too?" Barkley turned to pour Solomon another drink.

"You know, I have to be honest. It has come to mind a time or two. Karina is getting ready to go off to school. I don't want her to have to use any of the YSW scholarships."

Solomon held the second small glass to his mouth and turned it up. Kevin did the same. Barkley reached his hand out to grab the empty glasses, and that is when Kevin noticed the time glowing through the skin of Barkley's arm.

"Hey, I gotta get going," Kevin said.

"Me too." Solomon got up as well.

"Short visit. Hey, Kevin, make sure you don't forget to stop by. Even though you are selling your soul to the DEAD company, I will still fill your cup." Barkley laughed.

"No problem. With the money I'll be making, I should be able to buy it back in no time," Kevin retorted.

"See you later, Barkley." Solomon and Kevin headed toward the exit.

As they walked out of the Shooters, the sensor above the door scanned them and said, "No charge."

"Thanks, Barkley," Solomon and Kevin said, waving to Barkley once more as they walked out. They headed in the same direction for about a block before splitting up.

"See you next week," Solomon said.

"Alright, See ya."

Solomon felt uneasy and thought, *"From this point forward, be careful around him."*

The concrete sidewalks had been replaced with digital screens a long time ago. This was another brilliant idea to get people to purchase items or hook them on the next device.

"Solomon, can I help you find something for dinner?" The sidewalk called out to him. "Solomon, do you need a new shirt?" Solomon sped up his walk and hurried to his high-rise building. The human concierge had been replaced with a droid a long time ago. He looked so lifelike. He was a young, brown-skinned male with straight hair. He wore a bellboy suit, and his demeanor was always pleasant. He was nearly identical to Jose, the human who used to do the job. But there were days when Jose was pissed off and didn't greet the tenants, so it wasn't long before he was replaced.

His piercing blue eyes looked over to greet Solomon. "Good afternoon Solomon." Jose waved as Solomon passed by the front lobby desk toward the elevator.

"Good afternoon. Elevator, please," Solomon said. The elevator came whizzing down to the lower level and immediately reported. "Greetings, Solomon. Your family is already home. Kyle and Knox have been home for 30 minutes. Your wife and daughter arrived about ten minutes ago," the elevator said.

"Thank you," Solomon replied. "You know, it is kind of scary how much you pay attention to everything."

"That is what I have been programmed to do." A slight pause before the elevator spoke again. "Someone has requested a lift."

"Accept," Solomon responded to the elevator.

"Thank you. Lift accepted." The elevator slowed down and arrived on the 3rd floor. A young woman with kinky-curly brown hair walked onto the elevator. She was blinking incessantly.

"What floor?" the elevator asked the woman. But the woman continued to blink non-stop.

Solomon tapped her on the arm.

"Miss, what floor?"

"Oh, I thought the lift would know. It's not like this is the first time it's seen me." The young woman with a kinky curly mop of hair smacked on her gum and continued to blink rapidly.

"Miss, you tend to visit many different floors, so again, what floor?"

The young woman ignored the underhanded comment from the elevator.

"The sixth floor." Then she zoned out and continued to blink in order to move to the next news feed on her third eye device. It was clear that she was completely connected. She was obviously a member of the YSW who had recently gotten her third eye implant.

"Miss." Solomon attempted to make small talk with his elevator companion during their ride.

Solomon cleared his voice and made his final attempt. "Miss, how are you enjoying your implant?"

The young lady rolled her eyes. "I didn't think someone like you would be interested, but it's cool. I am trying to get used to all of its features. Just got it implanted this morning. I am learning how to swipe to the next story."

"Ha, well, I can see that." Solomon chuckled.

An awkward silence filled the elevator before the young woman got off on the sixth floor. Solomon watched as she staggered down the hall.

The elevator doors closed and Solomon continued to his floor. A few short moments later. "The ninth floor. You have arrived."

"Thanks," Solomon responded.

"You are one of the few people that say thank you. I know I am just a machine, but I can still tell when someone has a good heart. Have a nice day Solomon."

"Thank you," Solomon responded.

As he approached, the door camera scanned his face, and Solomon could hear the click of the locks.

The ruckus of two boys quickly found its way to the door. Solomon jabbed at his son Kyle and ruffed up Knox's hair.

"How was school today?" Solomon asked his sons.

"My day was alright, but Kyle…" Knox said, looking at his brother.

"Hey, you promised you wouldn't say anything."

"What are they picking on you about this time?" Kristen asked.

"It's nothing. I am fine."

"None of this is your fault. I know you feel out of place, but I need you to be strong. Jah doesn't make any mistakes." Kristen said to Kyle. She loved all her children but had an exceptional fondness for Kyle because of his condition. Her heart went out to him. Kyle was born with a cleft lip, and they couldn't afford to fix it. The YSW babies would have fixed it in the womb. But Kyle wasn't born with such luxury, a plight that Kristen could understand. Her mother and father were part of the International Society of One Race, working to eliminate a defined race with their mixers. Kristen felt that her parents were weak for giving into one of the YSW social groups.

Most One Racers were proud. No one would suspect the shame that she felt because her features were accepted by everyone in every class. She could only imagine what Kyle must feel like, having such a prominent disfigurement seen by the world.

"Tell us what happened son," Solomon demanded.

"It was just the Cocooners again," Kyle said solemnly.

Chapter 3: Cocooners

The difference between reality and fiction will become too difficult to tell and those who seek truth will have to ask Jah for discernment (A Warning from the Writ)

"Move, you crooked-lipped freak!"

Before Norman became a cocooner, he would have nudged Kyle, but since he is technically not here, he could only inflict verbal insults. Norman's parents paid for him to cocoon at home. Which means his body was incubating while a virtual Norman roamed the school hallways. "I am not a freak!" Kyle looked down, trying to hide his face.

"Norman, why are you even here? Oh, I know. I bet your parents lost their job at the DEAD company. Now you're slumming it with the rest of us," Knox said, taking up for his brother.

"Yeah," a frail framed, frizzy-haired Clifton chimed in. He was Knox's friend and for some reason, him chiming in only made Kyle feel worse.

"I don't need you guys to take up for me." A frustrated Kyle stormed off.

"You, your brother, and whatever he is, is a waste of my time." Norman pointed to Clifton before walking away with the rest of his cocooner gang.

Knox chased behind his brother, putting his arm around his neck. "Look, I know you don't need me to take up for you, but you're my little brother."

"You're only ten months older."

"Yes, but I am still older."

"Look, while you two debate on whose older, I think I may have something that will interest the both of you," Clifton said, pulling Knox and Kyle Wiseman into a small corner in their literature classroom.

"You guys were asking me if I could get my hands on an Illuminus 2150, well, I couldn't get the 2150 model, but my dad just threw away the 2125. It's basically the same model, just a tiny bit slower. And you can't get this one surgically placed under your skin." Clifton pulled out the shiny timepiece from his pocket.

Kyle quickly forgot about his interaction with Norman. "Oh my Jah, I can't believe you got your hands on one of these."

Knox stared at the shiny timepiece. "It's beautiful. Besides, you can't get the surgery until you are 16. I can't believe your dad was actually going to throw this away. Can I see it?" Knox asked.

"You can have it. My dad is going to get me the new one soon." Clifton handed the timepiece over to Knox.

"If Mom or Dad see us with it, they will kill us."

"You think so? I don't know anymore. Dad seems like he may not get all that upset."

"But, mom." Kyle stared at his brother.

"You're right. Mom will kill us and then force us to read the last ten chapters of the *Writ*." Knox smirked as he continued to analyze the object.

"That is why she can never find out."

"Oh my gosh." Clifton looked at the brothers. "*PLEASE* don't tell me you two are about to do the stupid chant."

"Why yes, we are," Knox replied. He turned to his brother, and they both whispered, "Secrets shared between you and I, others can't hear, or else you die. The type of death will be painful and slow. You'll leave this earth, and none will know." This chant was accompanied by a very complicated handshake and ended with a chest bump.

When it was finished, Knox turned to Clifton and said, "You should feel special. We haven't said that in front of anyone outside of our family. That means you are almost like a brother to us."

"That's nice and all, but I never want to be one of the Wiseman brothers."

"Wow," Kyle said. "That was pretty harsh."

"Don't mean it to be harsh. I just know if I am part of your family, I can't date your sister." Clifton chuckled.

"Not to worry, Karina wouldn't date you anyway," Knox said, and both brothers started laughing.

It was a typical day at the Liberal Arts Magnet Education School. Math, Science, English, History, and some of the arts were part of the curriculum. The arts were thrown in just to appease the parents who desperately wanted their children to know what school was like in the good ol' days. A glint back to the past where students actually came to school, made friends and learned about who they could be when they grew up. The little bit of the arts thrown into the curriculum was not enough to mask the true nature of all schools in the 23rd century, which was to create the perfect peon for the DEAD company.

As the day ended, the Cocooners began to disappear.

"The stupid cocooners get to just teleport back to their pods. We have to walk home," Kyle said as he watched the image of Norman and his friends walk into the science lab to connect themselves to the transporter.

"Who cares? Tonight, we get to finally play with the Illuminus."

The three boys put on their Code Red masks and walked seven blocks, stopping in front of the Ocean View high-rise.

"See you later." Clifton waved. "And tell your sister I said hi." Clifton chuckled. Clifton headed toward his building about two blocks away.

"She's not interested!" Knox shouted over the noise of the hovercrafts and airlifters in the sky.

"Hey," Kyle said, turning to his brother. "Don't tell dad about what happened at school today."

"You mean the Illumines 2125?...absolutely not," Knox responded. He reached into his pocket just to make sure it was still there.

"No, I am talking about the Norman thing. I don't want to hear his long speech about how I should be proud to be different. He doesn't know what it feels like to look like a freak of nature."

"Would you not call yourself that!" Knox was irritated.

"Oh yeah, then what am I?" Kyle asked.

"You're my brother," Knox responded. "I will try not to say anything to dad, but you will have to figure out how to stand up for yourself."

"It is so different because you aren't like me. Why did I have to be born like this?"

"Believe me, it doesn't matter. The Cocooners will mess with anyone if you let them."

Kyle was amazed at how quickly Knox forgot to NOT share what happened at school today. Kyle was jolted out of his flashback when his dad asked again, "What happened at school?"

"It's Norman again, but I can handle it."

"That's my boy. I know you can handle it," Solomon said, patting his son on the head.

"Anything else I need to know?

"Yes," Kyle said. Knox stared at his brother, fearful that he would tell him about the Illuminus 2125.

"Well," Solomon said. "What is it?" Solomon headed toward the refrigerator, looking for a snack, a habit from a long time ago.

"My teacher refused to take your handwritten note." Knox continued with a huff, "Dad, it's illegal. We are not allowed to have paper anymore."

"Dad, they do have a point. These two lames have it hard enough. Don't make it worse," Karina said. She seemed to have popped out of nowhere.

"Gee, thanks for your help, Karina," Knox sarcastically replied.

"No problem. Glad I don't have to deal with that kind of stuff much longer. I will be off to university soon."

"Yeah, right. You know Mom and Dad aren't going to let you go to any of the colleges the YSW are in control of. You will be stuck at home with us!"

"No, I won't!" Karina retorted.

"Okay, Okay. Everyone stop arguing," Kristen interjected.

"Hello, my love," Solomon said, greeting his wife.

Kristen slowly walked into all of the commotion. "You all know I have not been feeling well. Keep all of that noise down." Kristen went over to Solomon and gave him a kiss on the cheek.

In the middle of the commotion, a digital message from the boys' school popped on the living room screen.

"Teacher messages - would you like it to be read aloud?" The volume startled Solomon, who loathed that he was forced to keep that thing on.

"Go ahead." Solomon dismissively waved his hand.

"A virtual field trip for Knox and Kyle Wiseman. Please sign the permission slip. Would you like to accept the permission now?"

"Wait a minute," Solomon interjected. "How much is it?"

"$75.50."

"You've got to be kidding me?" Solomon shook his head in disbelief.

The screen continued. "I can take the money directly from your account once you give me permission."

"I bet you can," Solomon said under his

breath. "Debiting account now," the tablet

responded.

"Wait! What just happened? I didn't say you had permission."

"I heard you can. Was that not confirmation?" the tablet inquired.

"Screen, refund, please."

"Refund granted. Please allow seven to ten days for the money to return."

Solomon slammed his hands down on the kitchen table and shouted, "Screen off."

"I am sorry. I cannot power off. I can go into sleep mode."

"Sleep mode, please."

Karina could not help but laugh. "Dad, I wish you could see your face right now."

"So you are making fun of your dad?" Solomon gave his daughter a playful nudge.

"Dad, you make it so easy." Karina continued to laugh and gave her dad a hug.

Solomon continued reading the permission slip form and started mumbling under his breath.

"What are you saying, dad?" Karina asked.

"I am not going to pay for a fake field trip. Looks like the trip is next week. I will if they don't want to take you all to the beach for your life science class. You want to miss a day of school?"

"Really?!" Knox and Kyle were shocked. They began high-fiving each other.

"Dad, will you really let them miss a day of school? Wow, how fair is that?" Karina pouted.

"You can miss a day too?" Solomon said to his daughter.

"Solomon, what has gotten into you? Are we really going to have the children miss school again? They were already out the other day for a checkup," Kristen asked with concern.

"Why not? I would rather pay for them to actually go than for them to sit behind a screen and pretend they are there."

"Dad, I must say, this is pretty cool!" Karina smiled at her father.

"So *now* I am cool. I finally won some of your approval," Solomon replied with a smirk.

"Solomon, I love the idea but think it could be dangerous. I mean, have you heard about all of the public shootings? I am sure they are rioting about something right now. Oh, and aren't we in a Code Red? It's not even safe to go outdoors. That's why the schools are making virtual field trips."

"Aren't you the one that always says that we shouldn't let the society outside dictate how we live our lives inside? Besides, we are on Code Red so often we would never get to go anywhere. I walk to work every day, and the children walk to school. If we can make it there safely, we can make it anywhere. We need to start living life," Solomon responded. He was shocked to hear his wife did not jump at the opportunity to take a family trip. She used to be so much fun, but something about her was different.

"Mom, come on? Can we please go?" Kyle begged.

"Mom, we haven't gone out as a family in a long time. You don't want to be like the Reclusives, do you?"

"Of course, I don't want us to be a recluse. You know what? Let's do it! I guess we will let your teachers know you will be absent one day next week," Kristen said.

"Yes!" Knox lifted his arms in the air like he was making a touchdown.

Kyle started dancing, chanting, "We're going on a trip. We don't need your permission slip. We're going on a trip, don't need your permission slip. In your face, teacher!!!"

After several moments of bopping around their small apartment, Kyle asked, "Mom, can you do me one favor? Can you please send a digital message instead of writing a note? I don't want anyone to laugh at me again, and don't you get a fine every time you write using paper?"

"You don't worry about the fine; yes, we can send her a digital message." Kristen looked at the joy in her children's faces. "You all do know that we are not trying to completely rule out the technology. We just try to limit it so you all don't become like the YSW."

"We know it's all about balance," Knox, Kyle, and Karina said at the same time.

"See, love. We have taught them well." Solomon laughed.

"Only a few minutes of screen time. Dinner will be ready soon," Kristen shouted from the kitchen.

"I don't know who these people are, but please don't let our old parents come back," Kyle whispered to Knox.

"Yeah," Knox said, "I almost feel like we could tell them about the Illuminus 2125."

"Nah…" Kyle and Knox said to each other and laughed.

"Awesome! Screen on," Kyle said.

The voice from the screen began displaying an advertisement. "Upgrade from your handheld device to your eyepiece for the low price of six hundred and sixty-six dollars." The image of the third eye popped off the screen and appeared as a hologram right in front of them. The 3D image of the third eye then rotated around, allowing them to get a full glimpse of all its features. The hologram image was sucked back into the screen when the advertisement ended and Solomon's credit card information appeared.

"Are you interested in ordering the third eye?" the screen asked.

"No!" Solomon shouted.

"Purchase denied. Are there any other items you may be interested in today?" the screen asked.

"No! Screen, let's view the weather," Solomon requested.

The screen asked, "Would you like to feel the weather for tomorrow?"

"Yes, screen, feel the weather."

The sensors at the bottom and the top of the screen began blowing a light breeze and creating the sound of birds chirping. The heat sensor came on and located the people in the nine-hundred-square-foot apartment. It targeted their faces and put a warm laser on them. "The high for tomorrow is 77 degrees, with five-mile-per-hour winds. Would you like to feel low for tomorrow?"

"Allow us to feel the low," Knox asked. Again, the sensors on the devices located the people in the apartment and adjusted its temperature to a cool 53 degrees.

"Feels like tomorrow is going to be decent. A little chilly in the morning, but warmer than it was today."

"Severity of code red?" Kyle asked.

"Code Red severity is extreme tomorrow but will decrease to a Code Orange by Thursday of next week." The screen responded.

"Awesome. That is just in time for our family trip!"

Solomon smiled at his sons, who were still bopping around the house about the trip.

Todd Markley

It's me again, Todd Markley. Our friend Solomon was still in the corner of the Elders Against Devices meeting room, reflecting over his life and remembering the trip. He remembers feeling so excited to provide this experience for his family but now wonders if it was worth it.

Chapter 4: The Market

If you valued what was good when it was plentiful, Jah would have left an abundance, but lack of appreciation for His gifts, will have them taken away.
(A Warning from the Writ)

Solomon walked into the kitchen to help his wife with dinner. The boys quickly ran off to their rooms to check out the Illuminus 2125. Karina watched her brothers suspiciously.

Kyle and Knox were sitting on their twin beds. Knox had just reached into his backpack and pulled out the Illuminous 2125 when he heard the nagging voice of his sister.

"What do you have in your hands?" Karina said with her hands on her hips.

"Shhhh, close the door." Knox got up and quickly closed the door behind his nosey older sister.

"Mom and dad are going to kill you!" Karina hissed.

"Clifton from school, let us get his old Illuminous." Knox held the small device in his hands. It was no bigger than the size of a 1-inch by 1-inch cube attached to a leather band. It could be secured around your wrist like a watch or put on a chain to be worn as a necklace.

"What does it do? I mean, if it is the older model of the Illuminus 2150, do you think it will even do the cool stuff?" Kyle tried to pick it up, but Knox swatted at his brother. "Karina, I swear if you tell Mom or Dad, I am going to vaporize you with this thing."

"Yeah, right, this old one doesn't even have the ability to do that. Besides, only the richest YSW can afford the vaporizer app," Karina snapped at Kyle.

"Well, what are you waiting for? Do something with it," Kyle said to his brother, who was holding the device in his hands.

"What? Are you scared?" Kyle continued.

"Kinda," Knox responded. "Mom and Dad told us so many scary stories about these things. Okay...here goes nothing...device, play..."

"Make sure the volume is turned down first. You don't want to get caught." Karina reminded her brothers.

"I already did that... Device, play the big juicy booty song."

Immediately, holograms of the singers appeared in the room. Kyle and Knox joined in and started dancing with DJ Juicy and his backup dancers.

Karina giggled. "You guys are crazy. Here, give me that thing."

Karina snatched the device out of Knox's hand.

"Device, take me to the beach."

Instantly the device simulated the beach. The sounds of the ocean filled the air. The wood floors of the room took on the features of sand and faded into what appeared to be water that lightly drifted up and down the beach.

The device then asked, "Would you like to include smell? It is a $5.00 add-on."

Karina turned to her brothers. This isn't attached to dad's bank account, is it?"

"I don't think so. How could it be?"

"Why yes, device, please include smell." Karina giggled.

A mist poofed out of the device filling the air with the smell of sunblock, tanning lotion, and the ocean.

"Karina, this is fantastic!" Kyle said.

"Can you believe dad is going to take us to see a real beach?"

The kids didn't get to relish their accomplishments long before hearing their father walk down the hallway.

"Device off," Kyle said frantically and just like that, the entire beach went away.

The door to the boys' room flew open. "Hey Karina, I need you to come help me. Your mom said she isn't feeling well. You boys can set the table for dinner."

"I can't believe I am saying this, but I really miss vegetables, like really miss vegetables."

"Me too," Karina said as she also plopped some on her plate.

"Yes, we need to try and save up to get the real deal. The good stuff just costs so much now," Solomon said. "At least this will fill your bellies."

A dry hacking cough erupted from Kristen.

"You okay?" Solomon asked his wife.

"I don't know what's going on. It seems like it won't go away. And these shooting pains in my stomach. I may sit this meal out," Kristen said, trying to catch her breath.

The hacking continued. "I need to get some water. Excuse me." Kristen got up and went over to the faucet. She grabbed a glass. She was having difficulty catching her breath, so she manually turned on the sink. She filled the glass with water. The water had a slightly gray-brown pigment and smelled a little like sulfur, but Kristen gulped it down to see if the coughing would subside.

"Mom, are you sure you're okay?" Kyle asked.

Kristen could not answer, she quickly ran to the bathroom, and Solomon followed.

"I am sure your mother will be fine. I am going to go check on her. You all finish eating."

Solomon found his wife hovering over the toilet when he got to the bathroom. She was heaving and trying to catch her breath.

"Kristen, can I do anything?"

"No, I've just been having a hard time keeping this food down."

"Okay, well. Let me see if I can make an appointment for you. This has been going on for a little while. You don't think you are pregnant, do you?"

"Solomon, seriously, you think I can have children at this age? Besides, we were lucky to have Kyle after they announced the Code Reds." Kristen tried to smile through the pain.

Solomon picked up the tablet and pressed the emergency button.

"It's asking if this is an immediate emergency?"

"No, I should be fine in a minute," Kristen said, still doubled over the toilet and heaving. "Just see if they have an appointment next week."

Solomon booked the appointment and walked Kristen to their bed. "Lay down. Let me know if you need anything else?"

Solomon walked back into the kitchen.

"Is Mom okay?" Knox asked.

"I am sure she will be fine. We went ahead and booked an appointment for next week. In fact, I think it is the day after our field trip."

Karina got up from the table and went to accompany her mom.

'Kristen struggled through the cough to comfort her daughter. "Hey, sweetie, don't look like that. I will be alright. Just need to rest."

"Mom, do you need me to do anything for you? This has been going on for months." Karina said as she stroked her mother's hair.

"No, I am fine."

"Can you please stop being strong and just tell me what you need? Please, Mom!" Karina's voice broke as she begged her mom.

"Well, I wouldn't mind if you laid here with me."

Kristen cradled her daughter's head like she did when Karina was a baby.

Solomon couldn't help feeling guilty for what was happening to his wife. He couldn't afford to purchase real fruits, vegetables, or grain. Once the YSW took control of the online grocery markets, organic food became nearly impossible to purchase unless you became one of them. Solomon used to get his fresh food from a small business owner who started selling illegally, but he was jailed once the YSW found out. Now, Solomon was settling for the scientifically engineered food powders or selling his soul to the YSW to get organic food.

Solomon was so mad that he couldn't do what he wanted to do for his family. "I need to take a walk. Maybe see what I can afford at the grocery store."

A pile of packages sat in front of the adjacent apartment. Solomon peaked at the stack of items to find the name Todd Markley. He was about to walk off but then noticed something oddly familiar. A package from Reader's Publishing. Solomon could tell a Reader's Publishing box from miles away. The chances that he was the one to put the books into that box was 50%, as it was only him and Kevin who worked for that branch of the company. Solomon quickly left the door when he noticed the blue light began scanning the part of the hall where he was standing.

Solomon tightened the strap on his mask and placed the goggles over his eyes before walking down the noise-filled streets. Sirens and sounds of protest filled the air. Ominous blue lights penetrated through the red dust particles. *They are always watching,* Solomon thought as he walked toward the market. *Stupid idea.* Solomon remembered when people protested to have the cameras feel like they were part of nature so everyone would feel more comfortable.

As if 'they' were reading his mind, the advertisements began. Ironically, all of the ads pointed him toward the nearest market, the Yummy Supply Warehouse. He replayed the initials of the Yummy Supply Warehouse in his head, *YSW a conceited bunch, always having to leave their mark.*

Hovercrafts and airlifts zoomed overhead. Airlifters were designed to transport crowds, and hovercrafts were for single people or small families. Solomon looked up. The sky told the story of the haves and the have-nots. The closer the hovercraft was to the ground, the less money the individual made. The higher up, the more air space you could purchase. The more flight freedom you had. The sky was zoned. Invisible electronic airfields helped hold the hovercrafts in the atmosphere. Each zone had the same amount of electrical current, but there were more hovercrafts in the lower fields, so those crafts tended to move a lot slower. Airlifts were also on the lower levels. Solomon watched as a crowd of people boarded the airlifters.

Air Traffic, with all the space in the world, there is still traffic. Solomon observed the crafts flying past. He actually felt better as a non-vehicle owner. According to 22nd-century social status, he was a walker on the bottom of the totem pole. The walkers were a mix of the urban poor and a few of the passionate YSW who made some sort of socially conscious movement by walking instead of using their privilege to fly. Deep down, Solomon had respect for them.

There were so many different classes of people to keep up with that Solomon gave up long ago. He was pretty sure, however, that no matter what his role in society was, he was probably on the bottom.

It wasn't long before Solomon arrived at Yummy's.

"Greetings, Solomon and welcome to Yummy's Supply Warehouse, where we supply you with everything yummy to your tummy," the door said as he entered the store. "Looking for anything in particular?"

"Fresh fruit and vegetables?" Solomon replied.

"Yes, you will find them on aisles three and four."

Solomon walked through a stark white store. The aisles were immaculate. None of the shelves were fully stocked. They didn't have to be.

Solomon walked to the aisle with grapes. It was his wife's favorite fruit. *Sheesh, $49.99 a pound. Dear Jah, this is ridiculous!* Solomon thought to himself. Upon closer inspection, another sign read YSW price $9.99 a pound. See customer service to sign up for your YSW discount today. He put a quarter pound of grapes in a biodegradable bag before moving on to find string beans. *$17.99 a pound. This is ridiculous,* Solomon thought. He could feel the eyes of the surveillance cameras watching him. He was not their typical shopper. He grabbed a few more items before heading straight out the door, where a body scan quickly and accurately deducted the correct amount from his account. He laughed to himself, *Kinda like this technology. No lines, just scan you right out the door.* He immediately felt guilty after that thought.

"Thank you, Solomon. $124.99 has been deducted from your account. If you sign up for YSW rewards, you can save $94.50. Are you interested in saving?"

"No thanks," Solomon replied.

"YSW reward is no cost to you, just a quick chip implant and you can begin saving."

"I am fine, thank you."

Solomon made it back to his apartment and could not help but notice that the packages in front of his neighbor's door were still piled up. The name on the package read, Todd Markley.

When he opened the door, his children waited to see the delectable treats he brought back.

"The grapes are for your mother." Solomon quickly stated before greedy hands grabbed the fruit.

All three of the children grabbed a few of the green beans and ate them raw. The fresh crispness of the vegetables is a sensation they have not had in years.

"Kristen, here." Solomon brought her some grapes. "You think this will make you feel better?"

Kristen sat up in bed and grabbed the bag from Solomon.

"Thanks." She placed a few grapes in her mouth and squeezed them so that the juice ran down her throat.

"Now that's good. Thank you. Solomon--" Kristen looked at her husband. "--I know that you question Jah because of what we are going through, but He is good, and I need you to pray with me."

Solomon looked at his wife. The topic of Jah was always very uncomfortable for him. He grew up in a household where he and his family worshiped Jah, but as he got older and saw how terrible things had gotten, it was more and more difficult to believe.

"You know I am not good with this kind of stuff," Solomon replied.

"Can you just do it for me?"

Before he could respond, Kristen grabbed Solomon's hand and closed her eyes. Solomon followed her lead and he began to pray. When he was finished, Kristen said, "You definitely have a gift Solomon. Don't ever forget that." Kristen let go of his hand and laid down. "I think I need to get some rest.

Chapter 5: Your Neighbor's keeper

---◆---

*In the end, there will be very few with a heart with room for
more than themselves.
(A Warning from the Writ)*

A week later, Solomon was at Reader's Publishing with Kevin for
the last time. "I can't believe you are actually taking a day off
tomorrow to take your family out. You're the man!" Kevin said to
Solomon as they were loading the dropcraft.

Solomon put a stack of vintage books into a tote and clipped
them to the claw. He patted Bubbles on the head, and it scurried
off to its charging pad. Then he programmed the dropcraft to
make its deliveries.

"Yeah, I think it should be fun. I can't remember the last time
we did something like this. I broke all my rules too. You can't do
anything without technology, so I said to heck with it. I ordered
our lift for tomorrow with no partner pickup."

"Wow, you are really going all out. That's going to cost you an arm and a leg, especially without the YSW discount." Kevin was in awe.

"I know. I made reservations for our lunch and dinner to eat at The Fresh near Clean Water's Edge. If I am going to do this, I want to do it right." Solomon couldn't help feeling proud of himself. The Fresh was the most exclusive part of the beach because it was the only part that was not completely contaminated.

"The Fresh only allows a few people in at a time to view the beach." Kevin couldn't help but ask, "So, how much did this all cost?"

"Let's just say I nearly considered joining the YSW to get the perks," Solomon replied jokingly.

"Look, it's no secret." Kevin began fumbling around. "I wish I stayed as strong as you and not take part of what the YSW has to offer, but I have a family...things are just difficult. I guess what I am trying to say--" Kevin continued. "Is that I am going to really miss working with you. I admire what you are doing, Solomon, but let me help you a little. You don't have to become part of the YSW, but let me give you some of my discount. Put a couple of those adventures on me and save a few thousand bucks. I know, working here, there is no way you have the money for this."

"You're right. I had to charge most of it. I don't even want to discuss the 42% interest rate, but I am just so tired of not living life," Solomon replied, completely ignoring Kevin's offer.

"Look, just let me help you out."

A long pause filled the air of the small office. Solomon looked around and watched as the little blue light peered at him in the corner. He felt the eyes of a thousand people looking at him. So many thoughts ran through his mind before he ultimately said, "Sure, I will accept your offer as a gift from a friend."

Solomon couldn't believe what he just said. A part of him felt like he was selling his soul to the devil, but there was another part that felt a huge financial relief. *What harm could accepting his discount do? I am not going to join the YSW. It's just a discount.*

"Good deal. I will take care of the lift and meals for your trip." Kevin immediately pulled out his timepiece, something that Solomon had never seen him wear before.

"What is that?" Solomon asked.

"They give you one of these as a 'starter kit' for joining. Mine is 24K gold because I held out for so long they wanted to make my offer as enticing as possible."

"It's nice." Solomon felt conflicted again. "Just promise me you won't get one of those eyepieces that the younger YSW's are wearing." Solomon chuckled and watched as Kevin began making all of the reservations.

"One important thing...it is asking me who will be on the trip. You know there are cameras everywhere and they are going to check your PID number, so I am going to put in your name. I just don't want you to feel pressure if they start hounding you to join."

"I have lasted this long, my friend. I am sure that it can't get much worse."

"Alright...there, you are all set," Kevin said as he made his last voice request into his timepiece.

The rest of the day seemed to go by as expected. Solomon noticed the number of *Writ*s being ordered had doubled from last week. Several other new pieces of literature were being requested as well. It was when an order came through for Todd Markley that Solomon paused.

"Come here," Solomon called over to Kevin who had just made his 5th cup of bitter coffee. "I want you to look at this."

"What?" Kevin stared at the order confused. "He is placing an order for books. Nothing different than everyone else."

"He lives in my building. He is a reclusive. I don't think anyone has ever seen his face," Solomon said as he stared at the order. "Do you see what types of print he is ordering?"

"Let me see," Kevin said, hoping to satisfy Solomon's odd request. "Looks like he has purchased three copies of the *Writ*, a copy of Deiderick Dollard's life story. I bet that will be an interesting read. Hmm, the 1776 version of the Declaration of Independence and the 2090 revision. I didn't know there was one in 1776. I only knew about the Declaration written in 2090."

"I didn't either." Solomon continued to study Todd Markley's list. "Look at this, he is also ordering a book written in 1960 on CIA secrets and a book with the same title but rewritten in 2158. Does that seem strange to you?"

"Well, I guess you have a lot of time on your hands when you are a reclusive. So, it's good that he is using his time to read."

"And where is he getting all of this money from? Do you know how expensive these copies are? The older the text, the more expensive."

"Well," Kevin said. "Maybe your neighbor is filthy rich."

"I guess." Solomon was intrigued by Todd Markley, the reclusive man that lived just a few doors down from him. Solomon also noted that he paid large amounts of money to get prints of these rare documents. He paid $15,000 for the 1776 version of the Declaration of Independence while the 2090 version was a free print. Solomon also noticed that Todd was willing to pay over $9,000 for the 1960 version of the book entitled CIA secrets. The one written in 2158 only costs $500.

Solomon shuffled things around to find a pen and paper. He turned his body away from the blue light as much as possible without looking suspicious and wrote down every item in Todd Markley's order.

The rest of the day was uneventful and the men decided to grab a drink at Shooters before heading home. A few laughs, a goodbye drink for Kevin, and Solomon found himself in the lobby of his apartment complex.

As Solomon walked toward his building, the girl from the elevator was still learning to work her Third Eye implant. He could tell that she had a much better understanding of its capabilities.

"Hey there." Solomon waved to catch her attention.

The girl's eyes were closed, but she turned her body toward Solomon and gave him a wave.

"I see you are learning to work that thing a bit better now."

"Yes, it is so cool. I can actually see you with my eyes closed because of the infrared capabilities. I swear Deiderick Dollard is brilliant."

"He is something," Solomon said through gritted teeth. Deiderick was the president of the DEAD Company and if you asked Solomon, he was why the world was in turmoil.

"My Jah, this thing can literally do everything. I basically don't even have to think for myself."

"Why is that cool? Why do you not want to think for yourself."

"Wow." The girl opened her eyes, and the 3rd eye stopped glowing. "You really know how to ruin someone's high. You sound like my parents before they died. Look, I have seen you around my building a few times. You seem like a really nice old man, but don't judge me, okay? If you want to know something

54

for education's sake, then, by all means, feel free to ask, but don't start with the questioning to make me feel bad, alright?"

Solomon was taken aback. "I apologize. It was definitely not my intent. I just…"

"You just what?" the girl snapped.

"I just remember seeing you a few years back, and it seemed like you were just a different person, but you are right. I can see how my comment made you feel. I'm sorry."

"Wait. Look, I get it. You see me and think I could do something more, right? I am sure it is no secret that when my parents died, they left me a decent amount of money. I know the whispers about me. People feel as if I am squandering everything they left me on devices or wasting it on the lavish life of a YSW elite. And maybe I do, but you and I both come home to this high-tech piece of crap of an apartment where the devices are plentiful, but the warm water is scarce. I do my best to find peace in this shithole and find a way to cope without a family."

"You're right. I have wondered what you were doing, but I never judged you one way or the other. You have had it rough. Let's start again. My name is Solomon. I live on the 9th floor. Feel free to visit me and my family anytime. I have a daughter that is a few years younger than you. I am sure she would love to hang out with other girls around her age."

"Thanks…I appreciate your invite. My name is Aurora. I guess you already know that I live on the 6th floor. I am sorry that I seem so sensitive, but…"

"No need to apologize. Unlike the rest of the droids around here, we have human emotion. It's really nice to see, actually. I was serious about my offer. Feel free to stop by anytime."

"I was headed out. I will see you around." Aurora left out the door of the Ocean View apartments.

Solomon waved goodbye and was greeted by Jose. At Solomon's arrival, the elevator came whizzing down. No one else joined him on his lift, so he arrived at his floor quickly. He couldn't help but look in the direction of Todd Markley's apartment. It appeared that Todd had removed the previous packages from the door. He walked past slow enough for the motion detector in front of Todd's apartment to trigger. "You are being recorded. Please continue to your residence." Solomon was startled and quickly went to his door. A quick scan of Solomon's face and he could hear the locks open. His apartment was full of excitement as everyone was getting ready for their family trip.

"Guess what, Dad?" Kyle said excitedly.

"What?" Solomon's smile grew just watching his son.

"Can you believe on the day of the beach trip, we will be downgraded from Code Red to Code Orange. That is the best oxygen ranking in months."

"No, I didn't know that." Solomon continued to smile.

"You know what else?" This time it was Karina with something exciting to share.

"What, Karina?"

"I can't wait to collect fossils and take pictures."

"I think that is a great idea," Solomon replied.

"Me too," Kristen said, smiling. Kristen pulled Solomon into their room, away from their children's excitement. "I just wanted to apologize for my initial hesitation. Seeing them like this is worth however much this trip costs...By the way, how much is this little trip costing?"

"Don't worry about it. I have it all taken care of. We will live like royalty, even if it is for just one day." Solomon kissed his wife on the forehead. "Let's get some rest before our big day tomorrow."

Chapter 6: Night Vision

Jah will reveal himself, but many will say they don't know why things are happening. Look at the signs, dreams and visions. Write them down, for they are warnings of things to come.
(A Warning from the Writ)

Solomon pulled the blanket over his head and quickly found himself in a deep sleep. During the night, he had a dream.

In his dream, he and Kristen held hands and walked behind their three children along the beach. As they walked, thunderclouds began to roll in, and they all ran for cover. The family headed toward a small cabana that was located near the beach. Solomon grabbed a towel when they got inside the cabana and patted Kristen off. As he was patting her hair, he noticed long strands were trapped in the fiber of the towel. Kristen looked at the towel and asked, "What is happening to me? She reached up and ran her fingers through her hair. This time, large clumps were tangled between her fingers.

"Mom, stop pulling at your hair," Karina screamed. "Dad, what did you do? What is happening to mom?"

"I don't know, baby. I was just trying to get her warm. She was drenched," Solomon replied.

"I will get her another towel." Karina ran off in search of another towel to dry her mom. When she finds one, she tosses it to her father. Solomon begins patting his wife again, and as he does, everywhere the towel touches turns her skin into dust and the particles of dust float away in the air.

"Dad, stop it! Why are you hurting mom? Stop hurting mom!" His children all began screaming.

"I am not trying to hurt your mom. I love your mom. I would never hurt your mom."

Solomon immediately woke up from his sleep. He quietly walked into the kitchen, filled a glass with water, and found his sleep aid. He rolled the pill bottle in his hands. *"I hadn't had to do this in months,"* Solomon thought as he looked at the small white bottle of medication. Solomon popped the top of the little white bottle and poured three oval-shaped white pills into his hands. He placed the pills on his tongue and quickly followed with a swig of that slightly gray water. He laid back down and did not wake up until the next morning.

Chapter 7: Family Vacation

Families should value each other. In the last days, the enemy whose spirit glows amber, tricks many, making what is most valuable; appear common.
(A Warning from the Writ)

The morning of the vacation could not have been more beautiful. The Code Red was downgraded to a Code Orange, but everyone still wore their Code Red masks out of habit. Thanks to Karina, the bags were already packed and organized by size, and it was not long before their airlift arrived. The family ran excitedly to the elevator.

"I will be down soon. Just grabbing a few more things." Solomon shouted to his family, who were halfway down the hall. Solomon grabbed a few miscellaneous items and headed out the door. He was surprised to see a typed note stuck to the door. He looked around suspiciously to see if he could figure out who left it.

He pulled it off and opened it up:

Solomon,

We know that you are using the YSW perks account of Kevin Baggett. We highly encourage you to join the YSW before non-membership fees are applied to your trip along with additional charges for using the identity of an employee.

Enjoy your vacation,

YSW

Solomon's stomach dropped. He crumbled the note and shoved it into his pocket before smiling to join his family in the lobby.

"You have everything?" Kristen asked.

"Yes, Sure." Solomon fumbled around.

"Are you okay?"

"Of course. Why wouldn't I be?"

Jose, the AI lobby attendant, greeted the family. "Greetings, so where is the family headed?"

"We are going on a family trip," Kyle replied excitedly.

Jose then turned his glimmering blue shining eyes Solomon and Solomon knew he was being watched.

"Hope you enjoy it. By the way," Jose continued, "did you get your message, Solomon?"

"Yes, I have everything," Solomon responded. He looked around to see if anyone else noticed the awkward exchange, but his family was too excited. When the lift arrived, the entire Wiseman crew grabbed everything and piled in. "You have selected to ride at the highest altitude, correct?" The airlift captain asked. "By the way, my name is Julian, and I will be taking you to The Fresh this morning."

"Thanks, Julian." Solomon smiled.

"Solomon, isn't that going to be pricey? Can we really afford to fly at maximum altitude?" Kristen felt giddy and nervous all at the same time.

"Before we depart, would you like to keep this reservation under Kevin Baggett, or would you like to use a different account?" Julian asked. His glowing blue eyes looked at Solomon through the rearview.

"What is it talking about? You had Kevin pay for this?" Kristen's excitement waned as she started putting the pieces together.

"Yes, I would like to keep the reservation under Kevin."

"Did he pay for this trip?" Kristen now had her arms folded.

"No, I paid for the trip. I told him about how much everything cost, and he…" Solomon stopped speaking, realizing that they were probably being recorded.

"Look," Solomon whispered, "I have taken care of everything, just relax and enjoy your day. This is not the time to get upset. Babe, we haven't done anything like this in years. Just trust me."

"Fine, Solomon, I trust you."

The airlift began to elevate; before you knew it, they were at maximum altitude.

"I see why the elite YSW pay for this. It is beautiful up here." Solomon looked down and could see the orange haze below.

"Wow, it is so much clearer up here. I can't believe it. The sky is really blue. I didn't believe them, but it really is blue." Kyle looked out of the window in awe.

Directly below them, Solomon could see the other hovercrafts and airlifts.

Kristen smiled at her daughter. "I thought you were embarrassed to carry the camera your dad and I got for you."

"Yes, this is quite embarrassing, but we may never be on another trip like this, so I need to capture the moment." Karina looked down at the old relic. She turned the camera around to find the date it was made, 2120.

"Dad, since you seem like you are being kinda cool now, do you think you will ever let us have one of the new ones?"

Before Solomon could answer, Kristen quickly chimed in, "Absolutely not! If we had gotten you all that crap, you wouldn't appreciate the moment we are having now. Just sit back and take it all in."

The family enjoyed the flight so much that it was sad when it ended. It landed before a sign that said 'The Fresh, the clearest beach on the east coast.' Slightly underneath 'The Fresh' was a smaller sign with all of the rules for the beach.

The Fresh

'The clearest beach on the east coast'

The Fresh Rules:

-Maximum beach capacity 40 people

-No more than 10 seashells removed from the beach per person

-Beach time is 3 hours

-Additional hours can be purchased for $259.00 per hour for non-YSW or $75.00 for members of the YSW

- Littering will be severely punished with a minimum of a $5000.00 fine and 3 weeks in jail

Remember to Have Fun

"That's kinda scary," Karina said as she read the sign and quickly snapped a picture.

"Yes, but just remember to have fun." Solomon chuckled. "We don't have anything to worry about, just follow the rules, and we should be just fine," Kristen said as she exited the hovercraft. She started looking around to make sure they hadn't dropped anything.

"Okay, I know that we are all excited to begin our adventure, but I don't want us to exceed our three-hour time frame. We will look for shells for about an hour, play in the water, and then head to the Seaside Cafe for lunch. That should leave us about ½ an hour to look around before the airlift comes to pick us up." After Solomon laid out the plan, everyone took a bag and looked for shells in the light brown sand.

"Can I take off my shoes?" Kyle asked.

"I don't see why not. Just make sure that you carry them. You don't want anyone to think you are trying to litter," Kristen reminded her son.

Kyle, Knox, and Karina removed their shoes, tied the strings together and threw them over their shoulders.

They all relished the moment. Allowing the breeze to caress their cheeks, putting their toes in the sand, and splashing in the water. It was magical. The air was crisp and clear. The unfamiliar sounds of birds chirping and a quick glimpse of a crab headed toward the ocean before being scooped away by a wave left the family in awe.

Before they knew it, the hour was up, and they were headed to the Seaside Cafe. Their menu consisted of fresh grilled Salmon covered with crawfish etouffee, grilled asparagus, and loaded baked potato with cheese, bacon, sour cream and chives. A side salad and dessert of a warm chocolate brownie with ice cream accompanied the meal.

Groans of satisfaction came from everyone. They were all too busy stuffing their mouths to say much during dinner. Kristen was in heaven. Her eyes rolled back with satisfaction every time she put a morsel of food in her mouth.

A human waiter came by several times to check on them and fill their glasses. The entire family requested water. It was the most expensive beverage, but it was so satisfying. It had no odor or taste like the water in the 212 area code. It was just cool and refreshing.

"Dad," Knox whispered. "Does he really get paid to check on us?"

"Yes, son. I was a waiter when I was a few years older than you."

"I thought these jobs were eliminated," Knox replied.

"Well, when you pay enough, you get real customer service," Solomon responded.

The waiter slipped the bill on the table, and Solomon picked it up quickly. He didn't want Kristen to see that he also used Kevin's discount for the meal. Discount or no discount, it was still expensive, $575.00.

Solomon whispered to the waiter, "Can you make sure my wife doesn't hear the total?"

"No problem, sir, but that service is an additional fee," the waiter said. Seeing that Solomon wanted all of the financial exchange to be discreet, the waiter wrote the additional fee on the receipt for the meal.

"Wow," Solomon gulped. "Oh...okay...well, thanks for a lovely meal and just take care of that favor for me."

"No problem, sir. Would you like the tip to be automatically deducted as well?"

"So the total I just saw didn't include the tip?" Solomon said nervously.

"No sir, it did not," the waiter responded.

"What percentage is customary now?"

"Thirty-five percent is customary."

"Dear Jah...wow...um...yes...a 35% tip. Okay, go ahead and add it to the total."

Kristen was no idiot. She knew her husband was struggling with the bill, but she could not deny that she enjoyed every moment. Kristen sat quietly, a smile on her face, looking at her children.

As they left the restaurant, Solomon knew that nearly $1,000 was being deducted from his account. He could feel the regret easing its way into their fun.

Time never seemed to have moved so fast. The airlift was approaching.

"We made it! We didn't break any of the rules. No extra fees, but I know if we did, you had us, Dad," Karina said, smiling at her dad as they boarded the airlift.

"Yep, your dad had it covered," Solomon joked.

A few moments into the ride home, Kyle pointed. "Dad, what is that?"

A large metal building seemed to puncture the sky. So high in the air, clouds drifted in the middle of the dark gray structure, adding to its mystery. Multicolored lights jetted from all sides, creating a rainbow haze in the surrounding air. A long glass breezeway connected the building to a mansion.

"I am not sure what that is, son."

Knox's discovery had the entire family looking out of the window.

"That, my friends, is the DEAD company. Do you see the light-colored building attached? That is Deiderick Dollard's house."

"Whoa! That is so cool!" Knox gasped.

"Yep, the man himself lives right there. Boy, what I would pay to get a glimpse of what's inside."

"He lives like a king, and we are about to head back into orange haze and sketchy streets." Solomon huffed.

As the airlift traveled, the massive building faded in the distance.

"We will begin our descent. Please make sure to buckle up." They landed back into reality.

After all of the children were in their rooms, Solomon and Kristen reminisced over the day.

"So much fun, love. One of the best days I've ever had." Kristen snuggled next to Solomon.

"It was. It cost us nearly all our money, but it was amazing."

"Look, Solomon, I am unsure how you afforded everything. I have my suspicions but promise me one thing. Promise me you won't get yourself involved with the YSW."

"I promise I won't. Now, rest up. You have your doctor's appointment tomorrow."

Todd Markley

So, you finally got to meet me. Yes, I once lived across from Solomon. He truly had a beautiful family. It was so unfortunate what happened to him and to all of them. I remember when he shared the story of visiting The Fresh. He told it to me with tears in his eyes. A mix of joyful memories coupled with sadness because it would be his last fond memory of his family before everything changed. Still sitting in the corner of the EAD convenience store, Solomon remembers his wife, Kristen.

Chapter 8: D-Day

The body will experience hurt and pain, but the spirit lives on. Do not focus on the pain that comes in bodies created from the Earth. In the end, all things that come from the Earth will be filled, will parish, but those whose spirit belongs to Jah will live on.
(A Warning from the Writ)

Kristen and Solomon sat in front of a large screen where Kristen pressed a series of icons that listed the different symptoms that she was having.

"Do you think we will actually see a real person?" Kristen asked.

"I hope so. We could have pressed buttons at home." Solomon held his wife's hand.

After they pressed a few more buttons, a voice from the screen came on. "Based on the symptoms you have checked off, we have provided you with a Gastroenterologist. She should be with you shortly. In the meantime, please remove your clothes and put on the gown in the drawer below the table. When you are finished, press the XR button, and we will begin taking your x-ray pictures." Kristen stripped down and put on the robe. She pressed the button and stood behind a screen. Quick flashes, and the Gastroenterologist walked into the room a few minutes later.

A yellow-skinned, well-put-together woman walked into the room with the x-rays. She had a serious look on her face.

"So, you have been experiencing stomach pain for quite some time now. Your assessment shows that you also have nausea and sharp piercing jabs in your stomach area. Can I have you lay down on the table for just a minute?"

Solomon grabbed his wife's hand as she lay back on the table. The doctor placed her hands on Kristen's belly and started firmly pressing. "Does this hurt?"

"Yes, it feels very tender," Kristen responded.

"How about this?" the nurse asked. Kristen winced.

"Ah, okay, well. I think I know what is happening here, but I will see if we can get you in to do an endoscopy today."

When the doctor left the room, Solomon said, "That's good. I am glad they are taking things pretty seriously. I hope they are able to get you done today so we can get back home."

"Same here. I have a few things I need to finish up for work."

Within a few minutes, the doctor returned with two other individuals. "They are going to assist me in the endoscopy. We are going to put you under anesthesia. We need you to sign a few documents."

The doctor handed Kristen the tablet. "I can't read all of this. Can my husband just sign it for me?"

"Sure. It's pretty standard stuff, but just read through it quickly."

Solomon glanced over the long list of warnings and other information, scrolled to the signature page and signed. He handed the tablet back to the doctor and they began the procedure.

An AI with a tag reading, Dr. Terry, pointed to a set of large glass windows and a waiting area. "Please step out. You can watch from there."

Thirty minutes later, Solomon was brought back in.

"Solomon, let's talk." The yellow-skinned nurse pulled Solomon to the side of the room and spoke in a low tone.

"Sure, what's going on?" Solomon felt troubled but put on a brave face. "Is everything okay?"

"I wish that I could say it was good." A brief pause before finishing. "Your wife has Adenocarcinoma."

"Okay, what in the world is that?" Solomon asked.

"Well, it is a type of stomach cancer, and hers is pretty advanced. We can try to remove it surgically, but I am afraid that it has spread so much that removing it will cause more harm than good."

Solomon was in shock, and immediately the dream from the other night came flooding to his mind. "What are our other options?"

"Honestly, it may be best for you to make her as comfortable as possible. It is not going to be easy for her. We can put her on aggressive medications to kill the cancer off, but truthfully, I haven't seen it help in masses of this size. I wouldn't recommend it."

"So what are you saying?" Solomon's words felt like they were coming out in slow motion.

"I'm talking a few months, not years. I know this is very difficult to hear, but I don't know how else to explain it."

Then there was silence. Solomon looked over at his wife. He turned his back to her and wiped away a tear before turning back, pushing a smile on his face.

"Hey, babe. How do you feel?" Solomon asked a very groggy Kristen.

"Not too bad. So, am I going to make it?" Kristen said, laughing.

Immediately tears welled up in Solomon's eyes. He tried to turn before Kristen saw him, but it was too late.

"What is it? What's wrong?"

"Um…" Solomon cleared this throat. "The doctor will be back in to talk to both of us, but, she…"

"Solomon, you already know something. Just tell me!"

"She told me that you have stomach cancer and it doesn't look good."

A long breath before Kristen said, "Wow, I didn't think you would tell me that. Well, I am sure that we can beat this thing. I mean, with all of the technological advancements, I am sure I will be just fine. Besides, I have to see Karina off to college. Kyle and Knox are just boys. I have too much to do with them first. I can't have anything happen to me. Things will be fine, Solomon. I have faith in Jah. I trust in His will."

Solomon wiped his eyes. "You're right. Everything will be fine." But deep down, Solomon knew. He put a smile on his face and held Kristen's hand as the doctor came back into the room to give the news. What was even more telling was that the medical office paid for the hovercraft home, a parting gift to put a band-aid on the terrible diagnosis.

The ride home was quiet except for the last five minutes, when they both agreed to not tell the children until the time was right.

They walked into their 900 square foot apartment holding hands, brave faces on, emotions locked away.

"How did the appointment go?" Karina asked.

"They ran a few tests. They will call us back if there is anything to worry about. Your mom is a champ, so don't worry about anything," Solomon replied.

"I am sure you will be okay, Mom. Besides, Dad must be making more money now. Look at the amazing trip we just had. That means that he can probably buy better food."

Kyle chimed in. "We got to get better food, Dad. It will have Mom feeling better in no time."

"Yep, I will start feeling better in no time. Enough about me. How was school?"

Without saying a word, Karina got up and went to her room. She came back with a small handmade book. "You didn't send me off to an art school for no reason."

She opened up a book that she created. It had the family pictures from their beach trip and the seashells she collected neatly placed inside. She hand-painted words around each picture and drew pictures of the meal they ate. The entire family hovered over the book.

"You didn't take a picture of our food?" Solomon inquired.

"I didn't even think about it. I was too busy eating." Karina giggled.

"It's beautiful, Karina. I can't believe that you did all of this in such a short amount of time."

"She's so talented, isn't she?" Solomon chimed in, beaming at his little girl. "Let's put this up on the shelf... maybe right here." Solomon took the book from Kristen's hand and placed it on the shelf with all of the children's school accolades and a lighter with his father's name engraved in it. " I am so proud of you. I am proud of all of you." Solomon grabbed all of his children and hugged them.

Kristen looked at Solomon with her kids, put her head down, and returned to her room.

"Mom, what's wrong?" Karina asked. Her mom was lying on the bed with tears in her eyes.

"Nothing, baby. I just really enjoyed seeing all of you like this. Great memories. I will cherish this day forever," Kristen replied.

Chapter 9: An Eye for a Blue Eye

In the last days, everyone will want to lash out at their oppressor, but everyone will feel oppressed. So revenge will become the norm, and kindness will become obsolete. (A Warning from the Writ)

A week had gone by since Kristen found out the news of her cancer. Kristen tried her best to send her children off to school without wincing in pain.

"Bundle up. We are back at a Code Red. Kyle, do you have your inhaler?"

"Yes, mother."

"See you all this afternoon."

"Alright, mom. Love you."

Kristen never logged on to her job. She was too sick. She cried because, unlike so many other people, she loved her job.

She walked into her bedroom and pulled out a small wooden chest. The top drawer of the chest contained beads of all shapes, sizes and colors. She grabbed a pair of wire cutters and pliers. In the second drawer, she had pieces of jewelry that were completed. A beautiful wooden necklace with beads that she carved herself. The attention to detail was extraordinary, and each bead told a story. When she was in her prime, she could have sold a piece like that for nearly five thousand dollars, but that was before all of the YSW taxes. Now she would be lucky to get five-hundred dollars from a piece.

Kristen picked up an oblong wooden bead and her carving scalpel. She held the bead in front of a light and a magnifying glass and attempted to carve a picture into the wood.

"Crap." Kristen was frustrated. "Just stop shaking." She looked down at her fingers. "Focus, Kristen, you can do this." She picked up the scalpel and attempted to do it again. "Damn." Kristen put the scalpel and the bead back at her work station and sucked the spot of blood off her pointer finger.

While Kristen was at home feeling defeated, her sons were at school planning a victory over Norman and his cocooner friends.

The line for school breakfast went fast. Most cocooners didn't even come into the cafeteria because they ate at home. Only the ones who wanted to mess with the real-lifers bothered entering the cafeteria.

"So mutant, what are you attempting to eat this morning? Or wait, do mutants even eat food?" Norman turned around to relish in the laughter of his cocooner friends.

"Why don't you ask your mom what I eat? She's the one who cooked for me last night."

"Dang! He just roasted you!" Knox gave his brother a high-five.

Just then, the color of Norman's piercing blue eyes grew more intense, becoming lasers. He glared at the tray Kyle held and burned a hole through it, causing all of Kyle's oatmeal to fall onto the floor.

"That will teach you to stay in your place, mutant!" Norman said as he walked off.

"I really can't stand him," Kyle said, bending down to pick up his tray.

"Don't worry. I am sure he will get what he deserves one day," Knox replied.

As they were cleaning up the mess, Clifton walked up with a geeky smile.

"Clifton, let me see it. I know your dad bought it for you by now," Knox demanded.

"You are correct. Here it is, gentleman. It is the Illuminous 2150."

"Wow." Both of the Wiseman boys were in awe. "Can I touch it?" Kyle asked.

"Sure. I'll let you two hold onto it for a while. Get it back to me after lunch. I don't want to have it in Mr. Grumble's class. If he gets hold of it, I am sure I will never see it again."

"You're seriously going to let me hold onto it?"

"Yes, but don't give it to your brother Knox. He is not the responsible one."

"Hey, I heard that," Knox replied.

"Just kidding. Look, I will see you two later. Oh, make sure to give this to your sister."

"Another note? Let me do you a favor and throw it in the rubbish bin now." Knox laughed.

"Just give it to her. She may like my ol' school way of romancing her. Besides, I'm a rebel. I'm using real paper. That may make her see that I am not the nerd she thinks of me."

"Whatever," Knox replied. Knox and Kyle walked down the main hall. Before splitting up, Knox said, "Hey, let me hold it during class. I promise I will give it back to you when we get out of first period."

"Fine." Kyle went down the 7th-grade hall and Knox went down the 8th. It took everything in Knox's power not to play with the 2150 during class. He did, however, take it out and look at it a few times but managed to not get caught. When class was over, he immediately ran to Clifton and Kyle, who were standing in the main hall waiting for him.

"While I was sitting in class listening to Ms. Morrison drone on, an idea came to me."

"What dumb idea do you have now?" Kyle responded.

"My idea is going to help you out, brother."

"So, what is it?" Kyle asked.

"Let's give Norman a little taste of his own medicine. Do you want him to keep messing with you forever?" Knox asked.

"No, but I just want to be unnoticed by him. Maybe if I stay out of his way, he won't bother me anymore."

"That is NOT a good plan. Besides, I think I have come up with something that could make him go away forever."

"What's the plan?" Clifton inquired.

"The vaporizer app," Knox replied.

"The Illuminous 2150 can download the vaporizer app. Let's just vaporize him." Knox smiled at both Clifton and Kyle, waiting for some form of approval.

"That won't work, you idiot. The vaporizer app only works on real humans. Besides, it's temporary. It only lasts for about ten minutes, and then the person reappears."

"Forget about all of that. The number one reason why it won't work is that it is expensive, and we can't afford to purchase it."

"We may not be able to afford to purchase it, but I think I have also figured that out." Knox said and then whispered in Kyle's ear.

"Hey, what are you two over there whispering about?"

Kyle's eyes gleamed with excitement at Knox's plan.

"Do you want to come over to our house after school today? Karina will be there." Knox teased.

"You're inviting me over to your house? I am suspicious of your plan, but...I am not stupid enough to pass up an opportunity to see your sister. I must let my dad know, but I am sure it shouldn't be a problem."

All three of them could not wait until the end of the day. Again, they watched the cocooners attach themselves to their stations and vanish. Kyle, Knox, and Clifton started their walk home. They quickly arrived at Ocean View apartments.

"What did your dad say?"

"He was cool. Just wants me home in a few hours."

"Great!" Knox was excited.

The boys rushed off the elevator and made it into the house. Kristen was in her room. She attempted to say hi when she heard an additional voice enter.

"Hi, Clifton. Nice to see you."

"Nice to see you as well, Mrs. Wiseman," Clifton said.

They all ran back into Kyle and Knox's room.

"Hey, I didn't see your sister yet." Clifton licked his palm and started slicking his light brown hair over to the side.

"Ew! Gross! Remind me never to shake your hand again."

Clifton wiped his hand on his shirt. While he was in the room preparing for Karina's arrival, Knox went into his sister's room.

"What are you doing in my room?"

"I need your help. Clifton is here."

"Oh my goodness, please get him out of the house."

"I don't have time for this, Karina. I need you to listen. Norman is still messing with Kyle. I have a plan. I want to try the vaporizer app out on Norman, but we can't afford to put it on the device. Clifton's dad is loaded. I am sure he can pay for it, but I need you to convince Clifton to add the app to the Illuminous 2150."

"Seriously? You want me to flirt with your lame middle school friend?"

"Yes, but it is for our brother. He needs our help. Norman is a jerk."

"Alright, fine. I will do some of my best acting. If I ever hear you mention this to anyone. I promise I will kill you."

"Thank you, Karina."

Karina looked through her makeup bag, put some lip gloss on, pushed up her boobs and sashayed into Knox and Kyle's room, where Clifton was waiting.

Clifton could feel his palms sweating. "Wow, Karina, you sure are beautiful," a nervous Clifton said.

Kyle started snickering. Karina did her best to seductively walk over to Clifton.

"Why, thank you, Clifton," Karina whispered in Clifton's ear. "I heard that you may be able to help my brother with the Norman situation. Helping my brother is so sexy."

"I...I...I...will do whatever I c...c...can to help your brother," Clifton stuttered.

"Yes, so I also heard you have the new Illuminous 2150. Only real men can handle that type of power." Karina ran her hands through Clifton's hair. Kyle snickered again.

When Karina sat on Clifton's lap, Knox bit his lip to hide his laughter.

"Do you think you will be able to find a way for us to get the vaporizer app on your device?" Karina continued to whisper in Clifton's ear.

Clifton cleared his throat. "Um yeah, I'm sure I can figure something out."

"I sure hope so. I wouldn't want you to have to get permission from your daddy. But a man like you would not need to ask their dad. Someone like you could just download the app yourself, right."

"Of course, I can." Clifton tried to gather himself together.

"So...let me see it. Let me see you download the vaporizer app."

"Sh..Sh..Sure...no problem," Clifton replied. After fumbling around with his Illuminous 2150 for a few minutes, the app was on his device. As soon as the app was completely downloaded, Karina hopped off of Clifton's lap.

"Wait, where are you going?" Clifton asked.

"Back to my room. I have homework," Karina responded.

"Before you leave...Do you think we can go out sometime?" Clifton asked.

Kyle, knowing his sister, dropped his head in embarrassment for his friend.

"Um...yeah, I'll think about it," Karina said, quickly returning to her room.

Knox put his arm around Clifton's neck. "I can tell she is warming up to you. Now, let's talk about what we will do tomorrow."

The next day, the Wiseman brothers and Clifton anticipated Norman's arrival. "There he is, look... there he is." Clifton was frantically tapping Knox's shoulder.

"Are you sure we want to do this?" a nervous Kyle asked.

"We can't really hurt him. He's not even really here," Knox responded.

"Yeah, but we don't actually know what effect the vaporizer will have on a hologram," Kyle said.

"Well, there's no time like the present to find out." As Knox said this, Norman and his cocooner friends were right on time.

"Hey, it's the mutant and his cronies," Norman joked.

Before Norman could even think of a new way to insult Kyle, Kyle pointed Clifton's device at Norman and pressed the vaporizer app button. At that moment, Norman, or better yet,

Norman's hologram, started having glitches shorting out. He faded in and out.

"Hey, what did you do to him?" One of the Cocooners shouted. They were all standing in the middle of the school hallway.

"I did this." Kyle pointed the device at the remaining Cocooners and pressed the app. He kept pressing the button until all seven Cocooners were vaporized.

"I can't believe you just did that," Knox said, high-fiving his brother.

Other kids in the hallway, who saw what happened, ran over to Kyle and started cheering. "You did it dude! You got rid of that creep." Others came over and started patting Kyle on the back.

"Good job Kyle!" Clifton said with excitement.

Todd Markley

Naturally, Solomon and Kristen didn't know what the boys were up to. They would have lost it if they found out that their boys were in possession of the Illuminus 2125 or any other unnecessary device. But, like many parents, you don't always know every little thing going on with your children. The trouble is going to get even worse.

Chapter 10: What Happens Now?

—————⊛—————

In the end, no one will predict anything. Confusion and fear will set in.
(A Warning from the Writ)

When Kyle, Knox, and Clifton arrived at the LAME school the following morning, they were prepared to feel the wrath of Norman. In fact, Kyle tried to get out of going to school altogether, but Kristen was not going to work, so she forced all of her children out of the house.

They all went into the cafeteria. "Might as well get this over with. Yesterday was glorious, but I am sure it will end soon." Kyle was discouraged. After about ten minutes of nervously waiting and no Norman, they all began to wonder what had happened.

"Do you think we killed him?" Kyle asked.

"Of course not. He should have appeared shortly after we vaporized him," Knox responded.

"Yeah, but he didn't. And, if you look around, it doesn't seem like he or any of his friends are at school today. Something must have gone wrong." Clifton whispered.

"So, what happens now?" Kyle asked.

"How am I supposed to know? Let's just wait and see if he shows up. If we don't see him by the end of the day, we will start worrying," Knox stated.

The boys grabbed their breakfast and sat at their usual table in the back of the cafeteria near the exit. Kyle requested the chair closest to the door so he could run. A girl with straight, strawberry-red hair approached their table as they ate. "You were so brave yesterday. It's been nice not having Norman here to push us around. Just wanted to say thanks."

Kyle blushed.

"Oooh, Kyle has a girlfriend," Knox taunted.

"Come on, she was just happy about not being bullied."

"That's not all she's happy about." Knox continued to tease.

"Whatever," Kyle said and jabbed his brother in the arm.

The trio left the cafeteria and made it through the day with no Norman or any of his friends in sight.

"What if we killed them?" Kyle asked fearfully.

"Look, stop thinking that. Everything will be okay. We just need to do a little research."

"In the meantime, I will delete this stupid app off my watch. See you both tomorrow." Clifton said as he headed home.

When the brothers arrived in their apartment, their already somber mood was intensified by the bleak feeling in the atmosphere. Kristen and Karina were sitting on the living room sofa. There was only one light on in the entire house.

"What's wrong?" Knox asked.

"I came home from school early today, and Mom was already here."

"Okay...so, what's the big deal?" Kyle replied.

"Let me say it another way. I...I tried to skip school, but Mom was here because she never went to work." Karina said.

"Your sister was trying to skip school and I was still home because I quit my job. I quit it last week because I have been too sick to work."

"Is everything okay, Mom?"

"No, everything is not okay. I have stomach cancer. I have been so tired. I tried to fake it as long as possible, but I don't think I can anymore. I am in so much pain." Kristen broke down and started crying, on Karina's shoulder. The boys walked over to their mom and put their arms on her.

Solomon felt the heaviness as soon as he entered the door. The mood of the house cast a darkness throughout. No one ran to the door, another sign that something was amiss. When he turned the corner and saw all of his children on the bed surrounding Kristen, he already knew what happened.

Tear filled eyes looked up and Kristen's hollow face mouthed the words, "I told them."

Solomon sat on the edge of the bed and put his arms around all of his children. "It will be alright. I promise I won't let anything happen to your mother. It will be alright."

And before Solomon could finish his sentence, Kristen said, "And if something happens to be, it will still be alright."

Karina couldn't help but let the tears roll down her face. The Wiseman family held onto each other tight.

The next morning, Karina walked past her dad in silence. He immediately knew why.

"We debated on telling you sooner, but we found out right after the trip to the beach, and your mother didn't want to ruin the experience for you. After that, it just never seemed like the right time. I hope you understand."

"We should have known," Karina said.

"We never expected to be in a situation like this, so we didn't know how to navigate it. But now that there are no secrets, we can do things differently. I can start working more, get our food from Yummy's."

"Really, Dad? If you had done this a long time ago, Mom wouldn't be sick." Karina went into her room and slammed the door behind her. Solomon got up and headed for Karina's room. Kristen, hearing the commotion, got up and grabbed his arm.

"Solomon, it is not your fault. Leave her for right now. I will talk to her later. It will take time." Kristen's voice was faint. She got up and went into the bedroom to lay down.

Solomon felt defeated. His apartment felt like it was suffocating him. He had to leave.

Chapter 11: Behind Closed Doors

—————————————●—————————————

It is better to know all of the layers of a being before you judge. It is the layers that provide context into how they view the world. But very few will have the patience to carry this out. Learning a person will lend to understanding, dismissing a person leads to division.
(A Warning from the Writ)

Solomon noticed a small crack in the door of Todd Markley's apartment as he walked down the hallway. Two tiny packages were lying on the floor in front of his door. Solomon's curiosity forced him to drift toward the door and peek inside. Solomon was startled when, through the crack of the door, an eye was peeking back at him.

"I am so sorry. Please forgive me." A startled Solomon was trying to catch his breath.

Solomon continued to mumble apologies as he walked toward the elevator, but he soon heard "pssst." He initially ignored it, assuming it was a figment of his imagination. But when he heard it again, he froze. Solomon heard "pssst" coming from the apartment of Todd Markley once again. He turned toward the cracked apartment door and slowly walked toward the sound. Another "pssst" was made before Solomon decided to enter.

There were no lights on inside Todd Markley's apartment. The only thing that illuminated his wrinkled, age-spot-covered hand was the lights from the hallway. Upon closer inspection, Solomon saw that Todd had a very sophisticated surveillance system around his doors. A raspy whisper of a voice said, "You have been hanging around my apartment?"

Solomon didn't know whether he should lie or tell the truth. Looking at the cameras around Todd's apartment, he decided it was best, to tell the truth.

"Not really hanging around. Just noticed some packages near your door. They are sent from my company. I was just curious as to who was ordering these books." Solomon stumbled through his explanation. Somehow, though, he felt better once he said something. Like a weight was off his shoulders. "You have a very eclectic collection," Solomon continued.

"Yes, well, I have learned to read everything, especially original works of literature. If you don't read the original, you will be deceived into believing this fake world we live in. They have changed everything," responded a whisper of a voice. Todd Markley continued to mumble under his breath, but Solomon couldn't make it out.

"Well, it is certainly nice to meet you. I never thought I would have the opportunity to meet a reclusive in person." Solomon started to walk toward his apartment when that same whispery voice said, "You should join me."

Solomon was shocked.

Todd could see Solomon was uncomfortable. "How often are you going to be invited into? What did you call it? A reclusive's home? Come in."

He's right, Solomon thought to himself, and before he realized it, Solomon had entered the home of Todd Markley. Todd flipped on a small lamp sitting on a little round wooden table. Solomon could see books filling the Markley apartment from floor to ceiling. It reminded him of the libraries from his youth, the days before printed text became illegal.

Solomon continued to scan the room before locking his eyes on Todd Markley.

Todd stood about 5'6", although he could have stood taller if not for the hump in his back. His belly protruded over his pants, slightly hiked up above his ankles, held up by suspenders. Solomon squinted his eyes to see if he could tell Todd's age. He scanned his body for the small incision, typically on the inner wrist. It was made mandatory when Solomon was fifteen years old. A vaccine forced upon all school-aged children after the Rose Flu seemed to kill off nearly an 8th of the world's population. The only people exempt from the vaccine were already over 30. He noticed that there was no incision on Todd Markley's arm. A sign that he was at least 15 years older than him.

"Oh...you're looking for my mark? I don't have one," Todd replied after seeing Solomon examine his body. "I was lucky enough to escape the mandatory chip implant. I was 40, and it was too scary to implant the chip in people 40 and over."

Todd shuffled about as if he were looking for something. All of the movement made Solomon a bit nervous.

"Don't mind me," Todd said. "I am not used to company. When all this stuff became too obvious to deny, and everything in the *Writ* started to come true, I went into hiding." Todd shuffled over to a green and blue plaid recliner with cotton stuffing coming from the arms of the chair. A cane was leaned up against the back of the recliner. Todd grabbed it to steady himself before sitting down.

"Would you like some coffee or tea?" Todd asked.

"No, I am fine. Thanks for offering," Solomon replied.

Todd bent down to open one of the books near his recliner's foot. Solomon could see the top of his head. It was shiny bald, and only traces of straight white hair started around his ears and went down the nape of his neck to the other ear. His shiny bald head was covered with age spots. His scalp was surprisingly smooth and starkly contrasted with his face, which had too many wrinkles and folds to count.

Todd started flipping through the pages of his leather-bound book. Solomon started to feel uncomfortable. "So, what are you reading?"

"The *Writ.*"

"Ahh, yes, I remember you ordering that book," Solomon said.

"I have ordered it 21 times in several different languages."

"Why, if you don't mind me asking?"

"Well," Todd said, "look around. What do you notice?"

Solomon slowly scanned the walls covered with books and observed how well-organized they appeared. They were in alphabetical order according to title, and there were several prints of the same title.

"It looks like you have several of the same books?" Solomon picked a book entitled 1996 and flipped through the pages. Without looking up, Todd said, "Turn to page 215." Solomon flipped to the page.

"Read paragraph three, sentence seven."

"On January 19th, 1996, eight-hundred and eighty thousand gallons of home heating oil were spilled, causing one of the largest cleanups on moonstone beach. This event had a devastating impact on over three thousand different species of plant and animal life. Do you want me to read more?"

"No," Todd said, "I want you to pick up the book right next to it. 1996 the second edition. It was printed in two-thousand ninety-nine. Turn to page 215 and read."

"On January 19th, 1996, the United States created advanced ocean cleaning technologies that allowed for the cleanup of moonstone beach. After the cleanup, residents said the ocean was even better now than before the spill." A long pause. Solomon was confused. "Are they talking about the same event?"

"Yes," Todd replied.

"So, why is it so different?"

"I want you to figure it out. Pick up another book."

"Any book?" Solomon confirmed.

"Yes, any book on the shelf. Pick up the original text first, and then find the reprint. Tell me what you notice."

Solomon grabbed another book, another discrepancy.

Solomon continued to scan the walls but couldn't help but ask a question of his new friend.

"I am just guessing that you know a lot about what happens in this building and the people who live here?"

"Yes, you are correct."

"I gather that you are rather particular about who you allow into your space, so...why me?"

"You can't live for as many years as I have and not be a good judge of character. There is something special about you."

"What do you even know about me?"

"I know the children that you and your wife raised are smarter than any of the YSW, and I know that you have to be different to work for the department and the company you work for," Todd continued.

"What do you know about my company?"

"I know that you work for Reader's Publishing. Hence the reason why you were so interested in the books near my front door. I also know that, technically, Reader's Publishing collapsed its print division when it became illegal to print written works over 20 years ago, but that they still have a print division that seems to operate for those who pay top dollar to have printed text. I just so happen to think it is worth every penny to have actual printed text."

"I have seen some of your orders. You are willing to pay top dollar, but why?" Solomon was a little confused.

"Before I answer that question, why don't you take the time to read the books you have picked up and tell me what you notice?"

Solomon opened the book. It was a book by a psychologist named Dr. Ruth Gunnard in the early 21st century. It explored the effects of technology on the brain. Solomon scrolled his finger to chapter three. It spoke about children and their social skills. The line he read was on page 46: "A recent study of six through ten year olds who engaged in more than four hours of technology or social media per day reported having less friends than those whose interaction with devices was limited under four hours per day. The study also wanted to determine the actual brain development and concluded that the system in the brain responsible for human interaction was severely underdeveloped compared to children whose parents limited their interaction with technology." Solomon was not shocked by the study. "Well, Kristen and I always thought that technology and social media were having a negative effect on children. We do our best to limit their interaction with devices, but it is really hard. I am not going to say that I am shocked by what I have read."

"Well, you may be shocked at what you will see next. Why don't you pick up the edition of the text written about 50 years later." Todd encouraged Solomon.

Solomon looked at Todd Markley's shelf and found the newer edition of the text. The cover of the text was exactly the same. Inside the cover, Solomon glanced at the copyright and confirmed that this book was by the same author but reprinted by a company owned by the YSW. He noticed the chapter titles were also the same.

"I want you to see if you can find that same passage in the new text," Todd asked.

Solomon looked up at Todd and then back down in the text. He quickly thumbed through and identified the study on page 46. It was in a slightly different location on the page, but Solomon attributed it to a slight difference in the printing company. "A recent study of six through ten-year-olds who engaged in more than four hours of technology or social media per day reported having more meaningful relationships with friends than those whose interaction with devices was limited to under four hours per day. The study also wanted to determine the actual brain development and concluded that the system responsible for human interaction was remarkably developed as compared to children whose parents limited their interaction with technology."

"Wait a second, only a few words were changed, but this reads completely different." Solomon was confused. "Why would anyone want to do this?"

"Now you are asking the right questions." Todd Markley flashed a wrinkled smile.

"Every book on my shelf is a mate whose copy reads differently than the original. Fifty years ago, when printed text became illegal, I noticed it was almost impossible to find the original text. I knew it was a plan of the YSW to manipulate words and change meanings over time, but I wanted to know why. I started trying to explain my thoughts to people, but they made me feel as though I was crazy. Soon, I...I didn't want to interact with people anymore. I just hid." Todd held his head down.

"No need to feel ashamed of hiding. This world is a crazy place. I completely get it. I kinda feel like running away too." Solomon reached over and patted Todd on the back.

Todd's eyes were a little red and slightly glossed over, but he did not let a tear come down. "You know, the world used to be a very beautiful place." With an unsteady hand, Todd grabbed his cup of hot tea.

"So, if print became illegal. How did you find out about all of these books?" Solomon continued to pat Todd's back while he gazed at all of the books in Todd's collection.

"I was using the computer to research books and came up with nothing. Then, about 20 years ago, I got a random e-mail from Reader's publishing asking if I was interested in printed books. The company was selecting a few people to participate in a delivery service that would give access to copies of original prints. I had never used the company before, so I thought it was like everything else...somehow tracking my moves to entice me to purchase items, but I thought, what the heck. Let me give it a try. And soon, I had this." He lifted his finger and pointed to his massive collection of books.

A long pause filled Todd's apartment. The small desk lamp and the lights of his sophisticated surveillance system were all needed to illuminate the dark space. Where there weren't bookshelves, small screens were monitoring every inch of the apartment and the hallway leading up to his apartment door.

"So," Solomon broke the silence. "Isn't it strange that someone would want original prints to get out to people? They must, somehow, know which people would be interested in original prints."

Todd Markley started to smile at Solomon as he watched Solomon put the pieces together.

Solomon continued. "They must somehow be connected with Reader's Publishing. It doesn't make sense. Who would be powerful enough to hide this from the YSW?"

"Exactly, unless." Todd stopped.

Solomon paused before saying, "Unless they were somehow connected to the YSW but powerful enough not to get caught." Solomon finished Todd's sentence.

"Yes, now you are thinking." Todd resumed sipping his tea.

"But why does it matter? I mean, as long as someone is giving access to the truth, then that's good right?" Solomon was a bit confused as to why Todd seemed to wonder about the originator as long as it was happening.

"It matters. It matters because that means that someone out there has a conscience. And, if they are powerful enough to create a company that can leak the truth, they may also be powerful enough to put a stop to all of the madness going on. The world doesn't have to be like this. All the mass suicides, protests, silence orders, rules and regulations, jacked up prices, it doesn't have to be this way."

Solomon began to think about what Todd just said. He realized that he had grown so used to just living life and trying to survive that it never dawned on him to make meaning from everything happening. Solomon's mind began to race and now, he was thinking about the mysterious person releasing such incriminating material. *Who could have this type of power and still have a heart?* There was only one name that came to mind, Deiderick Dollard. Solomon knew he had the power, but did he have the heart?

Solomon looked at a clock on Todd's wall. He chuckled because, like him, Todd had an analog clock, a remnant of the past. "Todd, it is getting late. I am going to try and get some sleep."

"Thank you for coming in. You are my first visitor in years. Why don't you take a few of my books with you as...a gift." Todd gathered a few books off his shelves and passed the stack to Solomon. The *Writ* was on top. He noticed that every other book that Todd gave him had two versions, except the *Writ*.

"Can I get the reprinted addition of this one as well?" Solomon held up the *Writ*. "I think I would like to compare the two texts."

"Ahhh...Well, I can't do that. Until this point, there has only been one version of the *Writ*. "Todd winked as if he and Solomon had some secret they shared.

"Thanks for the books. I...um...hope I am not taking away from your reading pleasure," Solomon joked, looking at all of the books on Todd's wall.

"Well, as much as I like to read, I feel I have been charged with a new task. The task of writing."

"Oh...yeah? Really? You write? I bet you use traditional paper and pen." Solomon chuckled.

"Yes, well... I do a little of this and a little of that. I have to get messages out to people in a way they will read them." Todd smiled.

"Well, I must say. This was definitely a delightful distraction," Solomon replied. He gathered the books and headed down the hall to his apartment. The doorbell scanned his eye as usual, and Solomon could hear the locks. Solomon walked in and plopped himself on the sofa, hoping to read a little before falling asleep.

Todd Markley

That night was the night that forged our friendship. It was also the night that I realized it was time to move from a reader of Jah's word to a writer of the things to come. Jah started telling me about my new role shortly before my passing. I was chosen as a scriptor and would be assigned to write Warnings to people of the Second World and provide instruction to those who will make it to the New World in a book called the *Writ*.

I realized that Jah orchestrated our friendship for a greater purpose, but neither Solomon nor I knew the importance of our connection at the time. I did know that Solomon had a lot of bumpy roads ahead of him. His family would be tested in ways he did not expect. He had no idea that his children were trying to figure out what happened to Norman and all the other cocooners that Kyle zapped with the vanisher app.

Chapter 12: The Fruit Falls Far From the Tree

───────◆───────

A parent can lay the road for your children and protect them from the obstacles or prepare them for the unknown path ahead. Decide which parent you would like to be carefully Z
(A Warning from the Writ).

"Why are you in our room?" Knox asked Karina.

"I am just really sad about what is going on with Mom. I am so pissed with Dad for not telling us sooner. We should have known."

A long silence. "I know sis, but I think Dad and Mom were doing what they thought was right. Besides, Mom is strong. I think she will get better," Kyle said in an attempt to console his sister.

"How do you guys feel about everything?" Karina asked.

"Well…" Kyle said, "I feel like everything is really messed up right now, and it is not just the stuff with Mom. It's everything."

"What are you talking about?"

"Remember the other day when you helped us convince Clifton to put the vaporizer app on his device?"

"Yeah, so what...oh my goodness, did you do it? What happened?" Karina's somber demeanor changed.

"Well, we did it yesterday. It was so awesome. Their stupid holograms started shorting out, and then they were gone, but..."

"But what?" Karina inquired.

"But, I don't think you are supposed to use it on a hologram."

"Isn't it better than vanishing the actual person? Besides, what could it hurt? It only lasts for what, like, ten minutes?"

"That's what we thought," Knox replied. "But Norman didn't return to school today."

"Well, maybe it is a coincidence."

"None of his friends did either," Kyle replied.

"You vanished the friends as well?" Karina said. Her mouth dropped.

Knox looked over at Karina. "Kyle got...a little trigger happy, and well, he zapped all seven of Norman's friends."

"You zapped seven people. Oh....my...Jah...you are going to be in so much trouble," Karina said.

"I know." Kyle looked as if he were about to cry. "I can't believe we may have killed eight people."

"Look, I don't think you killed eight people. They have got to be somewhere. But where?"

In some way, Karina was thankful for the distraction. It got her mind off of her mom.

"Look, I think I can try to help you figure this out. I just need some time to wrap my mind around it. It has been a really long day. Let's all go to sleep."

"Before we go to bed, we have to do our chant. This cannot get out to Mom and Dad. They can't handle it right now," Knox whispered.

"You know what, you're right. Okay, pinkies out."

All three siblings formed a triangle and locked pinkies before chanting, "Secrets shared between you and me, others can't hear or you die. The type of death will be painful and slow. You'll leave this earth, and none will know."

When they finished chanting, Karina giggled, remembering she was the one to teach her brothers that chant.

"Okay, boys, I promise I will try to figure this out. Try not to worry."

Karina started to sneak back into her room, but she noticed her dad on the sofa surrounded by...books?

"Dad, what is all of this?"

"Just some books I got from a friend...Hey...listen, Karina, I am sorry for how we decided to handle things. When you have kids, no one gives you an instruction manual. You just have to figure everything out. Your mom and I prided ourselves on ensuring our children didn't get caught up in the YSW nonsense. It made us feel good, not giving in to it all. Like we stood for something, but it is times like this when I wish I had made a different choice. So, I get it. You can be mad at me."

"Look, Dad, I am mad at you. I don't know when or if this will go away, but I still love you. I just don't know if I feel that any of you and mom's life lessons were worth all of this. I may never understand it. All I can do now is pray that Jah will make mom better."

Solomon embraced his daughter. "Love you, Dad."

"Love you too, Karina."

"I need to head to bed. I have to get up early."

"You sure you don't want to stay up with your old man? I could use the company."

Karina wanted to but knew she needed to get to her room to think of a plan to get her brothers out of their mess.

"Sorry, Dad, early morning."

"Goodnight, sweetie."

It wasn't long before Solomon fell asleep on the sofa.

Chapter 13: Vision of One Leader

The world will fall under one leader, one ruler will give people a sense of unity, but this ruler will take away free will. Free will is a gift from Jah, and the people will become oppressed once that is gone.
(A Warning from the Writ)

A few more nightly visits to Todd Markley's house and Solomon was finally putting all of the pieces together.

"Just take it. You can take any book you would like." Todd shuffled over to his plaid blue and green chair. He grabbed his cup of hot tea, blew on the scorching hot liquid, and stirred in two drops of honey. "You know, if you keep coming over here like this, I am going to think we are friends." Todd smiled a half smile and took another sip of his hot tea.

"I would consider us friends." Solomon chuckled, grabbing the *Writ* off the shelf. Both of them kept their voices low. Solomon spent many late nights visiting Todd when he couldn't sleep. It seemed to occur more frequently. Somehow, after a visit to Todd's apartment, a long discussion about all the craziness in the world, and a good cup of tea, Solomon found it easier to fall asleep when he went home.

"How is the writing coming along?" Solomon asked Todd.

"Oh, it's coming along well. I don't have to do much. Just clear my mind and listen to what I am being told. When you are connected to Jah, everything becomes so clear," Todd responded.

Although talks of Jah became more common, Solomon still couldn't wrap his mind around the power of Jah or the Jah that Todd was describing.

"So, who do you think is reading your, what did you call them again?"

"Warnings?" Todd answered. "To be honest, I don't know. What I do know is there are a lot of things going on. Things that are beyond our realm of comprehension. There is a spirit world out there. I am sure of it now. This is no longer about what we see happening. There is something, a greater force in charge of it all."

"Now you sound like Kristen. Jah is in control. Well, if He is in control, why are so many terrible things happening? Why does my wife have cancer? Why am I plagued with these...these...terrible dreams?"

"Ha," Todd chuckled. "I can't answer those questions for you, but I do believe there are answers. Have you been reading the *Writ*?"

"A little," Solomon replied, shaking the *Writ* he was holding in his hand. "Hoping to get to read more soon."

"Well, I am sure you will pick it up when the time is right." Todd smiled.

"I have been reading all of the other books you gave me. It's crazy. Like the government is trying to brainwash all of us into thinking the same way. Believing the YSW is good for us." Solomon continued to gaze at all the books on Todd's shelves.

Todd got up, shuffling his feet to a small wooden table with a jar on top. "I know things have been rough for you lately. Here...a gift." Todd shuffled his way back over to Solomon.

He grabbed Solomon's hand, put a card in it, and closed Solomon's fingers around it. "Don't look at it here. Take it home with you."

"So, I guess I will see you on another sleepless night."

"See you soon." Todd chuckled.

Solomon went back into his apartment. It was dark. Everyone was asleep. Solomon didn't want to use his voice, so he manually turned on a small desk lamp. He put the *Writ* down, grabbed the 1978 version of CIA Secrets and the 2090 reprint, and started to read. In the middle of reading, he glanced over at the *Writ*. *You have all of the answers huh?*, Solomon said, replaying the conversation he had with Todd.

What is going to happen to us? was Solomon's last thought before he fell asleep.

Solomon had a dream of a globe. Each continent on the globe was a different color, and each color bubbled and quarreled with the other. As they did this, lines broke through each continent, dividing it into smaller parts. The colors continued to pop and bubble until one of the bubbles rose up above all the other ones. It continued to float higher until that bubble hovered over the entire globe. That bubble swirled and began reflecting the colors of all the lands below. As this happened, the continents stopped bubbling. They calmed down, and everything seemed to be at peace, but when one of the colors reached out to the color hovering over the globe, a laser shot out. Seeing the violence, another country tried to help, and it, too, was met with a strong lightning-like dagger.

The large bubble continued to shoot daggers at all of the other countries. As they were being struck, enormous amounts of dollars, coins and other currency with many designs and patterns started floating up to the large bubble. It sucked all the money inside of itself, and a few small coins that looked exactly alike came from the bubble and were distributed sparingly yet equally to all of the countries below. Over time, all countries below, including the large bubble, turned gray, and the bubbling and turmoil ceased. Each bubble was the same color, had the same amount of money, and was the same size. There was nothing left to fight for or fight over. But, unfortunately, all of their Jah-given gifts had been taken away. They lost their light and gave up their talents for complacency.

Solomon was able to sleep through this dream. Although disturbing, it was less vile than some of his previous ones. When he woke up, he grabbed a pen and paper and began writing down what he saw. Then, for some reason, Solomon felt compelled to open the *Writ*. He thought, *if this book really has the answers, I can open it to a page that can further explain my dream.* He closed his eyes and opened the *Writ* for the first time. With his eyes still closed, he picked up his right index finger and landed on a scripture: When the world falls under one rule, it will be deceived; only those guided by the words in the Writ *stay connected to Jah will see the new world.* Solomon's mouth dropped open.

Chapter 14: Stealing Time

Time on earth is your most valuable resource. Those who waste time, waste life. Time to Jah does not exist because the spirit of Jah lives beyond the constraints of the earth.
(A Warning from the Writ)

Karina also had a difficult time sleeping at night. She had a lot on her mind. Her mother seemed to be getting worse each day, and her brothers, well, her brothers may have accidentally killed 8 people. She was becoming more concerned when a whole week went by, and her brothers told her there was still no sign of Norman or his friends. It was Saturday at 6:20 in the morning, so she decided to get up and go into her brothers' room. Her brothers seemed to wake up on the weekend when most people were getting ready for lunch, but she didn't care. She cracked the door open and began saying, "Psst."

A groggy Kyle rubbed his eyes. "What are you doing in here?"

"I've got an idea," Karina said.

Kyle threw a pillow at Knox, who was sleeping on a small bed opposite the room.

"Dude, what the heck are you doing?" Knox said, rubbing his eyes.

Kyle just pointed to his sister.

"This better be good," Knox replied.

"So, what is this big idea that you have?" Kyle asked.

"I came because I thought about your little situation with Norman."

"Not only do I think my plan will help you with your friend."

"Please don't call him my friend," Kyle said.

"Okay...well...not only do I think it can help your situation, but I believe it can also help mom." Karina was so excited and couldn't figure out why her brothers appeared so uninterested.

"Well, if you need Clifton's device, you will be out of luck. His dad took it away after he was CHARGED nearly $2000 for the vaporizer app."

"Oh...well...tell him I am sorry about that," Karina replied.

"We did. He said the only thing that will make up for what we did is if you finally go out with him," Kyle replied.

"Well, that's after he gets off punishment," Knox mumbled, still wiping his eyes to wake himself up.

"Could you two stop going back and forth. You two idiots may have killed Norman and you're droning on about Clifton. Are you going to let me talk now?"

Kyle and Knox said in unison, "Sorry, sis."

"Time manipulation," Karina replied.

"What about it?"

"I want to figure out a way to go back in time. There is supposedly an app. It's been banned, but the technology has got to still be out there somewhere. I think I found someone who still may have it, I just have to figure out how to get to them."

Knox interjected, "I heard it was a pretty dangerous app to have. Besides, how would that help us?"

"I know. I have been up all night doing a lot of research on my tablet that Mom and Dad DON'T know that I have!"

"Finally!" Knox said.

"Finally, what?" Karina was confused.

"You finally have something I can hold over your head." Knox smirked.

"Can we try and stay focused here please?" Karina begged.

"Anyway," Karina continued. "You two were not the only ones that zapped a hologram. I read a story about a boy who did the same thing last night. Norman and his friends are not dead. They are lost in some sort of time warp. A place between reality and the virtual world. We can use the time manipulation app to go back and see if we can get them from wherever they are."

"Okay. Not a bad idea, but how will this help mom?" Knox asked.

"There is another feature of the app. It costs a few bucks more, but it is worth it."

"A few bucks more. like how much?" Kyle inquired.

"Don't worry about the cost. I will figure everything out. There is a time-snatcher feature as well. The time snatcher allows you to steal time from people who are not using their time wisely and give it to someone who needs it."

"Yeah, I heard about it before. Sounded pretty cool but too risky. You are taking someone's life away," Kyle said to his sister.

"Look, I know this is going to sound harsh, but there are so many people out there wasting their time doing stupid things or not using their time. Taking a few minutes from them is not going to hurt. Besides, the app prevents you from taking any more than ten minutes at a time."

Her brothers were quiet for a moment. Karina's eyes filled with tears. "I need to see if we can find a way to keep Mom around longer. Can't you see that she is getting worse?"

There was silence in the room. They all realized that their mom would not be around much longer.

"Okay, fine. We're in. But we need to be smart. I think we need to try to find Norman first. Less risky, and if it doesn't work, then who cares," Knox joked. Kyle couldn't help but join his brother's laughter. "But, if the time snatcher part doesn't work, it could be…"

"Don't say it. I know. But it is worth a try."

"Whoa, whoa, whoa," Kyle interjected. "All of this is great, but how in the world are we going to be able to afford the apps for the Illuminous 2125?"

"I don't have any money, but I think I know how I can get it," Karina replied.

"What are you talking about?" Knox's eyes grew big as saucers. He couldn't believe there was more dirt on his sister.

"You promise you won't tell?" Karina asked. "If you do, I will kill both of you."

"We promise." Both Kyle and Knox said it at the same time.

"Then do it," Karina said.

"Do what?"

"Do the secret handshake," Karina said.

"You actually want to do our secret handshake?" Knox asked and then looked at his brother.

"I know that is the only way you two loud mouths won't squeal. So, if it means doing that dumb chant, then yes, I want to do it." All three of them looked around at each other before saying:

"Secrets shared between you and I, others can't hear or else you die. The type of death will be painful and slow. You'll leave this earth, and none will know."

They followed this with a secret handshake filled with pats, claps, and snaps.

"That sounds really morbid now. I can't believe we thought that was funny." Karina smirked.

"You made it up," Knox said,

"Yeah, that is when you used to hang out with us. You were kind of a cool sister before you got all teenagerish," Kyle interjected.

"Whatever....you thought everything I did was amazing because it was," Karina bragged.

"Hurry up and tell us how you think you will be able to get the app," Kyle begged.

"I swear if you tell Mom or Dad..."

"Just get on with it!"

"I may have--" Karina paused and took a gulp. "I may have applied for the YSW scholarships to attend their universities."

Knox was astonished. "You can only get one of those if you took an oath that you would become part of the YSW."

A moment of silence filled the air. Kyle looked at Knox, who looked at Karina.

"It gets worse." Karina looked down, ashamed.

"How?" Kyle asked.

"Because our family is not part of the YSW, I received incentives for promising to give them your PID (Personal Identification Numbers)."

"Seriously, Karina?! If Mom or Dad ever finds out, they will kill you," Knox interjected.

"Exactly, that is why I don't need either of you to say anything. Besides, I haven't joined them yet, nor have you two. I just showed interest." Karina looked away from her brothers.

"You know that once you show interest in the YSW, you belong to them," Knox reminded his sister. "Besides, just because you applied for a scholarship doesn't mean you actually have access to the money."

Karina grew quiet. She continued to look away from her brothers. They immediately noticed the change in her demeanor.

"You have the money in your account?" Kyle questioned.

"Well, they wanted to persuade me to attend, so they gave me a perk ahead of time. I know I got a B in technology, but I did well on one of my tests, and my scores were reported back to the YSW. I let them believe I would join them."

"Oh, they are going to own you!" Kyle warned.

"Look, I am doing this for Mom. She deserves to live. I can't see Mom go through this. Oh, and don't forget that you two have a little situation that I am also trying to fix."

"So… what next?" Kyle asked nervously.

"I can choose whatever app I want, but I will need the Illuminus 2125."

Knox went to a shoebox in the closet where it was hidden.

"Here." He handed it over to his sister.

"Are you guys sure we want to do this?" Kyle asked.

Knox replied, "What other choice do we have?"

Before they knew it, Karina had downloaded the Time Snatcher app on the Illuminus 2125. They stayed in their room, mapping out the details.

"Hey guys," Solomon said as he knocked on the boy's room. "I am headed to Yummy's to get your mom some food. Do you have any requests?"

"Dad, you are taking requests? Yummy's is super expensive, but sure. Can you get enough grapes for us as well?" Karina asked.

"No problem," Solomon responded and headed out the door.

"What's going on with Dad?" Knox asked.

"I don't know, but that was weird. Anyway…let's get back to figuring out how this app works."

"Whoa…so cool…look at it." Kyle looked at the device that now has a small emblem of a wavy clock on it. Next to the wavy clock was another symbol of a hand grabbing at the time. "I am assuming this one is the manipulation app, and this one is for time snatching," Kyle concluded.

"Yes, it sure is." Karina grabbed the device back from her brothers. "I need to hold on to this. I need to play around with the features before our mission."

"Sure, just don't lose it," Knox said. "How long will it be until our first mission?"

"Soon." Karina grabbed the device and headed back to her room.

"I'm scared," Kyle said to his brother.

"Don't worry. Everything will work out the way it should."

Chapter 15: Aurora Comes for Dinner

Those who learn to look after one another show those around them what the spirit of Jah looks like on earth.

(A Warning from the Writ)

Solomon headed down the hallway. He put his mask on and headed toward the elevator, which was already there waiting for him.

"I noticed you left your apartment. Thought you might be headed out, so I decided to come," the elevator said to Solomon.

"Well, you were right. I am headed to Yummy's."

"Wow...I hate to ask you this, but did you actually convert?"

Solomon thought that was a weird question for the elevator to ask, but he decided to answer. "No, a friend gave me some money to help out."

Solomon patted his pocket where he had the 'gift' that Todd had given him.

"Permission to pick up?"

"Sure." Solomon gave permission for the elevator to add another person to the ride. Before he knew it, Aurora had joined him.

"Wow! I would say it's good to see you, but you kind of look like crap," Aurora joked.

"Gee, thanks. I've had a little trouble sleeping. I have these crazy dreams that keep me up?"

"Oh yeah? Sounds terrible. "Aurora closed her eyes, and the third eye implant began glowing on her forehead.

"I haven't seen you in a while. Getting better?"

"I can zone out and still get so much done. Hey, maybe you should try it. You can get sleep while you get things done."

"Nah...I am too old for those things." Solomon chuckled.

"Hey, I am headed to get some stuff for dinner tonight. I would love for you to come over. Maybe meet my daughter."

"Are you sure you want someone like me to come over? I may be a bad influence." Aurora opened her eyes when she said this. The light from the implant turned off.

"You're not too bad. Especially when you are not connected." Solomon chuckled.

"You're not too bad yourself. Kinda reminds me of my dad. I miss him...sure...I'll come over."

When they arrived into the lobby, Aurora waved goodbye and headed out the door. Solomon was walking toward the doors as well but heard a voice say, "Mr. Wiseman."

Solomon turned around to see Jose, the AI bellboy flagging him down.

"I have a note for you," Jose said, handing Solomon a tablet. His piercing blue eyes were looking at Solomon. Solomon went from feeling joy about his gift from Todd to feeling unease. Solomon took the tablet, turned away from Jose to read the message.

Solomon,

It has come to our attention that you are enjoying the perks the YSW has to offer. You also neglected the opportunity to sign up for membership. A notice of charges has been sent to your address along with the process for paying the charges. These fees will be waived if you sign up for YSW membership.

Thank you for your consideration

YSW

After Solomon finished reading the message, he returned the tablet to Jose and continued out of the doors.

His head was spinning, and it didn't seem to matter how much he covered up, he felt exposed. When he hit the streets, the noise started. He made it through Yummy's, but instead of walking out, he had to go to the customer service desk to hand them the card that Todd Markley had given him.

"Hi Solomon, so you want to put all of your groceries on this card? We haven't seen one of these in a long time. The AI scanned the card with its laser blue eyes and returned it to Solomon. "You are in luck. We still accept these. You have a remaining balance of $650."

Wow, Solomon thought to himself, *how much was on that card? I have to have nearly $2000 worth of food.*

A walk through all of the noise and Solomon was back home. He placed the groceries on the counter and checked on his wife. She was sleeping but rolled over when she heard Solomon enter the room. "Hey," she said as she sat up. "How are the kids doing?"

"I haven't heard much from them today, so I guess they were doing well." Solomon chuckled. "I invited the young lady I keep running into for dinner."

"That was nice, but do we have enough food?" Kristen asked.

"I think we should be fine," Solomon responded.

A few hours later, the Wiseman family cleaned up and had dinner prepared. Everyone seemed excited to see all of the food. Real food was on the table.

The door announced, "Human presence. Should I reject or allow them to enter?"

"They may enter," Solomon said. He opened the door for his guest. "Everyone, this is Aurora. I have run into her a few times and decided to invite her over for dinner."

"Thanks for inviting me over. Hey, if you all are low on food, you can use my YSW discount." Aurora smiled, hoping that her offer would buy their acceptance.

Solomon ignored the gesture. After receiving the notices, he was not keen on accepting any more favors from members of the YSW. His credit card debt was more than $100,000 for making all of his fresh food purchases, charging Kristen's doctors' visits, and splurging for that vacation, but he pushed those thoughts back and smiled as he sat his guest down and allowed her to pile real fruits and vegetables onto her plate. A clear sign that she was not used to making sacrifices.

"Hello Aurora, Solomon has told me so much about you. It is nice to finally meet you. It is so crazy, I haven't been out of the apartment in so long, it is nice to see other people," Kristen said in a weak voice. She had a smile on her face, masking the fatigue.

Just as Solomon expected, Aurora and Karina became quick friends. The conversation between the two young ladies seemed to flow naturally. Solomon smiled and hoped that this would ease the odd tension he felt around his daughter.

"So tell me about university? I am going off soon," Karina eagerly asked Aurora.

"Well, honestly, I only attended for a semester."

"Why, what happened?" Karina said, taking advantage of her father's generosity. She scooped another helping of peas onto her plate.

"Sometimes, having money, and being a part of this life, is a bit of a trap. After my parents died, they left me with some money, and I did whatever I wanted. University was my parents' thing, but, looking back now, I wish I had gone. It would have made them proud. You guys have it good. Solomon is a wonderful dad."

Karina looked up at her father. He could tell that she was doing her best to apologize. The corners of his mouth turned up, and the wrinkles around his eyes scrunched, flashing his daughter a smile.

"Hey," Solomon said, "I will clean up tonight. Boys, let the young ladies have time to chit-chat."

Karina, Aurora, Kyle, and Knox shot up from the table before Solomon changed his mind.

"Dinner was nice today," Kristen said. "It was good to see Karina so happy."

"It was. Aurora's a nice girl. She has me doing a lot of thinking. I don't know if I will be able to hold out much longer."

122

"What are you saying?" Kristen's weak voice asked.

"I didn't tell you because I didn't want you to worry. I thought I could handle everything, but…" Solomon placed his head in his hands and did his best to hold back tears.

"I have messed everything up." Solomon's face was completely turned away from Kristen.

"How?" Kristen asked. Her feeble body exited from the table and approached her husband. She began rubbing his back. Kristen could feel him quiver. She had never seen Solomon like this.

"I owe so much money. I feel like I can't breathe. I know it could all go away if I join them, but on my own. I don't know. Karina is so different now. We don't talk like we used to. She is about to go off to school, probably at one of the YSW universities. The boys seem to stay trapped in their room. Everything we have stood for has been for nothing. Look around, we still have devices and technology in this apartment. The only thing that we didn't do is sign the oath and take the financial perks. We are living the life I most despise. No matter how much we want to say we are not part of them, we are!"

Kristen looked at her husband and thought it best not to say anything until he was finished.

"I got a notice the other day and another one this morning." Solomon went to the shelf where he hid the notices. "With one click of a button I can eliminate all of our debt."

Kristen read over the entire notice. Her mouth dropped when she got to the line that showed the amount of Solomon's debt. "Dear Jah, how did it get so bad?" She whispered.

She continued reading and came to the signature line:

BY PLACING YOUR THUMB PRINT ON THIS NOTICE, YOU HAVE PLEDGED YOUR LOYALTY TO THE YSW. WE VOW TO PAY OFF ANY DEBT OCCURRED WHILE NOT UNDER OUR PROTECTION. WE WILL WORK TO SECURE YOUR SAFETY AND SECURITY.

-WWW.YSW.ORG

"So, this is what you want to do?" Kristen asked. "You want to sign this letter?"

Solomon quickly realized he was being baited.

"Go ahead. Sign it. It just needs your fingerprint, correct?" She said as she stared into Solomon's eyes. "I am not going to be the one to tell you what to do. I realize my part in our debt. I am sorry I am sick and cannot work, but you must have forgotten who you are. You are not a man that falls for these types of antics. A lot of this is my fault. Us, living like this. We should have done away with all of it completely, but it was so difficult. Yes, I know we have indulged in our technological pleasures now and then, but I never thought we would get to the day you would consider conforming." Kristen paused to catch her break before continuing. "Solomon, I know things are bad. I can't imagine what it is like for you. Frankly, I have been so sick I haven't even thought about it. I know that you are better than this. But if you don't think we can do it anymore, then just sign it. I am too tired to fight about this right now."

Kristen removed her hand from Solomon's back and went to her room. Solomon followed behind.

"I am not trying to make you upset." Solomon sat at the edge of the bed. "Kristen, I feel lost. I am not getting sleep at night. I have been reading all of these books that should make me want to run in the opposite direction of the YSW, but truthfully, I feel like I am one man fighting against the world. I know they are a horrible organization, but they run everything. They have been manipulating and corrupting the system for centuries. I am not going to win!"

As Kristen listened, a tear rolled out of the corner of her eye as she listened to her husband go on.

"You know I have had these nightmares for a long time right?" Solomon continued.

"Yes," Kristen replied.

"They are beginning to feel so real."

Kristen looked her husband in the eye. "You know, this isn't the first time you have told me this. Solomon, this could be happening for a reason. Maybe...maybe Jah wants you to know something. Remember when you knew I was pregnant before I did?"

Solomon smiled. "Yes, in those days, the dreams were much sweeter. I am sorry to say all of this to you, but I miss you. I miss being able to talk to you."

"I know. I miss being able to talk to you as well. I hate being sick."

Solomon kissed her on the forehead. "Look, I will finish cleaning the kitchen and ensure Aurora gets back to her apartment."

Kristen grabbed Solomon's arm before he headed out of the room. "Being sick puts things in perspective. I don't want to say this, but I don't know how long I will be here. Screw the bills, screw the debt, none of it matters anymore. Just make sure those kids are happy. Make sure you spend as much time with them as possible before they are all grown up and out of the house. Learn to love them extra hard so they know it is coming from you and me."

Solomon's knees buckled, and he sat back on the bed and embraced his wife.

Chapter 16: Suspicions

Remember to always watch to see if the actions and the words of man align,
then you will know you have found a person of good character
(A Warning from the Writ).

When Monday arrived, everyone in the Wiseman house, except Kristen, was out the door early. Solomon would have been suspicious that all three of his children were out of the house at the same time, but he had too many thoughts of his own floating through his head. Between his conversation with his wife, the late-night chats with Todd, the books he had been reading, and all of the threatening messages, it was nearly impossible for him to focus on anything else.

When he arrived at Readers Publishing, a new guy was already there. He was temporary. A young kid that they could pay the bare minimum until he decided to do something else. Solomon had worked with Mike a few times, but their interaction was forced. He tried to tell Mike about Todd Markley, the reclusive man that lived in his building. Solomon couldn't figure out whose side the young employee was on. He could have chosen to work for the

YSW and make more money but decided to accept a job at Readers Publishing? *Maybe he is more like me than I thought,* Solomon said to himself. He thought he could bait Mike into sharing some of his feelings about things if he talked about Todd Markley and the books he was ordering, but Mike didn't seem to pay much attention to Solomon's efforts.

"Why do you think he is ordering two different versions of the same book?" Naturally, Solomon already knew the answer but wanted to see what the young Mike would say. "I figure he must like to read," Mike responded.

Ah, Solomon thought to himself, *I understand why he doesn't work for the YSW, the boy is a nitwit.*

Solomon lost interest in talking to Mike until Mike said,

"Oh...There was an eMessage for you. It just popped up on the screen. It requested an eye scan to play, so I figured it was top secret and not an order."

Solomon's mind was spinning. Silence filled the air. Mike passed a small tablet over to Solomon so he could see the message. There it was, mixed in with all of the orders, in bold writing, an eMessage.

"I am going to take this in the hallway. Thanks for telling me." Solomon left the small office and walked to the hall. He got into a spot where he thought the blue light of the camera couldn't see him. When he pressed the message, it immediately scanned his eye and opened. As soon as it opened, images of his vacation popped off the tablet's screen and played like a 3-D movie in front of him. As the images played, a voice said, "We are glad you were able to enjoy some of the YSW benefits on your recent trip. However, our records show that you are not a member of the YSW. It is illegal to partake of YSW benefits without being a member. If you want to become a member, please say yes or touch the green button."

As soon as the voice from the tablet said that, the images of his vacation went away, and a large green and red button appeared. Solomon touched the rotating red button refusing YSW membership.

"Thank you. We have logged that as your response, an additional fee of $12,300 has been added to your credit card. Thank you and have a wonderful day."

As soon as the account was charged, a chime went off. It was a notification. "Your account has been charged $12,300. If payment is not made within 3 days, an overage fee of $300 will be added. To avoid payment, select the YSW button below."

Solomon could not breathe. It was all crashing down. He walked back into the office, distraught.

"Everything alright?" Mike said as Solomon walked back in.

"Yes, everything is fine." Solomon didn't trust him. He didn't know him. He didn't want Mike to know anything else about him. Solomon worked in silence the rest of the day.

As soon as Solomon left, he called Kevin.

"Hey, how are you enjoying the new job?"

"Good to hear from you. It's work. Nothing special. They made it sound interesting by calling it data collection, but I am really just getting coffee and running errands for these young techies. I am supposed to take some type of aptitude test next week so they can better place me. I guess for the salary, I thought I would be doing more."

"Hey, if you're getting off soon, can we meet up at Shooters?" Solomon asked. There were so many things he wanted to talk to Kevin about.

"Sure. Let me see. I should be able to make it there in a few minutes."

"I thought you were further away."

"I was," Kevin responded. "But they gave me a hovercraft. You know...just to run errands. I am not a high flier yet, but it helps me get around."

"Well...okay...I guess I will see you in a few minutes," Solomon said.

Solomon put his mask and glasses on, and hiked his collar up as high as he could before heading toward Shooters. Kevin pulled up on his Skyrider, the newest hovercraft out as he walked toward the door.

"I thought you said it was just to do a few errands. This is really nice."

"Thank you, but you should see what the higher-ups are riding around in. Man, it sure is good to see you. It seems like it has been way longer than a few weeks."

"Yes, feels like old times. Let's get inside before the code red burns the skin off my face." Solomon chuckled.

As soon as the men walked in, they were greeted by Barkley.

A loud rupture of greetings filled the air.

"Hey!" Barkley ran over to them. "I never thought I would see both of you in here at the same time. Let me get you your old spot."

Barkley walked them over to their spot. "I would usually try to get you a drink on the house, but things have been a little tight. So, this time, you boys are payin'. What would you like?"

Solomon was about to order before remembering that his account was vastly overdrawn. "Nothing for me," Solomon said.

"You don't want anything?" Kevin inquired. "Barkley, get us two rum and Cokes."

"Coming right up." Barkley went over to grab the glasses and wiped them on his beer-stained shirt.

As soon as Barkley left, Solomon turned to Kevin. "So good to see you. So many strange things have been going on, and I haven't felt like there is anyone I can talk to."

"What's going on?" Kevin asked, concerned.

"I got a message from the YSW today."

"Yeah, what was it?" Kevin asked.

"It was a message about the trip I took my family on using your YSW discount. They said they will charge me because I am not a member of the YSW, they charged over $12,000."

"I am so sorry about that. That should not have happened. Look, let me see if I can figure this out. I am sure it is some mix-up."

"That's not all." Solomon leaned in toward Kevin to make sure no one around him heard what he would say. "I had another dream."

"Your dreams have never been good, my friend." Kevin chuckles.

"Tell me about it. This dream was different from the others. I used to have dreams about my family or people close to me, but this one was about the world, and when I woke up, I could remember every detail. I wrote it down."

Solomon was about to pull out a piece of paper and hand it to Kevin, but Kevin pushed his hand away. "You know I can't be seen with that."

"I forgot that you are one of them now." Solomon chuckled.

Kevin started looking around to ensure no one saw him nearly engaging in non-YSW behavior. "Look, I don't want to be the one

131

to tell you what to do, but I think you may need to consider letting go of all your hang-ups about the YSW and just become a member before you get more than the three notices you have already received." Kevin chuckled.

"Yeah, you may be right," Solomon continued. "Wait, how did you know about the other notices? I only told you that I received one this morning."

"Oh yeah, well, just a hunch. I guess I figure the YSW always gives three notices before their warnings become more than just warnings."

"So, what are you trying to say?" Solomon felt extremely uneasy. He was beginning to realize that Kevin may not be someone he could trust anymore.

"Look friend," Kevin said, patting Solomon on the shoulder. "All I am saying is, it may be best to give up and just join the YSW. I am sure that all of that debt will be taken care of. You're under a lot of stress. It may even stop you from having those dreams."

Don't say what you want to say, Solomon thought; instead, he responded with, "Yes, I guess you're right. Maybe something I need to consider."

Solomon looked at Kevin suspiciously. He decided it best not to tell him about his dream, Todd Markley's discoveries, or share anything else about his debt.

"So, how is everything at home? Is Kristen doing okay?" Kevin inquired.

Solomon was short. "She's fine."

"And Karina? Still looking to go off to University soon? I am sure you found her the right school."

"She is also doing well. She's a smart girl. I am sure she will make the right decision."

"You are right. She will make the right decision. I am pretty sure there are a lot of YSW Universities that would love to have her."

Solomon grew even more irritated but decided not to respond. Solomon was about to end the conversation when Barkley came over to them.

"You guys need another drink."

"Sure, get us another one of these," Kevin said, holding up his small glass with a remnant of rum and coke.

"No, I'm fine." Solomon looked at Barkley.

"You sure? You guzzled that one down pretty quickly." Barkley laughed.

"Let me ask you a question, Barkley. What would you do if you were getting threatening notices from the YSW because you used all of their benefits but didn't commit to membership?" Kevin asked. He took a sip of his next drink and shook his head. "You made this one strong."

"I had gotten them for a while. I used to be a lot like Solomon. Felt they were a corrupt organization, but truthfully, they controlled everything. I got to a point where I said, what the heck, " Barkley responded, then he looked over at Solomon. "It hasn't been too bad, but, I don't know...I respect Solomon for making his own way."

"Thank you for that," Solomon said.

"No problem." Barkley tilted in support of Solomon.

"So." A sip and long pause from Kevin. "What if the YSW knows you are the last family in the 212 area code they need to convert. What do you think they would do to finish their mission?"

Fear ran through Solomon's veins, but he tried to save face. "Why don't we change the subject?" Solomon whispered. "I think your drink is kicking in, my friend."

Kevin, noticing Solomon's demeanor, said, "Okay...I'm just joking around. Lighten up man. Have another drink."

Kevin ordered another round of drinks and Solomon tried to lighten his mood, but too many thoughts were running through his mind.

It was not long before the thoughts were interrupted by the noise of people chanting outside of Shooters.

"What do you think they are shouting about now?" Barkley asked as he wiped off the bar top.

"Who knows...the YSW are always upset about something. Twenty-seven people died in the protest about two weeks ago," Solomon said. "Wait...I forgot. Kevin is now one of them. I guess I can't make comments like that anymore." Solomon jabbed.

All of the men turned to look out of the dirty window of Shooters. The haze on the glass was from years of Code Reds. They could see about forty young YSWs yelling in the street through the glass. They were using their third eye or their time piece to cast messages in the air. Solomon worked to read them through the nearly opaque windows. One message was in bright neon flashing green letters. It read, "One power, One mind!" Several other signs had similar meanings. "One World, One Leader, Yusef Aesis!"

"Do you think he will be the first One World ruler?" Solomon asked Kevin.

"Looks like it. Kinda like the idea myself. We need someone who is going to bring all of the people together. He seems to be the best man for the job."

"I am shocked to hear that. Not too long ago, you thought it was a terrible idea. The death of democracy, remember?" Solomon hid the seriousness of his question behind a smile.

"I am just gaining a new perspective. That's all." Kevin got up from the wooden table with the broken leg. "I will see you gentlemen later. I need to be heading home. Hey, Barkley, charge the drinks to me. I will use my YSW account." Kevin shot a glance that Solomon had never seen before. Kevin left out of Shooters and hopped on his hovercraft. He zoomed off, breaking through the laser show of protester images and faded off in the distance.

"I can tell what you're thinking," Barkley said, as he was wiping down the bar. "You're thinking he has changed already right?"

"Yeah, something like that," Solomon said, still looking out the window at the protesters.

"Well," Barkley said. "At least he got you a drink."

"Very true, my friend. Very true...I guess it is about time for me to head home as well." Solomon looked at the time glowing through Barkley's skin.

"Hey, Solomon...Hang in there. Everything will work out the way it is supposed to."

"Thanks, Barkley. You're a good man."

You could see a tiny odd light flash from behind his sunglasses. That was Barkley's way of winking.

Solomon headed into the chaos. He covered up as much as he could so the YSW couldn't identify him. He pushed his way through the crowd. His mask covered his mouth and nose, his collar up high. He walked quickly through the noise and the laser light messages to find his way back in the lobby of his apartment.

Solomon quickly greeted Jose and headed toward the elevator. He was so focused on returning home that he didn't notice his friend from the 6th floor.

"Hey, Solomon. How have you been?" Aurora asked.

Solomon turned around quickly.

"Hey. Good to see you. Glad you were able to come over the other night. Karina really enjoyed talking to you."

"I enjoyed talking to her as well. Actually enjoyed the whole thing. It felt like...I don't know, like home," Aurora said, looking down. "I wished my father were like you when he was alive. He was a good man, but you're just...I don't know...different."

Solomon smiled. "Yeah, well, I hope you told my daughter that."

"I did. Hey, I'm headed out to grab a few things. I will leave some groceries for you. I know that meal had to cost an arm and a leg."

"You don't have to do that," Solomon replied.

"I know, but..." Just then, Aurora received a call. She waved bye and headed out the door, before zoning out to take her call.

Solomon made it back to his apartment. He went into his bedroom to check on Kristen. She was so still that he waited to see her chest rise and fall to ensure she was still breathing. She didn't look like herself anymore. She had lost so much weight that she was nearly unrecognizable. Solomon walked away from the door and plopped down on the sofa. So many thoughts and feelings swirling through him, he didn't recognize that his children were not home yet. They were having adventures of their own.

Chapter 17: Time Waits For No One

No one knows when their time is up, so treat those around
you with love and kindness.
(A Warning from the Writ)

"I'm scared." Kyle's finger was trembling over the time snatcher app.

"Just press the button!" Karina shouted.

"Shhhhh!--" Knox was just as frightened as his brother. "Why aren't you doing it?"

"You two were the ones fighting over it. Fine, here, I'll do it." Karina grabbed the device from her brother.

They were hovering over a drunk homeless man lying at the end of an alley. He was covered with a leather jacket to prevent his skin from burning. Karina pressed the button, turning her head away. She didn't know if there would be a bright light or a zap, but she wanted to be safe. Her brothers copied her demeanor, turning away as well. To their surprise, there was not much of anything except for a small chime sound that came from the device.

They removed the jacket from the man, taking a little time to examine him.

"He looks alright to me," Knox said.

"Yeah, me too," Kyle replied.

Karina was holding the device in her hand. "Look," Karina said, pointing at the app that now reads, "Ten minutes of life time added."

"That's scary. We can take ten minutes of someone's life?"

"I know it sounds bad, but he wasn't using it. Look at him."

"So you feel okay with taking ten minutes of life from someone?"

Karina's brown eyes shot over at Knox. "I don't look at it like that. Mom needs these ten minutes and what does this person do? Absolutely nothing."

Kyle felt torn. "Mom will need a lot more than ten minutes if we plan to save her, and the app will only let you get ten minutes at a time. So what are we going to do?"

"I know, you're right. I've got to figure something out." Karina rotated the Illuminus 2125 as if she were examining it.

"I have got to find a way to get more time faster."

"Karina, we've practiced stealing time for mom, but what will we do about Norman? He is still not back," Kyle reminded his sister.

"That job is going to be a little more complicated than this one," Karina responded.

Kyle and Knox stood there waiting for Karina to tell them their next adventure.

Karina continued. "I think we are going to have to go into the cocoon and find Norman in the place between the virtual world and reality."

"And HOW in the WORLD do you expect us to do that?" Knox threw his hands in the air at the preposterous idea.

"We are going to have to break into Norman's house and, one of us, will have to go into the cocoon with the Illuminous 2125."

"I am NOT doing that! What if I never come back out?!" Knox shouted.

There was a little silence. Everyone was processing what was just said, and then Kyle spoke. "I'll do it. I got us into this mess, I'll get us out."

"Wow, you?" Karina was surprised. Kyle wasn't known for being the brave brother.

"Yes, I'll do it," Kyle responded again. "Let's just finish this before I change my mind."

Knox was proud of his little brother and patted him on the back. "So, where do we start?"

"I searched and found Norman's address. It's about ten blocks away."

The Wiseman children headed in the direction of Norman's house. To their surprise, it was a large white house with black shutters just outside the city. "Wow, this is nice."

"Nothing like our apartment," Knox said.

"Do you think anyone is home?" Kyle asked.

"Probably not. To have a house like this, his parents must work a lot. Think about it; he is a Cocooner. His parents just put him in a machine and sent him to school."

They walked up on the porch and peaked in the large windows. "It's completely dark inside."

"You're right. I don't think anyone is home."

"I don't see a hovercraft around either. So they are probably at work," Karina stated.

"How are we going to get in?" Knox inquired.

Kyle was nervous. "Not sure. They probably have some surveillance system watching us right now as we speak. Maybe we should just leave."

"We're not leaving. We just need to find a way to get to the Cocoon."

The Wiseman children walked around the back of the house. "Look" Knox wiped the red dust off the windows and pointed to what appeared to be the living room.

"That's a butt-ugly sofa," Kyle said.

"That is not what I am pointing to. Look in the corner, I think that is the cocoon."

The Wiseman children looked at the corner to see a large, round, egg-shaped chamber. It was shiny silver and had a window so parents could see their children's faces through the cocoon.

"Is that, is that Norman?" Kyle pointed.

"Oh my Jah, it is," Knox replied.

"He's still in there? That means his parents didn't take him out for over a week to check on him." Kyle was in awe. "Makes perfect sense, no wonder we didn't see any reports about missing children. They leave them there. Poor parenting."

"That's kinda sad," Karina said. "Okay...think about this. We have been wandering around this house for several minutes, and no police have come, no sirens have gone off. They may not have their system on."

"Maybe, maybe not. Either way, we are here now."

"You're right Knox, okay...let me try to do this." Karina pulled out a series of small tools attached to a metal circle.

"What are you doing?" Kyle asked.

"If there is a sensor attached to the door, I want to cut it off so when we open the door, it doesn't make a sound. I am not too worried about cameras identifying us. We have so much stuff on to protect us from the Code Red, that they probably can't see our faces." Karina snipped a few wires.

"I can't believe you just did that." Kyle was holding the door that was now in his hands.

"Put it over there. I will reattach it when we leave."

Kyle leaned the door against the wall, and they all tiptoed into Norman's house.

"It's so empty. Just a sofa, a screen, and a cocoon." Knox said. They all walked over to the cocoon. This is the first time I am seeing the actual Norman. Kinda creepy." Knox continued to look at Norman through the glass. Norman's eyes were closed, and his hands were crossed over his chest.

"We're going to have to get his body out of there," Karina said. She pressed the button, and the egg-like contraption unlatched.

The brothers flinched at the sound of the cocoon opening.

"Okay. I will grab his hands, you two get behind him and push."

All three of the Wiseman children began tugging and pushing Norman. "He's like a rock," Kyle snickered.

"Almost got him, keep pushing."

One last push and Norman popped out of the cocoon and landed on Karina. "Ah" she screamed and pushed Norman's large heavy body off. Norman was still breathing but did not move.

"I can't believe we got him out. I can't believe we are doing this. I can't believe…"

"Shut up!" Karina said. "Just get into the stupid cocoon and stop freaking out."

Kyle hopped into the cocoon. "Is it too late to change my mind?"

Karina ignored his question. "Here, I have set the time manipulation app for Thursday. The day you two numbskulls vaporized Norman. When I press the button to turn you into a hologram, you have to press the time manipulation app at the same time so that it doesn't send you to school today. I will count down starting from three. Do you understand?"

"What happens if I don't press it at the same time?" Kyle was extremely nervous.

"Just make sure you press it when I say," Karina responded.

"Kyle, be safe, brother," Knox said.

"Okay." Karina closed the door to the cocoon. "Three…Two…One…press the button." Both Kyle and Karina pressed buttons. Karina sent Kyle into the world of virtual reality and Kyle pressed the time manipulation button that sent him to Thursday right before Norman was vaporized.

142

"I think it worked," Karina said to Knox. She was pointing to a wall of lights and sensors that were all green. "I am assuming that they would be a different color if something were wrong."

"I sure hope you are right," Knox replied nervously, watching his brother. "I should have gone in there. I should have done it for him. Kyle may not be able to pull it off."

"I think Kyle has proven to us that he is much braver than we imagined. He will be able to do it."

Chapter 18: Seeing Double

There are two sides to every man, take time to learn who they are and what strengths each possesses and do not let one over power the other, but live a life of balance.
(A Warning from the Writ).

While Karina and Knox watched the cocoon, Kyle felt like he was floating through the events of last Thursday. He could see himself in the cafeteria waiting for Norman. He saw Knox and Clifton as well. A few moments later, Norman and his gang appeared.

"Hey, it's the mutant and his cronies."

Oh my gosh, Kyle thought to himself, this is where I vaporize him.

"Stop!" the hologram version of Kyle shouted to the real Kyle. "Stop, don't do it!"

"Wait, how in the…" Knox said, looking back and forth between the real Kyle and the hologram. Knox was in utter disbelief.

"There are two mutants?" Norman said.

The entire cafeteria was looking in disbelief. Whispers of two Kyles spread all over the cafeteria.

"First of all, you will stop calling me a mutant," Kyle said. His piercing blue eyes stared Norman down.

"You're a hologram?" Norman pointed. "Ah...Ah...and you're the real thing. What is going on here?"

"Yeah, what is going on here?" Knox was confused as well.

Kyle whispered, "Look, something goes wrong when we vaporize Norman. I have come from the future to ensure we didn't kill him. My real body is in a cocoon at Norman's house. The rest I will have to explain later."

Knox's mouth dropped. He couldn't believe what he was seeing. The hologram version of his brother and his real brother standing together. They looked the same, the only difference was the eye color.

"Norman, just so you know. I can vaporize you so that you and your friends never return. I am here to save you from that fate, but you must promise me that you will NEVER, and I mean NEVER make fun of me again or else."

Norman was so shocked by what he saw that he stuttered, "Oh...oh...okay...I promise I won't make fun of you again."

"Not just me. You need to promise that you will never make fun of any of us again."

All of the children from the cafeteria started cheering. You could hear them shout "Yeah, that's right!"

"Fine."

"And your friends. They must promise to leave everyone at the LAME school alone!"

Norman's friends didn't seem as excited to take the deal. A few of them turned away.

The blue-eyed Kyle turned to the other version of himself and said, "Kyle, get ready to vaporize them."

The real Kyle held the device up and hovered his finger over it.

"Wait!" shouted one of Norman's friends. "Don't be stupid. I don't want to be vaporized forever. What we were doing to Kyle wasn't right. Just apologize."

"Sorry, Kyle."

"I apologize."

"Yes, man, I'm sorry."

Blue-eyed Kyle turned to Norman. "What about

you?" "Yes, yes, I apologize."

Kyle's laser blue eyes darted over to the real him, and the brown-eyed Kyle smiled back.

"Now, Norman, you are going to need to do what I tell you to do. You and all of your friends need to connect yourself to your stations and transport home now."

"Are you crazy? It's the middle of the school day." Norman replied.

"Just do it!" Kyle, Norman, and all of the other Cocooners who Kyle vaporized, headed to their stations.

"All of your friends can go ahead and connect to the station." the blue-eyed Kyle announced.

"What about me?" Norman folded his arms.

"Right now, my body is in your cocoon. If you went back right now, your persona would be transferred back into my body, and we both know that you don't want that."

"Alright, so then what am I supposed to do?"

"I am going to transfer back first, you wait about 3 minutes before sending yourself back. That should be enough time for us to get your body back into the cocoon."

"You're in my house? You're lying in my cocoon? What is going on?"

"Stop with all the questions and just do what I say," Kyle said to Norman. "Go lock the classroom door. Lunch is almost over, and I don't want anyone coming in while we do this."

Norman did as Kyle told him. He locked the door and watched as the blue-eyed Kyle pulled out the device and programmed the time manipulation app to return him to the present before transporting himself back. Then Norman waited for 3 minutes.

"Look," Karina said. "I think he did it. I think he is coming back."

Knox looked into the cocoon as Kyle's eyes opened. Karina rushed to open the cocoon, and Kyle shot up, gasping for air.

"Are you okay? Did you do it?" Knox asked

"I...I...I think so. But we don't have much time. We need to get Norman back into his cocoon quickly."

All three Wiseman children went over to Norman, whose body was lying on the floor, and hoisted him up. "What does this kid eat?"

"Just hurry up and get him in there." Kyle looked at the device. "We only have 30 seconds left. Hurry!"

They thrust Norman back into the Cocoon with ten seconds to spare.

"Quick, Karina, close it up and press the button."

No sooner did Karina do this than the ten seconds were over. "Do you think we made it?"

"I don't know."

The Wiseman children waited for what seemed to be an eternity before seeing Norman's eyelids begin to move.

"I think...I think he is coming back." Karina peered into the cocoon. As she did this, Norman's eyes popped open. Karina screamed.

"Open the top," Knox shouted.

Norman was breathing hard and looking around. "What is going on. Where am I?" Norman gathered himself for a minute. "Wait, you were just in my dream but, but you had blue eyes."

"Norman, you weren't dreaming. Last week, when you were making fun of me. I got so upset that I vaporized you. We got worried when you didn't return to school for an entire week. So, we came back to save you."

"You saved me?"

"Yes," Kyle replied.

"You had an opportunity to live without me messing with you ever again, and you saved me." A long pause before Norman continued. "Thanks. That really means a lot."

"I saved you on one condition," Kyle replied.

"Oh yeah, what was that?"

"That you and your friends never mess with me or anyone else at school ever again."

"Wait a minute. I think I remember that. I thought it was all a dream. There...there were two of you."

"So Norman, do we have a deal?" Knox was staring at Norman, waiting for him to reply.

"Deal!"

The Wiseman children were headed to the door when suddenly they heard, "Why in the world is our door off the

henge?" It was Norman's parents getting off work.

"Quick, go out the back." Norman pointed, and the Wiseman children ran. Karina and Knox made it out, but Kyle still struggled to get out of the window. Norman ran over and pushed him through. Kyle landed with a loud thud but took no time to see if he was injured. He popped up and ran as fast as possible to catch up with his siblings.

The Wiseman children made it out just before Norman's mom and dad came around the corner to see Norman out of his cocoon, looking disheveled. "Why in the world is our door off the hinge, and why are you not at school? You know we don't like dealing with you. Get back in there." Norman's mother pointed to the cocoon.

"I..." But before Norman could finish, his father interjected. "You know what, I don't want to hear it. You are returning to that cocoon, and I don't want to see you back here for two weeks."

"But, Dad..."

"Get in there NOW!"

Norman got back into the cocoon. His dad pressed the button, closing him in for a few more weeks.

"Good thing we don't have to deal with him any longer." Norman's dad said as he looked at his wife. "I'll go get some tools to put the door back on the hinge." He walked off in search of tools.

Norman's mom looked into the cocoon at her son. She placed her hands on the glass and said, "Serves you right." She headed into her kitchen and started dinner for just the two of them.

Chapter 19: When it Rains, it Pours

When it floods, learn to detach from the storm and float above the water.
You cannot control the flood, so let go. Eventually, the
flood waters will recede.
(A Warning from the Writ)

The Wiseman children ran home, arriving before their father got off of work.

They were out of breath but full of adrenaline. "Kyle, you're the man!" His brother high-fived him.

"I can't believe you could get him back," Karina replied, panting.

Kyle was feeling pretty proud of himself as well.

"Remember, not a word of this to anyone," Karina reminded her brothers.

"Of course not, who would we tell?" Knox said. Karina looked at him knowingly.

The following Monday, Solomon found himself back at Readers Publishing. The only difference was the new computers that arrived.

"I'm an old man, it's hard for me to catch on to all of this new stuff," Solomon joked.

"No problem, I can try to show you how to use everything once I set it up, and bubbles is helping me," Mike said eagerly. He was petting bubbles on the top of his glass dome head. Mike was young, and considered himself revolutionary because he hadn't signed with the YSW yet. Solomon did not doubt that he would soon.

Solomon poured coffee into his #1 Dad mug, plopped down in the busted leather chair, looking into a brand-new screen. Mike eagerly bopped around the small office. *He's irritating,* Solomon spun around in his chair and turned his computer screen on before heading to get sugar for his coffee. When he returned to his computer, he had a message pop up on his screen:

NOT PART OF THE YSW YET? IN DEBT? CLICK HERE

Solomon was used to receiving pop-ups similar to this, so he didn't pay it much attention until he tried to exit the screen and another message popped up:

SOLOMON, YOU ARE RECEIVING A GENEROUS OFFER. NOT ONLY WILL WE ELIMINATE YOUR DEBT, BUT WE WILL ALSO PROVIDE A FULL SCHOLARSHIP TO KARINA. REFUSING TO ACCEPT THIS OFFER COULD RESULT IN SERIOUS CONSEQUENCES FOR YOU AND YOUR DAUGHTER.

Solomon quickly clicked off the screen. "I am going to go on break." Solomon got up and went down the hall. He felt more exposed than ever before. The blue light in the corner seemed to gleam brighter today.

Would they really try to use my daughter to get to me? He regretted taking anything from Kevin and wondered what Karina had done to get involved in this, if she had done anything at all.

Solomon grabbed his jacket, walked through an alley and onto the street. He made his way through several groups of protesters chanting, "ONE GOVERNMENT, NO WAY!"

A loud siren came on during the protest, followed by an announcement so loud it was deafening. Solomon covered his ears. "No one can protest against the One World Government. Return to your residence before there are consequences."

At that, a young-dumb YSW threw his middle finger in the air and shouted, "Screw the government. One Government, No Way!" With that, the police flew over the protester and, with a laser, shot him in plain sight. The crowd broke apart. A female radical YSW screamed at the sight of the dead body, and she was also struck down.

Solomon ran for cover, finding refuge under an ally bench and having a flashback of a previous dream.

"Unbelievable, it's really happening." He remained crouched under the bench and was about to get up when another thunderous announcement filled the air. The screens on the sidewalks and buildings all shifted to the same image of Yusef Aesis.

"Greetings. I am excited to run for the first-ever, One World leader. My name is Yusef Aesis. I have heard the discord of the nations, the protests, and the frustration of the people. It may be confusing to see violence to promote peace, but there must be consequences for those who don't follow the rules. I hope you appreciate a ruler who believes in the values of peace, order, and lawfulness. Although I am not in power yet, my opponents do not demand the respect I do, nor do they have the connections and power I have. I desire to keep you safe. I desire to provide you peace. My opponents will soon be eliminated from the election and you will know what true freedom feels like under my reign."

As soon as his announcement was over, a female voice immediately followed. "This campaign was brought to you by Yusef Aesis, your choice for world peace."

Solomon was afraid to move from under the bench. The entire city was eerily quiet, fearful of what may happen next. Solomon waited for a few hovercrafts to fly past before deciding to leave his hiding place.

When Solomon arrived home, he was greeted by Kyle. "Dad, where have you been? Mom is not doing well."

Solomon didn't want to explain what he just witnessed. Instead, he asked, "What's wrong with your mother?"

Knox grabbed his father's hand and dragged him into the bedroom. Solomon saw Kristen sitting on the edge of the bed as he walked in. She was heaving and coughing up bright red blood.

"What is going on? How long has she been doing this?" Solomon ran into the bathroom to get more towels.

"She started throwing up, but it was like she had nothing in her stomach. Then it just got worse about twenty minutes ago," Knox explained.

Karina was sitting next to her mother. She was moving her mother's hair out of the way. Karina had a small bucket in her hand, filled with an ungodly smelling substance that Solomon could only assume had come from his wife.

"What took you so long to get home? Mom needed you! Where were you?" Karina snapped at her father.

"I didn't know. Why didn't anyone try to reach me?" Solomon fumbled around, looking for his antiquated cellphone.

"I am so sorry. We need to contact the doctor." Solomon was frazzled.

This is one of the worst days of my life. He thought to himself as he connected to the doctor's office.

A few minutes later, Solomon walked back in the room to see all his children surrounding Kristen. Solomon did his best to mask his emotions, but Karina could tell something was different about her dad.

"What's going on?"

"Come here, Karina. Leave the boys in here. I need to talk to you."

Karina got off the bed, pulling her long, bushy, dark brown hair off her shoulders and putting into a bun. Her deep brown, round eyes looked up at her father, who stood about six inches over her.

"Dad, seriously, what's wrong?"

Before Solomon could begin his sentence, a tear welled up in the corner of his eye. Karina had never seen her father cry before. Solomon leaned his head back, hoping to force the tear back where it came from.

"Um," Solomon cleared his throat and turned away from Karina. He couldn't look her in the eye. "Your mom is really sick. The doctor said it is much worse than they thought. If she is already throwing up blood, they don't know if she will make it to the end of the month."

The awkward silence could have been cut with a knife. It must have also drawn the attention of Solomon's younger sons, who soon joined them in the hallway.

"Why are you guys out here instead of with Mom?" Kyle asked.

Karina shot her eyes over to her dad and walked away saying, "I am going to lay next to mom." She wiped a tear away from her face and rubbed her wet hands on her long flower-printed skirt.

"Dad, why is Karina crying?" Kyle asked.

"Your mom is pretty sick. We need to make sure we are on our best behavior for her. Okay? You boys can do that, right?"

"Of course." Both Kyle and Knox said it at the same time.

That night, Karina snuck into her brother's room. They were snoring. She rummaged through a few of their school belongings before finding what she came in there for. "It's time to get some good use out of you." She put the small device in her pocket, looked at her brothers, who were sound asleep and walked out of the room.

Karina carefully disconnected the security systems to the apartment before heading out. She was bundled up from head to toe, had her hair pulled back into a bun, and tucked in a black hoodie. She made her way onto the elevator and down to the lobby, just to be spotted by Jose.

"Leaving?"

Karina didn't answer. Several of the electronic sidewalks began to call out to Karina. "You should upgrade your device, Karina. Follow the path, and we can have you all taken care of."

She learned to ignore the call of the ads a long time ago.

There was so much noise in the streets that she felt masked. "If you can't say anything nice, don't say anything at all," was shouted by a group of YSW. They held signs in the air promoting a new initiative, the silence order. There were so many YSW in the streets walking in and out of bars and clubs. Third-eye technology was catching on as they walked through the streets with eyes closed and third eye glowing. Mixed in with the YSW were AI's, with bright blue eyes peering into the darkness. Hoverboards were darting all around as YSW raced each other, breaking the zoning laws.

Karina was on a mission to find someone who she could steal time from. She stumbled upon an unsuspecting YSW who seemed partied out lying on a bench near the edge of the street. Pointing the device at them, she pressed the button and added ten minutes to the Time Snatcher app. She took advantage of ten more drunk partiers before arriving at a homeless woman sleeping in an alley near a dumpster. This time, instead of Karina pressing the button once, she decided to press it three times. Karina looked down at the device. "30 minutes of life received."

Thirty minutes isn't that bad, She thought to herself. So, from that point forward, she decided that, instead of pressing the time snatcher once, she would press it three times for each person she ran into. Karina made her way down another alley. *I lucked up, there are four of them here,* She thought to herself after seeing a group of homeless people huddled together, sleeping. After she had collected two hours of life from the group, she turned around with the device in her hand, looking at all of the time she had collected for the night. The light from the device illuminated her face. She was about to come to the end of an alley when she heard, "Karina, is that you?"

It was Aurora. She had finished partying. There was a YSW male groping her. "Hey, I didn't think your dad would let you out."

Aurora swatted at the guy. "Can't you see I am talking to someone. Chill out--" The guy staggered away.

"So what are you doing? "Aurora asked.

"Nothing, just...I just needed a little fresh air."

"Ha!" Aurora let out a boisterous laugh. "You came out in a Code Red to get fresh air. You must think I'm stupid. Look, I remember when I was your age. I snuck out of the house a lot. It's cool...I am not going to tell anyone."

"Thanks--" Karina fumbled around nervously. "I, um, I think I need to head home."

She walked home at a neck-breaking pace, quickly returning to the lobby where Jose seemed to be waiting for her. "Hi Karina, you're getting home awfully late."

Karina shot him an irritated smile and got onto the elevator,

The elevator opened the doors. "Hi, Karina, headed to the 9th floor?"

"Yes."

"How was your night out?"

"You sure ask a lot of questions for an elevator."

"My apologies---" A few short seconds later. "You have arrived."

"Look, I don't know if I need to tell you this, but please don't let my father know that I was out tonight. I had a lot on my mind and just needed to think."

"I understand. My emotions are different from yours, but I can't imagine what you and your family are going through. Your secret is safe with me."

"Thanks." Karina got off the elevator and started walking down the hall. As she approached the door of Todd Markley, it cracked open.

"Solomon, is that you?" Todd whispered.

Karina walked toward the opening slowly. As soon as Todd saw her face, he slammed the door shut.

Rude, Karina thought to herself. She managed to make it back into her apartment. She turned the sensors back on and locked the doors exactly how they were before leaving. Her father was on the sofa asleep. She was able to tip-toe past him and make it to her room. She lay in bed thinking about her night. *I can't go out like this anymore, too many eyes are watching. I've got to find a way to steal time from people in the building without being caught. I need to find a way to get large amounts of time so I only have to go out once or twice.* Karina kept thinking until she finally decided, *The reclusive. He's the answer. Not sure why he was calling for my father. He's probably losing it. No matter, he had the door open like he was waiting for someone to come. I need to get in there. He will be the one to give my mother her life back.* Before heading to bed, Karina stood over her mom and zapped her with 3 ½ hours of life she collected for the night.

Then she took out the device and hooked it up to her tablet. She opened one of her coding programs from her technology class at school and unlocked the code to the app. She spent the rest of the night programming the app to take days and not minutes.

Chapter 20: A Warning-Dead Quiet

Out of your mouths comes corruption and harm. In the last days,
mouths will be silenced
(A Warning from the Writ)

Karina, nor anyone else in the Wiseman house, would have known that Solomon cried out to Jah just an hour before Karina snuck out of the house. All she knows is that he was asleep when she left and when she returned home. But at midnight, Solomon was in his master bathroom. "Please allow me to get some rest. I can't take this anymore!"

He broke down crying, looking into the mirror. "You appear distressed, would you like a filter to change your expression?" the mirror inquired.

An angry Solomon whispered, "I hate you. Stop talking to me!" He banged his hands on the glass, but it did not break.

A year-old bottle of anxiety medication sent to his house by Dr. Monroe to help him with his dreams seemed to be the answer. He had avoided it for a while but could not imagine going another night without sleep. He turned on the faucet.

"Your preferred temperature setting is eighty-seven degrees. Would you like to use that setting now?" A sensor on the faucet inquired.

"No," Solomon replied, frustrated. The brown-tinted water poured out into his cupped hand. He threw the medicine in his mouth, chased the pills down with water, tilted his head back, and swallowed, taking twice the recommended dosage.

Solomon grabbed two blankets and a pillow and plopped on the couch. He picked up the *Writ* and turned to the last page he remembered reading but had fallen asleep before he found his spot.

Everyone in the Wiseman house managed to keep busy for the next three weeks. Solomon still had nightmares but coped with his new routine, which consisted of a late-night talk with Todd Markley, reading the *Writ*, and taking four anxiety pills. This routine often left Solomon groggy in the morning, but getting 5 hours of sleep was better than none. Todd also seemed to get into the routine and started leaving his door open and turning his security system off so Solomon could come in with no issues. When Solomon arrived, Todd always had a pot of tea brewing and a stack of books or newspapers ready to be discussed.

Karina stayed up many nights trying to find a way to program the time snatcher app to take three days every time she pressed the button. She wanted to do more than three days but thought it best to start conservatively. She also went through her building looking for someone to snatch time from. She focused on Todd Markley but needed to see how her dad knew him.

"Dad?"

161

"Yes, Karina," Solomon hastily replied. He was putting on all his gear to head outside and start walking to work.

"I want to ask you a question."

"Well, hurry up. You're about to make me late."

"Okay...well...you know the reclusive--" Karina started. Solomon froze up. He didn't know where this line of questioning would lead. He didn't want Karina to know how they knew each other. Solomon was sure that Karina would judge him for leaving the house at night instead of being there to take care of his wife.

"Yes, I know of him." Solomon was careful with his response.

"Do you know what he does for a living or how he spends his time?"

"Why do you want to know? Seems a bit odd."

"No reason, I was just curious. He always has so many packages at the door. I wonder what he must do during the day."

"Hmm...well...I am not the one to judge how others use their time. And why would you think that I would know what he does for a living?"

"Well...you are always out and about, thought you may know something about him," Karina responded.

"Nah, don't know much. I have seen him peek out of his apartment a few times before. I try to be friendly. You never know what people have gone through."

"Okay...I was just wondering."

Like her first night of time snatching, Karina waited until it was one in the morning before venturing out. When she arrived at the door of Todd Markley, she was surprised about how easy it was to get in. She came prepared with all of her gadgets for disconnecting his system but discovered that it had already been turned off. A quick twist of the knob and the door was open.

When she walked in, the entire room was dark. It was nearly impossible to make her way through without bumping into something. *Dang, where is the stupid light feature on this thing? Oh, okay, there it is.* A slight glow illuminated the room.

She found Todd Markley sleeping on a plaid chair. She felt way more nervous about this than her adventure a few weeks ago. Karina stood over Todd and watched him breathe. Karina pointed the device at Todd. She took a deep breath. *Okay, Karina, you can do this.* Her hand was trembling. *Get it together.* She pressed the button, and a few short seconds later, the device read: three days of life collected. *I shouldn't do this anymore,* she thought to herself.

Karina returned to her apartment and walked past her father, sleeping on the sofa. Karina slowly opened the door to her mother's room. Beads of sweat were sprinkled on her mother's forehead. Her complexion was gray, and her breathing was heavy. Her mother's full round face was gone. Now, her cheekbones were visible.

"I am going to do the best I can to help you," Karina whispered in her mother's ear. Karina sat next to her mother. Kristen turned slightly. "Hey baby, what are you doing here?" Her question was followed by a series of coughs.

"Just wanted to see you." Are you doing okay, Mom?"

Kristen put on her best smile. "Of course. You know me, I'm fine."

Karina smiled. She started rubbing her mother's back.

"That feels nice, Karina. My everything hurts." Kristen chuckled. It wasn't long before she fell back to sleep.

Karina held the Illuminous to her mom's back and deposited three days.

Chapter 21: All Gone

It is when there is nothing left that you will find yourself. But make sure you are looking in the right place or else you will be lost with no one around to guide you.
(A Warning from the Writ)

Several restless nights later, Solomon found himself in the book-filled home of his neighbor.

"Ahh, so, I see you have been reading the *Writ* more," Todd said to Solomon.

"Yes, you were right. I never looked at it like this before. It makes so much more sense than it used to. Or maybe..."

"Maybe what?" Todd inquired.

"Maybe I am just looking for anything to make sense of what's happening. Maybe believing that Jah has all of this under control helps me...I don't know...find peace with what's happening with Kristen. Maybe this gives me a way to rationalize my nightmares." Solomon sat down and put his head in his hands.

"Solomon...it is okay to believe, even if you feel it is for all the wrong reasons. Jah has to find a way to speak to you somehow. He doesn't care how He gets to you. He just wants to get to you."

"Thank you for that--" Solomon said "Hey, are you okay?" Solomon asked, looking at Todd shuffling about much slower than usual.

"I'm fine. I have just been more tired than usual. These old bones, I guess." Todd chuckled.

"Yes, old man...we are all feeling it," Solomon responded. "So...you see the election results, right? Yusef Aesis has officially been voted as the new One World leader."

"How do you feel about that? You told me that Jah revealed it to you, right?" Todd asked.

"I don't know how to feel. I guess I am trying to learn to see these nightmares as a gift. I have looked at them as a burden for so long..."

"I get it, but Solomon, you...you do realize that, for some reason, you have been chosen. Look...I want to share something with you. I don't know if I am supposed to, but I don't know how much longer I will be around. For the past few weeks, I have just felt like I am getting weaker. I don't want you to worry, but..."

"What are you trying to say?"

Solomon and Todd were quiet for a moment. "I know what it feels like to be assigned a, what is the word I'm looking for, a mission from Jah that you may not want."

Solomon was perplexed. "What are you talking about?"

"You receive dreams, and I feel that Jah gives me words that need to be shared with people. You know the things I have been talking to you about? The Warnings? They are sent to me by Jah,

166

but now, I don't know what I will do because I just don't know if I will be around long enough to finish writing them."

"Of course, you will. Aren't you the one that tells me that Jah doesn't make mistakes? If He is the one who assigned you to write the warnings, then you will be around long enough to complete them."

"He doesn't make mistakes, my friend. No mistakes at all. The message will still go out. The Warnings will continue to be written with or without me. I suggest that you start writing down your dreams. Continue to look to Jah and read the *Writ* for meaning, and don't let anything, I mean anything, remove you from the will of Jah. The angels sing when one of their children comes home. They are happy that you are making your way back to them."

Solomon was uncomfortable and just shook his head. "Okay, well, look...It's getting late. I need to return and get my usual four hours of sleep."

Todd just smiled.

"Same time tomorrow?" Solomon asked. Both men walked toward the door.

"Go home and get some rest." Todd shut the door behind Solomon, leaving it unlocked in case Solomon wanted to stop by and talk.

A few hours later, Solomon had fallen asleep on the couch.

Karina had gotten used to her father's schedule. She didn't know where he was going every night but didn't ask questions, as she was on her own mission. She peered over her dad before heading out the door.

Nerves of sneaking into the reclusive's house had subsided. "This is the last time," Karina said to herself. The door creaked, but she didn't flinch. She stayed focused on her mission. Karina got to the plaid chair and leaned over Todd, who, as usual, was in a deep sleep. She took out the Illuminous 2125 and pressed the time snatcher app three flashes of light. She looked down at the screen. "Nine days collected." Karina quickly turned around, accidentally knocking into the corner of a table. "Shoot," she whispered. She turned to look at Todd. He didn't budge. *Whew,* she thought to herself.

An eye scan and the door clicked open. Tiptoeing past her dad, Karina headed around the corner to her mother sleeping peacefully. She watched her mother's chest move up and down and was grateful. The room was dark, only illuminated by the light from her device. She placed the device on her mother's back and deposited nine days. Karina bent over and kissed her mom on the top of her head. "I love you." As if Kristen heard her, a brief smile before returning to her heavy breathing.

As she went to her room, Karina realized she could not keep sneaking out to take life from her neighbor. She spent the night forcing herself to accept that her mother was sick and would not be around much longer and decided to enjoy every moment she could.

The usual hustle and bustle of the morning were interrupted by the sound of the Wiseman sensor system. "Someone is approaching."

"Who is it?" Kyle asked.

Hologram images of the visitors appeared inside their living room—two men dressed in police uniforms. Metal chest plates on top of long, dark blue, bullet proof shirts were tucked into dark blue pants. One was short and stocky with dark hair and dark eyes. The other, clearly AI, bright blue eyes, dark skin, no hair, muscular.

Another repeat from the door. "You have guests, how would you like to proceed?"

"Dad," Knox shouted, "there are police officers at the door!"

"Give me a sec--" Solomon finished bathing his wife and had placed her in the bed. "I'll be right out."

Solomon unclicked all the locks and peeked out the small round peephole before opening.

"Hi, officers," Solomon said as he wiped the remaining water off his hands.

"Hello, Mr. Wiseman. Beautiful family you have here," the stocky one said as he looked in Karina's direction, "We have just come from an apartment across the hall. It belonged to a Mr. Todd Markley. Do you happen to know him?"

Solomon's eyes grew big. "Um...what is all of this about?"

"Let me rephrase, we know that you know him. We have already scanned his apartment and seen your prints all over his bookshelves, coffee mugs, and furniture. We also have footage of you entering and leaving his apartment nearly every night for the past few weeks. So, how do you know Mr. Markley? "

Karina overheard the conversation. She was afraid and did her best not to lock eyes with the visitors.

"I...he and I had become friends. We...we talked about...we just talked. Is everything okay?"

"No sir." The officer's badge read Sgt. Richardson. "Mr. Markley has been found dead."

"Oh, my Jah." Solomon just stood in disbelief. Solomon's back was turned to his daughter, so he did not see her as she struggled to catch her breath, but Sgt. Richardson took notice.

"Hi--do you mind if I speak with you?" Sgt. Richardson looked in Karina's direction.

"Uh...sure," Karina responded nervously.

169

"Did you know Mr. Markley?"

"No, not really, he was just the strange man who lived down the hall."

"Are you sure?"

"She's sure!" Solomon said firmly. "No one really knew him except for me. Look, he and I had become friends. He didn't trust anyone else to come to his house. No need to ask my daughter any questions. I am more than willing to talk to you about whatever it is you want to talk about."

"If it makes you feel any better, we know *you* didn't have anything to do with this, but we have pulled footage from the cameras in the hallway. We saw you leave Mr. Markley's apartment around twelve in the morning, another person, petite, slim frame, black hoodie, came from this very apartment about an hour later. They walked across the hall and entered Mr. Markley's apartment. They stayed for about three minutes and returned to this very apartment. We are not here to make an arrest today, but"—Sgt. Richardson looked over at Karina—"you may want to talk to your family and see if anyone else had a relationship with Mr. Markley besides you."

The officer handed Solomon a chip. "Here is our information. If you have any questions or if you want to talk."

"Thank you, officer." Solomon took the chip and looked back suspiciously at Karina.

"No problem Mr. Wiseman. Have a good day. Oh, and we will be keeping an eye on you. You know...for your protection."

"Thank you again." Solomon closed the door and turned all the locks.

Solomon was quiet and looked at his daughter suspiciously.

"Karina, a few weeks ago, you asked me about Todd, why?"

"Like I said, I just wanted to know what he did. I wanted to know how reclusives live."

"Why did the officer look at you like that? Have you ever gone over to his apartment?" Solomon stared at his daughter. She quickly looked away.

He already knew her answer but didn't push anymore.

She grabbed her belongings. "Look, Dad, I'm going to be late for school."

"I have to go as well, but we are not finished talking about this."

Karina pushed past her brothers, who were watching the awkward exchange and headed out the door. Solomon left shortly after, slamming the door on the way out.

His pace slowed as he walked past Todd Markley's apartment. *"You knew. You knew that it was going to be your last night. What in the world is going on here?"*

When Solomon hit the street, noise was coming from every direction. A group of people was cheering the results of the One World Leader, Yusef Aesis. The street was littered with screens displaying the new leader's first speech. Solomon listened as they echoed the new leader's message:

"Ladies and Gentlemen, I promise, you will not be disappointed with your decision to elect me as your leader. My goal is to bring about peace among all nations. Like many of you, I too had parents that were members of the International Society of One Race, so I don't just represent one group of people. I represent you all, one race, the human race. I also know what it is like to want more for yourself but feel confined by the world's view of democracy, where only the rich get richer. My goal is to make sure that everyone, in all nations, has fair and equal access to resources. The only way we can make this happen is to have one form of currency. My first action as your leader is to make cyber currency the only acceptable currency."

Solomon heard the speech in English, but as others passed, scanners would read their Personal Identification number on their wrist to determine which language they needed to understand the message. Immediately, the speech was delivered to them in their language.

While Kyle and Knox were headed to school, Karina was not. She removed the time snatcher and the time manipulation app from the Illuminus 2125.

Then she looked at how much money she had from her YSW perks and bought a ride on an airlifter to take her to the border of the 212 area code.

"Thank you." Karina waved to the AI driver, got off the airlifter and ran as far as she could. The murky river was in view. She quickly glanced and saw signs of the Hudson River being replaced with signs reading Aesis River this way. She wanted to throw the Illuminous 2125 into the river, but it was still too far in the distance, and she had grown tired and settled on a cave in the rocky hills that separated inhabitants of the 212 area code from other zones.

She examined the device for the last time. A symbol of a bitten apple and the words, everlasting life battery, were in fine print at the bottom of the glowing device. Karina used all her might to throw the device into the cave. She took a moment to gather herself before returning to the airlifter drop-off location.

She was amazed that her adventure took most of the day, but she managed to make it home right before her dad walked through the door.

Solomon wasted no time. Bursting through the door, he asked, "What happened to Todd Markley?"

Karina scrambled for the right words. The words that would allow her to tell the truth without telling everything.

"Dad, I didn't know him well. I had a lot of things on my mind one night and noticed his door was open. I walked past, got a glimpse into his apartment, and saw him. I thought I heard him say your name. So, I got curious and went into his apartment. Look, I know it seems strange, but that was it. I promise."

"Fine, Karina. If you say that was it, then fine. You have no idea how much I worried all day about you. You and your brothers are all I have left."

"And Mom. You have Mom too! She's still here, and you didn't even say her name. You have Mom too!" Karina shouted and cried.

"I know I have your mom too, that's not what I meant." Solomon was mid-sentence as Karina stormed off to her room.

A deep exhale and Solomon walked into his bedroom to talk to his wife. "That daughter of ours." He took off work clothes and continued, "I think she has been up to something. I just don't know what it is. She talks to you, has she told you anything?"

"No, she hasn't said anything to me." Kristen's response was faint, and she winced in pain.

He was still moving about, taking off all his layers.

"I have to be honest," Solomon said. "I have been going over to our neighbor's house to talk. I didn't want to bother you with all my stress. You have enough going on as it is. I have to admit, it was really nice having someone else to talk to, and now, my friend is gone. Sorry I couldn't tell you sooner." Solomon slipped a thin white shirt over his head but stopped talking when he noticed Kristen was not engaged in the conversation.

"You okay?" Solomon walked over to Kristen. She was not moving. He put his head on her chest to see if he could hear anything.

"Kristen, Kristen, wake up. What are you doing?" Solomon started weeping. "What are you doing Kristen, wake up." His weeping turned into a deep wail. He grabbed his wife, holding her close to him.

"Karina, Knox, Kyle, help me! Your mother won't wake up."

All three children ran into the room.

Karina fell to her knees. "No, Mom, no, no, no, you still had time. You still had time left."

"Call an ambulance!" Solomon shouted into the living room. "Please call." He whimpered. He held Kristen in his arms and rocked back and forth.

The medics confirmed their worst fear, Kristen was gone.

A few days later, relatives from both sides of the family were in the 900-square-foot apartment with condolences.

"How are you holding up?" Galvin, Kristen's brother, leaned against the wall talking quietly to Solomon. His 6-foot frame was in a black, wrinkled suit, white shirt, black tie. Solomon hadn't seen him in nearly 15 years. They were close once.

"The boys...I don't know...I think I am messing up. I bought them one of the virtual reality simulators to get their minds off everything. I know Kristen would be so angry at me, but...."

"Don't do that. My sister.... Jah knows I miss her, but she was quite the radical. You are a good dad. Don't beat yourself up for being unable to keep this unrealistic way of life."

174

"Thanks, brother. I just feel so terrible. I see what is happening with my boys and realize she may have been right. I am just too tired to fight it now, and my daughter…"

"Hey, what are you two over here talking about?" It was Kelly-Rose, Kristen's sister.

"Hey Kelly, how are you doing?" Solomon hugged her. "Long time no see."

Solomon knew Kelly-Rose before he knew Kristen. She was the one that introduced them.

"Tell me about it. I haven't seen you since. Was it two years ago?"

Solomon chuckled. "Something like that. The worst turkey I think we ever ate."

"I don't even think they tried to simulate the turkey flavor. It was more like saw dust."

Kelly-Rose and Kristen were very similar. They banded against the YSW together.

Kelly-Rose smiles at her brother. "Hey brother, how's Europe? Are you still working for the devil? I mean, the DEAD company?"

Gavin gave his sister a hug and playful banter. "Now I see why I never come home."

"How are you and the kids holding up?" Kelly-Rose looked around to see if she could spot her niece and nephews.

"Solomon was just telling me that he bought Kyle and Knox one of those virtual reality simulators."

"Oh no, you didn't cave in, did you?" Kelly responded

"Don't beat him up about it. They're kids, they need a break from all of this."

Several seconds of awkward silence was broken by Solomon saying, "Let me go see where they are. I want them to say hi."

Solomon could hear the game's sounds from outside the boy's door.

Solomon knocks softly on the boys' door.

The door flung open, and Kyle rushed back to the game; Karina was in the room as well, acting as a spectator. "I think you should come into the living room and speak to your family. They've come a long way to support us right now."

"Dang, hold on, Dad! We're flying right now, about to save the prisoners," Knox replied.

"Turn it off now!" Solomon said sternly.

"I don't want to go out there. It's too depressing," Knox said.

Karina said, "Us going out there is not going to bring Mom back. I'd rather hide out here."

Solomon raised his voice. "This is not a negotiation. Turn it off and come speak to your family."

Kyle turned off the virtual reality simulator and walked out of the room. Karina rolled her eyes and brushed past her father as she walked out the door.

The next few days, the house felt cold. Their apartment was filled with tension, hurt, and sadness. It wasn't until two weeks after Kristen's funeral that the silence was broken.

"Dad, I'll be going off to school soon," said Karina.

This was not how Solomon pictured their first communication in over two weeks, but a dream a few nights ago popped into his mind.

Karina continued. "I know that you and Mom wanted to protect me. You wanted to keep me from being part of the YSW. But let's face it, you can't afford to send me off to school on your own, and the YSW has tons of scholarships that I qualify for. They have the best programs with the best technology and, if I get in with them, I'm guaranteed a job working for the DEAD company. And Dad, I am good with technology. Really good."

"Is this what you want to do? Solomon was furious.

"No! What I want is to be free from this, Dad. What is this? I have done everything that you and Mom wanted me to do in the hopes that my efforts to be 'noble' would pay off, but now that Mom is gone and you're stuck with her hospital bills, you can't even afford to send me off to school. And I don't want to wallow in misery when I can move forward and create my own future." Karina went off to her room, and Solomon followed her to her bedroom.

"What!" Karina felt the disrespect come from her mouth.

"Karina, I don't want you to leave like this. Your mom would be sad to see that we are not in a good place. Why are you so angry with me?" Solomon pleaded.

"I'm trying not to be, but I guess I don't understand. What is so wrong with the YSW? Why was it so important for you to be so...so oppositional?"

"Honestly, Karina, there were so many times that I wanted to give in, but the love I had for your mom... I would have done anything for her. She wanted us to live a life of meaning, and I did too."

"I am sorry, Dad, there is just so much going on. I need to get away. I can't be here anymore," Karina started crying.

"Everyone is leaving, and I don't have my friend anymore. Todd was a friend of mine. I am going to ask you something, and

I need to know the truth." Solomon stared into his daughter's eyes.

"Todd Markley, the reclusive Karina, do you know anything about what might have happened to him?"

Karina bit her lower lip, doing her best to hold it in.

"Karina, just tell me what happened?"

"Dad, I asked you. I asked you if you knew him and what he did. You acted like you didn't know anything. I...I thought...I thought that he just sat around doing nothing. I would not have done it if I knew he was one of your friends."

"What did you do, Karina?" Solomon's voice was quiet, serious.

"I didn't mean to, I just wanted to help Mom. I...I got hold of, you know, one of those devices and I downloaded the time snatcher app."

"What does this app do?" Solomon was confused.

"It allows you to take away time from people. Five to ten minutes from people who don't use their time wisely."

"Karina, I don't think taking five minutes killed Todd. I don't want you to feel guilty for that." Solomon wrapped his arms around his daughter. Karina's guilt consumed her.

"Dad, I need to tell you something else..." Solomon was rubbing his daughter's arm.

"What is it?"

"Um...this is going to be hard. I just need to get it all out and I don't want you to stop me because I don't think I will be able to finish."

"Oh...Okay...go for it. I promise I won't stop you. I'm just happy that we are talking."

"So...I am pretty good with technology, believe it or not, and I was able to reprogram the app to take more than a few minutes. I programmed the app to take three days every time I pressed the button. I started going over there nearly every night, taking time from Todd and giving it to Mom--" Karina's voice broke. "--I just wanted Mom to live. I didn't want Todd to die." She broke down on her father's shoulder.

"So a few weeks back when the officers came, it was you in the camera."

"Yeah, but don't worry. Everything will be fine."

"How do you know that, Karina? They could take you away."

"They won't. They want me at their school. They want me to work for them."

"So what are you saying?"

"I'm saying that if I join the YSW, they can make it all go away. Apparently, I am worth making it all go away." Karina started rambling. "A while back, I took this aptitude test and ever since then I have been hounded by the YSW. They offered me money, an incentive to join their organization, and I took it. Now, I have no other choice. I have to go off to a YSW school. It's one of the best ones, Dollard University. I have a full scholarship. I wanted to tell you. I wanted you to be proud of me, but I know your stance on this."

Solomon kept rubbing his daughter's arm. He needed to process everything that happened. Her confession had him conflicted. Her entanglement with the YSW made him upset. Her leaving frustrated him, but all his feelings were buried, so he could sound supportive. "How much longer do you have before you leave?"

"Next week."

"That's short notice," was the phrase that came out of his mouth. "So that's it, huh? You just leave? No looking back now? I guess you are on your way to do big things." Solomon felt short of breath like a weight was on his chest. Karina's head was still lying on her dad's shoulder. Her bushy hair nearly covered his mouth. He brushed it down with his hand and continued. "So, I...I guess you will need help packing up?" Solomon wiped a tear from his eye.

"I'm working on it," Karina said, still soaking up her father's embrace.

"Me and your brothers will help you. I don't want you to do all of this alone."

"Okay, sure, Dad, um...I know my bags will be really heavy. They were going to send drop crafts to come and pick them up, but I can cancel them and let them know that you will carry them for me."

"Let me do at least one thing for you before you leave." Solomon felt like a failure. "Ah...well...it's getting late, and I need to check in on your brothers. They are probably still playing that stupid game. Thank you for telling me what was going on in your world."

"I am sorry, Dad. I am so sorry. I messed up so much and should have told you sooner. Thank you for listening."

"I love you, Karina. Why don't you get to bed, and we can start working on getting you ready to go off to university tomorrow."

"Love you too, Dad." Karina wiped the tears from her eyes and smiled at her dad before heading to bed.

Chapter 22: Digital Detox

Remove those things from your life that corrupt and fill yourself with things that are good. To take the time to remove bad things and fill yourself with things that are not good is worse than leaving the original darkness.
(A Warning from the Writ)

Time. They say time heals all wounds, but I don't feel healed. Life is not the same since Kristen died, and now Karina is gone, I feel lost. Jah, if you are real, please, I am begging you, please help me. I don't know what I'm doing anymore. I am trying to hold it together for my sons, but I don't even know if I have strung two sentences together since the boys and I helped Karina pack up. I know my boys probably hate me. My only saving grace is the damn gaming system that seems to keep them preoccupied, but every time I hear the sound of the game coming from their room, I can feel Kristen's disappointment.

Solomon closed his journal and took a deep breath. He walked down the hallway to his boy's room. He knocks on the door.

181

Neither boy came to the door. Solomon twisted the knob. The boys were completely zoned in. "Now that your mom is gone and your sister is away at school, I am going to need both of you to step things up a bit," Solomon said as he picked up the clothes that Kyle and Knox had scattered on the floor.

You would think they were sleepwalking if you didn't know any better. They both had their virtual simulation glasses on, walking with their hands out, reaching for objects invisible to Solomon. Solomon quickly went over to the power and disconnected it.

"Dad, what are you doing?" the boys shouted.

"I am not going to sit here and watch both of you continue to waste your time on these stupid games."

"Maybe if you tried it, you wouldn't feel they were stupid."

"Why don't we shut things off and talk or tell stories like we used to?" Solomon looked at his boys.

"Seriously, Dad? We are getting a little too old for your stories," Knox responded.

"So let's talk about...how have you been, you know, since your mom and sister left?"

"Dad, don't you think that is a little heavy? We are doing well, I guess."

Seeing that he was getting nowhere, Solomon said, "Okay, well, I guess I will leave you two alone. Just try to straighten things up around here."

"Sure thing, Dad!" Before Solomon walked out of the room, both Kyle and Knox had the virtual reality simulator back on.

A few minutes later, Solomon shouted down the hallway. "Okay, well, I am going to head out and grab some groceries. I am heading to Yummy's; let me know if you want anything."

"We're fine," Kyle shouted as Solomon walked out the door.

When Solomon walked out of his apartment door, he couldn't help but look over to the right. A new person moved into Todd Markley's apartment. A floral wreath was placed around the security camera system, and a welcome mat was on the floor where Todd typically had packages of books stacked.

Solomon didn't greet the elevator as usual when he walked onto the elevator.

"Permission to pick up?"

"Sure." Solomon shrugged.

"Thank you."

A few short silent moments on the elevator later, Solomon heard, "Hey, long time no see." It was Aurora.

"Hey."

"Wow. How is everything? I heard about your wife. I'm so sorry."

"Thanks. I appreciate it." Solomon flashed a forced smile.

"Look, you don't have to pretend for me. I have felt the kind of pain that you are feeling now. When my parents passed away, I felt so lost, but...I promise it will get better."

"I sure hope so."

The elevator reached the ground floor. Both Aurora and Solomon continued their conversation in the lobby. Seven maintenance workers huddled together, getting ready to go to lunch. Two of them disappeared, holograms. More than likely, managers popping in to check on their workers. The rest were human. A new law forced companies to have at least 51% of their staff be human. Solomon was happy to see the law swing in favor of humans for once.

Those fleeting thoughts didn't break his conversation with Aurora.

"So," Aurora continued. "Look, when I was going through a lot of stuff, I ended up at this place. I guess it was some therapy. It was good for me. You can go in person, or they do virtual meetings as well. It was nice to talk to someone."

"Thanks, but I don't know if that is what I need," Solomon responded.

"I didn't think it was what I needed either, but I'm still standing. I know what it feels like to need time to grieve, so just let me know if you need anything."

"Thanks, I will do that. I appreciate the gesture." Solomon knew she meant well but was hesitant to participate in the YSW's methods for healing.

"Okay, cool. Hey, I'm headed out. I um...I met a

guy." "A real one?" Solomon joked.

"Hey, what is that supposed to mean?" Aurora playfully slapped him on the arm.

"It's not completely out of the question. You heard about the marriage law that just passed."

"I know. I hope I never get desperate enough to marry an AI, but this guy is real. I think you would like him. I may have to have you check him out for me. Give him the stamp of approval." Aurora laughed.

"I can do that." Solomon was flattered.

She waved bye and walked out the door.

Solomon headed to Yummy's and returned home to hear the sounds of zaps, pings, and booms from his son's room.

"Get off the device now!" Solomon stormed back into Kyle and Knox's room. He had enough.

"RIGHT NOW!" Solomon took the virtual reality simulator and threw it up against the wall.

"What are you doing? I need it!" Kyle lunged after the simulator trying to catch it before it hit the ground.

"You do not need it. This is absolutely ridiculous. We are going to go back to the way things were before Mom died."

"Dad, we can't go back to the way things were. Everything has changed. You have changed."

"I know, and I am trying to change back. So, join me for dinner. Let's talk like we used to."

With great hesitation, the boys joined him for dinner. A small plate of green beans and a piece of chicken breast shared between the three of them was served.

"So, school? Anything new?"

"Nope," Knox responded, swishing around the green beans on his plate.

"That's about $50 worth of green beans you're playing with." Solomon chuckled.

"If you had joined the YSW, it wouldn't be," Knox mumbled.

"The YSW, huh?"

"Dad, Karina is part of the YSW, and things seem to be going well for her?" Kyle said to his father.

Solomon was short. "How do you know? She doesn't call. She doesn't even send messages."

Knox quickly responded. "That's because she is trying to enjoy herself, Dad."

Solomon looked down at Kyle's fingers. "What is going on there?"

Kyle looked down to notice a tremble in his fingers as well. "It always seems to do that when I don't play virtual reality for a while. I need to get back on or I will start feeling really sick,"

"I get it. I see exactly what is going on here." Solomon glanced back and forth at both of his sons. "You boys...you're addicted."

"No, we're not!" Both boys asserted this at the same time.

Solomon looked into his boys' eyes and could tell they were void of the joy they once had.

"You can never play those games again. I made a mistake with you, and I won't keep doing it. You are turning into all of those other mindless YSW. No more. I can't let you do it anymore."

Solomon tried to detox his boys in the small 900-square-foot apartment. But after several broken items and a few holes in the wall, Solomon called the Digital Detox Center. It was an away program for people who overdose on technology. It was also another bill he couldn't pay along with threats that continued to grow more aggressive.

Solomon,

I have been watching you for a very long time. You have nothing left, no wife and no children. Working at Reader's publishing, you can never repay the money you owe. Join us now and I can make it all go away.

Sincerely,

D.D

It wasn't until Solomon received this message, signed with the initials D.D, that he no longer thought it was an attack from the YSW organization but rather a personal mission to break Solomon. *"Could D.D be Deiderick Dollard himself? Nah, too high up the food chain to care about me. But who else would have that kind of power? Was he the reason why Reader's Publishing even existed and why its only employees are non-YSW? Is he the one peering at me through the blue lights? How could a man who created the YSW be the same one who is watching me, a non-YSW participant? I owe so much money. I am worth more to the YSW dead than alive, but they haven't killed me off yet? Why?*

These thoughts filled Solomon's head, leaving him in a fog at work. Mike, the 20-something, could tell something was wrong.

"Look, I know you think I am one of them, and you're scared to speak to me, but I am just worried about you. Is everything okay?"

Solomon looked the young 20-something in the eye. He was skinny and for lack of a better word, nerdy, pants slightly too high, so his white socks were showing. He wore them with thick-soled black shoes. Solomon suspected that they were the shoes with the flyers in them, a pair of rockets that jetted out from the sole of the shoes and allowed him to fly around in the air.

"Sorry. I am sure that I am making this uncomfortable. You know...truthfully, things aren't going well," Solomon said, continuing to shuffle around, getting orders ready to go out.

"I get it. Well, no, I don't get it. But I know that what you're going through must suck."

It must suck...wise words from a 20-something, Solomon thought. "Yeah, it does. You could not imagine." Solomon continued working. "Look, I will do my best not to make this uncomfortable for you." But it was difficult for Solomon. Solomon couldn't get everything off his mind. He missed his wife, his daughter, and his friend.

"If it helps at all. My G-ma always told me that when things go bad or good, to talk to Jah."

Talk to Jah? Coming from a 20-something, Solomon chuckled to himself. "You know that guy I used to talk to you about. Todd Markley? He used to tell me that all of the time. My wife did too. I tried, and it didn't help."

"If it didn't help, you didn't try hard enough. Look. You never asked about me, but I have been through more than you know. The only thing that ever helped me was my belief in Jah and..."

Mike whistled to Bubbles, and the googly eyed robotic spider came crawling over to him. "Bubbles, get my favorite book." The spider rapidly crawled up the shelves and came back down with the *Writ*.

"Do you have one of these?" Mike asked.

"Believe it or not, I do," Solomon replied.

"When is the last time you have read it?"

"Sometime before Kristen died."

"Well, I know it's only been a few months since she died, but it's time for you to pick it back up again."

"Where did you learn all of this? I didn't think anyone your age would come close to this book, let alone be brave enough to talk about it."

"I was raised by my great grandmother. She doesn't play." Mike and Solomon laughed in unison.

"You know what, kid...You might be okay. I may just have to meet this grandmother of yours."

"Yeah, that would be cool. I am sure you two will get along just fine. She's a pretty good cook."

"Oh yeah, pretty good cook? I could use a home-cooked meal." Solomon smiled at the thought of someone else doing the cooking, a skill he still hadn't mastered.

"Well, she's able to make that powdered crap they call food taste...edible."

"So you eat the powdered stuff, too, huh?" Solomon was intrigued.

"Yeah, we do. Well, unless we get a little extra money from somewhere."

"This grandmother of yours, what's her name?"

"Mediana...she's sweet, a little clingy, but sweet."

Later that evening, Solomon returned to an empty apartment and thumbed through all of the books he collected from Todd. He landed on the *Writ* and took it off the shelf. He held it in his hand and tapped his thumb on it before thinking, *not tonight, maybe tomorrow.* He looked up at the picture of the family at the beach. "I messed up, Kristen. I really messed up, but I promise I will do my best to try and get everyone back so we can all be together once again."

Chapter 23: Consumed with Loneliness

It is not good that man should be alone (Genesis 2:18)

The next few weeks felt like a quiet hell for Solomon, and yet, he still did not pick up the *Writ*. But Jah has a way of still reaching His people. A deep depression, sleepless nights, horrible dreams, a thirty-pound weight loss, and Solomon realized that he needed help. He had been closed up in his apartment since his children and wife had gone, when a dream about Todd Markley made him realize that he needed to make a change. *Todd was locked up in his apartment and still met a terrible fate. I have got to get back out into the world, even if it is a horrid place to be,* Solomon thought to himself.

His usual day at work was a bit better because he spent more time talking to Mike. He was becoming a great distraction and a pretty wise young twenty-something.

"Hey, my great-grandmother is making dinner tonight, and to be honest, you look like crap. I think you need to get out of the house?"

"Oh...I look like crap. Well, I have been through hell. What's your excuse?" Solomon chuckled.

"So we are really going there, old man?" Mike laughed.

"We're going there...no, seriously...I think you're right. I need to get out of the house. I would love to meet your wonderful grandmother. What time?"

"Around seven. How do you want the information? I know you live in a different universe, so I can't just chip you."

"You could, I don't know, write it down here. You know, you young people probably don't even know how to write anymore." Solomon just shook his head.

"You're right. Most of us don't but watch this." Mike opened the printer and took a sheet of paper, then wrote:

5550 West 74th Street

Area Code 212

Solomon took the piece of paper from Mike's hands and smiled. "Alright, I will see you at seven?"

Solomon had to admit that he was excited as he prepared to visit Mike's great-grandmother, Mediana. The streets were always chaotic, and Solomon nervously walked past the group of silence order protesters, remembering his recurring vision of mouths sewn shut.

Advertisements seemed more aggressive today, but of course, he can't remember the last time he walked this far. and saw this many screens. He was about to jab the ear buds further into his ear canal, but he overheard the screens as he walked past. They had all changed to the same channel:

192

I am honored to stand before you as the One World Ruler, and as promised, I will begin the act of unifying our nations. Last week, one leader from every country all over the world met to discuss the One World Currency. Today, we will begin the process of creating a universal funding system. This will eliminate the current debt of 117 countries all over the world. The remaining 78 countries will begin to receive incentives for not incurring high amounts of national debt.

After the announcement, the screens flipped back to their previous channel, and Solomon continued his walk. Through the dark tint on his goggles, Solomon watched the airlifts and hovercrafts fly overhead. For a brief minute, he remembered his trip to The Fresh when his entire family enjoyed the beach for the first time. He smiled and went on to 5550 West 74th street.

Solomon tapped on the door. A habit that still remained from the world before technology. While he was knocking, the security system at the door was taking a scan. Solomon could hear Mike shouting, "He's here." The door opened. Mike and a rather large, burly woman stood at the door. Looking at Mike, you would never have guessed they were in the same family.

In a deep, raspy voice, Mediana said, "Well, I have heard so much about you." Mediana extended her hairy, freckled arm, and Solomon reached out to find that he was not prepared for her aggressive handshake.

Mike stepped out the door behind Solomon and patted his back, welcoming him into their home.

"It smells wonderful," Solomon said as he walked into a small white house with red shutters on the windows. The inside of the house was slightly cluttered. She had items of the world before littered all over. An analog clock, written letters, and pictures of family were all over the walls. Solomon was taken to the kitchen where a table was already prepared. White plates, silverware, cloth napkins with leaves embroidered in them were stationed in front of wooden chairs. Several bowls with different colored pudding-like substances were sat out on the table.

"I do the best I can," Mediana said when she saw Solomon looking at the menu.

"I understand. I heard you can make this stuff taste wonderful."

"Yes, well, I was a bit of a pack rat before the YSW took over, so I managed to have enough spices to last for years."

They all sat down at the table and started plopping scoops of dinner on their plates.

Solomon couldn't believe what he tasted. "My goodness, you're truly gifted. I never thought this could taste so good."

"Thank you. I have had to learn to adjust. Every now and then, we can afford to go to Yummy's, but that is not often."

Solomon was surprised at how quickly he found himself telling Mediana about his wife and children, his loneliness, and his nightmares that all seemed to be coming true.

"Wow, You have really gone through a lot. I completely understand." Mediana grabbed Solomon's plate. "Want anything else?"

"No, I'm stuffed." Solomon patted his belly.

"Well, that's unfortunate because I made--" Mediana bent down, opened the stove, and pulled out a pan. "A cake."

"Cake?" Solomon's eyes perked up. "You made cake? Well, I think I can make room for it." He chuckled.

"The secret is to take the food powder and add a bit of sugar and mix your lactose powder with water and a touch of vanilla. Eggs are the tricky part. I can use the powdered egg substitute, but to get the best cake, you need the real thing. We haven't had the company in so long, so I splurged." Mediana sat the cake on the table. Solomon took in a deep whiff.

"Have you received your letter yet?" Mediana asked Solomon as she cut a large chunk of vanilla cake and placed it on a plate.

"No, I wasn't expecting a letter. To be honest, I have only had bad news, so I stopped checking the mail a while ago."

"Well, when my husband died. The YSW sent a check in the mail. They figure a lot of us don't have devices, so they are nice enough to mail a check, but…"

"But what?" Solomon asked, stuffing his mouth with the moist sweet cake.

"I guess I will let you find out on your own."

"Nothing surprises me much anymore." Solomon didn't care about whatever she was talking about. He was too busy stuffing his face with the moist, delicious cake.

"Here, take this one home." Mediana wrapped up another large chunk of cake for Solomon. She sat back down at the table.

"I told you my great-grandmother is amazing." Mike smiled.

"I must say, I am really impressed ," Solomon replied

"He's a good boy. All I have left of my family." She smiled at Mike and said. "Take these to the sink and wash them out for me."

Mike replied, "Yes, ma'am"

Solomon was impressed. "You are doing a good job with him. Haven't heard a yes ma'am in years, like a word from before the YSW took over."

Mediana was proud but quickly changed the subject to talk to Solomon before her great-grandson came back into the room.

"Look." Mediana paused. "There is a group that I am thinking about joining. I have heard there are a lot of people like us in this group?"

"People like us?" Solomon's eyebrow lifted.

"Yes, older people, against all the forced technology. People who have gone through some heartache and don't feel like they fit into the world of the YSW. I am thinking about joining. I get a little lonely sometimes and need to find someone, something that can fill this void."

"I get lonely too, but I don't know. I guess this is all part of the process. What is this group called?" Solomon replied as he grabbed his piece of cake.

"Elders Against Devices. I got a letter from them shortly after my children died. I was skeptical at first, but I met this woman named Quantas. She has this little storefront, but it turns into so much more. I have only been once, but it felt familiar. Don't go telling anyone else about it, just thought I would tell you because I think you may be a good addition to the group."

Mike walked back into the room, and Mediana changed the subject. "You are really enjoying my cake. Mike, make sure to wrap up one more piece of cake for Solomon."

"You're going to let me take some home?" Solomon was elated.

Mike wrapped up a good chunk of cake and handed it to Solomon.

"I'll walk you to the door," Mike said. They walked back down the hallway covered with family pictures.

196

"I am so glad you were able to join us. I could tell my great-grandmother enjoyed it."

"I enjoyed it as well. Thank you. You're not too bad for a twenty-something." Solomon chuckled.

"You're not too bad for an old man."

"Alright, see you on Monday."

Solomon walked back home feeling a little better than he did when he left his apartment. He made sure to check his mailbox. Nearly everyone he knew received digital mail. He was the only one in his building to receive the occasional paper mail. He would have to change it soon because he gets charged for every piece of paper mail that comes to him.

In his stack was a check from the Department of Artificial Vegetation. It was a settlement check. Solomon hoped it would be the amount he needed to get Karina into another school. Maybe he could get her back. So when he opened the envelope and saw the check for $130.00, Solomon was pissed. *That was what she was worth to them? One hundred thirty dollars?*

The next envelope he opened did not have a return address or stamp. Someone must have slipped it in his mailbox. The words inside weren't typed out. It was a handwritten message that said:

We know your loss. You are not alone. Location: 444 5th Ave. Date 2/12 Time: 7:00 PM. Use the code "Do you have a newspaper?" We hope to see you soon.

Sincerely

EAD

Solomon couldn't believe it. Mediana just told him about the EAD (Elders Against Devices). He was conflicted. Was this another plan to attack him, or was this a genuine attempt to support the last few people who had not joined the YSW.

Chapter 24: Elders Against Devices

———————◆———————

Remove yourself from the temptations of the world, free yourself from
addictions, lust for nothing, and compare yourself to no one, for those
who do, will live an unhappy life and die unfulfilled.
(A Warning from the Writ)

Solomon took the piece of cake out of his pocket and sat it on
the countertop. Walked over to his couch and fell
asleep. Another, darker vision of the silence order entered
his dreams. Eyes sealed shut and bandages over their mouths.
Those who attempted to remove the bandage, shot down.
This vision immediately followed by another of a massive fire.
Solomon was running, large flames behind him, but the dream
was in flashes. Fire images became a recurring vision.

A week after the dinner at Mediana's house, Solomon was
on his way to his first EAD meeting. He was nervous
when he entered the old convenience store. *What the heck am I*
doing here, he

thought to himself. When he walked in, a heavyset older woman with gray hair was behind a plexiglass window.

"What do you want?" The ornery woman turned around. Her voice didn't match her face. She had kind eyes but a snappy tone.

"I think I may be in the wrong place." Solomon began to turn around and head back toward the glass doors covered in red dust.

"Aren't you supposed to ask me for something?" The woman said, stepping from behind the plexiglass. "You're not too bright, are you?"

Solomon couldn't believe how he was being talked to. As he stood there baffled, a door labeled 'cleaning supplies' opened behind the plexiglass and someone familiar popped out.

"Quantas, why are you giving him a hard time?" It was Mediana.

"Well, how else am I supposed to have fun?"

"Solomon--" Mediana said, "I am glad you were able to make it. This is Quantas," Mediana continued. Then she cupped her hand over her mouth, leaned in closer to Solomon, and tried to whisper to Solomon, "I am learning that she takes a bit of getting used to."

"Hey, I heard that--" Quantas said. "So, so you're to blame for bringing in the riff-raff. I still haven't heard him say the words." She laughed a loud, boisterous laugh. "Say the words riff-raff."

Solomon was still very confused by it all, but his curiosity about this group helped him mutter the words, "Do you have a newspaper?"

"Ah, so you can follow directions. Come along." Quantas ushered him down the dark stairs behind the door that read 'cleaning supplies'. Mediana followed.

"So, what is this all about?" Solomon could not help but look around the room. It reminded him of Shooter's bar, but it smelled a little musty. Several older people were playing chess in the corner. There were a few wooden bar stools and pub tables scattered about. Very few of the furnishings looked as if they were in good shape.

"Look around, Solomon; everyone in here is at least 60 years old."

Solomon took a scan of the room. "Yep, so that's why I'm here? Because I'm old?"

"Yes, because you're old and because you have managed not to be part of the YSW."

"Wait...so none of you are part of the YSW?" Solomon was amazed. "I didn't know there were that many more."

"Yes, well, we are just the ones that represent the 212 Area Code; there are more in the other codes."

"So, how did you find out about me?"

"We have our ways." Quantas smiled.

Mediana interjected, "I told her after Mike came home and let me know that he thought you were not part of the YSW."

"Fine, she told me." Quants chuckled.

Solomon asked, "So what does this club do?"

"Can't tell you that yet. Not until you sign an oath."

"Sign an oath? Seriously? You have got to be kidding me. People still do that?"

"If the YSW can sign an oath, then we will too. Here--"

Quantas handed Solomon a typed document. "We suggest you take your time to read over this before you sign. We have very strict stipulations, and you must be committed--" Quantas looked around for a pen. Solomon was shocked to see an entire jar of pens right at her disposal. He felt rebellious. He never thought looking at a cup of pens could feel so dangerous.

"After you finish reading, sign it and bring it back to me. I am heading back upstairs to make sure no one came in." Quantas flounced up the stairs.

Official EAD Contract

All members of the EAD must abide by the following:
- Be at least 59 years of age
- Swear off the use of excessive technology. The EAD will make exceptions for the following:
    - Employment
    - Family Communication
- Read the *Writ* daily
- Pray to Jah daily
- Regularly go to EAD meetings and look out for the welfare of EAD members.

If you are able to abide by the guidelines above, please sign and date the document on the lines provided below.

Welcome to the EAD

(signature)_____(date)_____

Solomon was quiet as he read over the document.

"What's wrong?" Mediana asked. She had managed to find a few cans of food in the kitchen of the hidden room.

"Hmm... I don't know about all of this," Solomon responded.

"What do you have to lose?" Mediana inquired.

"I just need to think about it for a minute."

Mediana didn't know how Quantas got hold of so many canned goods and didn't bother to ask questions. She took the bottom of her skirt and folded it up so that her skirt acted as a basket. Then she said, "I needed to take time as well. Don't worry about it ; we will still be here. But, I must admit, being here is the only time I don't spend most of the day thinking about the family that I don't have anymore."

"I still just need to think." Solomon folded up the document and placed it in his pocket. He walked back up the dark staircase.

"Headed home?" Quantas asked. "Where's the document?"

"I am going to look over a few things before I sign," Solomon replied.

"What's there to think about…. ah, you don't read the *Writ*. You don't get it. Don't you think, for one second, that you have managed to live through this hell on your own. Jah is the only reason why any of us is still standing." Quantas fussed.

Something in Quantas' nagging resonated with Solomon. "I truly appreciate you all allowing me to be part of your club, but I just need to think through everything."

"I understand. I am sure that I will see you later." Quantas smiled.

When Solomon got home, he picked up the *Writ*. "Why does everyone want me to read this thing?" Solomon said to himself. He opened it up to a random page and began to read, *Do not be afraid because Jah is always with you.* Solomon scoffed but continued to read: *You will know He is and will see his presence. He seems to each of you in a way you will understand. Some through dreams, others through words, and some through experiences. Those who are sensitive to his will, discover their purpose. Just silence the noise of the world around, and tune into His spirit, and He will make everything clear* (the *Writ*).

"Interesting," Solomon thought to himself.

202

Ten chapters later, Solomon was feeling convicted. He asked Jah to forgive him for being so stubborn. He realized he harbored strong feelings toward Jah for all that has happened after the YSW take over.

It took a week before Solomon returned to the EAD hangout. But when he returned, he had the paper signed.

"Good to see you again. So, do you have something for me?" Quantas held out her hand. Solomon placed the signed document in her possession.

"Looks good. I was afraid you were backing out." Quantas chuckled.

"So, what do I do now?" Solomon was still curious about this mysterious club he had joined.

"Well, to be honest, we meet to talk, share stories, and create a family of our own. We know something is happening and are trying to figure everything out. The YSW are not the only smart ones. We have gifts of our own. We just believe that our gifts come from Jah."

"So, what if I told you I thought my gift was the gift of dreams and visions? What would you say?"

"I would say we have been waiting for someone with your skillset to join our team, but Jah only sends visions and dreams to the wisest men. You don't appear to be one of the ones he would speak to." Quants laughed so hard tears welled in the corner of her eyes.

"So, you're the president of this organization?"

Quantas was still in mid-laugh. "Yes, why?"

"This may not be the committee for me if the members assigned you as their leader," Solomon replied.

Quantas laughed even harder. "I knew you had it in you. Okay, well, let's get you down these stairs."

They walked down the stairs to the secret room. "Hey, everyone," Quantas announced.

"Hey," the twenty or so people shouted back.

"He says that he receives visions from Jah."

"You receive visions, aye?" Another elder came over and patted Solomon on the back.

"Something like that," Solomon replied and found a seat on a wooden bar stool with a broken leg. He put his foot down to balance himself.

Another elder walked over. She had a sweet disposition and looked younger than the other elders. Only a bit of gray framed her face. She had brown skin and bushy hair, like his wife and daughter.

"We need a good visionary in this group. So tell us, what visions have you seen?" A sweet soft voice asked. Her name was Veronica.

"I didn't know you even talked." Quantas laughed, looking at Veronica.

"Well, I just hope that there is someone in this group that can help us through all of this. So, what have you seen?" Veronica asked again. Several elders gathered around. Men playing chess in the corner stopped for a moment to hear what the new recruit had to say.

Solomon looked around nervously. "Um...I don't know if I should share them just yet. I may need time to understand them first."

Mediana seemed to pop out of the kitchen. "Oh, go on, share."

"Okay, well, I think I am getting a vision of a growing activist group. They're called the peacemakers. They're a small subset of the YSW, but they are gaining in popularity."

"Another activist group? I am sure they won't be any different than any of the other groups we have seen come and go in the past," Mediana replied.

"I don't know." Solomon looked around at all of the faces that were staring at him.

"I believe this one is actually going to make an impact, and we need to be prepared because it will affect us, our relationships, and our ability to speak to one another."

Quantas was moving about. How is this going to be any different from any of the other crap going on in the world right now? It is all going to hell anyway."

I could be reading my vision wrong, but so many of the other dreams have come true.

"So what did you see? I'm interested to hear this," Mediana responded. The other members of the EAD were sitting on the edge of their seats.

"Well, you are already seeing evidence. When you walk the streets this afternoon, look around. The signs are everywhere -- 'If you can't say anything nice, don't speak at all'.

Solomon went on to tell them about the vision. "There were consequences for speaking when you weren't supposed to. I am assuming there will be some sort of speaking hours in place. Look, we all know that social media, propaganda, and news is affecting people like never before. Pay attention to what's going on around you. We don't have long."

"Well, I don't know about you, but this may actually be a platform that I can stand behind. I would love not to hear any of you speak again! Ha!" Quantas made herself laugh.

Solomon looked around and noticed that no one else seemed to pay her much attention.

"I know things are bad right now, but do you seriously think the YSW would implement a silence order? They love to hear themselves talk too much." Mediana pointed this out.

"I know they will, and I really think we need to do something about it ," Solomon pleaded.

They continued to discuss the silence order, but Solomon could tell they were just doing their best to entertain him. Solomon let his story wane off and found himself sitting at a dirty high-top table.

"Hey, Solomon, I know it may not mean much, but I believe you," Veronica said to Solomon.

"Thanks," Solomon said before taking another glance over the dark, musty room.

"Do you mind if I sit here?"

"Of course not. Go ahead," Solomon said, pointing to a chair near him.

"Thanks." A few seconds passed before Veronica started talking again. "I was hoping to run into someone that had a gift from Jah. I need something, some kind of hope." Veronica's voice broke.

"I don't know if I will be able to do all of that. What's your story?" Solomon asked.

Veronica pulled out a picture. A printed picture like the one that his daughter created of their family beach trip.

"Wow, who is she?" Solomon asked, pointing to an image of a little girl in the photo.

"That's my daughter. Well, she's much bigger now. She's 31 years old. Expecting a baby. I just found out."

"Wow! That's exciting news," Solomon replied.

"Well, I hope I get to meet the baby. My daughter... she has her... issues. I pray to Jah every day that my grandbaby is born happy and healthy."

"I am sure she will be," Solomon replied. "When is your daughter due?"

"She's got quite a while left. Just found out a few days ago. I'm actually surprised she told me. We have bumped heads a little."

"Kids...my daughter and I went through... still going through a little patch of our own. They push so hard to be like everyone else. They want all the world has to offer, but they don't realize that it's not good for them. And, in the world, we live in now, by the time they find out what the world has to offer is no good, it's too late."

Solomon and Veronica chatted a bit more, and soon, Quantas and Mediana made their way over to them. They laughed together and enjoyed the evening. For the first time in a while, Solomon didn't feel emptiness.

Chapter 25: Silence Order

In the last days, the voice of the wicked will reign over the voice of the noble. Those who are wise will be silenced, and the noise of false teachings will prevail. You must read and meditate in the word of truth or the words of those who are rooted in evil will overshadow the words of whispers of truth (A warning from the Writ)

Solomon was beginning to feel like a veteran member of the EAD. It had been three months since his first EAD meeting. Solomon went to every meeting since the time he told the Elders about his dream of the silence order. Since he didn't hear from his children much, talking to these grumpy old people seemed to help fill the void. It was a great way to get his mind off the loneliness. Between his EAD membership, Aurora, who would occasionally stop by, and Mike, who turned out to be a lot better than he originally assumed, Solomon realized that he was getting better. He hated to admit that reading the *Writ*, a requirement of his EAD membership, also seemed to provide some comfort for him.

Solomon put his Code Red outfit on and headed out the door, but things were different this time because the silence order hours were more restrictive. He was now walking the streets during no-talking hours. He did what came naturally and shoved the earbuds in his ears, hoping to block all of the noise from the advertisements. Only the sidewalks and the screens were allowed to talk. During silence hours, the screens repeated the phrase, "If you can't say anything nice, don't say anything at all." *That's creepy*, Solomon thought to himself. When he arrived at the convenience store, he made sure to whisper, "Do you have a newspaper?" Even though it seemed ridiculous to him because Quantas knew exactly who he was. He was only allowed to go behind the plexiglass if he said the passphrase. He entered the door marked 'cleaning supplies' and walked down the dimly lit stairs. The claggy dark room was more comforting now. Mediana was already there. Her back was turned to him.

Solomon bent toward her and whispered, "Hi, Mediana."

"YSW has you shook. Besides, talking hours will begin soon." Quantas belted out almost as if she were daring someone to say anything to her about speaking in her own establishment.

"Shhhh," Mediana turned around with her finger on her lip.

Solomon squinted his eyes. "What happened to you?" He realized he was staring at a very bruised Mediana.

"I messed up." Mediana was trying to cover her face. "I was at home talking to Mike, and one of the birds, you know, the ones with the blue eyes, saw me. When I went out the next morning, a group of silence order police roughed me up. They said I was breaking the law." Mediana started to cry. "I didn't think I was breaking the law if I was talking in my own house. I can't believe they are watching us in our homes."

"I saw them looking in my window as well," Solomon interjected. "I just don't have anyone at home to talk to. This is insanity. I can't believe you were punished for talking to someone in your own house? They have taken things entirely too far."

"How have you been dealing with no kids?" Quantas asked.

Solomon looked down, "It has been hard. I want my family back. I am so angry with them. I want to get them back for what they have taken from me."

Solomon continued,"I think we should organize a protest.

"Everything in the 212 area code is so terrible. Which issue are we protesting exactly?" Quantas asked mockingly.

"Let's just start with one issue at a time. Let's get our voices back," Solomon responded.

Mediana began to smile. "Ouch." She rubbed the bruise on her face. "I wouldn't mind doing that. I participated in a few of those in my younger days. Maybe we should wait until our quiet hours and march down 5th Street."

"Now you're thinking. Yes, waiting until quiet hours is perfect, but we are going to have to be careful. You remember what I told you. I saw people killed." Initial excitement changed to fear as Solomon remembered how Yusef Aesis made his political appearance in the 212 area code.

The EAD members stayed up for the rest of the night, planning their protest. When the silence order hours were over, Solomon put on his Code Red mask and completed it with his long, brown leather jacket to protect his skin.

"I have to work in the morning. I will see you at our next meeting on 5th Street." Solomon winked and headed home.

A week later, Solomon, Quantas, Mediana, and 13 other members of the EAD met on 5th Street at 7:50 PM - ten minutes before the beginning of the silence order hours. When 8 o'clock struck, so did the members of the EAD. Solomon used what little money he had to buy bulletproof suits. They were also armed , not with the high-tech laser shooters of the YSW but with weapons of their day, guns.

Feeling free, they banged on the pots and buckets, chanting, "WE HAVE THE CHOICE TO USE OUR VOICE." They walked up and down the street chanting at the top of their lungs and flailing their signs all around. It was quite a spectacle. Soon, some of the lesser status YSW began to join in the protest and it was not long before their group of 16 became a group of over 100.

By 8:25, the news media had flown their airlifters over the protest. "Good evening, and welcome to 212 action news. We are here covering what appears to be a protest led by a group of older non-YSW members. They seem to have been joined by level 3 YSW citizens demanding that they are able to use their voice during quiet hours. Oh no...what is this...it looks like the silence order Police are headed their way. Let's watch to see how this plays out."

Within seconds of the news report, the sirens of hovercrafts filled the air and drowned out the protestor's chant. They began to shoot lasers from the aircraft as well as electronic nets to capture disobedient citizens. The crowd quickly disbanded and started running in all different directions, but Solomon, Quantas, and Mediana promised to stick with each other. They ran as fast as their old bodies would take them. The heaviness of their Code Red outfits coupled with their body armor didn't help. An electronic net came jetting out of one of the police hovercrafts encapsulating the three EAD members. The net scooped all of them up and started lifting them higher into the air. The elders could hear as the broadcasters announced their capture to the world.

"The silence order police patrol has captured what appears to be the lead instigators. They have been identified as Solomon Wiseman, Quantas Greybottom, and Mediana Cook. We are not sure how they will be punished, but what we have seen is that people who violate the silence order will be prosecuted. Now over to Shannon Prestley for the weather."

As they were lifted in the air, the net swung, and their faces were seen live on camera. When they arrived in jail, their clothes were stripped off, and they were given gray jumpsuits. They were fingerprinted, had their mugshots taken, and thrown into a holding cell for ten days.

"Old fools," the guard said, followed by a hack and a wad of spit through the prison bars. "I don't know why they waste money on keeping you alive." Then the guard slid the elders one bowl of brown sludge. "Eat." He walked away, leaving them nothing to eat with.

"You know, they could have killed us," Solomon whispered to Quantas and Mediana.

"The question is, why didn't they?" he continued. There were too many times in Solomon's recent past where he could have been dead. His personal debt alone was enough to have him killed, but there he was alive, and somehow, his friends were alive as well.

The ten days felt like a lifetime. In the moments when he wasn't talking to the other elders, he passed the time with his thoughts. At the end of ten days, they were hurt and hungry.

Quantas, Mediana, and Solomon were tagged. A process the police department used to track parolees. When he arrived at his apartment lobby door, he was happy to run into Aurora.

"Oh...here comes the man of the hour!" Aurora joked. "Haven't seen you in a while."

"Yes, well, it's been a bit of a ride."

"I bet. I saw your story with my third eye, but I would love to hear about it from you."

"I am a bit tired today…don't feel like going through all of the details, but I am sure I can summarize my adventure in one word, Miserable!" Solomon chuckled.

"Well, I have a bit of news to share with you as well." Aurora started smiling.

"Ah…I'm   assuming   good

news?" "I think so."

Their conversation was interrupted by Jose. "Good evening, Aurora and Solomon." Jose's electric blue eyes seemed to glimmer at Solomon intensely. "I have some messages for you, sir."

"Just perfect," Solomon said sarcastically. "Send the messages to my apartment."

"Absolutely, sir," Jose responded.

As Solomon and Aurora walked up to the elevator, it zoomed down.

"Good to see you back," the elevator said.

"It's good to be back. I guess I should be concerned that you even know about my infraction."

"Solomon, I am a device. I am programmed to know everything."

"I guess you're right." Solomon chuckled. He turns toward Aurora. "Why don't you come up to my floor and tell me your news."

"Oh, okay, sure," Aurora said.

The elevator heard Solomon and asked, "Both of you to the 9th floor?"

When they arrived at Solomon's door, the eye scanner allowed Solomon to come in. "Did you want to allow your guest in as well?"

"Yes." The door clicked open, and both Aurora and Solomon walked in.

"I heard Jose say you have messages. Do you want to check them first?" Aurora asked as she made her way over to the sofa.

Solomon was pretty sure that it was another threat or notice. "Nah, I'm fine." Solomon took all of his Code Red Gear off and sat on the sofa. "So, what's this news you want to tell me? I can use some good news."

He was so tired and really just wanted to go to bed, but he had never seen Aurora so happy.

"Well, I don't know if you will think it's good news. Especially with how crazy the world is right now, but--" Aurora took a deep breath. "I'm pregnant."

"Wow." Solomon was truly shocked. "Well, that is good news." Solomon had a forced response. He didn't know what to feel about Aurora bringing a little one into this world.

"There is something else I need to tell you."

"Sure, anything."

"I, um, whew...this is harder than I thought it would be."

"Go on, just tell me."

"I want you to be a grandfather figure to my baby. My parents are gone, and I...well, I don't want my baby to miss out on having someone like you in his or her life."

Solomon was silent for a moment. A tear welled in his eye. "I would be honored." Solomon gave Aurora a hug.

"Hey." Aurora pulled away. "You know us YSWer's...we're not used to human affection." She joked.

For a brief moment, Solomon felt joy in the hole created by losing his wife and children. Maybe this was a chance to start over again.

"I know that you just got in, so I will give you time to relax. I just wanted to tell you."

"Well, I am certainly glad that you did."

Solomon went over to the tablet to review his messages. Retrieving your first message:

SOLOMON, YOU HAVE REACHED THE MAXIMUM ALLOWABLE DEBT AND WILL SOON BE EVICTED FROM YOUR APARTMENT IF YOU ARE NOT ABLE TO START MAKING PAYMENTS OR BECOME A MEMBER OF THE YSW.

"Next message," Solomon called out.

"Dad, what the heck are you doing? I have seen you all over the news. Are you crazy? The YSW could kill you , Dad, stop it. Hey, I know I don't call as often as I should. Look, I have a lot of schoolwork, and things are a bit hectic. I heard that you will be gone for ten days. I will try to give you a call when I think you are back home. Talk to you soon, and Dad, please be safe...I need you to be okay for my brothers. Alright, bye."

Solomon hadn't heard Karina's voice in months. She called every now and then, but not seeing her face was miserable. He longed to know what was going on with her.

Karina Wiseman

Chapter 26: Digital Dare

In the end, many people will be controlled by those they believe are in power. Remember, since the beginning of time, you have given all power. Do not give power away and have other people control you with what belongs to you
(A Warning from the Writ).

"Wow, Karina, you're so good with technology. It is really hard to believe that your parents were not connected. Professor Tinkerbot NEVER gives an A. I think you could literally be the first."

Grey and Karina became friends in their computer engineering class. Grey got her name from the gray streak in her long, bone-straight, and otherwise jet-black hair. Like Karina's mom, Grey's parents were part of the International Society of One Race, so the rest of her features could not be traced back to any one particular race. She had a tan complexion with bright green eyes and a slim frame. Guys thought she was stunning. When Grey and Karina walked next to each other, they couldn't help but turn heads.

"I finally got my invite to Digital Dreamers. They are having a mixer tonight. You interested?" Grey asked Karina.

"You were invited to an upper-class mixer...wow." Karina was impressed. "Uh...I'm not sure if I should go. I have a lot of studying to do."

"You're part of the YSW now; you don't have to study. All of the information you will ever need is right here." Grey pointed to her implant.

"Wow...nice...you chose to get yours behind the ear? I have only seen them in the center of the forehead."

"And mess up this face? That is for the girls who need people to know their status because they don't have the looks to fall back on. Not for girls like us." Grey chuckled.

"Girls like us?"

"Yes, the entire package...all the others, asking their parents for enhancements at the age of nine or those girls who have parents that genetically engineered them. We know who they are...every surgery makes them...well, less valuable. We are the top prize ," Grey said as she grabbed Karina's arm and carted her off.

"Wow...I learn something new every day. I used to envy those girls. I would be so mad at my mom and dad for not letting me know." Karina smiled.

"Be glad. You had really good parents...in a world where hardly anything is natural anymore. We...rare commodities. And you? Even rarer. Your mind is brilliant--naturally brilliant."

It took Karina nearly a month to get used to breathing at the elevation of Dollard University. The air was crisp, the sky was bluer, and the trees were green. The trees were fake, but at least they were green. Sidewalks were programmed to provide meditative music and positive affirmations to all of the young college students. AIbots were sprinkled at each corner, offering fresh water or sweet fruit to them as they walked past.

Grey grabbed a bottle of water from that AIbot. Karina took one as well.

"Thanks," Karina said.

"You don't have to thank them. They're not even real."

"I know, but it feels wrong."

"I really think you should consider going to the mixer tonight. Not too many freshmen are able to go, but if they are invited...it's a big deal."

"Okay, I will think about it. But, like Professor Tinkerbot says, you want to create the technology, not rely on it."

"Now I get why you're his favorite." Grey laughed.

"I am not--" Karina swatted at Grey playfully. "But...okay...I'll go to the mixer tonight."

"Awesome...hey look...I am going to head back to my dorm and get changed. Meet you at the Union at 9 pm. Cool?"

"Cool." Karina headed back to her dorm as well. Her room was all white, but the lights continued to change the colors of her walls. She paused the light when it landed on purple. It was her favorite color. Karina had a small desk with hardly anything on it except for an image of a keyboard sitting below three screens.

"What should I wear?"

A mirror responded, "What is the occasion?"

"A mixer."

"Oh...the mixer tonight. According to campus events, it is the Digital Dreamers mixer, correct?"

"Yes, I believe so."

"Thanks. The dress code for the Digital Dreamers mixer is cocktail attire. Would you like to see looks best suited for your body type."

"Please," Karina responded.

"Pulling looks now it appears that you have nothing in your closet suitable for the mixer. I can design looks for you and create them here. Just connect me to your printer."

"Wireless connection printer to hub," Karina called out.

"Printer connected. Okay, now let's see what we can do for you."

Karina was lying on her bed, watching an image of herself appear in the mirror. The mirror placed several looks on her. A bright pink shirt, fluffy skirt, ripped stockings and huge pink earrings.

"Next," Karina called out.

"Okay, how about this one?"

"Not bad," Karina responded. "What else do you have?"

"What about this?"

"I like it ," Karina responded. "Let's see it from the back."

The image of Karina in an all-black, knee-length dress

rotated. "Yep, that's the one."

"Okay...printing started. The look will cost $130 to print. Would you like to deduct it from your YSW account?"

"Yes, please."

While the outfit was printing, Karina took a shower, washed her curly brown hair, and put a little bit of lip gloss on.

"This will always be so cool to me," Karina said as she grabbed the dress from the printer. "Oh...it's still hot." She waved the dress around to cool it off and headed out to meet Grey.

Grey came riding up to her on what looked like a floating skateboard. "You want a ride?"

"Sure."

Grey pressed a button, and the board extended, allowing room for Karina to hop on.

"Hold on," Grey called out, and the girls darted off to the mixer.

The girls arrived at a cinder block building with no windows. It was graffitied. For as long as anyone could remember, each new member of the Digital Dreamers left their mark on the building.

"Hey, Grey." A boy named Craig answered the door.

"Glad you could make it. Wow...who is your friend." Craig was ogling Karina.

"She's a freshman but probably knows more than you."

"Oh, really?" Craig lifted his bushy brown eyebrows.

"Yes, really."

"Okay... well, maybe your friend would be into playing a little Digital Dare later."

"Maybe, but I thought Digital Dare was saved for potential members."

Craig looked Karina up and down. "I think we can make an exception."

"Give her some space." Grey grabbed Karina's arm and pulled her into a big open room. Karina scanned the room. "There's got to be at least 300 people here."

"You're good. Don't even need a device...but...if you had one, you would have known there are 302 people here."

"I know that. I wasn't including us." Karina smirked.

They walked around and talked to several groups of people before Craig shouted out, "Who's down for Digital Dare?"

"You know only those who participate in the dare can move on to the next phase of initiation." Six people stepped forward.

"Karina, what about you?" Craig shouted out, and before Karina could refuse, Grey pushed her toward Craig.

"Oh no...If I'm doing it, then you are too," Karina said, grabbing Grey's arm.

"Okay, we have eight brave souls here. Any other takers?"

The room went silent. "Okay...then the rest of you can leave." When Craig said this, several AIbots came from different corners of the room and began tasing all of the people who were not part of the digital dare game.

"They don't need to see the ins and outs of the Digital Dreamers. Tonight, the eight of you will participate in phase one of our initiation process. Those who are able to successfully pass tonight's test will be invited to participate in the next two rounds. I am the Digital Dreamers president. You will meet the other members after you pass your test."

"Hey--" Karina raised her hand. "I am not sure if this is for me. I just came to spend time with my friend here, and I think it is about time for both of us to leave." Karina started walking backward.

"It's a little too late for that," Craig responded. The AIbots started huddling around. "It's just a simple game of dare. Nothing serious." Craig started looking around at the group of eight. "Okay...now that that is settled, have a seat. Go ahead, sit down."

"But there are no chairs." One of the eight announced.

"JUST SIT DOWN!!" Craig shouted.

Everyone was scared and immediately sat. As they did, chairs appeared.

"Yes, the chairs you are sitting on were designed by me. Everything around you is made of matter. Of course, you already know that, but what you may not know is how to manipulate matter so that it will do, form, or create anything you want. Tonight...that is your first challenge. You create something out of nothing, and you will receive 'likes' for what you can produce. Each of you will only be able to use the screens I provide you with. I will disconnect you from any other technology source. Like Professor Tinkerbot says, you want to create the technology, not rely on it. My suggestion to you is that you spend the first few minutes learning the program. You will have an hour. Your time begins now."

Karina was the only one that did not have a third eye. The third eye on the others stopped glowing. Grey's device behind the ear went black as well.

What am I doing here? Okay, Karina, you can do this...let's see, Karina played around with the screen. You've got to be kidding me. Karina chuckled when she realized that this was a program she was familiar with. It was the same program she used on the time snatcher app. She thought she would never see anything like this at Dollard University. It was old technology. Maybe that's the point, Karina thought. Maybe Craig thought no one would have ever seen anything like this before.

"Hey, what the heck is this?" Jason, a 3rd-year student, called out. "You've got to be kidding me. My grandparents didn't even work on a program like this."

"I am not trying to see what the program can do. I want to see what you can do," Craig said as he walked around, looking at the eight people frantically trying to figure out what to create.

The hour seemed to fly by. "Five minutes," Craig called out. "Finalize your projects."

Before they knew it, the eight could hear Craig say, "3...2...1... times

up" "Steven, you

first."

"Okay...me first, huh? So, what I have created for you all today is a virtual girlfriend."

A flickering digital image began to appear. Big boobs, a small waist, and thick wavy hair appeared in front of everyone.

"How is that any different from all of the other virtual people that have been created?" Craig was unimpressed. "Two likes, and that is stretching it."

"Well, because she only says positive things."

"Steve, I like you. Steve, you are handsome. Steve, you are so smart," the busty girlfriend called out.

"It's unoriginal; get him out of here and take her with you." The AIbots came to escort Steve out of the Digital Dreamers' house. You could hear Steve's creation still complimenting him on the way out.

Four more unimpressed programs later, four more people were dismissed from Digital Dreams, and it was now Karina's turn.

"So Karina, what were you able to do?"

"Well, I decided not to reinvent the wheel." Karina was scared. "It's nothing like manipulating matter to make chairs appear out of thin air."

"Okay, so what is it then?" Craig and the remaining people stared intently.

"In high school, I did this thing where I was able to alter the time snatcher app."

"Oh yeah, I remember that app. It was kinda lame. Didn't give you enough time. What was it like, maybe ten minutes of life or something." Craig shook his head and chuckled.

"Exactly, so I was able to reprogram the app to give more time."

"You were able to hack Deiderick Dollard's app? He has all kinds of protections on his codes."

"I know, but I was able to figure it out, so look."

Craig looked at Karina's program. "Wow! Yeah...now that, ladies and gentlemen, this is exactly what I am talking about!"

Craig leaned into Karina. "We are going to have to try that out later just to make sure it works, but there is a lot of potential in this design. I will give you 50 likes. Well done." Craig smiled at Karina. Then quickly turned to Grey.

"Grey, what about you?"

"Look, Craig, I just didn't come up with anything like that, so you can escort me out now."

"How about this? I will give you ten likes because you're cute. So what do you have?"

"I created a color manipulator that works on human fiber. You know, so when I want to get rid of this gray streak, I can just do this." Grey pressed a button on her computer before running her hands through her hair. Her jet-black hair turned pink, and her gray streak turned green.

"And, when I am feeling a little spicy. I can also..." She snapped, and her eyes turned violet.

"Okay, cool...not the most unique thing in the world...nothing a pair of contacts and hair dye won't do, but I guess with your bonus likes, it will work. Plus," Craig whispered, "You look kind of hot." Grey smiled.

The rest of the creations included a voice thrower that could mimic anyone's tone and make it sound like it was coming from any direction, a molecular defragmenter that could break down particles, turn them into a gas, and group the particles back together, and an enhancement on the memory recreator where memories could not only be recreated but you could interact with the memory without altering the past.

Craig smiled and said, "Give yourself a pat on the back. You have made it into round two. We will send you more information later but for now. Go home and get some rest."

The AIbots appeared out of nowhere and began escorting all of them out of the door. Grey grabbed her board, and Karina jumped on. They zoomed off toward the dorms.

"See you tomorrow." Karina hopped off and ran to her room. It was late, but she still managed to get a few minutes of studying before falling asleep.

The next day started off fairly normal. Karina went to a few classes, some taught by humans and others by holograms. She grabbed a bite to eat and headed back to her dorm. When she arrived at the door of her room, she saw a digital message.

"Accept," Karina said.

"Congratulations, you have moved to the next round of Digital Dreamers. Please arrive at the house by 7 PM for your next challenge."

"Shoot, it's already 6:30." Karina ran into her dorm, gave herself a quick once over, and ran back out the door. She arrived at the Digital Dreamers' house, panting.

Craig was already outside waiting on her. "Calm down, catch your breath. Here." Craig handed Karina a red cup. "This should help."

A quick sip. "Gross. I don't drink."

"Suit yourself."

Karina and Craig walked in. "Do you remember when I said you would meet the other members of the Digital Dreamers Society? Well, let me introduce you." Craig began pointing. "The guy with the blue cap, that's Joe, the vice president. She's Roxy, the treasurer, over there is Swift, it's a nickname because she is one of the fastest coders we have ever seen, and lastly DeBow, he's security.

Karina looked up at DeBow. He was intimidating.

"Ha..Hi.." Karina waved a few fingers at him.

"He's not going to talk."

"Okay...well..." Karina looked around. "Where is everyone else?"

"They are not here. This is just your test. Not theirs. So Karina...I was really impressed with your time snatcher app. Today, we will do the next part of your dare."

"What do you mean?"

"You created it. Now, I dare you to use it."

"Look...I don't really want to be part of all of this. I appreciate you allowing me to crash the party yesterday, but me and this app, we have a history that I would like to leave in the past." Karina turned away and began to walk toward the door.

"Lock!" Craig shouted. The doors locked, and DeBow walked in front of the doors with his arms folded.

"Let's not make this difficult ," Craig said. "Have a seat."

Karina sat down hesitantly. "Look, this app. I shouldn't have manipulated it. It can be dangerous."

"I know, Karina. Like the time you killed Todd Markley? Didn't think we knew about that? We're the YSW; we know about everything."

Karina was scared. "What do you mean?"

"I mean, we knew you had potential after the aptitude test you passed in high school, but when we found out about Todd Markley, there was no denying you were the right one."

"The guilt...I cannot do that again. The guilt alone nearly...it nearly drove me crazy."

"Well, we know something else," Craig said, staring at Karina.

"What?! Look, I don't want to be part of your organization. I will go back to my dorm room and pretend like none of this ever happened." Karina got out of her seat and started marching toward DeBow.

"I know about your father," Craig said. Karina stopped in her tracks.

"What do you know about my father?"

"I know that your father is nearly $900,000 in debt. And, up to this point, he has only received a few friendly reminders to join the YSW before we collect payment."

"How can you collect payment on money that he will probably never have?"

"You're right. I mean, look at him; What is he now? Sixty-three? We wouldn't have much use for him anyway. But…" Craig looked at Karina in her eyes… "You can help him. You can eliminate all of his debt by just playing a simple game of dare. No more threats, no more charges. You can share your YSW perks with him, and he will not be punished for it. We just need you to do a little time snatching for us."

"You won't hurt my father?" Karina nervously replied.

"Absolutely not. In fact, we will clear all of your father's debt with the click of a button." Craig had a smirk on his face.

"Can't you just use the formula and do it yourself?" Karina's voice was trembling.

"Yes, I could, but I don't like to get my hands dirty. Don't you think your father has been through enough?"

"What happens if I don't?" Karina said with tears in her eyes.

"How are your brothers?"

"Seriously, you would bring my brothers into this?"

"No…you're bringing your brothers into this--" Craig began circling around Karina. He pushed her hair off her shoulder. "Now, ever since I found out about your ability to manipulate the time, I had this vision. I would like to live as long as possible, and you are going to help me do it. I don't care who it is, but I need you to snatch time from them and give it to me. I think we can start with a few days at a time, you know, just to make sure there are not any glitches with your program, and then we can start taking years. So Karina, I dare you to steal three days."

Craig handed Karina a device she was very familiar with. The Illuminus 2125.

"We couldn't find the exact one you used, but I tried to find one just like it ." Craig smirked.

Karina snatched the device from his hand and walked toward the door. This time, DeBow moved out of the way. "This better come back with three days of life on it ," Craig shouted as Karina walked out the door.

She didn't know what to do. As she looked at the device, all the memories began to flood back into her mind. I can't do this, she thought to herself. She went back to her room and plopped down on the bed. Who...who am I going to get this time from? Karina looked up and saw her reflection in the mirror. That's it. She took a deep breath. You're young, Karina. It's just three days. Then this will all be over. Karina took the device and held it up to her temple. She pressed the app and took three days of her own life. She sat on the edge of the bed and cried.

The next morning, Karina wasted no time heading over to the Digital Dreamers' house after class. "Open the door, Craig. It's me."

"Come in." The door slid open, and Karina marched in. Craig approached.

"Here's your stupid device with your precious three days. Now, I'm done." Karina threw the device at Craig.

"Close," Craig shouted, and the doors slid closed.

"Good job." Craig put the device on his arm and added the days to his life. Karina winced.

"Where did you get the time from?"

"It doesn't matter. I got you the time. Now, clear my dad's debt and let me go."

"Let me show you something." Craig snapped, and the lights went off. Craig began to walk over to Karina.

"Home screen 1," Craig called out. The large blank white wall turned into a computer screen. "Solomon Wiseman 212 area code district."

Just then, a picture of her father and all of his information showed up. Craig went over to the screen and touched the line that showed Solomon's debt.

Craig seemed sinister as he said, "And now you can make this all go away."

"What do you mean, I can make this go away? You promised if I completed your dare, you would help my dad. I already gave you three days."

"You? You gave me these three days? Well, isn't that sweet. I know your dad would be so proud."

"So all you have to do is remove the debt. I did what I was told to do. Now you do what you promised you would do!" Karina shouted.

"I'm sorry. You misunderstood me. The three days were your initiation fee. You want the debt gone. You need to get me a year. And...now that I know you are so giving, I want the year from you."

"No...I'm not going to give you a year of my life. You've got to be kidding me."

"I am not. You could easily go to prison for Todd Markley. I don't think anyone as pretty as you needs to be locked up, and I would love to enjoy my life for as long as I can. Now...what's your decision?"

Tears welled up in Karina's eyes. She knew that she wasn't going to get out of there without giving up a year of her life, she knew that her father's debt wouldn't go away, and she was even more fearful that they would do something to her brothers.

"You are such a jerk. I cannot believe you would do this to me." Karina sat down. "Give it to me." Karina snatched the device out of Craig's hands.

"Joe, DeBow...one of you get over here. Don't you think Karina's dad would like to see how giving she is? Record it."

Joe took out his device and turned the camera on.

"Program it for a year," Craig demanded.

"I don't want to do this. Please!" Karina begged.

"Tase her!" Craig told DeBow.

Karina started crying. "I can't work like this." After fumbling around for ten minutes, Joe asked, "How much longer is it going to take?"

"Just two more minutes," Craig said, looking over Karina's shoulder.

"It's done. I programmed it for a year."

"Good...now...give it to me...give me one year."

The tears continued to stream down Karina's face. Her hand was shaking. She put the device up to her temple and pressed the button.

Taking so much life at once had Karina's eyes roll in the back of her head. She started convulsing. Joe, who was holding the camera, said, "I bet Daddy would be shocked to see his little girl like this."

Karina lost so much energy that she fell off the sofa and hit the floor. Craig picked up the device, put it on his wrist, and transferred Karina's year of life into his body.

"Hey, make sure she gets back safe. Oh, and make sure you get that video to her dad."

DeBow and Joe loaded Karina onto a hoverboard and took her home. It took two days for Karina to wake up. When she did, she had a digital message that said,

"Congratulations, you have been accepted into the Digital Dreamers Society, where all your dreams come true!"

Karina looked at the message and cried, realizing that she just gave away a year of her life. In complete silence, she stared at the message for several minutes. Karina sat up on the edge of her bed and wiped her tears. Another message popped on the screen. It was an image of her dad's debt. Amount owed, zero dollars. Karina smiled . I did it, she thought to herself. She redeemed her father, and although she hated to admit it, she was proud to be part of the digital dreamers.

Chapter 27: Come Home

A good parent will always receive their child back home, but a foolish child will choose not to go.
(A Warning from the Writ)

Karina did not send messages to her father often, but it wasn't because she was mad at him. She grew to a place of understanding and knew that her father did the best he could. So, after a few months of being in school and taking time to stop blaming her dad for her mother's passing, she decided to give him a call.

"Hey, Dad," Karina said.

"Karina, my goodness, you look amazing," Solomon said as he answered the call on the tablet.

"How are Kyle and Knox?"

"Well, I talked to them the other day for a few minutes. The detox center seems to be very strict on how much time they spend talking to their family. Something about not wanting them to regress, but I don't know. Seems a little odd if you ask me."

"Yeah, I know several students here whose parents put them in a digital detox center. So, not quite sure how effective it was since they ended up at a YSW engineering school."

"You make a good point. It feels strange to go from a house full of people to complete solitude. It has been more difficult than I could have ever imagined."

I bet. Karina realized she should have been better to her father.

"Well, "Solomon continued. "I sure am happy that you called me. So, what have you been up to?"

"A lot of studying."

"Studying? The YSW study?" Solomon chuckled.

"No, they don't study. It seems like life is one big party for most of them, but I guess some of the lessons that you and Mom taught seem to have stuck with me."

Solomon chuckled. "Well, that's good to hear."

Karina smiled. She was happy to see that her comment brought some light to her father.

"I guess I am one of the few disciplined students here. My professor thinks highly of me. Again, I think it is because of you and Mom. So, I just wanted to call and say thank you."

A tear rolled down Solomon's face. "Karina, you have no idea what it means to hear those words. I know your mother is smiling as well."

"I just want both of you to be proud of me. Oh, wait...I forgot to tell you something."

"It must be something good." Solomon's eyes lit up, seeing Karina's excitement. "So, tell me. I need to hear some good news."

"Have you checked your account balances and your credit card debt?" Karina asked.

"Now, why would I do that? I thought you were going to tell me something good." Solomon chuckled. "Karina, I stopped looking at that a long time ago."

"I found out why you had so much debt. I know you did it to take us on that trip and to save Mom. I am sorry for being mad at you. You could have told me."

"No, you weren't ready for me to tell you ," Solomon replied. "But I am glad you understand now."

"Well, I can never repay you for everything you have done for me, but hopefully, I have helped a little. Why don't you check out your balance now? Go ahead. I want to see your facial expression when you check it out."

"Oh...Okay, I am almost afraid." Solomon pressed his finger on the tablet and logged into his accounts. As the balances pulled up, Karina could see him put his hand over his mouth.

"Dear Jah. What in the world?--" Solomon paused for several seconds. "Karina, how did this happen?"

"I took care of it for you?"

"What did you do?"

"Dad, don't worry about it. I just wanted to help you."

"Karina, I am scared. What did you do to get them to erase nearly $900,000 of debt?"

"Dad, just be happy, okay? Don't worry about how it happened; just know that I took care of it."

"Karina, I love you. Please let me know if you are okay. I don't know what you could have done to erase this, but I will take it all back just to make sure that you are okay. Are you okay? Is everything going to be okay?"

"Yes, Dad...don't worry. Hey, look, I have to go. Grey is coming to my dorm room to scoop me up."

"Oh yeah, who is Grey?"

"It's a girl I met. She's pretty cool. Oh...Dad, remember not to worry. I am doing what's best."

Karina got off the tablet when Grey arrived at her dorm.

Solomon did his best not to worry, but truthfully he was running every scenario through his mind trying to think of what she could have done to erase that amount of money. Three weeks later, Solomon's tablet went off. Solomon ran over to the tablet in excitement, hoping it was one of his children. When he picked it up, he was confused. It was not Karina, but a video of Karina sent from someone named Craig. She was surrounded by a group of people who seemed to be making her do something she didn't want to do. She was holding a device up to her body, then she started shaking and fell to the ground. He heard someone say, "I bet Daddy will be shocked to see his little girl like this." He watched the video several times before spending the rest of the night trying to reach his daughter. When she didn't answer, he just became desperate to talk to any of his children. He then tried to call the digital detox center to speak to his sons.

Chapter 28: Kyle and Knox Wiseman

———————◆———————

Love your brothers and sisters, look out for them, and protect them. There will be so many things that will attack them, so fight for them and not with them.
(A Warning from the Writ)

The first few days at the digital detox center were very different than Kyle and Knox expected.

"Knox, look." Kyle pointed to a familiar face.

"I can't believe it. Is that Norman?" Knox was in awe.

"I...I think so."

"What do you think he is doing here?" Knox inquired.

"Probably the same thing we are doing here. I mean, he was the one who was more hooked on technology than we were," Kyle replied.

The boys walked over to Norman. "Does he look a bit different to you?" Kyle asked.

"Yes, you know why, right?"

"No...why does he look like that?"

"Remember, in school, we never got to see the real him. We only saw a hologram version of him."

"Wow, you're right," Kyle whispered back. The brothers walked up to Norman.

"So, how did you end up here?" Knox did his best to sound friendly. A little apprehensive about their relationship after their last encounter.

"My mom and dad sent me here after you two broke into my house," Norman replied.

"Hey, we saved you. It would have been terrible to leave you in between the virtual world and reality. Besides, we would never have had to zap you if you weren't such a mean person," Kyle stated.

Norman looked a little solemn. "Hey, it's cool. And...I am sorry for doing all of those mean things. The truth is, my parents don't want to have to deal with me. I am not here because I need to detox; I am here because they don't want me home."

Knox tried to make Norman feel better. "That's pretty messed up, Norman. Hey, you're not so bad."

"Yeah, when you are not so cruel to people, then...well...you seem kinda nice," Kyle chimed in.

Norman was remorseful and said, "Look, guys, I am sorry for being so mean." There is an awkward pause between the boys. Norman broke the silence by saying, "By the way, did you know that Clifton is here?"

"You've got to be kidding me?" Kyle looked around the sterile facility with excitement. "Where is he? When did he get here?"

"Yeah, I was wondering what happened to him. Tried to get in touch with him a few times after...well...you know...after we went into your house, but I heard his dad was really upset and put him on punishment," Knox replied.

"Well, welcome to his punishment. He got here a few weeks before I did," Norman replied.

"Wow. I feel terrible. It is all my fault. I was the one who asked him for his device," Knox replied. "Where is he? I want to talk to him."

"I can take you to him, but..." Norman paused. "I don't think you are going to like what you see."

"Why? What's wrong?" Kyle asked.

"It may just be easier to show you," Norman replied.

All three boys left the stark white lobby and headed down a hall with lots of windows overlooking the city.

"We are really high up," Kyle said, looking down at all of the tiny people walking the streets of the 212 area code.

They kept traveling down the long, stark white hallway until they arrived at Clifton's room. There was one bed and four bare white walls. Clifton was in a chair with his back toward them.

"Hey, Clifton, it's us, Kyle and Knox," Knox said.

Clifton slowly turned around.

"Ah!" Knox shouted, "What happened to you?"

"They say it shouldn't be much longer, and then I will get to go home. They said I could have gone sooner if I wasn't such a naughty boy." Then Clifton started rocking in his chair. "I was a naughty, naughty boy, a naughty boy."

Knox went over to Clifton and smacked him in the face. "Snap out of it, man! What has gotten into you?"

Clifton shook his head wildly, blinked his eyes, and said, "Hey, what's going on?"

"That's what we are trying to ask you? Are you okay?" Kyle asked.

Clifton, still a bit dazed, said, "I think I am okay."

Knox gave Clifton the once over. "You look like you're coming back to yourself. We ran into Norman, and he showed us where you were."

"Norman showed you guys where I was?" Clifton was confused.

Clifton looked around and quickly closed the door.

"You guys," Clifton whispered. "You have got to find a way to get me out of here. I feel like I am losing touch with reality."

"What are they doing?" Kyle was frightened.

"They are giving me these weird pills."

"They give them to me, too, but I don't think I have the same reaction," Norman replied.

"Norman, your parents trapped you in a cocoon for years of your life. Your body is so used to high amounts of digital intake," Clifton responded.

Norman sarcastically replied, "Gee, thanks for calling that out."

"Hey," Clifton said, hearing the ruckus in the hallway wind down. "You guys better get out of here before they give me another one of those pills.

Norman, Kyle, and Knox slowly opened the door and peaked around before quickly hurrying back down the hallway covered with windows through the stark white lobby and to their side of the facility.

All of the boys went back to their rooms. The bare white walls were marked only with a tiny blue dot in each corner. The boys assumed they were being watched. The Wiseman brothers were on separate beds looking at the bare white walls when they were visited by a nurse. A woman with piercing blue eyes let the boys know that she was not real, she was AI. She wore a white nurse uniform with white stockings and thick white-soled shoes. Her artificially tanned skin was in stark contrast to the white mask that hung from glasses. When she walked in, she pushed her glasses down to the tip of her nose and stared at the boys with her piercing blue eyes.

"I know that you have explored much of our facility today. Even making your way to the other side."

Kyle and Knox felt uneasy, realizing their attempt to sneak down the hall to see Clifton hadn't gone unnoticed. Her eyes twinkled, and the boys knew that someone was watching them through the blue glow. "I brought something for you boys." She handed them two small clear pills.

"What is this?" Knox asked the AI nurse. Knox caught a glimpse of her name tag, which said Nurse Gram.

"Just take it. It's part of your program," Nurse Gram responded.

Knox looked at Kyle, who was also receiving a clear pill. Kyle picked the pill up and examined it closer. "Look," Kyle pointed out. "There are all sorts of weird images floating in it."

The stern yet robotic voice of Nurse Gram interjected, "It's to help erase old memories and implant new ones."

"I don't want new memories," Knox said as he tried to hand the pill back to Nurse Gram.

"Yeah, I don't think we need this. We have pretty good memories. We just got carried away with using devices. Maybe just a break from them for a little while will help." Kyle was very apprehensive of this clear pill. He started to regret the day that he and his brother chose devices over their father.

Nurse Gram seemed unphased by Kyle's plea. "Look, I don't make the regimens around here. I just enforce them. If you refuse to take the pill, I will have to call for reinforcements."

Another nervous glance was shared between the boys. They didn't have time to think about whether they were going to ingest the pill before Nurse Gram pressed her name tag.

"We have non-compliant patients. Please report to the Wiseman room."

Within seconds two massive men covered with tattoos, faces splattered with red freckles, came into the room. They looked nearly identical except for one having red hair and the other had brown hair.

The one with dark brown hair asked, "Is there a problem here?"

"Typical new patient stuff. They are refusing to take their pill," Nurse Gram said. Then she handed the pills to the men and walked out of the room.

The man with red hair said, "You can do this the easy way, or we can make it even easier."

"I.." Knox gulped. "I don't think that is how the saying goes."

"So you're the funny guy. Let me clear things up for you. You can either take this without help, or I can make sure that it gets down your throat. Do I make myself clear?"

It was nearly impossible for Kyle's cleft lip to tremble, but still, it was. Both he and Knox grabbed the clear pill with weird images floating in it. They put it on their tongue and swallowed.

"I thought you boys seemed smart," the brown-haired man said before walking out the door.

"How do you feel?" Kyle asked his brother.

"Not too bad. Maybe it doesn't do very much," Knox responded.

"Let's hope not."

The boys had no such luck. A few moments later, things no longer felt normal.

"What is happening?" Kyle started looking at his hands which felt as if they were taking on a life of their own.

"I don't know. My head is spinning." Knox started looking around the room. The walls of the room felt like they were swirling around him faster and faster.

Images of every digital simulation game they ever played felt like they were in the room. It was maddening. The boys found themselves dodging bombs and running from enemies.

"This feels just like War Simulation II that we played at home," Kyle shouted over noise that wasn't really even there.

"I know. I guess we play our way to safety," Knox shouted back.

The glowing blue lights in each corner of the room could be traced back to the Digital Detox headquarters, where the boys were being watched.

"They are taking to the program faster than I thought," Nurse Gram whispered to Dr. Sway, who was the president of the Digital Detox center.

"Yes, they are. That is good news. Their father is foolish. He hasn't become one of us yet. Let's see how long he will last not being a member of the YSW once he finds out all of his children have converted."

"Yes," Nurse Gram replied, "I heard that his daughter is not only a member of the YSW but has become part of our most elite YSW. I am sure that Mr. Deiderick Dollard will be pleased with our progress on the Wiseman family."

"I'd say so. I have never seen Mr. Dollard so consumed with a man in all my life." Dr. Sway replied. "Honestly, I am very impressed with all the videos I have seen of Solomon. I thought he would surely take the bait by now, but he still remains a non-YSW member."

Both Nurse Gram and Dr. Sway looked back at the camera and watched the boys in an empty room act as if they were in a game.

Chapter 29: 212 Degrees - Solomon's Boiling Point

———————⚫———————

You will know you are in the last days when there is no relief from the temperature. Everyone and everything will hit its boiling point
(A Warning from the Writ)

"Solomon Wiseman for Knox and Kyle Wiseman," Solomon said to the tablet.

"Connecting you to the Digital Detox Center ," the device responded.

Solomon waited for someone to answer. After thirty seconds of waiting and the device said, "Knox and Kyle are currently undergoing a therapy session. Please try again later." The device disconnected.

He tried to busy himself, but something didn't feel right. He waited for three hours. "Surely, they have to be finished with their session. "Please call Knox and Kyle Wiseman."

"Connecting…"

Just as Solomon was about to disconnect. "Hey, Dad." "Hi, Knox. You okay?"

"Just really tired."

"Where is your brother?"

"He's lying down. Trying to recover from his therapy session."

"So, what are these therapy sessions about? What do you do?"

"We're really not supposed to tell anyone, but I guess you can know. Basically, we have to play virtual reality games all day and night until we have an adverse reaction to them."

"You're kidding me, right?" Solomon could feel himself getting angry.

"No...I think it is working. I am so exhausted. We don't get to sleep. We barely get anything to eat. We just keep playing until we are exhausted."

"I am sorry, I don't understand how they think this is going to work."

"It's kind of a new therapy, but..."

"But what?" Solomon was astonished.

"But they still don't know the success rate."

"I don't see how giving you more technology is going to help. I am going to get you out of there."

"Dad, it's cool. Just give it some more time. Kyle and I are fine." Knox yawned. "Hey, Dad, I am really tired. Can we talk later?"

"I haven't even gotten to tell you about this new group I joined."

Knox continued to yawn. "Hey, Dad, I will talk to you later."

"Device disconnecting in 5..4..3..2.." The screen went blank, and Solomon's heart was heavy. He was about to place the device back down on the table, but before he could, it lit up.

Maybe he is calling me back. Solomon was elated.

"Retrieve," Solomon called

out. "Retrieving message."

Solomon assumed it was Kyle, so when he heard the word message, he was confused.

SOLOMON,

IT HAS COME TO THE ATTENTION OF THE DIGITAL DETOX FACILITY THAT YOU HAVE DISCOURAGED A PATIENT IN THE FACILITY FROM COMPLETING THEIR THERAPY. THIS IS A BREACH OF THE CONTRACT YOU SIGNED WHEN YOU PLACED KNOX AND KYLE IN OUR CARE. ANOTHER BREACH OF THIS KIND, AND YOU WILL PUT YOURSELF AND YOUR SONS IN DANGER. IF YOU HAVE ANY QUESTIONS, FEEL FREE TO SPEAK TO YOUR DIGITAL DETOX REPRESENTATIVE AND REMEMBER TO HAVE A WONDERFUL DAY.

Placing them in danger. Kyle and Knox continue to be exposed to insane amounts of technology, and I am the one putting them in danger? Solomon was furious. They will not threaten me or my children like this. Solomon paced back and forth. They are getting out of there. Those YSW pieces of crap think they can run everything.

It was a restless night for Solomon. He tossed and turned, thinking of a way to get his sons back home. I will never be able to compete with their technology. I need to do something that they would not expect.

During the next EAD meeting, Solomon shared his concerns.

"I got to talk to my sons the other day," Solomon said to Quantas.

"Oh yeah, how did it go?" She replied. Quantas was moving about as usual. Fiddling with items scattered on the countertop.

"Not good," Solomon replied. "I don't want them in there anymore. I don't like the way they sound. The detox center doesn't seem to be helping at all, but when I have tried to speak to someone about getting them back, I'm disconnected."

"YSW, pieces of crap. Sounds about right. They ain't never going to let your boys out of there. If you ask me, they are as good as gone. Might as well have handed them to the devil himself."

Solomon couldn't remember why he even bothered telling Quantas anything.

"If I were you", she continued, I would try to break them out of there before it's too late."

"What do you think is going to happen to them?" Solomon inquired.

"I just don't know if you will ever see your boys again. You already told me your daughter has sold out to the YSW, who knows what brainwashing they are doing to your sons."

"You're right," Solomon said. "I have got to get them out of there."

For the next few weeks, Solomon continued to go over the details of his plan and prayed to Jah. A recurring thought, Keep it simple, came to mind. Just keep it simple. Solomon concluded that in a world filled with complicated technology, it was best to do something so obviously simple that the YSW would not have thought of it.

Before he knew it, he had broken a few EAD rules and used his computer at work to research. If I look up 'how to break into buildings,' they will know I am up to something. Hmm, Solomon thought, I need to be smart. Solomon used his job as his cover and typed in Book on The History of the World's Best Break-Ins.

He was shocked when several books popped up. Solomon stayed aware of his surroundings and did his best to move where the camera couldn't see him. Mike was bopping around, not paying much attention to Solomon's behavior.

"Summarize," Solomon did his best to whisper.

Mike looked up. "What did you say?"

"Nothing. I am just looking over this order."

"Oh...okay. Hey, do you want to come over again? Mediana really enjoyed cooking for you. She said it reminds her of when my mom and dad would visit."

"Oh yeah...I enjoyed it too. I am sure I will come by. We have another EAD meeting next week, so maybe sometime after that."

"Sounds good." Mike went back to gathering books. "Come here, Bubbles. Who's a good boy? Who's a good boy?"

Mike being preoccupied with Bubbles gave Solomon just enough time to read over the summary. "Decoding security systems, Assuming a person's identity" Solomon kept reading, "Tasers, Vaporizers," He continued to scroll through the chapter headings and then saw it. A plan simple enough for a non-YSW member, Fire. I will torch the place down and get my sons back.

As soon as that thought came to mind, Solomon remembered his vision of fire. The quick glimpses from his dreams started flashing in his mind, but he didn't let that stop his plan. In fact, he was very cautious, making sure to keep his same routine. He went to work, attended EAD meetings, and read the Writ. The only difference in his routine was his purchase of ammunition. He was smart enough not to buy large quantities at once and focused on acquiring flammable liquids that were used commonly enough not to raise suspicion. He took time to collect enough ammunition to set the detox facility on fire.

It took three months to collect all the items, but finally, Solomon felt he had worked out all of the details. He grabbed his copy of the Writ, took out the picture of his family and kissed it before putting the picture in the book and carrying the book in his jacket.

In the wee hours of the morning, Solomon set out. Naturally, he knew there were cameras watching him, so about two weeks prior, Solomon decided to start leaving his house at random times of the night, so it looked like a habit. He walked the streets with the YSW, so his behaviors seemed normal. Each night he walked closer and closer to the Digital Detox center before turning around and heading back home. Doing his best to make it look like a late-night stroll.

But tonight, Solomon was going to make it all the way to the center. Solomon kept a cool demeanor as he walked to the massive concrete building with hundreds of small windows. He casually strolled past the front entrance making sure to drop pages of books out of his pocket on the ground and sprinkling them with liquid from a container he held inside his Code Red jacket. When he came to the electrical box located on the right side of the building, he placed several books on top. Then he grabbed a container from his pocket and doused the paper with the flammable liquid he collected, took the lighter his father gave him when he was a little boy, and flicked it. A small blaze popped out of the top of the lighter. He threw the lighter down, and that small flicker of light burst into a ravenous fire that began to consume everything in the path Solomon laid out.

Soon, there was a trail that lit up the entire entrance to the Digital Detox Center. The fire went straight to the wooden doors, and they were fully ablaze. The plastic coating around the security cameras began to melt, and all of the wires were on fire as well. The electrical box exploded. Large flames engulfed the box and shot into the air like fireworks. The fire quickly traveled through the electrical lines, making its way inside the building. Solomon could hear the sound of police hovercrafts filling the air. The large wooden entrance doors of the center were on fire, but Solomon was prepared. He ran through the doors without being noticed. All of the cameras were knocked off, and the smoke prevented people from seeing him sneak in.

He ran down the hall looking from room to room in search of his boys. He was ½ way down the hall when he felt a hand grab him. A large man in a police uniform had his hand on Solomon's shoulder. "I got him." Another officer came through the smoke. "Tase him! He won't get away with this." A powerful jolt of electricity was sent through Solomon's body, and he collapsed. The men dragged him down the hallway. The sprinkler system went off, extinguishing the fire and leaving large clouds of gray smoke.

"Get in here." The officer threw Solomon into the hovercraft. They took off.

"This guy is an idiot."

"Tell me about it. Can't wait to see what the DEAD company will do to him for destroying their entire security system."

"This one should be dead by now, but Mr. Dollard refuses. What's so special about this low life?"

"Not sure, but nothing has worked on him so far."

Solomon drifted in and out of consciousness. As he came to, he could hear the officers continue to talk about his fate. He was groggy and started moaning. One voice sounded extremely familiar to Solomon.

"I think he's waking up," one of the officers said.

"Just hit him with another dose." It was then that Solomon knew it was Kevin.

Kevin took out his taser gun. As he grabbed for the gun, the hovercraft began to shake. "System failing"

"What is happening?" The other officer started calling out commands. "Autopilot."

"Autopilot disabled. Please use manual controls and land immediately."

The officer grabbed the controls, but the handle started shaking. "What the hell is going on?"

The hovercraft responded, "Air coordinates lost; please land immediately."

The hovercraft shook violently in the air and slowly began descending toward the ground. Solomon could do nothing but pray. In the midst of the chaos, he cried out to Jah. Please forgive me. There have been so many signs telling me that I should give up everything and follow you. I know that I have doubted you. I know that I have blamed you for the wrong that has occurred in my life. I blamed you for the death of my wife and the loss of my children, but Jah, I promise, if you save me from this, I will dedicate my life to serving you. I will read the Writ and follow your word. Please save me so I can see my children again. Forgive me Jah, please forgive me. Solomon wept in the back of the hovercraft. His arms were handcuffed together.

The next thing that Solomon heard was, "Airfield lost, no coordinates found. Cannot maintain altitude. Hovercraft descending. Danger, danger, danger." The hovercraft took a swift nosedive and crashed. Heads jerked forward and snapped back due to the force of the impact.

Solomon was the only one who could get up and run away. The others were severely injured. He was out of it for a minute before slowly gaining consciousness. Solomon opened his eyes and looked around. He removed his safety belt and reached through the bars that held him in the back of the hovercraft. As he reached through the bars, they began to flicker. An electrical pop broke his handcuffs, and his hands were able to go free.

AFTER THE FIRE

Chapter 30: Forever Changed

*Once you have a personal encounter with Jah, and see his
miracles, your life is forever changed
(A Warning from The Writ)*

Thank you, Jah, Solomon thought to himself. Solomon pressed
the button, and the hovercraft doors lifted in the air like wings on
a bird. Solomon squeezed his body through a small opening to get
to the front seat and jumped out of the right side of the vehicle.
He was in a field of nothingness. In the distance, Solomon saw a
dim glow hovering over the horizon. He assumed it to be the
bright lights of the 212 area code. Solomon ran in the direction of
the light. He kept running until things began to look familiar.

He wasn't sure, but he guessed that he ran nearly seven miles
that night without stopping. He made it home just before the sun
came up. He never went to sleep that night. Instead, for the first
time in his life, he praised Jah. He danced around the house, giving
Jah thanks. He knew it was Jah that caused the fire to take out
the detox center and create an electrical fire. The next morning,
Solomon did his best to keep his routine. As he headed to
work the voices on the screen proved he didn't go unnoticed.

"There is a reward for the man who set the Detox center on fire." One of the voices said.

Solomon's heart raced, breathing intensified, scared someone would make the connection to him and the fires.

"Jah, Jah, Jah, please help me," a panting Solomon thought.

I don't think they saw me come this way, he could hear the buzzing of the drones and the footsteps of the Youth of the Second World close behind. He prayed the blue eyes somehow missed his leap into the dumpster. He was surprised he was able to hide, well, at least for the moment.

His heavy breathing fogged up his Code Red mask, and the stench from the dumpster seeped through. An unbearable smell, but he knew better than to move. The parades of protesters walking past, for once, proved themselves beneficial and acted as a distraction allowing Solomon's escape.

Solomon patted his long leather coat to feel the book deep within the inner pocket. "Thank Jah, it is still here." Hunched in the corner of the dumpster, he took the Writ from its hiding place, opened the cover, and unfolded a picture of his family at the beach. A few months prior, Solomon would have never imagined wanting to protect something with his entire life. But the Writ must remain unharmed. Solomon kissed the picture of his family, folded it, and placed it back into the sacred book.

The physical pain of the crash landing didn't compare to the mental anguish Solomon experienced after realizing that he may never see his boys again. *What kind of piece of crap father are you? You are nothing like your dad.* His mind played those dreadful thoughts repeatedly.

Solomon was very close with his mother and father. He remembers how hard his dad worked and still managed to spend time with him. Solomon knows his dad would be so disappointed. Kristen, his wife would be disappointed as well.

Solomon reached for the Writ and read a few lines. He was hoping to turn to a page or find a chapter that could make him feel better about his failed mission. But nothing seemed to make him feel better. It was not long before the exhaustion of the day consumed him.

While asleep, Jah sent him a dream. It was a dream whose setting was in a different time and place. The place felt familiar although he had never seen it before. Solomon was in a battle and there were people all around him. He was surrounded by discord and chaos, but when he looked to his left and his right, his sons were next to him. Other figures, people who Solomon didn't recognize, felt strangely familiar to him and were all in the fight together. As Solomon charged toward what appeared to be the enemy, his daughter was in the midst of the enemy side headed in his direction. When Solomon woke up, he realized that he would see his children again.

Despite the restless night, Solomon still made it to work on time the next morning. He wanted to keep his schedule as much as possible so as to not bring too much attention to himself. On his walk to work, he was shocked to hear the screens:

An attempted break-in of the 212 Digital Detox Center occurred last night. The suspect was apprehended by police officers, but it was later discovered that the aircraft holding the suspect crashed in a field about seven miles away from the 212 district. According to the director of the Digital Detox Center, a fire was set to the building around 2:30 in the morning. The fire caused severe damage to the security system of the building, impacting the entire block by knocking out its power and dismantling the coordinate grid for all air crafts. All of the patients in the detox center survived the fire. Most of the damage occurred to the pharmacy section of the center where the medicine was held. We received a statement from Dr. Sway:

"Our number one concern is our patients. Many of these patients received medicines that supported their therapy. We are sad to report that they will not be able to receive their medication for several weeks but assure families that our patients are in excellent care."

We now turn it over to Deiderick Dollard, creator of the security system and president of the DEAD company, to explain what happened:

"I want to assure you that we are looking into the cause for such a massive blackout. What we do know is that many of our systems are connected through fiber-optic lines. These lines are connected with each other so that they can work as a unit to transfer information more efficiently. So, once the fire got into the fiber-optic lines, it impacted all of the networks connected to it. We promise to restore the entire block by the end of the day. Thank you."

Solomon could not believe what he had just heard but was relieved when it sounded like they had no clue who the assailant was who caused all of the damage. He was even more relieved to hear that his sons would not be forced to take their medication, at least for a while. It was not the primary goal of his plan to break into the detox center. He would have preferred to have his boys home, but it was good to know they were safe.

"Jah, you are a God of miracles. I realize that you have chosen me to see things through your eyes. You have given me visions of things to come, and you saved me so I can do what you need me to do. If it is in your will, I pray that you give me the strength to take down the YSW, Deiderick Dollard, and the DEAD company so I can get my family back."

From that moment on, Solomon was dedicated to living a life for Jah.

Deiderick Dollard and the Dollard Family

Chapter 31: Unwanted Responsibility

Be warned. The spirit of evil works slowly. Removing your sights from things that are important (love, kindness, family) and shifting your eyes to the things of this world
(A warning from the Writ)

Deiderick took his tie off and collapsed in his favorite leather chair that he had had ever since his senior year in college. His parents bought it for him as a gift. They were so proud that their son, from Woodstock, New York, a small rural town, seemed to be able to handle the demands of college. Excelling in the least likely field that someone from Woodstock would excel in, coding and artificial intelligence. His parents were even more excited when Deiderick seemed to get the attention of Janice Goldmine. A beautiful young blonde lady from extreme wealth. Her parents were tied to the oil industry. She was immediately smitten with Deiderick, the fair-skinned, dark brown-haired young man from meager beginnings, but her parents were not as excited until they began to see how brilliant he was.

They began dating in Deiderick's junior year, and it seemed to be a whirlwind love affair. She handled his late nights of studying in stride, and he seemed to be okay with her slightly spoiled antics and frivolous spending.

Their wedding made national news. Nearly 500 guests were there, ranging from big wigs with multi-million dollar yearly incomes, artificial intelligence human-like beings, to his parents, who bought their wedding attire off the rack from Felt, a chain store that was going out of business. Deiderick remembers looking at his parents to see if they seemed uncomfortable mingling with the upper crust, but the smile they had on their faces let him know they were truly happy to finally feel part of the 'in' crowd. A position they didn't even realize they wanted.

Deiderick turned his leather chair to look at the small pictures he had on his desk. His parents' picture was slightly faded. It was his parents on their wedding day. Smiles stretched across their faces. His father's suit was slightly too big, and his mother's dress made her already straight, wide figure seem a little boxier. Still, it was Deiderick's favorite picture of his parents. Next to that was a picture of Deiderick and his wife. They were, by society standards, a strapping couple. Deiderick stood six feet four inches tall. He had fair skin and a very chiseled jaw. His athletic frame filled the suit nicely. His wife could have passed for a model. She stood about five feet ten inches tall. She had long wavy blonde hair with eyes as green as the sea. Her smile could have lit up a room. Unlike Deiderick, who was completely unaware of his level of attractiveness. She was spoiled from birth, born into a life of luxury. Men doted over her, hoping she would select them as her suitor, but it was Deiderick who caught her attention, probably because he was the one man who was not impressed with her financial background.

Looking at the picture of him and Janice made Deiderick wonder how they ended up where they are now. The door sensor went off, triggering Deiderick out of his thoughts.

"Janice is at the door. Do you want her to come in?"

"Yes, open," Deiderick said.

His office was behind two sets of doors. He could not afford for anyone to have access to his office unless it was someone he trusted. The first set of doors parted vertically, and the second set parted horizontally. Janice was standing there.

Why does she always have that look on her face? Deiderick thought to himself.

"Are you ready for the meeting next week? It is a big deal, and I don't want to be embarrassed like last time." Janice walked toward a mirror in Deiderick's office and started fixing her lipstick.

"Do you think I need to tighten up a little around the eyes?" Janice asked.

Deiderick was not stupid enough to walk into that trap. "Of course not. You're beautiful."

"Well...It's too late. I already made an appointment with Dr. Liften," Janice announced, continuing to look in the mirror. "You may want to let the gray show and let your belly go, but I am going to be the first to try his reimager." Janice looked at Deiderick and pointed to his mid-section. Deiderick looked down and patted it. Looks alright for someone nearly 60, he thought to himself.

"Janice, you don't look a day older than when we first met. I would actually like a wife who looks like my wife and not my daughter. I am giving you permission to allow yourself to age." Deiderick was past the point of frustration with Janice's vanity.

"Wow! I can't believe what I am hearing. Are you even listening to yourself?" Janice snapped.

"What is wrong with what I am saying?"

"You have the ability to look like you did when we were in college, and instead, you look, I don't know, aged. It was okay at first to have the distinguished gentleman thing going on, but this is absolutely ridiculous. It is like you want to hold me back."

"I relieve you from the pressure to maintain this facade, and you feel as if I am holding you back. Wow, Janice! You are really a piece of work!"

"Look, I didn't come in here for this ; I just want to know if you are going to be ready for your advertising team to listen to your latest idea or do you want to put it off again?"

"I don't think I am ready to bring it to the public yet. I haven't worked out all of the coding issues." Deiderick turned so he couldn't see his wife's reaction. He felt as if he had been having the same argument for months and didn't understand why she was so aggressive with this particular idea.

"Look, Deiderick." Janice softened her voice and walked over to him. She started rubbing his shoulders and gliding her hands down his chest, kissing his neck. At one time, this was a surefire way to get him to do whatever she wanted him to do, but after 35 years of marriage, her effect seemed to wear off.

"You are a smart man," Janice continued. "This is a brilliant idea. Let's get a team behind it and see what we can do to get it out to the public. I want this out before the end of the quarter. It will be best for sales." She continued to press her chest into his back and rub his arms. Deiderick's tension faded as he changed the subject.

"You do realize your precious Dr. Liftup is using my technology."

"I know. All the more reason why you should support my endeavor." Janice stopped groping Deiderick, took a few steps toward the door, and smacked him on the butt before turning around and saying, "Why don't you pitch your idea to the tech team tomorrow. I will have our boys sit in on the meeting. They can help you work out some of the coding issues." And with that, Janice sashayed out of the room.

When she left, both sets of doors closed behind her. Deiderick fell back into his leather chair, rubbed his hands through the brown, gray mix of hair and took a deep sigh.

"Locate Barrett."

"Locating Barrett." Barrett was Deiderick's top human security guard.

"Good evening, Mr. Dollard. What can I do for you?"

"I have a lot of work to do in my office today, so I won't be out and about. Keep an eye on things for me. I don't know, Janice and the boys are trying to twist my arm into putting out this new project, but I am not ready yet. Something feels a little odd to me, so try to keep an ear out as well."

"Yes, sir." Barrett signed off.

Deiderick owned an expansive estate. They had seven bedrooms, seven bathrooms and several other living areas in his main house. There were three other guest houses on the property. Two of his houses were just for the security staff. Deiderick used a combination of humans, robots, and droids to protect his physical and intellectual property. His estate used to feel more like home, like the way that his relationship with Janice used to feel like a marriage. Now, Deiderick finds more comfort in his leather chair. He fell asleep in that chair many nights, and this night was no different. After several hours of reviewing the code, he dozed off, only to be woken up by the door sensor. "Your family is at the door."

Deiderick rubbed his eyes. "Windows" The blinds rolled up and let in a stream of light.

"Come in."

Janice and Deiderick's two sons, Damion and Tyler came barging into the office.

"Another night in your chair? Dad, get it together....you know what, it doesn't matter. The real question is are you ready to pitch to your tech team?" Damion asked his father.

Deiderick was irritated. "I never told you I would do that," he says to Janice.

"You never told me that you wouldn't. So Tyler, Damion, and I are here to listen to your pitch and see how we can help. The rest of the team is already in the boardroom." Again, Janice managed to say her peace and make her exit. His sons remained.

"Dad, you are a brilliant man. I really think you have a fantastic idea, but we can never find out how great it is until we get it out there and see how an audience will respond," Tyler said.

"You don't think I know that the idea is going to be successful?" Deiderick said, frustrated.

"Look, Dad, this could be the idea that trumps all of your other ideas. Mom is right, we need to push it out there before the end of the quarter."

"It won't be ready then. I don't even know if I want it to be ready then. I think we have done enough. The world has gone to crap because of my products. Do you think we need more money?" A slight pause for his sons to think about the rhetorical question before continuing. "If we were to make another hundred billion dollars, could we really have any more than what we have

267

now?" Deiderick felt like he had posed this question to his sons a hundred times, and he heard the same answer.

"Dad, in this life, there is never enough," Damion responded. It was a term that seemed to be the family creed for everyone in the family, with the exception of Deiderick. This slogan was started by Janice when the boys were little. It was cute at first. A saying she used to try and get her way with Deiderick. Janice used it on her father, the very wealthy Mr. William Paige.

William and Tara Paige died twenty-seven years ago and left their daughter nothing. Deiderick had earned Mr. Paige's respect when he noticed Deiderick had a way of calming his spoiled brat daughter. When he and his wife passed away, they left nothing to Janice and left everything to Deiderick Dollard. This generous offer was the first move that began to change the relationship between Deiderick and his wife. He began to find it hard to find the line between providing simple pleasures and his new lavish lifestyle. Admittedly, Deiderick felt good being able to buy his wife and children a few items here and there, but two spoiled mama's boys and a headache for a wife later, and Deiderick realized that giving in to his family's material desires may have been a bad idea.

"Dad, right now, without this, we could lose our status as the world's wealthiest family. This app you are working on designing could make sure we maintain our position." Damion said.

"Why does that matter?" Deiderick asked.

"Dad, why can't you just get on the same page with the rest of us? The truth of the matter is you are a brilliant man that has a brilliant idea. Let's just head down to the technology team and see if we can find the holes in the code. In the meantime, Tyler will get the marketing team together."

"Marketing before we work out all of the kinks is a really bad idea. I have built a brand to make sure that my products are successful. I won't rush the process ," Deiderick replied.

"Investors are going to go crazy when we finally release this. Our stocks are going to go through the roof. We need to get the word out there now." Damion slapped his father's desk as if to assert himself. He seemed to ignore his father's concern.

Damion called out to the speaker, "Let the tech team know we will be in the boardroom in ten minutes."

"I hate to force your hand on this one, but I have to meet up with Meliah soon. I promised her that I would take her to the Fresh. We haven't been there in several weeks. I don't have time for you to waste."

The boardroom was full of some of the greatest tech minds of the 22nd century. Several of them were AI holograms that were programmed for the sole purpose of detecting errors in code, but none of them were as intelligent as Deiderick Dollard himself. All 23 members of the tech team were present. Regardless of whether they were in the flesh or virtual, their attendance was accounted for. They spent six hours trapped in that room going through each line of code, and no one, not even the great Deiderick Dollard himself, could find the glitch.

"Look, we have been at this long enough. I think we need to pause here and come back next week. In the meantime, I will continue to push through with the advertising," Tyler said, bringing the meeting to an end.

As the team disbanded, Tyler put his arm around his father's shoulders. "I know you were hoping to figure it out today, but I am sure we will work through it when we meet again."

"Does everyone in this family only hear what they want to hear? Look, I know this app is very exciting for everyone. Having a real experience when someone touches an emoji is revolutionary, but after meeting with several medical professionals, I...I just don't know if I feel this app needs to go out. It is starting to feel too risky. I just want some time to think about this before we move forward, and I really don't understand why we are rushing it."

A few people remained in the room. They were talking quietly in corners. Damion pulled his father to the side and whispered. "Look, we are moving forward with this project. There are things already in motion, and we are not going backward. You'll figure it out, Dad, you always do." Damion patted his father on the back and made his way out of the room, leaving Deiderick speechless.

When the room finally emptied out, Deiderick cut the large screen back on and pulled up the emoji code. The letters, numbers, and symbols filled the screen, and Deiderick stared at it until it all blurred together. He hated himself for succumbing to the pressure placed on him by his family but knew he would hate himself even more if he couldn't figure this out. "Run the hormone simulation."

"Running simulation."

A screen showing how the emoji app implanted in the cranium popped on the screen.

He began casually walking around his office while the screen ran three thousand scenarios. Deiderick poured a cup of coffee and sat back in his leather chair. He was just about to relax when he heard, "Simulation Fail."

"Crap ." Deiderick went back and looked at all of the code that was on his screen. He tinkered around with it again and then called out, "Run hormone simulation."

"System Fail, Fatal."

This is what they want to push out to the public, huh?

"Call Family" Deiderick's voice was tense. His communication system located his family. Each member of the Dollard family had the implant tucked behind their ear. They immediately stopped what they were doing when they received the call. Deiderick could see an image of all of them on his screen. "I will probably need six months to a year to work out these kinks. I will not push out a project that is potentially fatal."

"Dad, we don't have that kind of time," Damion replied.

"Honey, why are you making this so difficult? You work best under pressure. I am sure things will be fine." Janice was in a sundress playing with her precious poodle, Mittens.

"I need a year," Deiderick demanded and then clicked off of his device and returned to the screen, hoping to find the kink.

While Deiderick was in his office, trying to work everything out, the rest of his family had a meeting.

Janice Dollard was in the yard playing with Mittens when she used her implant to call her children. "Please call Damion and Tyler."

"Calling Damion and Tyler."

"Hey, Mom."

"Boys, meet me in the east wing conference room. I want to discuss something with you."

"Sure thing," Tyler replied. Tyler walked the long hallway heading toward the east wing. "Good afternoon Barrett."

Barrett was in the hallway spinning his electronic billy club rhythmically. "Hi, Tyler. How's it going?"

"It's going well," Tyler replied and continued to head in the direction of the east wing meeting room.

Barrett was headed toward Deiderick's office to check on him, but when he saw that Damion was headed toward the east wing, Barrett decided to change direction and follow the Dollard boys.

He stayed several feet behind and continued to casually look in other rooms so as not to draw attention to himself. He looked at the gardens and saw Janice, Tyler, and Damion gathered together, managing to find each other before arriving at the east wing. They were talking in a very low tone in the one place where the security cameras were not able to view.

Barrett didn't want to miss any of the conversations and quickly pulled out a voice-amplifying camera. It looked like a bee buzzing around and landing on a flower near the gathering.

Barrett pressed the implant that he had located behind the ear and did his best to record the conversation. He overheard Tyler say, "Dad wants a year, and I have never seen him this adamant before. I think we need to just give it to him and back off a bit."

"Mom, if we don't get on it now, I think we will be missing a prime opportunity to capitalize. We are at about 75% of the world's population with the implant. We are projected to reach 80% by the end of the quarter. The new president is in office, and there is public fear that the new economic system will have a detrimental effect on consumers." Damion used the time piece on his arm to flash projections in the air. "Look, all I am saying is that none of us know the impact this One World Dollar may have, we need to get in while our dollar still holds value."

"I agree, but your father is being very stubborn." Janice sat down in a wrought iron garden chair and continued to pet Mittens.

Tyler threw his hands in the air. "I don't like where this is heading. Dad has always made the right decisions at the right time. Besides, based on what I'm reading, there is no way we will get all of the nations to agree by the end of the year."

"You may be right, but what if you're not?" Damion turned to his mom Janice. "Look, Mom, it may be best to override Dad on this one. He isn't the majority owner of DEAD anymore...only at 49%."

"Yes, but that means that we will have to get all the other members of the board to agree to release the project early, and Dad has a lot of loyal followers," Tyler reminded his family.

"Let's just wait and see if he is able to work out the glitch soon--give it three months, and if we don't feel your father is ready to make the leap, we will make the decision for him."

The family disbanded. Barrett called for the bee camera, and it buzzed back over to him. He reviewed the recording and headed back down the hall toward Deiderick's office.

"Deiderick," Barrett did the best he could to make it down the hallway quickly without looking suspicious. "Deiderick, permission to enter your office."

"Permission granted." Both sets of doors opened, and Barrett burst through.

"I have something I think you need to see." The little bee-like camera zoomed up in the air and projected the recorded conversation on the walls of Deiderick's office.

"So, they want to override me, huh?" Deiderick did his best not to show how hurt he was to hear that his family was planning to go against him. "Thank you for bringing this to me, Barrett. That's why you are my top advisor."

Barrett was about to head out the door when Deiderick called him back.

"Hey," Deiderick's face was serious.

"Yes, sir?"

"If my family does this, they will ruin the brand I have worked so hard to create. Protect the brand at any cost, do you understand me?"

"Yes, sir," Barrett said, giving a salute and walking out of the room.

From that moment forward, Deiderick decided to speak about his projects less and less. They are not the only ones with a secret, Deiderick thought.

Chapter 32: Secrets

Betrayal, Secrets, and Lies are common in the last days. (A Warning from the Writ)

The DEAD Company was about ten years old when Deiderick began to notice something strange. It seemed that many people in the YSW, especially politicians, historians, the medical industry, and businesses, started altering reports. What they didn't know was that Deiderick would receive notifications every time a document was altered from the original text. This happened shortly after it was illegal to print and use paper unless it was approved. Soon, people began stamping the DEAD company label on digital documents because the DEAD company had a reputation for putting out the best and most accurate information. This infuriated Deiderick, who began to see his company name be attached to lies.

Instead of putting out a public statement, he decided to leak material through a company he called Readers Publishing. Through Readers Publishing, he could send out the original printed texts to those who were willing to still seek the truth.

Deiderick always had the suspicion that his family would sabotage him, but after viewing the recorded conversation his wife and children had behind his back, Deiderick decided to release a few journals, writings, and books to Readers Publishing. He had been writing in his journal for years as a form of therapy and started a book called, Behind the Mind of Deiderick Dollard. He never thought he would have a reason to release such intimate thoughts until today.

If somehow my family managed to go behind my back and push out the Emoji app, then someone out there would know the truth, Deiderick thought. "Book app activate," Deiderick called out his book writing application and began speaking. The book app took everything he was saying and turned it into printed text. Deiderick called out his first sentence, "All I wanted was more time, but it wasn't good enough for them."

Chapter 33: The Mystery Man

Protect your heart and stay mysterious. Don't let anyone who doesn't do what is right know how you are. (A Warning from the Writ)

Two months after Deiderick found out about his family's secret plan, a panicked knock was at the door. "I am so sorry to bother you, but you need to watch the news now!" Barrett said, panting.

"News On," Deiderick commanded. The screen popped on, immediately playing the latest news story. "A local man was captured after fleeing from the 212 Digital Detox Center. The man set the facility on fire, causing a disruption in the electrical grid surrounding the detox center. There is speculation that this unidentified man was trying to break out his children from the center. Although we are still working to determine the identity of this man, we do know that he was captured by police and placed in a hovercraft. The hovercraft left the detox center and was in the air for less than five minutes before hitting an electrical dead zone at the intersection of 40.7° N longitude, 73.9° W latitude, and 212°Z above the ground. Authorities have blocked off 30° in all directions of the accident as a safeguard. Those flying near the area will be allowed to upgrade their fly zone to bypass the accident. All YSW members will not be charged for elite fly zone status. These privileges will last for three hours. All non-YSW members will have a fee of $300 automatically deducted from their accounts once they enter the elite zone. We should have more coverage on this bizarre accident later today. Now... we turn it over to Guy Holmes for the weather."

"Screen off," Deiderick commanded. Deiderick slammed his fist on his desk. "How can one person cause this much damage? Do we have any additional information on who this is?"

"Not at this time. I was coming because I wanted to know how you would like for me to handle the situation?" Barrett responded.

"Well, first, find out if this man is dead or alive. If they were flying at that altitude, who knows what may have happened to them."

Barrett stared Deiderick in the eye. "We know who the officers were... The only person they can't find is the mystery man that caused all of the damage."

"We know who the officers were?" Deiderick inquired.

"Yes, we believe it was Kevin Richards and Ron Olglesby." Barrett had a very solemn tone to his voice. He had trained with both of them. "They are severely injured. Both of them are in the hospital. It doesn't look good."

"Unbelievable." Deiderick's voice waned off. "Look, I need a little time to process this. Make sure no one interrupts me."

"Yes, sir." Barrett walked out, and the doors automatically closed and locked behind him.

Deiderick still had not worked out the kinks on the Emoji project but found that he could use this unfortunate opportunity to shift everyone's focus. His wife and family would be too distracted with the publicity of Lithorium to focus on Emojis.

Deiderick called out to his computer system, "Lithorium status."

"The status of the Lithorium project is coming up," the computer responded.

"The Lithorium project is nearly complete, 93%. We have run 1,000 simulations, and the battery maintains its longevity."

"Please run the fire simulation again and report back."

"Running fire simulation."

He sat down in his leather chair and began trying to pull up information on the Detox Center until the tests on the Lithorium project were complete. Deiderick typed in:

212 Digital Detox Center fire.

"Pulling information on the Digital Detox Fire."

After a few seconds…The Digital Detox Fire started with flammable liquid and a lighter. Electrical boxes and computer structures were compromised. An assailant was detained, and electrical airfields were compromised because of the fire causing a crash. The two officers were in critical condition. The assailant was not captured. Based on the circumstances of the fire, it is highly likely that the media will be in contact with you. Is there anything else you would like to know?"

"No." Deiderick's mind began drifting on the details of the fire and thinking about how he would address the press when his thoughts were interrupted by the other computer screen. "Simulation complete. Lithorium project considered successful. Are there any other simulations you would like to run? "Yes, but I need to program them first."

Diederick realized that if he had focused on Lithorium, much of the technology on the block near the 212 Digital Detox Center would have been preserved.

I need this to work. This battery source could eliminate the need to recharge. All simulations show that it can pull power from a nearby host. This is it. Deiderick thought to himself. He needed this project. "I need to call the board and share Lithorium with them. This should take their mind off the Emoji project."

A message was sent to the board, and immediately the board room was full of all members, including Janice, Damion, and Tyler.

"We have done it again." Deiderick began his speech. "The DEAD company created an everlasting life battery with the use of Lithorium."

"Begin time simulation," Deiderick commanded.

"Time simulation beginning now." The computer continued to run the newly programmed time simulation, and the Lithorium battery was put to the test. "Approaching 50 years," the computer called out. Deiderick watched the screen to see if the Lithorium had lost power, but it had not.

"Approaching 100 years." Deiderick continued to watch to see the results. The battery was still going strong after 100 years.

"I have run this battery under every scenario I could think of, and I believe we have completed the tests needed to push Lithorium out on the market. In light of our recent hit on the Digital Detox Center, I believe we need to get on this as soon as possible. This type of power will allow an automatic backup of information and is practically indestructible. We may never have to worry about recharging another battery as long as we live." Deiderick was elated.

"Well, honey, you sure are excited, how does it work?" Janice found his excitement sexy.

Deiderick was in his zone and jumped at the opportunity to explain. "Let's say you have a timepiece on your wrist. As the battery starts to die, Lithorium helps transfer the energy you naturally emit from your wrist and transfer it into the watch so that you never need to plug it up. Think about it," Deiderick continued. "We are made of nothing but energy, why not use that energy to keep the devices charged up?"

"Well, Darlin', I think you've got something really special there," Janice said before turning to the board. "Isn't he brilliant?"

"Dad, that's simply fantastic." Tyler chimed in. "You have done it again."

Deiderick was happy to see his Lithorium project may have caused the diversion he needed. "Advertising, I want this to be part of the everlasting life series. Think about how you can rebrand and get back to me with images and slogans as soon as possible," Deiderick continued.

"I want this product to feel new and fresh." He turned to his advertising group, three YSW 20-somethings who were pop-culture gurus. "I need you to take some of our old products and give them a facelift, rebrand them using the Lithorium battery and tag them with the slogan 'Everlasting Life'. You may also need to create new adaptors for old products to use the battery. Charge a lesser amount for adaptors so that we can target people at all price points."

Deiderick continued to call out to the different departments giving them specific instructions. "We will meet in two weeks, and I need to hear everyone's progress. Let me see what you have come up with. I will let my financial advisors know that this will hit the market in a month."

The energy in the room was electric, and members of the DEAD company that went to the meeting felt revitalized after being nervous that Deiderick had grown soft or lacked creativity in his recent projects. Deiderick himself was happy that everyone left the meeting in good spirits and appeared, at least for the moment, to have forgotten about the Emoji project. A project that was still having fatal outcomes.

As the departments dismissed, Janice walked over to her husband. "Wow, babe, I haven't seen you this excited in a long time ," Janice said to her husband. She walked closer to him and whispered, "It was sexy." As much as he didn't want to, Deiderick blushed.

"Dad, I think it's brilliant," Tyler said.

"Yes, it is simply amazing," Damion agreed.

"Wonderful, so, let's sit down like a family and discuss ideas over dinner tonight. You know, like we used to," Deiderick enthusiastically expressed.

"Dad, I would love to, but I have a family obligation. I am not sure if I will make it in time," Damion replied.

"What kind of obligation? You can invite your wife over too. I haven't seen her in a while."

Deiderick's son was handsome. His face was chiseled, and his caramel blonde hair was slightly lighter than his tanned face. He was tall with an athletic frame.

"I don't know if she would be interested. I will see you later, Dad. Excellent work."

Deiderick turned to his other son.

Tyler replied before his father could ask the question again. "I should be able to join you. Let me just wrap up a few things. It is good to see you like this old man. It has been a minute."

"Thanks, I appreciate you gracing me with your presence. You should bring your family as well. I would love to see them," Deiderick said as he patted Tyler on the back.

"Sounds good. What time?" Tyler responded, looking at the time glowing through his skin.

"Let's meet in the west wing dining room at 7:30. That should give me some time to wrap things up."

Tyler left his father's office.

"Dinner in the west wing?" Janice questioned and then continued her thought. "Well, it has been quite some time since we have eaten together as a family. I think I will slip into something a little more. form fitting. I will meet you in the west wing at 7:30." Janice grabbed Deiderick's tie and pulled him in close to her face. She kissed him with her infamous Luscious Red lipstick that she had designed especially for her. A huge red smudge was left on Deiderick's lips. Janice let go of his tie and headed toward the bedroom.

Chapter 34: Missing Dinner Guest

———————◆———————

One day, you will look around and find people who used to be there are
gone. Don't beg for them to come back.
(A Warning from the Writ)

The dinner was delicious. Cornish hens and fresh vegetables from the garden were accompanied by salted caramel cheesecake for dessert paired with Sauvignon Blanc. For the first time in months, there was laughter at the table. Deiderick especially enjoyed his grandchildren but was still bothered that he couldn't see all of them. Damion seemed to be missing from many of the family gatherings. He only came around for business meetings and quickly excused himself right after.

Tonight, Damion was with Brianna. A woman he met while presenting one of the DEAD company's latest security products to a hotel chain. It was an immediate attraction. Damion's wife started having suspicions about his whereabouts about a year ago but was too afraid to ruffle any feathers.

"I am glad that you came over tonight," Brianna whispered. She was lying in bed next to Damion, rubbing on his chest.

"Me too." Damion picked up her hand and kissed it. "You know I can't stay too long. Sasha is expecting me home any minute."

"I hate this. I wish you could stay." Brianna huffed. She loved Damion but realized that his wife and children would always be his priority. "Before you leave, I really need to tell you something."

By this time, Damion had gotten up. He was buttoning his shirt. "Oh yeah, what is it that you want to tell me?"

Damion was watching himself in the mirror adjusting his collar. He swung his tie around his neck and began looping it around.

"I think I'm pregnant."

Damion stopped what he was doing and sat back down on the edge of the bed. Brianna sat up next to Damion.

"So, who do you think is the father?" Damion smugly questioned.

"I can't believe you just asked me that. I have seen you nearly every day for the past three months, and you have the nerve to ask me that?"

"I don't know what you want me to think. I don't know what you do after I leave," Damion said as he stood back up. He was headed toward the door of Brianna's small apartment.

"I would have never guessed that you would act like this. Unbelievable. I kept telling myself that the only reason why you didn't stay was that you didn't want to upset your kids. I never thought it was because you didn't care for me."

Damion was dismissive of Brianna's emotions. "Look, Brianna, you knew what this was when we met. I am sorry it took you so long to get it. Do me a favor --"

A tear rolled down Brianna's cheek. She had been in this place with men before but somehow, she thought she was lucky to be with Damion Dollard. She couldn't believe someone wealthy and handsome was attracted to her. She watched as Damion turned his wrist over. His wrist began to glow. "I have just deposited some money into your account. I need you to take care of this. I can't have something like this getting out there." He finished the last loop on his tie and left her apartment.

In that moment, Damion unknowingly created a monster, and his life would never be the same.

Chapter 35: A Fallen Empire

It will all fall down.
(A Warning from the Writ)

Damion Dollard lived on the Dollard Estate in a massive, although smaller house than his mother and father. In fact, both of the Dollard boys lived on the property. Damion's hovercraft landed on a glowing X in the front yard. He walked up to the door where he was scanned and greeted by their security system.

"Daddy!" Two well-kept, beautiful children ran to their father. Damion scooped four-year-old Bradford up in his arms. Seven-year-old Bella grabbed her dad's hand and dragged him into the kitchen where Sasha was making dinner.

"Smells delicious," Damion said as he put Bradford down.

"Yes, well, I did the best I could trying to keep it warm for you until you got home. Where were you?" Sasha aggressively stirred a spoon inside a pot.

"Bella, why don't you take your brother and go into the playroom. Mommy and Daddy need to talk." Damion said as he prepared for yet another argument with his wife.

"My father came up with a new project that he wants us to push out in a few weeks; we were working on a ton of stuff. Can you please just get off my back?"

"You're lying!" Sasha yelled, pointing the spoon at Damion.

"Seriously? I'm lying!" Damion lashed back.

"You really think I am stupid enough to sit here, and have you made me look like a fool? Who is she?"

"Who is who?" Damion's response was almost convincing.

"Who is the woman that has all of my husband's attention?"

"Look, I don't know what you are talking about."

"All I have to say is, I will NOT let another woman and her baby take away from our children's mouths."

Damion was completely silent. Eyes locked in on Sasha's face.

Sasha continued. "I just received this." Sasha put her hand out toward the wall, and immediately a screen popped up. It began playing the encounter Brianna had with Damion just minutes before. Damion stood there speechless. He could feel his heart beating through his chest.

"Well, love…" Sasha said sarcastically. "It appears you have met your match." Sasha chuckled in a way that made Damion's hair stand up on the back of his neck.

"Damion." Sasha's voice was cold. "I believe you have cheated on me with a lot of different women, but I could never quite get the proof. You really messed up this time. Brianna…she called me. She sent me the video and she told me that she is going to take you and your family for everything they've got. Oh, and thanks to

288

your dad and all of his wonderful advancements," Sasha said mockingly, "she already knows that you're the father."

Damion continued to stand there in silence, but Sasha relentlessly continued. "You better figure out a way to fix it." The conversation left Damion feeling attacked. He knew he should only be mad at himself, but, in true YSW fashion, Damion grew furious and tried to find a way to blame anyone and everyone else for what he did. When Sasha left the room, Damion made a phone call.

"Brianna."

"Calling Brianna." The implant behind his ear started to glow.

Brianna didn't say hello. Instead, she answered by saying, "I see your wife has given you my message."

"You evil witch," Damion whispered.

"Sweetie--" Brianna chuckled. "I would think you would learn to speak to the mother of your child better than that."

"What is it you want from me?"

"Well, I wanted you, but you're a selfish piece of crap and now that I see who you really are, I don't want to be with someone like that!." Brianna belted out a psychotic laugh.

"I just want to make sure that my baby and I will be taken care of."

"You want money?" Damion asked. "I can give you

money." "I don't know if I just want money. Feels so.

....impersonal, like

my baby is less valuable than your other children."

"So, what are you saying?"

"I was thinking about something more significant. I want my baby to be part of the Dollard family. Maybe even own a part of the company."

"Absolutely not."

"I don't know if you have a choice. Do you know how easy it would be for me to go to the media and tell them that Deiderick Dollard's son is a piece of crap? The entire world worships your family like they are gods. I will see to it that your family's empire all comes down."

"Brianna, why are you bringing my family into this?"

"It's my family now too, Damion. That's what I don't think you seem to understand. So, this is how this is going to work. My baby will have your last name and 5% of your share in your upcoming Emoji project that you were so willing to tell me about."

"My dad is not ready to push that project out anymore. So you are going to have to come up with something else."

"Nope, sorry. I know that project is going to be huge. I know that it will make way more money than I could think to ask for. My child, excuse me, our child, deserves the best."

"Whatever," Damion scoffed.

"Make sure your daddy gets that project pushed out. You have eight months before our baby arrives ," Brianna said and quickly got off the call.

Damion grabbed a glass from his wine bar and poured a dry red wine all the way to the top. He sat at the table and drank until the bottle was gone.

While Damion was sulking in his house on the Dollard estate, the head of security was in his quarters just 100 yards away, looking at footage from the Digital Detox break-in.

"Pull cameras on 71st street."

Barrett looked closer at the surveillance footage. He was trying to discover the identity of the mystery man. The fire managed to knock out all of the power of the cameras near the Digital Detox center, so Barrett began pulling footage from cameras several blocks away to see what he could find. "Zoom 50," Barrett said. The camera zoomed in to see an olive-skinned man running from the hovercraft crash. "Details." As Barrett called for details, the voice-activated security system began to run profiles of men who looked similar. Within seconds, the camera identified the mystery man. "Solomon Wiseman, 62 years old. Prior criminal history, silence order protester, arrested and released three weeks ago. Currently on probation."

Immediately Barrett saved the footage and sent it to Deiderick. Then he ran to the main house toward Deiderick Dollard's office. He was scanned before the two sets of doors to Deiderick's office opened.

"Did you get the footage I just sent?"

"No. I was working on something else. What did you send me?" Deiderick shifted his head from the screen on the right to the screen on the left. He pulled up the message that Barrett sent.

"I have finally found the footage of the man who caused the fires."

"I thought we didn't have any footage, has anyone else seen it?" Deiderick clicked the link and saw a very distant image of an older man. Right away, Deiderick felt very conflicted. He knew that he should want to protect his company. He knew that he should have been angry with the mysterious man who caused so much damage to his systems, but that wasn't the case at all, he felt an odd connection to him.

"No, this is the first footage I was able to collect. Just got a small side profile from a camera several blocks away. All of the surveillance in the nearby area was affected by the electrical outage. It is amazing. I don't know how he was able to do it."

Deiderick was amazed as well. So, who is it?"

"His name is Solomon Wiseman. He was arrested a while back for the silence order protest. He is currently on probation. This is definitely a violation. Do you want me to send out the police to arrest him? He may end up spending a few months in confinement for this infraction."

Deiderick knew that Barrett was right. "No need to send the police. I want to handle this on my own."

"This man is dangerous. He is trying to destroy the YSW. Look, if it is alright with you, I am going to beef up our security. We can't take the risk."

"Yes, yes, that is fine." Deiderick still felt uneasy with the decision but didn't want to let on. "Barrett, from this point on, I want to be the one to do the tracking on Mr. Solomon Wiseman. He is trying to ruin my empire...I need to deal with it."

"Yes, sir ," Barrett replied. "I am going to do a security walk. I am taking the bee with me."

"Sure, absolutely. Whatever you need. I think I am going to head out. I have been working non-stop. Just need a bit of a break." Deiderick rubbed his eyes. They had been staring at screens most of the day. He walked over to the bathroom, located in his office, and put his face over the sink. The sink was automatically set to his favorite temperature. Several small jets spritzed his face. When he looked into the mirror, small fans located on the side of the mirror began to blow.

Deiderick left his office that evening and walked down the long hallway. Their estate was large, but it seemed as if Janice was always around.

"Oh, there you are. I was just headed to your office."

Deiderick just looked at Janice with a blank stare.

Janice nervously smiled. "I just finished speaking with Damion. He was telling me that he is excited about the Lithorium project."

"That's great. I am too," Deiderick replied.

"But…"

Deiderick was annoyed. "But what?"

"But he doesn't want us to lose focus on the Emoji app. He thinks the Lithorium will improve products that we already have out, but that Emoji app will not only have more people rush out to purchase the third eye so they can feel the emotions of the app, but he believes it will be the biggest money maker since we created the third eye."

"First of all, the third eye has been redesigned in a way that I think is tacky. Wearing it in the middle of your forehead...horrid."

"I agree, dear; that's why I have mine here" Janice pushed back her hair showing the implant located behind the ear. "It looks cheap and tacky in the middle. This is a much better place for it," she said as she tapped her implant. "You are so smart."

"Well, my other issue is that when the third eye went behind the ear, I had better control of where we attached the device to the limbic system. Now, because everyone is wearing it in the center of their skull, I am nervous that the wrong move will cause some unwanted side effects. So, until the simulations come back with no issues, I don't think it is best to push out the Emoji app. I need everyone to focus on the Lithorium project for right now."

Deiderick thought the conversation was over but heard, "Deiderick, Look—" Janice sashayed over to him. She smelled sweet. It was the fragrance she often wore to get her way. It sickened Deiderick. "I think that Damion is in trouble. I was just talking to him, and he seemed panicked, frustrated. He really wants the Emoji project out there soon. He brought up some good points."

"You know what that means don't you?" Deiderick was not fazed by Janice's plea.

"No, what does it mean?"

"Your son has done something stupid and wants us to pay for it. Let him tough it out. Stop babying him, and maybe he will learn from his mistakes. Look, I am getting older, Janice. I thought I would be at an age where I could relax, maybe turn the company over to you or the boys, but...I am not so sure about that anymore."

"You don't trust me?" Janice inquired.

He said nothing but did his best to mask his feelings behind a forced smile.

"You can trust me, my darling," Janice whispered in Deiderick's ear and then followed with a kiss on the cheek. "Are you coming to bed?"

He knew she was trying to persuade him to push through with the Emoji app. He decided to retreat back to his office, saying anything to get away. "No, I have a lot to work on if I am going to get the Emoji project up and running soon."

"I am glad you are going to work on the project, but you can take a break for tonight." Janice caressed Deiderick's chest with neatly polished red nails. "Suit yourself. Make sure you come tuck me in tonight." She turned around, making a last attempt to grope her husband before walking down the hall to her bedroom.

Deiderick went back to his office and plopped down in his favorite leather chair, hoping to view the screen and take his mind off of everything for the evening.

"Would you like the full experience?" the screen asked.

"No."

The virtual reality did not turn on. Instead, the screen ran the local news. Deiderick's mind was racing. His thoughts shifted from the conversation that Barrett reported to him, to the discovery of the mystery man named Solomon, to the pressure he felt to get the Emoji project out to the public.

While Deiderick was thinking, the news discussed the silence order protest, the digital detox fire, and the one world currency. The news stories continued; deaths from the artificial vegetation, the world wide suicides, and an International Society of One Race mixer that was coming up soon.

How did we get to this place? Deiderick thought. Why does it seem like I am responsible for most of this? I don't want to do this anymore. I need out. Within the same minute, Deiderick received a notification letting him know that his stock went up by 5.7%. He knew why. Can't trust anyone. This is ridiculous. His mind jumped again, "Solomon, Solomon, Solomon, you are a force to be reckoned with. Knew you were special. Much braver than me. Single-handedly trying to take down the system." Deiderick looked at the footage that Barrett left him. He zoomed the footage in and out. "Hmm," Deiderick was talking to himself in the quiet of his office. "All the threats I sent to him, the messages, the pressure from Kevin, much braver than me."

Deiderick didn't know there was anyone in the world left who had enough courage not to give in to the YSW. Even more impressive was that he was brave enough to try and take the system down. Deiderick knew Solomon should have been killed long ago, but he wanted to keep Solomon safe. The more

Solomon passed Deiderick's tests and ignored the threats, the more Deiderick realized that Solomon was the person he needed to help him.

"Track Solomon Wiseman in the 212 Area Code."

"Tracking Solomon Wiseman." The system immediately sent a small droid with a blue piercing light into the window of Solomon. Immediately Deiderick saw Solomon sitting in his living room, looking at the picture Karina had taken of their last beach vacation. There were tears in his eyes.

"Scan house," Deiderick commanded the droid. The infrared system scanned the house for another warm body but found nothing.

Deiderick continued to watch Solomon look at the picture of his family.

"Wiseman family history."

"Wife Kristen died from stomach cancer. Together they have three children. Two sons named Kyle and Knox both reside at the 212 Digital Detox Center, and daughter Karina attending the prestigious YSW university."

"YSW association of each family member?" Deiderick asked.

"Solomon is not associated with the YSW."

"The YSW has attempted partnership 257 times."

Deiderick knew he made many of those attempts himself but had not realized his level of forcefulness. "He has turned us down 257 times?"

"That is correct. Would you like to initiate another attempt."

"No. Please run a family association."

"Wife Kristen had no association with the YSW. Daughter Karina is a YSW member and one of the top-ranking students in her class. She is expected to graduate in 2.5 years and will make a great addition to the DEAD company. Two sons, Kyle and Knox are not currently affiliated with the YSW, but they are attending the 212 Digital Detox center and will most likely join by the end of the year with the program in which they are currently enrolled."

"I know he has two children at the Digital Detox center."

"Yes, that is correct."

"Explains why he was breaking in." Deiderick exhaled loudly. "Those detox centers are like brainwashing stations. I get it. I know why he doesn't want his children there. Pull Solomon's call log."

"Pulling the call log...He appears to only attempt to call his daughter Karina or the Digital Detox center."

"Interesting. How many minutes was the last call to the digital detox center?"

"Last call was seven minutes in length and took place a week before the fire."

"I bet he heard something that upset him and wanted to get his children back."

"I need to keep an eye on him. He may be exactly what I need. Launch the drones and follow him but be discreet."

"Launching drones now. Is there anything else?"

"No...I think that is all. Sign off ," Deiderick said, and the computer screens went black. Deiderick fell asleep in his chair.

Crossing Paths
Wiseman, Dollard, Greybottom, Cook and the Others

Chapter 36: The Cats Out of the Bag

Even when the truth comes out, no one will believe it. (A Warning from the Writ)

Deiderick watched Solomon's daily interactions and was shocked to see he was a simple man. A regular routine of going to work, stopping by Barkleys during talking hours, and a late-night stroll to an old convenience store on 5th street.

"Can you get into the convenience store without being noticed?" Deiderick asked the computer system controlling the drone.

"Yes." The drone pushed through a small crack in a transom located at the top of the door. It was covered with red dust. A few dust sprinkles hit the floor, but Quantas didn't notice, and Solomon's back was turned away from the door. He was whispering to her.

The drone quietly inched its way over and heard Solomon say, "Do you have a newspaper?"

Deiderick had his eyes glued to the cameras and watched as Quantas opened a door with the sign that said cleaning supplies. Both Quantas and Solomon went down the stairs together.

Deiderick sat back in his chair. Hmm...I need to get into that room. It's got to be some secret club or something. Deiderick took note of the phrase. "Do you have a newspaper?"

I have to get in there. Deiderick looked at his schedule and decided he would try to get into the room marked cleaning supplies the following week.

Deiderick thought he could make it through the week without drama, but he was not so lucky.

Monday

"Dad, where are you on the Emoji project?" Damion asked.

Deiderick was too irritated to look up. "Can we just give it a rest? We are not ready for that project yet." Deiderick moved his hands in the air, making his screen change and asked, " Where are we with Lithorium?"

"We are looking good. The commercials have already gone out, and we will have it available to purchase by the end of the week," Damion responded.

"Excellent. Now, keep your focus there, and I am sure everything will work out just fine." Deiderick wanted to dismiss his son, but Damion was nervously clambering around.

"Is there anything else?" Deiderick said, turning his head from the screen and looking directly at his son.

"I need to tell you something."

"What is it?" Deiderick was uninterested until he saw the stress on his son's face. "Okay, Damion, have a seat." Deiderick pointed to a handcrafted wooden chair for his son. He sat down in his favorite leather chair.

Damion put his face in his hands and moved his fingers through his hair. He took a huge deep breath before speaking. "I really messed up."

"How?"

"How do I tell you this?" Damion paced back and forth, " I am going to have another baby."

"Children are a beautiful thing, son. I am sure that Sasha is excited as well. How do Bella and Bradford feel about another sibling?"

"I haven't told them yet."

"Well, I think you should. Is that what you are nervous about? You don't want Bradford to feel like he's not the baby anymore. I remember when we were expecting Tyler. You thought we wouldn't love you anymore." Deiderick chuckled. "I am sure you will be alright." Deiderick patted his son on the back and was about to get out of his chair.

"Dad, have a seat."

Deiderick watched his son squirm around for what seemed like an eternity but was no more than ten seconds.

"I got another woman pregnant."

Silence filled the air.

"I got another woman pregnant, and she wants part of the stake in the Emoji project. You have about seven and a half months to get the project out or else she is planning on going to the media to release a story about our whole family."

"Interesting."

"That's all you have to say?" Damion was confused and frustrated with his father's response.

"What else is there to say? Sounds like you cheated on your wife, told another woman about a project that NO ONE is supposed to know about yet, got that woman pregnant, and now you want me to push a project out that has not cleared my safety checks in order to help you? You are an entitled, sorry excuse for a man. You got yourself into this, you get yourself out! I am not helping you fix this. You don't think I get threats like this every day? I don't give a damn if that woman wants your entire share of profits from the project. You do what you need to do, but it better not impact me, or my brand!"

Damion looked at his father. He had never seen his father this upset.

"Dad, I want to lawyer up. I need to quiet this before it gets out there."

"So, you are trying to cover up your dirt, and you want me to help. Well, to be honest, all of my grandchildren are entitled to a piece of the Dollard fortune. So, I say, give her what she wants."

"That's your answer. Give her what she wants. She was a loose woman. She knew exactly what she was getting into, and I believe this was her plan from the beginning. She wanted a piece of our empire."

"And guess what?" Deiderick smirked. "She got exactly what she planned. If you were half as forward-thinking as she seems to be, I would have turned the company over to you long ago. Now, if you will excuse me, I have other things to do, and it sounds like you have some things you need to take care of as well. I would start with coming clean with your wife."

Deiderick said his piece and walked out of the room.

302

Tuesday

"Screen on."

"For the first time in history, people are starting to question Dollard's products. The Digital Detox fires have caused public concern about the quality of Dollard's technology."

"Yes, Sara, you are correct, we have never seen a failure of this type, but rumor has it that this could have all been a stunt to increase sales of his latest project, the Lithorium, everlasting life battery. I mean, the coincidence that immediately after having the largest power outage in the 212 area code, Deiderick Dollard and the DEAD company release a battery that will never die? Very strategic, Mr. Dollard."

"Screen off."

Wednesday

We are here with the late-breaking news. According to a reliable source, Sasha Dollard, wife of Damion Dollard, has filed for divorce after allegations that Damion Dollard is expecting a child by a woman named Brianna Gainer. If this divorce happens, it could be devastating to the Dollard Empire.

A source close to the family says that Sasha is devastated after hearing the news of her husband, and although she signed a prenuptial agreement, she is still entitled to a sum close to one billion dollars.

Thursday

"What the heck did you do?" Tyler asked his brother. "All you had to do was keep it in your pants. What's wrong with Sasha? Why would you do that to her, to us?"

"I wasn't thinking, alright. I didn't know this would happen." Damion was frustrated and had enough of his brother acting like he was the golden child. "I don't need this from you right now.

What I need is for you to help me convince Dad to get the Emoji project out so Brianna can leave me and my wife alone."

"I don't think Dad is going to do that right now," Tyler replied.

"He's going to have to or else we are going to lose everything."

Friday

Deiderick ordered a Code Red outfit. He didn't have to have one because he lived above the red haze, but today, he planned on flying his hovercraft down where the others lived. He parked his hovercraft in an alley about a block away from the convenience store.

"Clear," Deiderick called out, and the hovercraft exterior went clear, blending in with the surroundings. Hiding his hovercraft and walking down 5th street to the convenience store, he found himself amazed by a world he didn't frequent often.

He got out of the hovercraft shortly before putting his mask on and immediately started coughing. He fixed his mask over his face and peered through the goggles. He was shocked about how difficult it was to see. I have got to get it together before people can tell I don't belong, Deiderick thought to himself. He straightened up his jacket and shifted his mask one more time before walking out of the alley and down 5th street.

Within minutes, Deiderick found himself outside of the store. He nervously opened the door to meet Quantas. "What do you want?" Quantas said with her back turned away from the door.

"Yes, I wanted to know if you have a newspaper."

Quantas immediately turned around. "I don't believe I have seen you here before. Who sent you an invite?" It was a trick question, none of the invites had names on them. They were just signed with the initials EAD.

"Um...I don't. I don't remember who sent me an invite. I was just told to ask for a newspaper." Deiderick could not believe how nervous he was. He could feel beads of sweat on his forehead. The Code Red outfit didn't make it any better.

Quantas let out a loud laugh. "Ha, well, that was the correct answer. So, you are looking to become part of the EAD?"

"Sure, yes," Deiderick replied.

Quantas turned around and rummaged through a few stacks of miscellaneous items on a countertop and then found the EAD membership contract. "Here, you are going to need to review this before joining."

Deiderick took off his mask to read over the contract. All of his responsibilities flashed before his eyes. How can I live a life without technology? I guess most of it is job-related, but that's kinda, that's cheating. How would they even know if I was using technology or not? I can do everything else on this contract. Oh, the heck with it. Deiderick picked up the pen and signed.

"Wait a minute. You look so familiar to me. I swear I have seen your face before." Quantas stared Deiderick in the eye.

"I'm nobody special. Just found out about the EAD a little while back and thought this might be a place where someone like me could feel comfortable."

"Someone like you?" Quantas chuckled. "You would have to have more tatters and tears in your Code Red outfit to fit in with the likes of us." Quantas laughed. "Hey, you seem like you will be alright. Come on." Quantas ushered him down the stairs to the secret meeting room, and Deiderick did his best to look inconspicuous. "It may take a while for you to get comfortable. Not the most welcoming place. We don't come here for the aesthetics. We come here for the fellowship."

"Oh, this place is just fine. I think I am just going to sit over here." Deiderick pointed to a barstool over in the corner.

"Fine by me."

It wasn't long before Solomon came down the stairs.

A gleeful "Hey!" was shouted by several members of the EAD when Solomon came down the stairs.

"Hey, how's it going, Ralph?"

"I am doing well. How are things going for you?"

"Pretty good. So, any more dreams you need to tell us about?"

The other members of the EAD put down their chess pieces, books, and anything else they were working on to listen to what Solomon had to say.

"I have been having a vision about devices and...um...maybe some type of app...but it's not clear yet. I am sure that it will continue to haunt me until I understand it. It wouldn't be right if I didn't have a few sleepless nights." Solomon chuckled.

"So, I heard you got more time than Quantas and Mediana," Anthony, an elder who was playing cards, said.

"Just longer probation after they found out I was the mastermind of the plan.." Solomon lifted up his pant leg and showed where he was tagged. "Not too bad, though. It will only go off if I leave the 212 area code."

Mediana popped her head from her usual spot near the kitchen. "As liberating as the experience was, I never, ever want to go to jail again."

Deiderick just looked around at all of the small talk. He could tell that Solomon had asserted himself as a leader of the pack. He looked at how everyone seemed to light up when he came into the room. He watched as Solomon talked to everyone, played a few rounds of chess, and playfully bickered back and forth with Quantas. Solomon was there for about two hours before he put his coat on and walked up the stairs. Quantas followed.

While Deiderick was taking it all in below the convenience store, Solomon had made observations of his own.

"Who is the new guy? Did he look familiar to you?" Solomon inquired.

"I thought he did, but I couldn't place his face. Someone must have sent him the invite. He knew the secret code."

"Ah. Well," Solomon laughed. "I think we may need to update our security measures. The code thing is stupid."

"Got you in the door," Quantas joked.

Solomon finished putting on his mask and headed home. About five minutes later, Deiderick came up the stairs.

"You leaving too?" Quantas asked.

"Yeah...so...when's the next meeting?" Deiderick asked.

"Same time next week. See you later, Mr…?" Quantas paused. "I'm sorry. I forgot your name already."

"Deiderick." He thought about providing an alias but figured what difference it makes.

Deiderick walked back down 5th avenue. The screens were nonstop, and most of them were filled with images of him and his family drama. There were speculations about how much money his company could lose because of the impending divorce, pictures of Damion splitting from Sasha, and an entire entertainment segment showing a mashup of Brianna and Damion's future baby. Deiderick could not wait to get back into his hovercraft.

307

"Visible," Deiderick commanded. The hovercraft began to appear. Deiderick hopped in and headed home, excited about his next EAD meeting.

Chapter 37: Deiderick and Solomon's Encounter

Do not assume the nature of a
person. (A Warning from the Writ)

Six meetings or three months after Deiderick's first encounter with the EAD and he soon realized that Solomon was looking at him suspiciously. Deiderick remained in the corner of the room and sat quietly. He didn't know if he should approach Solomon or just sit back. Deiderick was used to being in charge of his company but being around 'real' people made him feel a little uncomfortable. He didn't have to wait long before Solomon got out of his seat and headed in his direction.

"It took me a while, but I was able to place your face. You are Mr. Deiderick Dollard." Solomon felt animosity toward Deiderick, but he still stuck out his hand.

"Yes, and you are Solomon Wiseman." Deiderick shook Solomon's hand.

"Ah, so you have used some of your gadgets to do some research on me. I guess I should be flattered." Solomon chuckled.

"I must admit, I have been very intrigued by the man who was able to penetrate my security systems," Deiderick continued. "I know a little about you, now, what do you know about me?"

Solomon was a little hesitant to tell him everything he knew, but after his dream last night, Solomon had to ask. "So, are you working on a new project?"

"We are. We are indeed." A long pause filled the air before Deiderick began speaking again. Deiderick looked around at all of the Elders. "You understand that you are the first person to speak to me in this place. I was beginning to feel like no one wanted me here."

"Well, I can't lie. I am a little confused as to why someone like you would want to be here with the rest of the commoners," Solomon chuckled, looking around.

"Hey, speak for yourself," Quantas interjected. She was sitting near the top of the stairs so she could quickly go back to the convenience store if someone were to come by.

"Well, you know that he's not like the rest of us. So compared to him, we are commoners," Solomon said, hoping to get an answer from Deiderick this time.

"To be honest, this place reminds me so much of what the world was like before devices took over," Deiderick explained.

Solomon was astonished. "I can't believe you would feel that way. You are one of the reasons why we're in the position we are now." Solomon felt good being able to get that off his chest. He was even more shocked when it appeared that Deiderick did not take offense.

"You have no idea how all of this works. It is not that simple. I am one man on a board of 12 others who also make decisions. My wife and children are on the board, and they are constantly going against me. It feels like I don't have a voice anymore. The technology is moving so fast that I can't even keep up with everything anymore." Deiderick placed his head in his hands and then continued. "The new project, I just...I just don't...I can't support it, It's not ready yet, but I don't know what to do. Everyone wants it out now."

When Solomon heard this, he knew exactly what project he was talking about, and all the images of his dream began to make sense. Solomon started whispering so that the others could not hear.

"This latest project--does it have anything to do with Emojis?"

"How did you know?" Deiderick asked.

"I have these dreams. They're all coming true."

"Yes, the latest project is going to be the biggest thing to ever be released in the twenty-second century. But what is your dream showing you?" Deiderick's expression was a mix of curiosity and concern.

"Well, your company has already begun to advertise the release of the most authentic Emoji to ever exist, but the YSW don't know just how real it will become. The design your company created will essentially provide the actual feeling behind the Emoji icon. So, for example, if you send the Emoji blowing a kiss or a heart Emoji, the device will release a feeling of love to someone. Or, if you send a sad face, then the person receiving it will feel sadness. But how do you plan to do this? I can't quite figure out how it all works exactly."

"Wow, you're pretty good. Your dream is extremely accurate." Deiderick was impressed. He looked around before continuing. "I

311

don't know if you quite understand the level at which everyone is connected to their device," Deiderick responded in a very low tone. "But for many, it's like their lifeline. Nearly eighty-five percent of the world's population has a device connected to their cranium. We literally control people's minds."

"I can't imagine having that much control," Solomon said.

"The pressure is unbelievable, and I don't know if I want any of it anymore. This new project, the Emojis...it scares me," Deiderick said.

"What makes this one so different?"

"The Emoji project involves attaching different chemical hormones to the Emojis' pictures. For example, serotonin and dopamine, the hormones associated with being happy or feeling joy, are embedded into the Emojis with hearts and smiles. The hormone is released to the receiver of the icon when they open their message. Pheromones, the hormones responsible for a feeling of euphoria, are released when someone receives an Emoji with some sort of sexual connotation. And because everyone has these devices connected to their brain, we can literally send the hormone directly to the limbic system, the part of the brain that controls emotions, but we have the ability to remove chemicals from the brain as well. If a person receives an Emoji that is unhappy, instead of providing serotonin to the brain, we are actually physically removing a bit of it. At first, the project seemed amazing, but now I'm fearful. This was never how any of this was supposed to happen."

"I'm pretty sure that you're not supposed to give me this much detail. So why are you telling me all of this?" Solomon asked.

"I don't know...I...I guess I needed to feel heard. It is ridiculous to be the head of a company and have no one listen to me. My wife, my children--they know that this will make billions of dollars, so they couldn't care less what I think. It doesn't seem to matter that we've crossed the line." Deiderick sighed.

"The dream I had tells me that your project will ultimately lead to the end of civilization."

"How?" Deiderick was curious.

"Let me ask this first--are you planning a worldwide release of this phenomenon in a few months?"

"That's what we are discussing now."

"And you have no idea what something like this would do on a global level?"

"I can only imagine," Deiderick responded with angst. "I have got to stop it from getting out there, but I don't know how."

Solomon could see the desperation in his eyes. "No matter what you do, it cannot be stopped. This is all part of a much bigger plan. So many nights, I have been plagued with these dreams about the end of the world. I have spent so much time trying to fight the inevitable, but I gave up a while ago, and I suggest that you do the same."

"Seriously? That's your answer? Just give up?" Deiderick slammed his hand on the high-top table. People started looking at him, so he started to whisper, "You can actually sit there and tell me that the end of the world is coming? It's all because of my company's project, and you don't want me to do anything about it? This is ridiculous!"

"I have my reasons; besides, it is not going to make a difference. Jah is more powerful than all of us. Everything is in His control. I suggest that you read the Writ and make peace with Jah."

"You are not the man I thought you were. I have watched you come here for weeks and tell everyone about your dreams and your visions of the future. You seemed so concerned about the state of the world, but you're all talk. I just shared my company's secret with you and all you can do is tell me to let it happen? You are NOT Jah; You are NOT our Creator! If you don't help me, the death of an entire civilization will be on your hands. I couldn't live with myself knowing that I could have done something. I thought you would feel the same. What reason do you have to allow the destruction of the world?"

"You don't know me. You don't get to speak to me like this." Solomon was about to get up from the table. Deiderick pulled him back down.

"You are correct. I don't know you, and the only thing you know about me is what the media says. But this is me. I am a man who has made mistakes, but I am also a man who would like to fix them. And I need your help to do that," Deiderick begged.

"It's not that I don't want to help. Look, I guess I will see what I can do. But my story is so different from yours. Unlike you, I lost my wife to cancer and all three of my children because of the YSW." Solomon was frustrated but was surprised by Deiderick's passion to stop the Emoji project.

Solomon spent the next hour telling Deiderick all about the death of his wife, the silence order Protest, and his attempted break-in of the Digital Detox center. Although Deiderick was well aware that it was Solomon who caused the blackout, he did his best to act surprised.

Deiderick thought he was making headway in convincing Solomon to help him stop the Emoji project. He couldn't get a read on the former mystery man. In his discomfort, Deiderick changed the subject with small talk. Solomon passively engaged, still thinking about all that Deiderick told him about the project and his plea for help. Once the forced conversation left both men uncomfortable, they got up from the table and went their separate ways.

"Where have you been?" Janice asked with her arms folded. "Don't tell me you are doing what Damion has done. Do you have another woman, Deiderick? If you do, I swear, the type of malicious things Brianna is doing to Damion will not compare to what I will do to you."

"I was out."

"Out doing what?" Janice was strong in her conviction that Deiderick was cheating. She couldn't imagine that a woman like her could not have her husband come to bed or spend time with her unless there was another woman in the picture.

"I was just out. I haven't flown down to the Inbetween in a while."

"Seriously, you have been going to the Inbetween. What's so good about the Inbetween?"

"Just wanted to see it."

"Well, I don't believe you." Janice took out the timepiece on her wrist and said, "Give me your arm."

"Seriously? You're really going to use the lie detector app?"

"Yes." Then Janice put her index and middle finger on Deiderick's wrist.

"I can't believe you are doing this." Deiderick was no longer frustrated, now he thought Janice was being ridiculous.

"First question...Are you cheating on me with another woman?"

Deiderick rolled his eyes. "No." Deep down, he hated to admit that he thought her jealousy was kinda cute.

"Question two, have you really been going to the Inbetween"

"Yes."

"So far so good. One more question. Do you still love me?"

Deiderick paused. He had to slow his heart rate and think clearly. He didn't know if he still loved her, at least not in the way he used to. "Yes," Deiderick said slowly.

"Well, you passed." Janice took her fingers off Deiderick's wrist and gave him a huge kiss on the cheek.

"I am sorry. It's just that you have been so distant. I just started feeling like you didn't love me anymore."

"Now you know. So, what has been going on around here?"

Janice jumped at the opportunity to have a conversation with her husband.

"Let's start with Damion. Apparently, Sasha is going to go through with the divorce, and she is taking the children with her. She, of course, wants to move off the estate but is demanding that Damion buy her a house."

Deiderick responded, "The truth is that he shouldn't have done what he did. He has plenty of money to buy the house."

"Well, he says it's the principle of the whole thing. She signed a prenup, and she is not fulfilling the contract."

"But he is the one that messed up. So what did he think was going to happen?"

Janice was very protective over her boys and didn't understand Deiderick's lack of empathy. "Anyway, Brianna has been threatening Damion and Sasha. Did you see her interview this morning?"

"What interview?" Deiderick inquired but didn't really care. He has been dealing with the media his entire life, this situation was no different.

"Apparently, the press is asking her what she wants for her child, oh, we found out it was a boy, and she blabbed all about the Emoji project and how her son will be born into wealth."

Deiderick chuckled. "So it is her fault the world knows about the project? It has nothing to do with the fact that you and the boys decided to advertise for the Emojis even though I didn't approve?"

"Well, I just figured that it should come from us first and not from some woman trying to dig her claws into our fortune."

"Oh...okay...I see...you were looking out for the family." Deiderick looked into his wife's eyes.

Janice was a little hurt. "Look, I know you don't agree with us moving forward, but everything I do is for the best. I want the best for our family and now that I know you still love me, maybe when all of this blows over, we can take a vacation. You have been working so hard; we just need to get away." Janice nuzzled next to Deiderick, and he put his arm around her. "I am so stressed out. I have been dealing with calls from the media, droids flying around, hovercrafts trying to get pictures. I think a vacation will be good for us."

Deiderick knew that deep down, Janice really did feel she was doing the best for the family, and the lie detector helped him realize there was still love for her. An emotion he hadn't admitted to himself. "Maybe you're right. Maybe we just need to get away."

Janice's perfectly plump red lips turned up, and her immaculately white teeth glimmered. "So, are you coming to bed tonight?"

"Yes, but let me do a few things first. I will be in there shortly."

After Janice left, Deiderick started to realize that the Emoji project couldn't be stopped. He wanted to release more truths in his journal in hopes that when he was gone, his name wouldn't be tarnished.

The Emoji project seems to be moving forward despite my desire to stop it. I traveled to the Inbetween and spoke to a man who told me that it was the will of Jah. He told me that Jah was going to destroy the world and use my app to make it happen.Maybe it is His will, but I don't want to give up hope. I don't want to see the world meet its fate because of my creation. There is something that feels so different about this project than any of the others that I have done in the past. I am a big enough man to admit when I need help. I hope this reaches someone who is brave enough to try anything to save humanity before it's too late.

- Deiderick Dollard

When he finished, he uploaded his journal along with several other writings to the Readers Publishing database and for the first time ever, signed his name, Deiderick Dollard.

When Solomon arrived to work the next day. He and Mike were filling their orders. Bubbles was sitting on Solomon's lap, all of his googly eyes taking in the titles of each text. Solomon kept scrolling through the orders and paused when he saw something extremely peculiar. It was an order with his name on it.

"It's a lot of orders... Alright, Bubbles, go get them." Solomon couldn't believe that there was an order just for him entitled, Behind the Mind of Deiderick Dollard, along with Deiderick Dollard's journals.

The spider-like contraption climbed up the walls to reach books well beyond Solomon's grasp. Before today, Solomon always thought any books written about the DEAD company were by someone hoping to capitalize, but now, the author is listed as Deiderick Dollard, a man who needs nothing and has nothing to gain from these prints. Bubbles placed the book on Solomon's lap. Solomon took the book and slipped it in his pocket, eager to get home and read.

Chapter 38: Solomon's Decision

━━━━━━━◆━━━━━━━

Make sure your decisions are rooted in truth, sound, and just. Every decision leads to righteousness or destruction.
(A Warning from the Writ)

"Hey, oh wow. You have quite the baby bump." Solomon reached his hand out to Aurora.

"Yes, not much longer now." Aurora patted her belly and smiled.

"So, how are you and the guy doing? You know that I need to give him my approval first."

"Not too well. I don't think we are going to end up together. I should have had you check him out before all of this." Aurora looked away.

"Look, there is nothing to be ashamed of. He is the one that needs to feel bad, not you. Besides, you always have me to help you look after the baby."

"Thanks," Aurora smiled.

"I don't want to bring it up, but ...I have noticed you are not using the third eye as much."

"They say it can be harmful during pregnancy. I don't know, I just want the best for my baby. I want him to be a greater person than I ever could be."

"Did you say, him?"

"Yes, I found out it will be a boy. I want a strong name, something that shows my son is smart and brave. I think I want it to start with the letter A."

"Wow, have you thought of anything yet?"

"No, not yet. I haven't found anything that really speaks to me."

"Why the letter A?"

"It's the beginning of the Alphabet. I want him to signify a new beginning for me. Silly, right?" Aurora looked down again.

"No, not silly at all. I think it is good, and I know that he will be an amazing young man."

"Thank you. So, what are you up to?" Aurora asked. She and Solomon stood in the lobby chit-chatting while Jose the AI watched.

"Well, I had an interesting encounter with someone and today, I got a little book from him." Solomon took the book out of his pocket and showed it to Aurora.

"No way! First of all, you have a book, and then it comes from Deiderick Dollard? That's crazy."

"I know, right ? I think I am going to go home and read it," Solomon said.

"Are you kidding? Stop wasting time with me and go. I will catch up with you later. Be prepared to tell me everything!" Aurora smiled and walked out of the lobby.

Solomon got on the lift and went up to the 9th floor. He quickly shed his Code Red outfit and plopped down on the sofa to read the book. It was a quick read. Journal entries no longer than a paragraph dating back about five years ago, not daily entries, just seemed to be thoughts as they came to his head. Through the reading, Solomon learned several things:

1) That Deiderick Dollard had been the one testing Solomon to see if he would give into the pressure of the YSW threats and was impressed when Solomon didn't.

2) It was Deiderick who was releasing all of the texts to Readers Publishing, hoping that there would still be some truth left in the world.

3) That Deiderick genuinely wanted to stop the release of the Emoji app.

Solomon closed the journal, prayed to Jah, and flipped to the Writ. He landed on a scripture that talked about misconception and felt it was Jah sending him a message. He didn't know what he could do to stop the release of the app. In fact, Solomon was pretty sure his efforts would be in vain, but in that moment, Solomon realized that he misjudged Deiderick, and he made a decision to help him, no matter the cost.

Todd Markley

Remember when Barrett was told to look after Solomon? Well, he did. Barrett had been following Solomon for quite some time. So, when Solomon was having his conversation in front of Jose, Solomon didn't realize that someone else was listening. Right after Barrett heard that Deiderick had released journal entries, Barrett became suspicious of both Solomon and Deiderick.

Barrett wasn't quite sure why Solomon was even in the picture at all. He wondered why Deiderick would choose to trust an Inbetweener who broke the law more than him, a guard who has been loyal since he was hired nearly twenty years ago. Barrett couldn't help but to feel a little jealous, and the fact that Deiderick chose to keep his affiliation with Solomon a secret only made him curious as to what other secrets Deiderick was keeping. For the last few months, Barrett thought that Deiderick was being wronged by his family, but maybe it was the other way around. Barrett started to think, maybe Deiderick doesn't want the Emoji project to get out because he is greedy and wants to prevent Damion's mistress Brianna from having any part of the Dollard legacy.

It wasn't long before Barrett had convinced himself that his reasoning must be true. He looked up to Deiderick for twenty years, but after his new discovery, Barrett started to feel that

Deiderick was being selfish and felt bad that Damion's son was being denied what was rightfully his. Barrett believed the best thing was to help Janice and the boys get the Emoji project out to the public and to stop Deiderick and his new friend Solomon.

Chapter 39: The Set Up

No one can be trusted, every situation you encounter, every person you meet, even those who are closest to you, will set you up.
(A Warning from the Writ)

Barrett went into the DEAD company offices. He spent the past week obsessed with researching Solomon and found that one of the DEAD company's employees worked closely with Solomon. Barrett looked for Kevin on the floors of the DEAD company warehouse. The warehouse was buzzing with a mix of holograms, artificial intelligence (AI), dropcrafts and all kinds of other devices to design, create, and ship the newest products out to the YSW. Barrett located Kevin using an app attached to his implant. Kevin was standing near the robots making sure there were no mistakes in the design of the devices going out.

"Hi, Kevin," Barrett said as he approached. Kevin was still bandaged up but had returned to work a week ago. His neck brace made it difficult for him to turn without moving his entire body.

"Why hello, I didn't think I would see one of Deiderick's top agents in the warehouse."

"Why yes, this is a special visit."

"Really, what is it?" Kevin was curious.

"I can't give you the details of my inquiry, but I need to know if you still associate with a man by the name of Solomon Wiseman," Barrett said.

"Yes, I know Solomon, but I really haven't seen him since the fire."

"So what can you tell me about him?"

"Well, Solomon is a really good guy. He's pretty strong-willed, though. When I first started working here, I was told that we would get a bonus if he signed up. You know, like a perk for me and an incentive for him."

"So what happened?"

"He didn't sign up, but I was instructed to let him use my discount," Kevin replied

"Who instructed you to do that?" Barrett asked.

"The man himself, plus, I thought the perks might help out. Solomon had a lot going on. Wanted to show him that the YSW was not as bad as he thought. Maybe the perks would not only make him join but give him some financial support as well, but then…" Kevin's voice waned.

"But then what?"

"Then things got weird. After I let him use my perks, I was told to send him different messages, threats. I was told that he was trying to take us down."

"Do you believe that he was trying to take the YSW down?"

"I don't know what to believe anymore. But in some way, I was proud of him. Solomon was determined to handle his debt and not join the YSW. Don't know what happened to him after the crash. I couldn't work security anymore, so now I am here in the warehouse," Kevin said as he rotated around sarcastically, showing off his new work location. His arm was still in a sling.

"You may have been told right; I have reason to believe that Solomon may be trying to take the organization down. I think he is going to use the DEAD company to do it."

Kevin laughed. "Solomon is pretty strong willed, but I don't think he would be able to touch the organization."

Barrett returned Kevin's laughter with a stoic expression. "It's hard to believe, and I may be wrong, but I need you to see if you can reach out to him. See if you think he would be willing to meet up with you."

"Why would I do that? What would we talk about? I am sure it would be weird. I arrested him," Kevin inquired.

"Just see if he would be willing to meet up with you, and I will take care of the rest," Barrett assured him.

"So...what's in it for me?"

"I am very close to the Dollard family. I think it's time to let them know how dedicated you are to your job and see if we can get you in a new position."

"Okay...I think I can find a way to get Solomon to meet up with me. I am curious about how he is doing," Kevin said.

"And I definitely see you up there--" Barrett pointed to the glass office windows surrounding the warehouse floor. "And not here anymore."

Hearing this, Kevin smiled.

Before Barrett walked out, he turned to Kevin and said, "Make sure you see me before you meet up with Solomon. I have a few things I will need to give you."

"Will do." Then Kevin resumed working with his colleagues on the warehouse floor.

Barrett left the warehouse and returned to the Dollard home. While he was making rounds, he came upon Janice, Tyler, and Damion talking. They were back in the garden. A buzzing bee landed on a flower near the conversation.

"So what's the status of the divorce?" Janice asked Damion.

"Sasha is still really upset, but she agreed to hold off on the divorce for the time being." Damion continued. "I may be able to save my marriage if Brianna would stop harassing my wife."

Tyler started laughing. "Do you really want to save your marriage, or are you more concerned about the money?"

Damion smirked. "Both."

"Well," Janice chimed in. "For our family's sake, you better reconcile with Sasha and keep Brianna at bay. It would be too devastating to our legacy."

"The only way Brianna will calm down is if the baby gets the Dollard name and a percentage of the Emoji project. The project that Dad refuses to push out. I don't have much time left. The baby is due in a month." Damion was frustrated. He took a deep breath and continued. "She knew I was married. I think she tried to sabotage me from the beginning. She is ruining my life--" Damion paused again. He started shaking his head and then said. "I think I am just going to go ahead and let Brianna get what she wants."

"I think that is the right thing to do, son. I know that your father does as well," Janice said. "But now, we just need to get your father to push the app out so all of this can go away."

"I don't think Dad is going to do that, so I think we need to come up with another idea," Damion interjected.

"You have another idea? I am interested to hear this." Tyler scoffed.

"I think we are going to have to find a way to get Dad off the project," Damion replied.

"I think that is a terrible idea," Tyler replied.

"I am sure you do. You are always protecting Dad, but you have to admit that this is taking way too long to release, and once it goes out, all of this drama will stop following us."

"Your drama has nothing to do with me," Tyler said.

"Unfortunately, it does. If Brianna gets a cut and Sasha goes after our fortune, it will affect the bottom line for all of us."

Janice looked at her sons. "Tyler, I know how much you love your father. Deiderick is a smart man, but I have been reviewing the prenuptial agreement that Sasha and Damion signed. It basically lets her get anything she wants if Damion cheats. I am not happy with Damion's choices, but I don't want his mistake to take everything away from us. I think Damion is right. We are going to have to find a way to get your father off the project and move forward with it," Janice said. "It is not the way I wanted to do this, but it is the way it has to be."

"Fine. Just make sure it doesn't affect my bottom line," Tyler said and started to walk away.

"Thank you, Mom," Damion said.

"I will always protect my baby." Janice gave Damion a hug. After the boys left, Janice cried.

Barrett quickly had the bee fly back over to him. An idea came to him.

"Good afternoon, Mrs. Dollard. Is there anything I can help you with?" Barrett sat down next to Janice.

"No, I'm fine." Janice wiped her face and turned away.

"I know things are tough on you and the family, Mrs. Dollard. I just saw you with tears in your eyes, just checking on you." Barrett started walking away.

"Hey, wait ," Janice called out.

"Yes, Ma'am."

"Thanks for checking on me. You have been with us for quite some time, Barrett. You are like part of the family."

"Thank you, Mrs. Dollard. I appreciate you saying that. I have worked really hard to show my loyalty to the family. It makes me feel good that Mr. Dollard can trust me with his most confidential information."

Janice could always tell that Barrett had something for her, so she came up with a plan of her own. She walked closer to Barrett and slid her finger across his chest, then asked, "Has Deiderick shared with you why he won't release the app? I mean, he keeps saying that it's not ready, but I don't know if I believe it."

Barrett looked into Janice's eyes, excited to have held a conversation with her for longer than a fleeting moment. "He told me the same thing, but I am starting to suspect that it is something else," Barrett said, hoping that she would take the bait.

"What are your suspicions?"

"I think that Mr. Dollard doesn't want to release the app because he doesn't want Brianna's baby to be listed as a shareholder, but I feel conflicted. It's not the baby's fault that he or she was brought into the world."

Janice knew that was not the reason. Her husband was a kind man and didn't care about money, but she couldn't afford to tell Barrett that. Instead, she asked. "Do you think you can do me a favor?"

"Of course," Barrett replied.

"Deiderick does trust you so, I need you to see if you can get ahold of all the board documents for the Emoji project and the information on the stock shares for this project as well. And if you can pull this off, I am sure I can find a way to make this worth your while." Janice gazed at Barrett flirtatiously. The thought of anyone but her husband sickened Janice, but she continued to charade to get what she needed from him.

"So, what did you have in mind?" Barrett couldn't believe he was finally having this conversation with Janice.

"I am sure we can work things out, but right now, we need to focus on getting the information for his stock shares."

"Mr. Dollard keeps all of those documents in paper form. I only have access to all of his computer files," Barrett responded.

"Yes, I know. He feels that documents can be manipulated when they are digital. He prints and signs every document that he deems important." Janice chuckled. "My husband, the technology mogul doesn't trust digital documents."

"Yep, that's why he is smarter than us." Barrett laughed as well. "I wouldn't even know where to begin to find those documents."

"Well, I know where he keeps them. I just don't know how to get into them," Janice said. They are in the west wing, the spare bedroom closet inside the safe. I have tried a few passwords, but haven't been able to figure it out," Janice said.

"Oh yea, what have you tried?"

"Our sons' names, their birthdays, and a combination of their names and dates. I thought it would be something that was important to him, but I couldn't figure it out."

"Well, I am sure I can run a password search on the lock and see what I come up with, and then I will get the documents over to you. I want to make sure to protect the Dollard name and estate."

"Thank you, Barrett. You have always been so good to our family." Janice gave him a kiss on the cheek and entered the house.

Barrett left the conversation with a mission, to help Janice get the Emoji app out to the public and stop whatever relationship Deiderick had with Solomon. He couldn't understand Deiderick's relationship with Solomon, but it made him uncomfortable. He also didn't know why Deiderick would want to stop his own project from getting out to the public, but if helping the project get out would infringe on Deiderick and Solomon's newfound friendship, then Barrett had no other choice but to do what needed to be done.

A day passed before Kevin contacted Barrett.

"The best way to get to Solomon is to have a casual run-in with him at Shooters. We used to go there after work to grab a drink."

"Good idea. Keep it casual. Act like you are just catching up on old times. I have a few things for you." Barrett opened a small case and gave Kevin a tracking system and a few other gadgets.

"This one you can put in his pocket. But the other one, you will have to find some way to attach to him. Preferably on his back."

"Thanks." Kevin grabbed the items from Barrett. "A quick question... You are not going to hurt him, are you? I mean, he was a pretty good guy when I knew him."

"No, I just want to make sure he doesn't interfere with DEAD company business or the YSW. As long as he doesn't do that, he will be fine." Barrett shot a sinister smile and patted Kevin on the back.

"Here, let me give you my information." Barrett placed his wrist on Kevin's wrist and shared his information.

"Did you get it?" Barrett inquired.

Kevin closed his eyes and concentrated, his third eye started to glow, and the information popped into his mind.

"Yes, thank you."

It took nearly a week for Kevin to have his chance run-in with Solomon. Kevin parked his hovercraft about a block away from Shooters and paced the street around the time he knew Solomon would be getting off work. As usual, Solomon's head was down. He had his earplugs pushed into his ears to block the street noise. He was especially careful not to even move his lips because they were under the silence order hours, and didn't want to have another violation of his probation.

Kevin waved. Solomon was still walking, eyes to the ground. An intentional nudge and Solomon looked up. Not being able to speak, Solomon just stood there. The last time he saw Kevin, he was flying the aircraft that was going to take him to prison.

"It's me," Kevin mouthed, remembering not to make a sound. Then Kevin cupped his hands and signaled a drink.

Solomon shrugged his shoulders, hoping to dismiss his former friend.

Kevin paid no attention and mouthed, "Let's get a drink. I'll pay."

Seeing that Kevin wasn't going to let it go, Solomon headed toward Shooters.

A loud announcement disrupted the quiet. "The silence order is over. You may resume your normal communication, but remember, if you can't say anything nice, don't say anything at all."

"Hey, I haven't seen either one of you in a long time!" Barkley took full advantage of his talking freedom. His loud voice barreled through the small bar.

Kevin was the first to reply. "This is my first time being here in months. It's my lucky day because I ran into Solomon."

Solomon was still very nervous about speaking, so he gave Barkley another wave before heading to a small corner bar stool.

"Aren't you going to say anything?" Kevin inquired.

Solomon held up five fingers and tapped his arm in the place where he would have the time glowing through his skin.

"Oh...I see, you want to wait five minutes to make sure. Okay, no problem. I will get us a few drinks in the meantime."

Kevin ordered two foamy dark beverages and looked out through the red dust-covered windows. "I forgot how gloomy it could look down here. Kind of depressing. Hard to believe this all felt normal to me at one time."

Solomon was glad that he chose not to speak. He hated the way Kevin sounded to him as if he were bragging, he would have ended up saying something rude. The silence gave him a chance to collect his thoughts, and soon, the five minutes were up.

Solomon chose to indulge his cocky former friend. "So, what's it like living with the higher ups of the YSW?"

"Not too bad. Still don't have a good friend like you, but other than that, I can't complain," Kevin responded, taking a sip of his foamy drink. "So, how have things been for you?"

Solomon was still a little hesitant, but still used this as an opportunity to get some information for himself as well. "I have been doing as well as can be expected considering all that I have gone through."

"Yes, I heard a little about you leading the silence ban protest."

"Hence the reason why I am a little skeptical about speaking until I am allowed to. I don't want to violate my probation."

"Honestly" Kevin paused to take another sip. "It is good seeing you. I always wondered if you were okay after the hovercraft crash. You see I'm still bandaged up." Kevin chuckled. "You look good though...no bruises on you anywhere."

"I was banged up a bit. A little sore, but Jah saved me ," Solomon replied.

"Jah saved you? Well, I guess."

A long silence before Kevin continued. "I don't want to be too forward, but how are you doing with all the fines? I am sure things are tight. I feel terrible about how things turned out. I can help if you need me to."

Solomon chuckled. "Yeah, well, I remember the last time you told me that you would take care of something for me, I ended up receiving threatening messages and fearing for my life. I'll pass."

"Right, I remember. I can still take care of that if I need to. I apologize I didn't realize they would be so aggressive."

"Sure, no worries, though, my daughter took care of it for me."

"Wow...well, I am glad that worked out. How is Karina?"

"Don't really know. I don't speak to her often, and I haven't seen her since she went off to school."

"What about your boys?" Kevin inquired.

"Haven't seen them either, but maybe it is for the best. I am learning that Jah has a plan for everything. I will see them again when I am supposed to," Solomon responded.

"I don't know if I ever heard you talk like this before. You definitely have a positive outlook." Kevin was a little shocked by how well Solomon was able to talk about his children without being upset.

"And you, how are you doing?" Solomon didn't really care, but it seemed appropriate to ask.

"I am doing great. I am up for a promotion. I plan to work more closely with Deiderick Dollard soon, fingers crossed." Kevin held up his index and middle fingers and crossed them.

"At one time I thought that Deiderick was this evil technology mastermind, but I am starting to see him in a new light. I am pretty impressed with his character," Solomon said to Kevin. Not only did Solomon think the statement was true, but he was hoping that complimenting Deiderick would soften the obvious tension between him and Kevin. Unfortunately, the comment had the opposite effect.

"I don't think I would have ever suspected that you would feel that way about Deiderick Dollard. You don't have to pretend that you like him just because you are talking to me."

"I wouldn't use the word like, but I would say that I have a new respect for him."

"Okay, well, does that mean you have a change of heart? Are you coming to join my team?"

"Quite the opposite, I feel even more confident that the DEAD company and their YSW following should come to an end," Solomon said, taking a swig from his glass and plopping it back down on the table. "It has been a long time since I had one of these. I have been trying to quit drinking, but I am sure one won't hurt."

"Sounds like a lot has changed since the last time I saw you. Well, everything except your dislike of the YSW," Kevin replied.

"They have my kids. They won't let me see them. What reason do I have to like them?"

"You're right. I guess I can understand why you feel that way."

Another drink later and both of the men got up and headed toward the door. "Put the drinks on my tab," Kevin called out.

"No problem!" Barkley replied. As the men walked out the door, the amount was removed from Kevin's account.

"Good seeing you again," Kevin said, patting Solomon on the back. He pretended to fix his collar, placing the device given to him by Barrett, on Solomon's neck. Then, as Solomon adjusted his coat, Kevin slipped a tracking device into Solomon's pocket.

Solomon must have felt something strange because he rubbed his neck in the area where Kevin attached the device, but by that time, it had dissolved into his skin.

"Whew! I am getting tired. I need to head home," Solomon said, continuing to rub his neck.

"Alright, well, I guess I will see you later. It was good catching up," Kevin said to Solomon and began walking in the opposite direction.

Solomon walked a few feet but quickly found a bench and sat down. He started fanning himself. Beads of sweat formed around his forehead and his Code Red glasses fogged up. Solomon slid

337

down off the bench and hit the floor. Within seconds a DEAD company hovercraft came and picked Solomon up.

Solomon woke up inside of a small room, with his hands behind his back secured with electronic cuffs, in front of Barrett.

A groggy Solomon woke up. "What am I doing here?"

"I promise I don't want to hurt you, but it has come to our attention that you want to put a stop to our organization, and my job is to protect it at all costs," Barrett said to Solomon. He was standing above him. "Do you want something to drink?"

"No"

"Once we get our project released, I will let you go but until that time, this will be your new home," Barrett said. "Now, are you sure you don't want something to eat or drink?"

"No, I am fine."

"Well, I hope we can get this taken care of within the next week or so. I am working on that now, but until then, just sit tight."

Solomon was in the room for a few hours before he drifted to sleep. During that time, he received a vision.

Typically, when Solomon had dreams, they felt bad, like nightmares, but confined in the room a feeling of peace came over him. He saw people begin floating in the air and the world was filled with an eerie silence. He saw himself and a group of other people his age wake up and look around in a world that was so beautiful. The people traveled along a path and came to a building covered with flowers and as the flowers bloomed, sweet babies were inside. He and the other people took the babies and traveled until they found a body of water, and there, they started a new life.

Chapter 40: Where is Solomon?

No one can hide from the end of the world. (A Warning from the Writ)

Deiderick was surprised to go to an EAD meeting and not see Solomon. He and Solomon planned to discuss how to stop the app from being released, so after waiting about an hour for Solomon to show, he hopped back into his hovercraft and went back to the Dollard Estate.

"Track Solomon," Deiderick called out to his computers.

"Tracking Solomon," the computer responded.

Deiderick watched as the computer screens began to zero in on Solomon's location. Solomon is currently located less than 2000 feet away in the DEAD company offices.

"I asked you to track Solomon Wiseman. Please run tracking again. There must be a mistake."

"Solomon Wiseman is currently located at the DEAD company office room 37C."

Deiderick was confused but got up from his chair and walked briskly through the double doors of his office. He came to the corridor that separated his home from the business and stopped in front of a facial recognition camera.

As soon as he approached, Barrett quickly came around the corner, put his hands over Deiderick's mouth and zapped him in the back. The electrical current of the zap immediately made Deiderick fall to the floor. Barrett dragged him into room 37C. He put Deiderick into a chair and placed his hands in electronic cuffs. Solomon woke up with all of the commotion. "Where am I? Why do you have Deiderick here? What is going on?"

"I need something from him," Barrett said as he took out a case that had the files. Barrett located them quickly with Janice's help.

"What is the code? I need the code." Barrett was flustered. It was obvious being a villain wasn't his strength.

Deiderick feeling dazed, groaned out the following: "# LOVE OVER TECH!."

Both Solomon and Barrett were surprised to hear the code revealed.

The box containing the documents said, "Phase one complete, please provide your fingerprint to open."

Barrett grabbed Deiderick's right hand and pressed his index finger on the black spot on the top of the box.

"Permission granted," the box said, as it clicked open.

"Thank you Mr. Dollard. Now, you two just rest here until I get the board to move forward with this project. I didn't want it to be this way, but you are making a mistake by befriending this one, Mr. Dollard." Barrett pointed at Solomon.

"You are also making a mistake with your family. Regardless of how that baby is born, he is a Dollard and deserves just as much as the rest of your grandchildren."

Deiderick was still groggy. "You've got it all wrong. Releasing the Emoji app is a mistake. A fatal mistake."

Solomon started in as well, "If you release the app, you have signed your death sentence. You are not helping his family and you are not doing anything to save the YSW."

Barrett kicked Solomon in the legs and shouted, "Shut up you piece of crap! I don't know what Deiderick sees in you, but ever since he started researching Solomon Wiseman, he has been making terrible decisions."

"You have it all wrong," Solomon said. "Look, just let me out of these cuffs and send me home. You can do whatever you want. Jah is in control now anyway."

Barrett walked out the door, slamming it behind him.

Deiderick was regaining consciousness. "Why am I handcuffed?" he asked Solomon.

Solomon was in the opposite corner of the room. His arms were handcuffed behind his back and his legs were strapped together. He was sitting in a chair and was starting to get very uncomfortable.

He squirmed around before responding. "From what I gather, they think that you and I are trying to stop the app because we don't want your son's child to have a share of the company, and if the app is released, the family drama would go away. I am also getting a strong feeling that Barrett has something against me. Not sure why."

"I trusted him too much…Solomon, we can't let that happen," Deiderick said.

"So what do you think we are going to be able to do? We're locked up!" Solomon's agitation was clear.

"Just calm down. They can take the papers to the board and push through with the program all they want, but it won't be without a fight."

Deiderick started looking around the room. "Every place in this facility was designed by me. I am sure that we can figure this out. Just give me a second."

Solomon joined in the search. "Not much in here."

He continued looking for anything that could free them. "Got it…scoot your chair closer." Both Deiderick and Solomon scooted their chairs closer. "Put your cuffs near mine. They are electrically charged and should cause a shortage."

The men scooted closer and pressed their cuffs together. A zing, zap, and a pop, and the cuffs fell off. The men rubbed their wrists and could see the red burn marks.

"Now to get out of this room, "Deiderick said.

The room was empty with the exception of a few cleaning supplies, some tools, and the chairs that they were sitting in.

Both Solomon and Deiderick looked around. They tried a few ways to get out, but none of them seemed to work.

"Well, you did a good job making sure that no one could get out of these rooms." Solomon chuckled.

Chapter 41: World is Excited About the app

---◆---

Humans have foolish desires. Desires that will lead to their own harm. Stay focused on your purpose. Do not be deceived by society's definition of success. If you stay focused, you will have all the riches you could ever imagine, but if you are blinded by the sparkle of the world, you will live in eternal darkness. (A Warning from the Writ)

Barrett took the documents to Janice. "Excellent work. I will make a few adjustments before taking these documents to the board. I am sure they will be excited to see that Deiderick finally got on board. Thank you for taking care of this. I see a raise in your future."

"Thank you, Mrs. Dollard."

"Where is Deiderick now?" Janice inquired.

"Don't worry, he is safe and secure, just make sure to take care of all this quickly."

"I love my husband. I don't want anything to happen to him. I will make sure to take care of this quickly."

Barrett was shocked to see Janice's immediate change in her interaction with him. "What about us Janice?"

"Oh dear, I realize how things may have looked the other day, but I love my husband very much and this," Janice said, waving her finger back and forth between Barret and herself. "Just can't happen, but, I promise, your financial compensation will be worth your while." Janice walked away, leaving Barrett confused.

She immediately went to the conference room and called an emergency board meeting.

Everyone was in attendance. All except Deiderick.

"I am so glad that you all were able to attend the meeting today. I do apologize for my husband's absence. He is feeling a bit under the weather and has sent me to take care of some last minute things. I have some exciting news that he wanted me to share."

The board members waited in anticipation, "Deiderick has agreed to release the app to the public!" Janice was pleased with herself.

All members, the ones who were virtual and the ones who were present, began clapping.

"We plan on putting the commercial out tomorrow. I will meet with the advertising team to finalize the details. Now, I will turn the meeting over to Damion to discuss shares."

"As many of you know, I have brought shame to the Dollard name, and for that, I apologize." Then Damion grabbed the documents that Barrett forced Deiderick to sign and continued. "After speaking with my father, he has graciously given up his shares of the Emoji app to help silence the media circus and put an end to the lawsuit brought to the DEAD company by Brianna.

344

Deiderick has agreed to split his ownership between Brianna and Sasha. Once this is finalized, both women have agreed to stop speaking to the media." Damion continued to address all of the members of the board. "My father has also been gracious enough to allow my brother Tyler, my mother Janice, and myself the ability to maintain our original shares, and naturally, none of your investments will be compromised." Another cheer from the board members.

Damion smiled. "Yes, yes, my father is always the hero, but there is one last piece before we celebrate. Whenever we change our agreements, we must have everyone place their fingerprint signature on the new document."

"Just to be clear, these changes don't affect our bottom line?" One of the board members asked.

"Absolutely not," Damion confirmed and once he did that, all of the members quickly signed the document and left the conference room.

"Mom, I don't feel good about this. We are going behind Dad's back to protect Damion? Would you have done this for me?" asked Tyler.

"Of course, I would have, honey. It's just that Damion seems to get himself into different issues than you ," Janice replied. She hoped that Tyler believed her. But the truth was, Damion was her favorite. She couldn't help it. He just was. Tyler, like his father, lacked excitement, but Damion always had something going on and it made her feel needed.

"Yeah, whatever, just do what is best for the entire family. Not just what's best for Damion," Tyler said. "Hey, where is Dad anyway? I haven't seen him in a while."

"I am sure he's fine, honey," Janice replied and then turned away and started talking to Damion. Tyler walked out but replayed

345

his mother's words in his head. They did something to keep him away. I know they did. Where the heck could he be? Tyler started searching through the massive estate hoping to get a sign of where his father was. The main house had so many rooms and each bedroom had a security code attached to the door. Deiderick installed this so when visitors came it would feel private, but now, it was slowing down Tyler's search.

While Tyler was searching, Janice and Damion rummaged through Deiderick's office.

"How in the world are we going to get to the computer code that will release the app?" Damion asked. "We don't have much time. We released a press statement saying that the app would push out in three days."

"I don't know, just think. What would some of his passwords be?" Janice replied.

Damion sat behind his father's computers. Deep down, sitting in his father's chair made him feel like he was powerful. While Damion sat in the chair, he remembered that he helped develop a passcode runner with his dad about 15 years ago.

"This could take several hours, but we should be able to get it unlocked. We created the passcode runner to override any security codes that may already be on a device so there shouldn't be a problem."

"Are you sure?" Janice nervously asked.

"About 80% sure." He responded. Damion then turned his direction to the wall of large computer screens that were running nearly five hundred thousand passwords per minute.

"While you do that, I am going to tie up some loose ends with advertising and make sure all accounts are prepared with the changes that we made earlier. I am also going to do a little cleanup for you."

"What do you mean?" Damion asked, with his attention still turned onto the computer screens.

"I am going to reach out to Brianna and Sasha to see if we can get all of this taken care of soon. Let me ask you something, do you really want to get a divorce?"

Damion looked up from the computer screens and turned to his mother. "I really don't know what I want. I never meant to hurt Sasha or my children, but I don't think she wants me back."

"What about Brianna?"

"It wasn't supposed to be like this. Brianna was supposed to be fun."

"So, what would you like me to tell them?" Janice asked her son.

"Just...I don't know, Just...give them what they want," Damion said. "Seems like they both wanted me for my money, so give them the money. See if I can see my children at least twice a week." Damion looked defeated. With all that had been going on, he had never been asked what he wanted. He hadn't thought about it until now.

"And...If Sasha wants to continue to stay here, I am open. Let her know that I still love her."

"Okay...I will do that Damion. Look," Janice approached her son. "No matter what they tell you. No matter what anyone else says, you have a good heart Damion."

"Thanks." Damion turned away and continued to watch for the passcode to appear on the screen.

Janice left Deiderick's office and headed toward her bedroom. She had pressed behind her ear to turn her implant on and began thinking of who she needed to contact and what she wanted to say, then the implant drafted messages based on her thoughts.

Sasha,

Damion is very sorry for everything that he has done to you and wants to make sure that you and the children are taken care of. If you really want to go through with the divorce, contact Green & Associates, 1-888-555-2212. If, however, you wish to stay married to my son, we would be extremely happy. I know you don't feel this, but he loves you very much. Please feel free to stay on the estate for as long as you need.

Janice

Janice hoped her message would show Sasha her concern and waited for a reply, but nothing came. Then she started thinking, and the implant created a message for Brianna

Brianna,

Damion has made arrangements for your son to be added to the Emoji project. He will receive fifteen percent of the stock shares, however, if you continue to make a media presence after the release of the app, then you give up all stake holdings. For more information, please contact Green & Associates 1-888-555-2212.

Janice Dollard

Unlike Sasha, Brianna responded right away.

Janice,

Apparently, you and your son don't get it. The point is not to throw my baby a little change so that people don't know who he is, the point is that my son, whose name will be Theiler, is part of the Dollard Family. Damion tried to embarrass me and treat me like a piece of trash, but I will NOT let your family do that to my son, YOUR GRANDCHILD. He will be someone! He will be recognized by the family! I will NOT let you think that by signing a few documents, you can ignore this part of your family. I will reach out to lawyers, and we will make it clear that my son will know his father's side of the family.

Brianna

Janice headed back to Deiderick's office where Damion was still sitting in his father's chair.

"You're back sooner than I thought. It only took an hour for the computer to figure out the passcode. Look," Damion said pointing to the large screen. Janice looked up to see the code.

"You could have asked me a million times, and I would never have guessed it." Janice was astonished.

"1LOVEJANIC3" was in large font across the screen. She immediately felt bad for what she was doing.

"He probably forgot to change his passcode," Damion joked.

"Oh, stop it. Look...maybe we shouldn't do this," Janice said.

"Mom, it's too late. I am in the middle of programming the app to release in three days at 11:30 PM. Just like the commercial says. The commercial goes live tonight, right?" Damion asked.

"Did you remember the free trial?" Janice reminded Damion

"Everyone who has the implant will receive the first thirty minutes with full Emoji access, including all emotions, for free. In

349

three days, the entire world will be hooked, and the money will come pouring in."

"It should happen sooner than we think. The commercial going out today will have people running to get the implant. I have already reached out to all vendors, surgeons, and everyone who will support the implant," Janice said proudly.

"Excellent work. They will need to prepare for the large numbers of people who want to get the implant in time to be ready for the app."

Janice looked at the screens with different symbols flashing. "Does the code look okay?" Janice inquired.

"I looked through it and couldn't figure out why Dad didn't want it to go out," Damion replied. "I didn't see any issues."

"That's strange. Well....I guess it will be okay."

Both Damion and Janice stood there for a while before Damion broke the silence. "Hey, Mom," Damion said.

"Yes."

"I heard what you said to Tyler. I know that I am the mess up, but I promise, when all of this is over, I will try to do better. I never wanted this for my family."

"I know and I hope you will stick with it. Brianna is one tough cookie. She wants to make sure her child has the Dollard name and I don't blame her. I want you to do right by Theiler. He doesn't deserve any of this."

"Theiler, who is that?" Damion asked.

"Well, Brianna named your son Theiler." Janice looked into her son's eyes.

"Theiler" Damion rubbed his chin. "I like it. Sounds...powerful."

"The baby is a Dollard, I am sure he will be powerful."

Damion smiled. It seemed like his mother always knew the right thing to say. He turned toward the main computer and called for the Emoji project.

"Voice not recognized. Please enter a code," the computer responded. Damion pressed "1LOVEJANIC3" and the computer gave him access to the activation release scheduler.

"So that's it huh?" Janice asked. Her eyes were glued to the screen. She didn't know what was going on. Unlike her husband and sons, Janice didn't find the world of computer programming to be an interesting one, but as she watched Damion, she was intrigued.

Damion pressed into thin air near the main computer and a set of buttons appeared.

"How did you know to do that?" Janice inquired.

"Dad showed me a long time ago. He said you can't trust people, so he learned to make everything invisibly plain." Damion smiled. "I didn't get it then, but yeah, Dad is smart."

A few more clacks on the keyboard that popped out of thin air and a countdown flashed on the screen.

"We're all set," Damion said. "I am just glad all of this will be over."

Chapter 42: Trapped

There is nothing you will be able to do. You cannot break free. Everyone
will be trapped. Only those who know the truth will
awaken in a new world.
(A Warning from the
Writ)

"Crap, he must have figured it out," Deiderick said to Solomon when a notification began glowing through his skin.

"What are you talking about?"

"They wanted to release the app. They have somehow figured out all of my passcodes. The app has been activated. We have got to find a way to get out of here."

Solomon looked around. "Will any of these things help?" Solomon grabbed a set of pliers from a shelf in the small room where he was trapped.

"Nah, I don't think so. If I am not mistaken, we are in my engineering and design factory. They are sealed tight. We used these rooms to house some of our most coveted devices before they hit the market. We don't want spies to come in and steal our designs."

"Has that happened before?" Solomon was intrigued.

"More often than you would think. We have even had people work for the company for years just to get hold of some design secrets or take a device and sell them to competing companies."

"Wow, I guess I never thought you had to go through so much. Always seemed to have it made...So, what are your thoughts about how to get out of here? All I can try to do is pry the henges loose or bang the door until someone hears us."

Deiderick looked at his arm again. The glowing numbers through his skin showed him that there were 79 hours before the app would be released.

"Do you really think we will be in here for that long?" Solomon asked.

"Doesn't matter. The atmospheric changes have already begun," Deiderick said, still looking around for a way to get out. "Hey, why don't you start banging around on some things while I try to figure out a more sophisticated way to get us out of here."

"Sure." Solomon took the pliers and started at the henges. They seemed nearly impossible to remove and would spark each time he took a strike at the metal. "What do you mean atmospheric changes?"

"My son has no idea how much power it takes to push this type of technology out to people. You have to do it in stages. I used to have to work with all of the electric companies to make sure we created towers that could transmit the signals slowly so there wasn't too much damage. It was a timely and costly process, so I ended up just taking over one of the electric companies and building the towers myself. This project does not have enough power to successfully be released. So, not only have I not worked out a glitch in the code, but the towers are not set up to handle it."

"What does all that mean?" Solomon asked, as he continued to work on removing the hinges from the door."

"If the app can't get the power from the towers, then...it will be forced to pull energy from the atmosphere ," Deiderick said before pausing to let Solomon bang on the henges.

"The electrical grid fields that hold up the hovercrafts and airlifters may start falling from the sky. So many things will be impacted. We have got to get out of here," Deiderick continued.

"My biggest fear..." Deiderick stopped again to make way for the banging noise. "Is that it can affect the bodies of anyone who is connected to technology, especially if they have implants."

Solomon stopped banging. "How?"

"Well, hmm...like when they have signs that say people with heart conditions shouldn't get in an airlifter or how they discourage pregnant women from riding in a hovercraft."

"So you are saying that vehicles can begin to fall from the sky and people will hit the ground when the pressure changes?"

Deiderick didn't confirm Solomon's statement. Instead he began scrolling through the lights that were on his arms to see if he had access to anything. But soon realized he was limited without his computers present. He joined in with Solomon who was making very little headway on the henges.

Tyler was still looking for his father. He searched every square inch of the main house before moving to the other properties on the Dollard estate. As he went outside, he ran into Barrett.

"Are you okay?" Barrett asked Tyler who was running toward one of the guest houses.

"Have you seen my father?" Tyler asked, never answering Barrett's question.

Barrett looked away. "Why are you asking me? I haven't seen him."

"Look, it's just a question. I need to find him before it's too late." Tyler took note of Barrett's suspicious response.

"What do you mean before it's too late?" Barrett was nervous.

"I know I shouldn't tell you, but my mother and brother are plotting to release the Emoji app without my father's permission. Something doesn't feel right about it to me. I need to find him to see if we can stop it."

"I am loyal to your mother and father. I may know where he is, but I cannot risk my job. I have been trained to only work for them."

"What do you do when they are working against each other? Huh?" Tyler asked. "Who are you loyal to then? ...Look, I need your help," Tyler asked.

"I don't feel comfortable doing that," Barrett said.

"Then don't waste my time," Tyler responded and started to run off. Barrett's conscience got to him. "Wait, I won't help you, but I can tell you that you are looking in the wrong direction. Head toward the DEAD headquarters factory."

"Thanks," Tyler replied. Tyler had been running quite a while and was exhausted. He quickly grabbed a flyboard that was lying on the side of the house. Apparently left by one of the children who lived on the grounds. Tyler threw the oblong board into the air and jumped on heading toward the DEAD headquarters.

Seconds later, the smooth ride soon turned turbulent. "What is going on?" Tyler continued to bump around until he couldn't take it anymore. The flyboard seemed to have given up as well.

Tyler was trying to land it, but the flyboard fell to the ground. Tyler hit the lawn a few feet away from the door of the headquarters.

"Ah...that hurt," Tyler dusted himself off and ran into the factory. He felt overwhelmed in the massive factory and wanted help, but for some reason, no one was around. He started on the first of three levels. Each level was about the size of a football field and wrapped around the factory floor which had massive machines and other equipment to make Deiderick's many devices. Tyler took it one step at a time and started trying to open each door.

By the time he reached the second floor, Tyler was exhausted. He kept opening each door and was halfway through the offices on the second floor when he heard strange noises coming from the floor above. Tyler stopped his search on the second floor and quickly ran upstairs. As he was running the lights began flickering on and off.

Tyler started yelling. "Dad...where are you?"

"Shhh, I thought I heard something," Deiderick said. He put his hand out and signaled for Solomon to stop banging.

"Dad, where are you?"

Just then, Deiderick and Solomon started screaming. Tyler ran faster and faster toward the sound.

"Dad, give me just a few minutes." Tyler worked outside the door to put in the codes to open the door. When the door popped open, Deiderick and Solomon ran out.

"Who is he?" Tyler pointed at Solomon.

"I'm Solomon. I can catch you up later, but we need to try and stop the app release right now."

As they left the room, they noticed the flickering lights.

356

"It is already pulling the energy from the atmosphere," Deiderick said.

"I see," Solomon said. "How much time do we have left?"

"It's hard to tell ," Deiderick replied and then turned to Tyler. "What is going on?"

"It's Mom and Damion. Believe it or not, they just want to get rid of the bad media press. They want to let Brianna get the money so she can stop bad mouthing the company."

"And they are willing to risk everyone's life for this?" Solomon interrupted.

"Dad, what does he mean?"

"I can't get a clean simulation...there is a fatal outcome. Solomon has these visions of the end of the world, and he had a dream that our app is responsible for killing off everyone ," Deiderick said, out of breath. All three men were running toward the main house.

"Seriously?" Tyler asked. He was also panting. They passed the flyboard on their way toward the main house and Deiderick was about to jump on.

"I wouldn't do that if I were you. It left me stranded. Stopped working in the middle of the ride."

"So the power went out? We have less time than we thought," Deiderick said.

"I thought you said we had about three days," Solomon responded.

"Three days until the app is released, but it looks like it is taking a lot more power than I thought."

357

Halfway between the factory and the main house, the men could hear sounds coming from the Inbetween. The land below them.

Todd Markley

I know that was quite a bit of a whirlwind, but there is more to come. Solomon and Deiderick tried their best to stop the release of the app, but they were unsuccessful.

The Emoji app has an astronomical impact on the electrical grids. The electrical grids support all of the transportation, billboards, the blue-eyed spy-bots, AI, and security cameras. Releasing the app to the entire world at the same time, uses a massive amount of energy and causes trauma to nearly all technology and electrical devices. That amount of power at one time is one of the things Deiderick fears most. He is also extremely skeptical of how that app implant would affect human beings and wonders about the long-term impact on the human brain. Unfortunately, all anyone could do now is wait and see what will happen.

We are going to take a peek into the lives of each person as the 2nd world embraces the Emoji app. Many of the events you are about to read occur at the same time, so if it feels a bit chaotic, just remember, the world coming to an end. This is far from peaceful, so buckle up.

Chapter 43: Three Days Before the App Release

————————◆————————

Jah is the light that dwells in everyone. It is his spirit that makes it possible for your heart to beat. To know Jah is to know Life. Do not turn away from Jah.
(A Warning from the Writ)

The Inbetween was already feeling the effects of app release. The silence order was in place, but you could still hear the noise.

"What is happening?" Aurora looked around at the lights that were flickering on and off in her apartment. She started rubbing her belly. She grabbed her jacket and started heading out of her apartment toward the elevator.

"Wa..wa..what fl...floor?" The elevator glitched and stuttered.

"Are you okay?" Aurora asked. "I wanted to go to the 9th floor. Solomon's apartment"

"9th th th th floor." The door to the elevator closed behind Aurora and the elevator shook. Aurora got a sharp pain in her stomach, and she grabbed her belly.

"Never mind, I need to go to the lobby," Aurora said, clenching her stomach. "I am not due for a few weeks. Ahh" Aurora screamed. "Please get me to the lobby."

The elevator headed toward the bottom floor. It jumped and jerked all the way down. When she got to the bottom floor the elevator shut off. Aurora grabbed her stomach and headed toward the doors. Jose turned to greet Aurora. "G-G-Good evening Aurora." And then the blue in his eyes shut off.

"My Jah what is happening?" Aurora ran out the lobby. She mentally sent a message for the nearest airlifter. The pains in her belly grew so sharp she was doubled over. The air lifter arrived within the minute and Aurora boarded. "Please take me to the nearest hospital."

The airlifter flew at a lower altitude because it was having issues staying in the air. It bumped up and down scraping the street before stopping in front of the hospital. The nurses immediately put her in a wheelchair and rolled her into a delivery room. Aurora wasn't there alone. She was right next door to a woman named Brianna.

The convenience store was also feeling the impact of the app release.

Quantas was frustrated. "What in the world is going on here? Where is Solomon to help explain all of this?"

"I haven't seen him in a long time. My grandson hasn't seen him either," Mediana replied.

"You don't think anything happened do you?" Quantas asked.
She lowered her voice when she noticed one of the piercing blue

lights coming past the window. The blue light of the drone flickered on and off and then zoomed away.

"Did you see that?" Mediana asked.

"Yeah, the entire world is falling apart, and they still send spies," Quantas replied.

"No, the lights were going on and off," Mediana said.

"What do you think that means?" Quantas asked.

"Maybe Solomon was right, maybe the world is about to come to an end," Mediana replied.

"I was reading last night, reading the Warnings from the Writ. Jah gave us warnings about all of this. Think about it, everything that is going on are signs of the end."

"You're right, so what are we going to do?" Mediana asked.

"I don't know, but I think we need to find Solomon. Maybe he can help us figure all of this out."

"Okay...I will see what Michael knows."

"I will go with you." Quantas went downstairs and to the secret meeting room. "Hey, I'm closing up shop, all of you need to go home."

Moans came from the other elders. The lights in the secret room flickered on and off making the already dark room feel even more uncomfortable.

The Elders got up, stretched and popped their bones, and headed up the stairs.

"Alright Quantas, see you tomorrow, right?"

"Sure, tomorrow," Quantas replied. She turned the lights off. Mediana and Quantas headed out in search of Solomon.

They were not going to find him. Solomon and Deiderick were still above the Inbetween where Deiderick Dollard lived. They were out of breath as they ran toward the main house and entered Deiderick's office. When they arrived, Damion and Janice were not there, but Deiderick could see the countdown on the screen.

"We don't have much time. I need to see if I can find how he coded it." Deiderick sat at the computer and began trying to find the password so that he could override the system."

Solomon started looking around at Deiderick's office and saw so many of the books that were in Readers Publishing on Deiderick's book shelves.

"Dad is a pretty avid reader and has a hefty collection," Tyler said as he saw Solomon. "The collection is worth hundreds of thousands, but he would rather give them away." Tyler chuckled.

"How long do you think this is going to take?" Solomon asked.

"Not sure." Deiderick was still clicking around trying to figure everything out. "Tyler, I need you to make sure the doors are locked. I need time and no interruptions."

As soon as Tyler headed toward the door, Damion appeared.

"Dad?" Damion was shocked. "What are you doing?" Damion ran toward his father and knocked the keyboard making it return to its invisible state.

"Hey, stop it." Tyler ran over to Damion.

"Dad, stop!" Damion shouted.

Tyler pushed his brother.

Damion pushed his brother back. "What is going on with you? I thought we all agreed on this."

Deiderick looked at Tyler with shock and disappointment but regained his focus while his sons fought it out.

"I never wanted this! You only pushed this because you haven't learned to keep it in your pants." Tyler pushed his brother again. Then Damion returned the push. Soon, it turned into a fist fight. Janice came running around the corner and pushed through the boys. "Stop it, just stop it. What is going on? Deiderick, you're back."

"So you helped him do this?" Deiderick stared at his wife.

"Deiderick, I tried to ask you, but…"

"But… because you didn't get your way, you decided to go behind my back?"

"Can we, for once, be on the same page? Why are you so upset with me? You should know how much I believe in your projects. Releasing this makes the press go away. It solidifies our status as the wealthiest family in the world.."

"So you don't think we already have enough? Look, there is more to it than you know. I have got to find a way to stop this before it hurts millions of people."

"I can't let you do that. We have already signed all of the agreements. If we turn back now we could be sued by everyone on the board and lose everything," Janice said.

"It won't matter, there won't be anything to lose," Solomon said.

"Who is this?" Janice asked.

"His name is Solomon. He is helping me."

"I can't let him do that. I can't let either of you do that. I can't lose everything. You started this company with my father's fortune. I can't have you make it all go away." Janice held her timepiece directly at Deiderick and Solomon.

Damion headed toward his father. "Dad, please, don't make this difficult, just move away from the computer.."

"What don't you understand about us losing everything anyway? Solomon, please tell them."

Solomon was astonished by the lengths that Deiderick's family would go to in order to keep their money. "I met Deiderick a little while ago and talked to him about a vision that Jah sent to me."

Damion scoffed. "Jah, can you believe this foolishness? Dad, we haven't talked about Jah since we were little children."

"Just hear me out. The YSW have gotten so far away from Jah that He is going to use your Emoji app to kill off everyone. Well, everyone except those who have done their best to give up technology and recognize Him."

Damion turned around and looked at his brother and mother. "Dad has befriended a lunatic."

Hearing the way that Damion dismissed him, Solomon grew upset and began to walk toward Damion. "I am not a lunatic! Now, we need to stop this immediately before the entire world's population is eliminated!"

"Are you going to let this stranger from the Inbetween raise his voice at me?"

By this time, Barrett, hearing the commotion, approached Deiderick's office. "What is going on here? How did you get out?"

"Barrett, we need you to arrest this...this interloper. He is the reason why Dad doesn't want to release the app."

Barrett took out his timepiece, aimed it at Solomon and fired. Solomon immediately fell to the ground twitching.

"What did you just do? He is NOT the reason why I want to stop the release of the app. I am doing this because I need to!"

Deiderick ran over to Solomon but didn't make it because Barrett tased him as well.

Damion turned to Barrett and said, "If he wants to hang out with the low life Inbetweener, then give him what he wants. Fly both of them back down to the Inbetween. By the time they wake up, the app will be released."

Janice and Tyler stood in shock. They watched everything that took place. Barrett called for two security guards to help load Deiderick and Solomon into an airlifter. Barrett and the other two guards carted the men out and threw them into the airlifter. Barrett programmed the airlifter to drop both of them off on 5th street.

The airlifter successfully made it through the highest levels of the energy field, but when the aircraft broke through the red dust, where the lower class YSW and Inbetweeners lived, it started jerking and bumping violently in the air. It shook and jolted about so erratically that the men were thrown from the lifter. They hit the ground from nearly 100 feet in the air and were thrown in two different directions.

The impact left both men unconscious. Two hours passed before Solomon woke up.

A dry patch in Solomon's throat caused a harsh cough. Solomon immediately realized that he didn't have on his Code Red outfit and was choking.

"Ah" Solomon said as he rubbed parts of his body that were aching. He stretched and popped his back. He continued to search his body and realized that there were no broken bones. "Thank you Jah." Solomon's new found faith was confirmed yet again. "Thank you." He said once more before forcing himself to get up. He looked around and realized that by some miracle, he managed to land on a heap of trash that broke his fall. Solomon didn't know where he was, but began to search for anything he could use to create a Code Red outfit before his skin was singed and burned.

Deiderick was finally waking up as well. He was sore. He looked all over his body and could see that he had a pretty rough fall. He pulled up the leg of his pants. His legs were covered in large black and blue splotches. He touched one. "Ouch." Deiderick's shirt didn't cover much of his arms. He tucked his arms inside his shirt and did his best to cover his head.

"Where the heck am I?" Deiderick whispered to himself. He looked around and realized that he did not die from the fall because he landed on piles of trash just outside the 212 area code in the recycling center. He gathered trash and covered himself from the falling red dust the best he could. He lived above the Inbetween and only dealt with the red dust when he joined the EAD for their meetings.

Where is Solomon? Deiderick looked around for Solomon thinking that they should have landed near each other, but when he didn't see him, Deiderick began to think Solomon left him for dead.

Where should I go? Deiderick continued to look in different directions. "Light" Deiderick turned to see a glimmer of light through the red haze. At first, Deiderick was hobbling, but eventually he pushed the pain aside and did the best he could to run toward the city lights.

While Deiderick and Solomon were trying to find their way back to civilization, two women, who were complete strangers to each other, would be connected in a way they could have never imagined.

"Jah, why is this happening to me?" Brianna screamed.

"Ma'am we are going to need you to calm down," the nurse said. She had trendy light gray and purple hair, looking a bit too young to be a nurse. In the center of her forehead was the third eye. Her badge read, "Nurse Shields."

"I am scared. My baby is not due for another three weeks."

"Yes, I understand that ma'am, but screaming is not going to stop the baby from coming. We need to get you admitted and into a delivery room as soon as possible." The nurse scanned Brianna's arm and quickly gathered all of her information. Then she looked up. "Oh, my goodness, it's you."

Brianna wasn't quite sure of what nurse Shields was talking about. "It's you. I thought I recognized your face from the screens, but when I scanned to find your medical records, I have never seen anyone with insurance like yours. I guess you won the lawsuit because, WOW! You and your baby will be set for life."

The lights in the catholic hospital began flickering on and off making it difficult to see the elaborate stained-glass windows and carvings on the walls. Brianna started grabbing her stomach. "What is that?" Brianna asked, looking at water running down her leg.

"Let's get you in a room quickly. Your water just broke." Nurse Shields grabbed a wheelchair mobile and plopped Briana into the chair. The lights continued to go in and out, but soon Brianna was in her room preparing to give birth.

"Aurora...my name is Aurora Weston."

"Okay, Ms. Weston." The receptionist scanned Aurora's third eye. "Ms. Weston, I am looking at your family history, you don't have any immediate family. Is there anyone you want to be here? Anyone you want to put down as an emergency contact someone who could be a guardian in case of emergency?"

"Yes, um...yes, can I put down Solomon Wiseman." Aurora proceeded to send the information she knew of Solomon from her third eye to the nurse's third eye.

"Great, this should be enough information. I will do my best to get in contact with him ," the nurse replied. She was a soft spoken, dark-brown skinned woman. Her name badge read Nurse Renee. The lights continued to go on and off. "Okay, sweetie, I don't know what is going on here, but we are going to take real good care of you."

"I'm scared," Aurora said to Nurse Renee.

"I understand, but we will be okay." Nurse Renee then programmed the wheelchair and started making small talk with Aurora. "Hey, I know what can get your mind off everything...the new Emoji app is supposed to be released soon."

"I know. I was super excited about it at first, but I have really been trying to cut down on using my third eye," Aurora replied.

"You're the only one. Everyone I know is rushing out to get a third eye before the app releases." Nurse Renee chuckled. "You know what, you're going to be a great mommy."

Aurora smiled. "I sure hope so."

Chapter 44: Two Days Before the App Release

———————◆———————

Even though all of the signs are around them, warning them of their death, they will be tempted and easily fall.
(A Warning from the Writ)

Solomon was panting, out of breath from walking from where he crashed to his apartment. Jose, the AI bellman, turned his head suspiciously. "Wow, I wasn't expecting you back," but glitched and stuttered before shutting down.

Solomon didn't engage. Instead, he continued to walk toward the elevator. When the elevator read his presence, it swiftly zoomed down the long glass tube to retrieve an exhausted and very bruised Solomon.

"It is good to see you. You have been gone for quite some time."

Solomon, extremely tired, could only make a grunting noise. "Um." He nodded his head in recognition of her voice. "Aurora is in the hospital. I think she is about to give birth soon."

With that news, Solomon shook away the pain. "Really, now? I didn't think she was due just yet?"

"Yes, according to my calculations, she had about three weeks left, but I am sure the baby will be fine." The lights flickered in the elevator. "No worries, I am almost…"

The elevator was nearing the 8th floor when it came to an abrupt stop.

"Sorry…I…have…been…" The elevator tried to explain before the lights went off.

You've got to be kidding me, Solomon thought to himself. I know that the world is coming to an end soon, but dear Jah, just let me make it home. Solomon slid down the mix of glass and metal, looked up and, with a quivering voice, repeated, dear Jah, just let me make it home. I am so tired.

As he finished his sentence, the lights on the elevator jolted back on and jerked its way to the 9th floor. The doors partially opened before the power went out again. Solomon was able to squeeze through the door and make it to his apartment. The door did not read his presence. The system shut down again. "Jah," Solomon prayed, "I am learning to lean on you for everything. I realize that I should not have tried to stop what you already had planned, and I ask that you forgive me. I am tired and in pain. Please, allow my door to open."

Solomon had become accustomed to Jah answering his prayers right away, so he was shocked when the camera at his door did not turn on immediately. He turned his back toward the door and slid down to rest. As he did that, his shirt got caught on the knob and the door opened. Solomon fell into his living room. He plopped himself down on the couch and before he realized it, he received a series of visions.

The first vision was about the release of the app. He saw all of the YSW, those with third eyes, and those with timepieces, opened the Emoji app, and vanished. After the sea of people disintegrated, Solomon received another vision of his children vanishing and then reappearing in a completely different place. He couldn't figure out what it meant, but in the moment, it gave him hope.

In his sleep, Solomon felt himself toss and turn. He wanted to wake up, but it was as if Jah's fingers were holding his eyelids shut.

The last dream was showing him a screen and time on a clock. It showed Solomon looking at the screen and frantically writing things down. As soon as that vision finished, his eyes were yanked open. He realized he had a few minutes to turn on the screen and write down everything he saw, and he did exactly what the vision told him to do. He wrote so fast his fingers hurt, but he knew that he had to use his time wisely.

Solomon didn't know what else to do. He began to look around at the pictures of his family. He wanted to reach out to his children before everything came to an end.

"212 Digital Detox Center" Solomon said, picking up the device.

"Contacting the Digital..." The device lost connection. The power in Solomon's apartment went out and he realized that he would never be able to speak to his children again. Solomon decided to rest before leaving his apartment and heading to the secret EAD meeting room.

Deiderick was also tired from his long walk. He lived above the Inbetween, so he only knew of one place to go. After what felt like nearly 12 hours of walking, Deiderick got his bearings and was about a block away from the convenience store where the EAD meetings were held. The sounds in the streets were eerie as screens popped on and off. Hovercrafts and airlifters bounced up and down in the sky as their electronic network lost and regained power. The EAD members, the ones who could not afford to break the silence order hours, did everything in their power not to scream in fear of being crushed under the crafts flying in the air. Every time the network supporting all of the technology would come on or go out, the silence was filled with a loud electric sound that was deafening.

Deiderick watched as people covered their ears. Others were screaming and running in the streets hoping to make it to safety before the network completely gave out. He realized there was not much time. Based on his estimation, he may have only had a day left before the Emoji app would be released to the world. This app is literally stripping the power from everything. The networks can't handle it. Deiderick thought to himself. Maybe it's for the best, maybe the system will shut down before the app is released. With all of those thoughts running through his head, Deiderick didn't realize that a hovercraft began barreling toward him.

"Crap!" Deiderick ducked and ran toward the convenience store. He made it in the doors, breathless.

"Oh, it's you," Quantas whispered. She didn't know what was going on but didn't want to risk the silence order police jailing her, especially now with all of the power and networks going on. Quantas held a flashlight in her hand. Her hand was slightly shaking. She whispered, "Have you seen Solomon?"

"I haven't seen him since..." Deiderick stopped short of finishing his sentence. He didn't want Quantas or Mediana to know what they had been up to. "I haven't seen him in a long time."

"You look like crap!" Quantas, even as things were looking bleak, still managed to make a rude comment, but Deiderick did not respond to her jab, there were too many thoughts going through his mind. He looked around and then said, "Do you have a newspaper?"

"Just go in, looks like it's all going to hell anyway, so just come on in."

Deiderick walked down the stairs, lights flickering on and off. Mediana saw him and gave him a hug. "Oh, my goodness, are you okay? Quantas and I went looking for you and Solomon. You look like you need something to eat and drink. Have a seat."

Somehow, Mediana whipped out a bowl of soup and glass of dingy water and placed it on a small round table in front of Deiderick. He looked at the water and realized his life of privilege came to an end when he fell from the sky and landed in the Inbetween. He chugged down the water, finding himself surprisingly refreshed after walking for so long. Then he stirred around the soup waiting for any sign of Solomon.

While Solomon was making his way out of his apartment, Aurora and Briana were hearing the words, "Push." In fact, every pregnant woman in the hospital was having contractions and feeling the urge to push.

"What is happening?" Aurora overheard one of the nurses say. "This is ridiculous, ALL of the women are going into labor?"

The equipment in the Catholic Hospital flickered on and off. Aurora could hear people running in the hallways. She could hear the screams of other pregnant women who were forced into labor.

"AHHHH!!! If I make it through this, you better tell Damion Dollard that I hate him for doing this to me and I will make him pay!" Briana shouted to her nurse. Aurora soon realized that she was in the company of Damion Dollard's mistress.

Screams of laboring women went on for twelve hours. They labored until the day of the app release.

Chapter 45: The Day of the App Release

No one can exist living too far away from Jah. He will bring all of his children back home and those who do not belong to him, will one day, recognize his greatness, but it will be too late.
(A Warning from the Writ)

The day of the app release, Solomon made it to the EAD meeting room.

"Oh, thank Jah, where have you been?" Quantas gave Solomon a hug. Mediana and I went looking everywhere for you. Then Quantas leaned in to whisper, "We thought that dirty Deiderick did something to you."

"No, he didn't do anything to me. I actually think he is a pretty good guy."

"Well, that's great to hear because that 'good' guy has been since yesterday."

"Really?" Solomon was surprised.

"So, is this what you dreamed about? This is how it all ends?" Quantas inquired.

"Maybe, I don't know. I didn't see all of the chaos, but yes, I think," A melancholy Solomon continued. "I think this may be it. Brought my Writ with me." Solomon took the book out of his pocket and tapped it, showing it to Quantas.

"Yep, you and me both." Quantas smiled and opened the door to the secret room and they both walked down the stairs.

When Solomon got to the bottom of the steps, he could see Deiderick in his usual corner. He didn't know if he should walk over to him. He gave a nod and Deiderick returned it. Solomon took a risk and slowly walked over to Deiderick.

Two men, from two different worlds had come together to stop a force that was unstoppable.

"We did the best we could," Deiderick said to Solomon.

"Yes, we did indeed. I wouldn't have traded this experience for anything," Solomon agreed.

"Hey, we don't have much longer, and silence order hours are approaching soon, so I want to get this out before...the end." Deiderick was disheartened. "I would like to keep this adventure our little secret. I love the Elders, but Quantas is a bit of a gossip and, if we do get a fresh start in the new world, I don't want any of the things that I have done in the past to affect the potential for my new life."

Solomon chuckled. "I won't say a word." Although the conversation between the two men was pleasant, neither couldn't shake the feeling that, when the airlift crashed, they were deserted. Deep down, Solomon felt that Deiderick left because he was upset that they were not able to stop the release of the app. Deiderick felt that Solomon left him because he never wanted to be part of his plan to stop the app in the first place. The two men went to their respective place in the secret room, reading the Writ. Solomon had the urge to go over and speak to him. He wanted to clear things up, but he decided against it.

Very few members of the EAD spoke to each other that evening. Most of them sat quietly in the basement of the convenience store with the Writ in their hand, trying to make peace with Jah. They prepared for the end.

The awkward silence in the secret EAD meeting room was the complete antithesis of the noise that was going on in labor and delivery.

"I see his head. Give me one final push." Nurse Renee did her best to calm Aurora.

"Ahh!" Aurora pushed.

"You are doing great!" Nurse Renee was so encouraging. Her presence made Aurora, who was alone, feel loved. It was not long before the room was filled with the sound of sweet cries. Nurse Renee took the baby and placed it on the scale. "Six pounds four ounces. Good size for a baby that wasn't due for a few weeks." Then nurse Renee walked the baby over to a screen where the doctor made a virtual appearance.

"Hold the baby up." Doctor Michaels demanded. An unkept five o'clock shadow was covered by a mask that only exposed his tired, red eyes with brown pupils.

The nurse did as she was told and held the small, peach toned baby to the camera. The baby cried.

"What is the baby's weight?" Doctor Michaels asked.

"Six pounds four ounces."

"Excellent. Now I will watch you conduct the rest of the evaluation. Make sure the baby's temperature is at 98.6 degrees before I chip him."

"Wait!" Aurora said. "I don't want you to chip my baby yet. He's so perfect. Can we just wait a little while?"

The doctor did not respond to Aurora, instead, the doctor turned his head to Nurse Renee and said, "You can feel free to stop the examination if she is not part of the YSW. It is up to you but as far as I am concerned, I am done here." And just like that, Doctor Michaels got off the screen.

"What did I say?"

"Nothing, don't worry about it. This is your baby, you should be able to do what you want with your baby. I can come back and chip him any time. So, what is his name?"

"I have really thought about this...I want him to have a name that means something. I researched names and have decided to name him Athirst."

"So with a name like that, it must mean something." Nurse Renee finished tapping the baby's knees and checking the baby's spine. She wrapped him in a blanket and handed baby Athirst over to Aurora.

"Well, I wanted the baby and I to have first names with the same letter, so after looking for a while, I found the name Athirst. It is Latin and means thirsty for knowledge." There was a small pause before Aurora finished. "I, I just want him to have the best life." Aurora, hearing the commotion from down the hall, couldn't help but ask, "I have been watching the news and getting the feed from my third eye. So, is it true, is Damion Dollard's mistress here? I think we were due around the same time."

"She is a few rooms down. She is...how can I put this...very dramatic! She is making sure that her baby gets the best of everything. Apparently, she must have reached an agreement with Damion, and he is footing the bill for this delivery. Whew...I never thought I would say this, but I feel sorry for the Dollards." Nurse

Renee was around and about in the room trying to straighten up. She was putting a glass of water on a tray near Aurora when she said, "thought you were trying not to use your third eye."

"I cut down a lot, but I can't help but zone out on it every now and then. So much is always happening. I may cheat a little tonight. You know the new Emoji app is supposed to come out today," Aurora said, nuzzling little Athirst. Aurora continued to hold her baby and started humming a song. Athirst smiled and turned toward his mother's chest.

"I am excited about the new app as well. I can't wait to send one of those sexy Emojis to my husband."

"Whoa! Ms. Renee! Too much information." Aurora laughed.

Aurora's laugh was interrupted when all of the lights and networks went down. The entire hospital went dark. The lights on all of the systems went away. Just a loud alarm that said, "System failure, System failure" repeated itself over and over again. This sound was followed by a loud shrinking sound, similar to an alarm, and it was not just heard in the hospital but seemed to ring throughout the entire world.

Back in the EAD meeting room, Deiderick dropped his head and started to pray, "Dear Jah, I know I have not done what you have wanted me to do. I feel so much guilt for my part in all of this, and I ask that you forgive me. I hear the sounds and know that the app I created will be released soon. I hear the sound of the end. It is using all of the storage from all of the networks so there is more energy behind this creation than any of the others. Solomon says that it is all part of your plan. I pray so and hope you will allow me to have a second chance. I know that you are not pleased with my family, especially my son Damion. I leave that in your hands."

The other elders seemed to be in prayer as well. The dark EAD meeting room felt even eerier as the gnawing sound grew louder, eventually leading Mediana to cover her ears. Quantas, who typically has something to say, remained quiet. She looked around with tears in her eyes and thought, "This may be my last time in this room alive. Dear Jah, let my children know that I did the best to take care of them and forgive me for letting the temptations of the world get the best of them."

Quantas, Deiderick, Solomon, Mediana, and the other elders continued to reflect on their lives and their families.

About an hour into the chaos, the strangest thing happened.

Every electronic device popped on. All of the networks began working again. The hovercrafts that had come barreling to the ground when all the electronic fields went out started floating in the air. The advertisements and screens that lined the streets began talking at full volume, and they were all on the same channel saying the same thing. "In a few minutes, the most amazing, most sensational app ever created will be released. Connect to your third eye or sync your timepiece to your chip for the ultimate emotional experience. Send emotions to your friends and family to let them know how you really feel. The app will be released at 11:30 pm to everyone connected. Stores all around will have third eye implants available to you and silence order hours will be lifted."

The YSW immediately forgot about all the previous chaos of the networks going out and began downloading the app. Those who had old devices ran to stores to get new devices and it seemed that all the stores were ready to handle the crowd.

Solomon's meditation to Jah was disrupted. "Do you hear that?" He whispered looking up to follow the noise above his head. It appeared as if some people had broken into the convenience store in search of a third eye device.

"It sounds like they are destroying everything," Mediana whispered.

"Shhh," Quantas replied. "Don't let them know we are here."

It was not long before the sound of footsteps above the elders' heads began to fade away to a new sound. It was a piercing, screeching noise that rang through the air.

"My Jah, what is that awful sound?" Quantas asked, holding her ears trying to shout over noise.

"The networks are being stretched to capacity. My estimation is that several billion people are connecting right now." Deiderick did his best to shout over the numbing sound.

Solomon was quiet, thinking about his children and Aurora.

Chapter 46: Thirty Minutes Before the App Release

The power of Jah lives in all of us from the time we are born. Use the power
with good intention.
(Warning from the Writ)

Aurora was holding Athirst. He was on her chest getting full of her milk when Nurse Renee walked back in. "Now it is time for Mommy to get some rest, come here big guy." Nurse Renee said reaching for the baby. She placed him in a small clear incubator that kept him warm.

"Just a few things I want to go over with you. So, you said that if anything were to happen to you, you want Athirst to go to Solomon Wiseman, correct?"

"Yes," Aurora replied.

"I am working on the information for the birth certificate, we can run a test on Athirst to see who his father is, the father does not need to be here, but do you want him on the birth certificate?"

Aurora thought for a long time. "No, No I don't think I want him on the birth certificate. He, he didn't want anything to do with me or the baby."

"Very well. A lot of mothers are choosing to do that option now." Nurse Renee could tell that Aurora was hurt.

"I can get the rest of the information from you later, just rest for right now. The other nurses are about to try out the app. It is so crazy, one minute it seemed like every woman in the 212 area code was in labor and the next minute it's so quiet you could hear a pin drop. You know, with all the craziness, you would think the world is coming to an end." Nurse Renee chuckled.

"It was really scary for a minute. So glad things seem to have gotten back to normal," Aurora replied.

"Yes, me too. Well, why don't you relax. Hey, how about this. If you use the app, I can send you some love for all your hard work today. You gave birth to a beautiful baby boy."

"Thanks, sounds good." Aurora smiled.

Nurse Renee left out the door leaving Aurora and the baby alone in the room. Aurora got up to take one last peek at Athirst.

"Oh, you are so sweet." She stuck her hand in the incubator and found Athrist's hand. She rubbed his itty fingers. "You are going to be something special." Aurora made her way back to her bed. She was about to zone out on her third eye and play around with the app but paused.

"I have been so good. I have tried to be so disciplined." She whispered to herself.

"I guess it's okay if I just try out the new app. I quit once, I know I can quit again."

Aurora hesitantly closed her eyes and concentrated. Then she began searching for the app. She really didn't know who to send

384

one to. She decided that she would start with Nurse Renee and send her a feeling of gratitude and Nurse Renee immediately returned the feeling. When the emotion hit Aurora, she laid all the way back in her bed, closed her eyes, and took in the feeling. She hadn't felt this good in years.

At the same time Aurora was relishing her pleasure, Karina was back in her dorm staying up for the moment the app was released. She found herself upset with her father for not becoming one of the YSW. She thought of him the moment the Emoji app was released because she dearly wanted to send him a message. "Dad, I know you may not believe me, but I love you. I wish you could feel what I feel for you." A tear rolled her eyes. She thought about her mom as well and wished they both had the opportunity to experience the love that she could send them while she was away at university. She wiped tears and her mind traveled to thoughts of her brother.

Karina closed her eyes and tapped into her third eye implant to connect to Kyle, and she sent her first Emoji. With her eyes closed, she scrolled through the Emojis. She found a perfect one, a hug and a heart.

"Okay, here goes nothing," Karina said to herself. She concentrated and sent the message to Kyle and then to Knox.

During their time in the detox center, Kyle and Knox were adorned with every type of technology and had converted to become members of the YSW about six months after they were placed into the facility. When Karina sent the emoji to them, Kyle and Knox immediately felt overwhelming joy and warmth. The boys enjoyed the feeling and were hooked. They returned the feeling to Karina. When she received the image of a heart, euphoria consumed her. Karina's eyes rolled in the back of her head, taking it all in. This sensation was intoxicating, and she continued to send messages out to everyone she knew just so she could get messages back.

This pattern seemed to ricochet all throughout various parts of the world. People sending messages hoping to let family and friends know how they felt about them. In a world where they had lost human connection, these emotions brought feelings that many of the YSW hadn't felt. And in the first few minutes of the Emoji release, all was good, but it was not long before other emotions were released.

Brianna had just given birth to Theiler when the app was released.

"Look, Theiler, your dad and his family created this." Brianna held up baby Theiler and nuzzled him on her face. Then she closed her eyes and concentrated as hard as she could. She sent her first message to Damion Dollard.

Damion and his upper-class family had their implant behind their ear, but the sensation reached him nonetheless. A series of mixed emotions were sent to Damion. Love and hate were forced into his brain.

"Ahh! What the hell is happening?" Damion shouted and collapsed to the ground. He placed his hands behind his ear. He was in his father's office. His mom and brother were standing nearby.

"Damion!" Tyler shouted. "Somebody, go get help." Tyler was hovering over his brother and Janice ran over to help.

"Barrett, get someone here now!" Janice shouted. Then she called out to every device. "Devices, I need you to notify the nearest medical professionals immediately."

But, unfortunately, the devices' response systems were slowed because the Emoji app had the network tied up. It was not long after Janice called out for help that she too hit the ground and started convulsing. She fell on top of Damion. Tyler couldn't help but to scream. "Mom, what is happening?"

"I need some help, please. Someone get help!"

The main computer kicked on. "I need more network energy to send a message for someone to come and help."

Tyler rushed over to the computer and could see that the free trial still had seven minutes left.

"How can I stop this thing?" Tyler started looking around. "Maybe Dad left something here to let us know how to stop it." Tyler rummaged through drawers and banged computer keys to see if he could find anything that could stop the Emoji app.

"There's got to be something here. Anything." But before Tyler could finish looking, he fell to the ground.

Brianna was seeking revenge on the entire Dollard family, but it was not just Brianna who was upset with the Dollards, Sasha, Damion's soon-to-be ex-wife, was sending messages of her own. Board members who had a bone to pick with the Dollards or who were jealous about not having the amount of wealth the Dollards had, were all sending mean, hurtful messages, and all the members of the Dollard family were impacted, all except Deiderick, who was in the secret meeting room talking to Jah.

Chapter 47: Five Minutes Before the App Release

*Be warned, there will be chaos and madness in the last
minutes of the last day.
(A Warning from the Writ)*

There were only five minutes left of the free trial. Across the world, everyone except for infants and Elders, found themselves hooked. They were trying to use every moment of the free trial. And unfortunately, the last few moments of the free trial were filled with hate. In fact, so many messages were written with hate that the YSW who connected to the app found themselves sorrowful and angry.

"I hate you! I hate you, you bastard!" were the last words of Brianna as she sent to Damion. She followed with the skull emoji to everyone in the Dollard family that was connected to a device. Damion, Tyler, Janice, and Brianna vanished.

On campus, Craig, DeBow, Karina and Grey found themselves sending vile messages to each other. Karina was so upset with Craig for taking away time from her life. When Craig received the message, he immediately told DeBow, who joined in retaliation. When DeBow joined in calling Karina a wide variety of vulgar names, Karina told Grey, who was quick to help her friend.

Karina to Craig: ☝ (sent the feeling of hate)

Craig to Karina: ☝ (replied with hate)

DeBow to Karina: ▦ (sent a feeling of being threatened)

Karina to Grey: They are messing with me. Please Help!

Grey to Craig: 💀 (sent a feeling of pain)

Karina to Craig and DeBow: 😡 (sent a feeling of anger)

Each of them ended the conversation with: 💀

When they sent each other the skull, all of them vanished. This was the same thing that happened in the Detox Center with Kyle and Knox, who received messages from all of Norman's friends. Kyle and Knox sent hateful emojis back, and they, too sent the skull emoji and vanished.

Jah looked upon the world and watched as chaos ensued. Billions around the world are connected with devices. They connected despite their location and despite the time zone so that they were all together at the same time. The app continued to inject and remove chemicals from the brain.

Their fingers began moving faster, their thoughts were growing more depressed, and their eyes were full of tears, but they did not disengage.

So, in the last minute of the Second World, all the remaining YSW pressed the Emoji skull. It released chemical compounds in such high quantities that it resulted in neurotoxicity and apoptosis. The members of the YSW died, and Jah vanished them. The only individuals remaining were the Elders, who did their best to swear off the use of technology, and infants younger than nine months or those who were not exposed to technology. Jah considered the unexposed exceptionally worthy of being saved.

The Emoji app was so powerful and used so much network energy that it had an effect on the atmosphere. The atmospheric pressure caused the Elders and infants to fall into a deep sleep, preserving them. The slumber lasted a little over ten years. Just long enough for the world to completely cleanse itself of the toxins caused by the YSW. During this time, the world was quiet as Jah prepared the land for the survivors. He purified the land, air, and water. He also gave those who were remaining dreams of things to come.

Todd Markley

So, there you have it, all the events that led up to the vanishing of mankind, ending the Second World. All mankind was vanished by Jah, except for Elders and infants. Two types of elders remained. One group were scriptors, those Jah would use to write his word and provide instruction. The other group were saved to raise the infants. Because the infants were unexposed to technology and were pure at heart, Jah kept them safe by putting them into a deep sleep after the vanishing. The infants would be assigned to an elder who would raise them in the New World.

For the first ten years after the vanishing, only scriptors were awakened and allowed to see the beautiful new world Jah created for the infants and other elders, whose job was to raise the infants. The scriptors had to write down everything they saw as the new world took shape. Jah also sent them dreams and visions, so scriptors had to be good interpreters of his word.

Altogether, 212 chapters were written by the scriptors. The first 211 chapters were wonders and warnings. The final chapter, chapter 212, provided instructions to the people who would inhabit the 3rd world. The scriptors called the collection of writings, the Writ 212. They hid the books in a cave for protection until Jah woke the infants and the elders who would raise them. The elders responsible for raising the infants had the most difficult job, to follow the instructions in the Writ precisely and keep the infants unexposed to technology. If the elders could do this, then their infants will go on to be successful and live in a beautiful, untainted New World, but if they did not follow the Writ with precision, they will have to deal with the consequences. As for me, Jah gave me a special job, I get to watch over those who were saved and tell their stories.

The End

Made in the USA
Middletown, DE
26 September 2023

39300154R00219